Cold Road to Imber

Jonathan Part

Cold Road to Imber

To Sarah, Pixlie and Ben.

This took longer than I'd hoped.

Sorry!

All the characters in this book are fictitious but the story is based around actual events. I've outlined a historical description of the two places central to the story, which I hope might be helpful.

IMBER

The village of Imber lies in the middle of Salisbury Plain and has been abandoned since the Second World War. In 1943 the American army needed to requisition the village for vital training prior to the D-Day invasion. The inhabitants were told that they had to leave within six weeks. They were asked to find their own accommodation and received no recompense for their loss, except the cost of moving their furniture. Most of the villagers left willingly, believing they would be able to return once the war had ended. However, despite several petitions and rallies over the years, particularly in 1961, the request to reclaim the village was never granted. The remains of the village are now open to the public for a few days each year. One of the last inhabitants was buried there recently at St Giles' church.

BERLIN

In 1952 the newly formed German Democratic Republic, or East Germany as the West called it, closed its border with West Germany, denying its citizens access to the West. However, within East Germany lay the city of Berlin which still had a Western sector, occupied by America, France and Britain, and an Eastern sector, occupied by Russia. Here it was still possible to cross the border between the two halves of the city because it was too complicated for the four, occupying powers to regulate. Roads and stations remained open and many people lived in one half of the city and had family, friends and jobs in the other. This situation remained largely unchanged until the Berlin Wall was erected by the East German government in 1961 to prevent the steady loss of East German refugees to West Berlin. At this point about 3.5 million East Germans had already left, approximately 20% of the entire East German population. After the Berlin Wall was completed, East German citizens were not allowed to cross to the West, unless in exceptional circumstances, until the Wall was dismantled in November 1989.

PROLOGUE

NOVEMBER 10th 1938,   EAST BERLIN

From a distant place she hears her mother's voice, not much above a whisper, rousing her gently from the deepest sleep.

"Katja, darling, don't be afraid, Mutti needs to get you dressed."

She smells her mother's musky perfume as she's lifted from the bed, which gives her comfort, because instinctively she knows something is wrong. There's no glimmer of dawn light behind the curtains, no sense that morning is upon them and it's time to get ready for school. Encouraged by her mother's soft words she rises from the bed, the floorboards cold beneath her feet. She shivers as her nightdress is removed, replaced by a vest and pants, her senses awakening now, acute enough to consider a glance at her bedside clock. It's just gone two o'clock.

"What's happening, Mutti? Why must I get up?"

"Quiet now, darling."

She can hear her father talking in murmurs downstairs. Her mother pulls a thick jumper over her head. She raises her arms, at her mother's request, and pushes her hands up the sleeves. The second voice downstairs is familiar, though the tone is more urgent than she's used to. It's her uncle. But why is he here and why does he sound so serious? Remembering her mother's plea, she refrains from asking. Even in the darkness she can sense her mother's unease; the way she fumbles with the buttons on her coat, trying to do them up too quickly, her breathing uneven and shallow.

"Come, Katja, we must go now. But remember, quiet as a

1

mouse."

She accepts her mother's hand and steps out of the room onto the landing. The door to her parents' bedroom is wide open, which usually it wouldn't be. On the unmade bed she sees an untidy pile of clothes beside an open suitcase. Both look somehow abandoned, as if they belonged to a different story, which she would never hear. At the bottom of the stairs her uncle greets her with an embrace, even a smile, and a little joke about his favourite, grown-up niece. It reassures her. But then she sees her father emerge hastily from his study, some important-looking documents in his hand which he thrusts into his overcoat.

Her uncle shifts his gaze, his smile faltering. "All set?"

"All set."

She hadn't spotted the large suitcase which her uncle now picks up as he leads them to the front door. She steps forward, holding her mother's warm hand again, her father following, closing the door behind him. Her uncle's van is parked in the shadows, between two streetlights. She's ridden in it before, on his round of bakery deliveries, always enjoying his light banter with the shopkeepers and their comments on his bread. This time her uncle directs them to climb into the back, where the bread is usually kept, under the canvas frame. He has laid out three upturned bread baskets for them to sit on. She settles where her mother suggests, watching her face for some clue to their circumstance. But darkness shrouds them again as her uncle draws the canvas closed. "Don't worry, Katja, darling. You try to sleep now. When you wake up, everything will be fine."

She trusts her mother's words but still she is afraid. As the van bumps along the cobble-stoned street she can hear distant shouts and the crack of a pistol. And she wonders if it has anything to do with all the broken glass she saw in the streets yesterday, and the ransacked shops, and neighbours of hers who were shouted out and abused by other families as they walked their children home from school.

NOVEMBER 1st 1943,   IMBER, SALISBURY PLAIN

Alec watches from his bedroom window as his mother hangs washing on the line, her fingers raw and chapped from regular immersion in ice cold water. He should be at school today but the building is host to a meeting, requested by the army, with the senior villagers.

No one in Imber knows why. There are rumours, spread from the pub, that it might be about the road and drainage scheme. But there are always rumours.

Beyond his back yard a field dotted with oak and elm trees stretches to the crest of the Plain. He often imagines there are Germans camped the other side of the hill, waiting to capture him when he lies asleep. But his father, on leave for two weeks, has reassured him that they are far, far away. Much further than Salisbury, which is the furthest he's ever been.

His father left for the meeting over an hour ago. Alec feels impatient now, anxious for him to return so that he can he recount gripping stories of the desert; of camels and pyramids and Bedouin tribesmen and the Germans who run like baby rats when his father chases after them in his tank. The war will be over soon, his father says. He hopes so. His mother cries for a week every time his father leaves.

She clasps a peg to the sheet then holds it tightly; unnecessary, Alec thinks, given the remarkably clement and windless skies. He follows her gaze to see that his father is at last walking along the grass path towards their back yard. His handsome face, chiselled

3

by God and nature, betrays no emotion. It is this, he sees from his mother's inertia, that she fears. The absence of a smile.

He watches his father open the picket-fence gate and walk towards her, his hands resting gently upon her shoulders, a few soft words spoken like a prayer, as she drops the sheet back to the wash basket, where it lies crumpled and cold and forgotten. He guides her back into the scullery and below him Alec hears the scrape of a chair across the tiled floor; muffled voices that he cannot quite make out before his mother shouts and starts to sob uncontrollably. He falls back to his bed, his pillow wrapped about his ears, and stares at the view from his window. Now a solitary patch of blue sky.

Eventually he hears his father call for him. He doesn't want to go downstairs. If he does, he senses that his life will change forever. But his father calls again and he must go.

1

SEPTEMBER 1954,   EAST BERLIN

Framed by the roofline of the opposite tenement block she admires a cobalt blue sky. The sun throws a patch of light onto the courtyard below her where a young girl and boy squeal with excitement. Probably a brother and sister, she thinks. It is only seven o'clock in the morning. A Saturday. Judging by the empty pram they spin across the concrete, Kitty imagines their parents are still in bed, tucked either side of their latest offspring, perhaps. She recognises faces in her tenement block now, after a year of living here, but she doesn't really know anyone. Except for Ursula. If she meets a resident in the stairwell she bids them good morning or good evening. But to say any more would invite questions.

Her packing is rudimentary. She considers the open suitcase lying on her bed, mentally ticking off her short list; a grey suit, three blouses, two thick skirts, two cardigans, underwear, a towel, her wash bag and a bottle of her favourite perfume; Memoire Cherie. Her supervisor at the Aussenpolitischer Nachrichtendienst (Foreign Intelligence Service) has authorised her to buy more appropriate clothes in London. She tried her best not to grin when he told her. She loves clothes. She tells herself it's in the blood; her mother was - is very stylish. Opposite her narrow bed stands a chest of drawers. An ashtray, a small mirror and a guidebook to English Cities lie on its surface. She turns the key in the drawer and removes two of three passports, one American, one West German. The East German passport, the only unforged one, she leaves in the drawer. She also takes a plane ticket and half of the English bank notes. There's bound to be more assignments.

The sound of someone coughing from the other side of the wall distracts her briefly.

She smiles. "Ich bin für eine Weile unterwegs. Leider müssen sie jemand anderen zum Belauschen finden. Wiedersehen ." *I'm away a while. Sorry, but you'll have to find someone else to eavesdrop on. Bye for now."*

There is no response. She glances around the room one last time and steps along the narrow passage into a modest living room which doubles as a kitchenette. Sitting in one of the two uncomfortable armchairs she finds Ursula, sipping coffee, returned from her night shift at the printing works.

"When did you get back?" she asks.

Ursula looks up from her morning paper, dropping her cigarette ash onto her plate. "I don't know. Two thirty, three? They're working us hard at the moment. The SED wants lots more posters apparently." She notices Kitty's suitcase. "Are you off somewhere?"

"To see my cousin. He's sick again. And there's no other relatives to help him."

"I'm sorry. Same thing?"

"Shitty, huh?" Kitty adopts a mournful guise but she knows she's not fooling Ursula. They've known each other since kindergarten. But Ursula knows better than to enquire too deeply. "You should go back to bed, Ursula, my darling. You look exhausted."

"I couldn't sleep. How long will you be gone?"

"Maybe a while. Work's given me dispensation."

"That would never happen at the factory. Please look after yourself, Katja."

"I promise." Despite the pretty, dimpled face her friend looks older than her twenty-three years; bleary eyes framed by deep purple shadows and hair that lies flat and lifeless. A part of Kitty feels she is betraying Ursula by leaving. They have brought such comfort to one another through difficult times. But her assignment can't be jeopardised and she appreciates the fact that Ursula instinctively seems to understand. She drops her suitcase and crosses the room, arms extended. The warmth and deep affection of their embrace ratifies her assumptions.

"Take care, darling," she says, turning to the door.

Ursula flops back to her seat. She smiles. "You look very beautiful today."

"So will you. When you've had some sleep." Others tell Kitty she is beautiful. But coming from Ursula it means something. It is more than skin deep.

As she reaches for the door handle Ursula stops her again. "I mean it, Katja. Look after yourself. For me."

She manages to find a smile before stepping out into the long, dim corridor. The first door she passes bears a large sign, Gothic letters on a white background. *Attention! Electricity. Entry forbidden.* She wraps on the door. "Wiedersehen. Viel Spass ohne mich" *See you again. Have fun without me.* Without waiting for a response, she hurries down the corridor to the stairwell.

Fehrbelliner Strasse is deserted; a residential street of identical, five storey tenement buildings, all bearing the pockmarked scars of heavy shelling. Workers have planted a few fledgling trees along the road in the vain hope they might distract from the bruised facades. There's barely a car on the road. Kitty turns down the broader Invaliden Strasse, ignoring the mountains of rubble and ragged brickwork which once constituted people's homes. She sees it every day, the destruction unleashed by war; a palette of abuse. The walk to the U Bahn takes around fifteen minutes. She doesn't hurry; it draws attention.

Alighting the underground train at Oranienburger Strasse, she heads south, towards the airport. Her compartment is surprisingly busy; some going to work, others visiting relatives or loved ones maybe? She's the only one with a suitcase. Shortly before the train passes the border from the eastern to the western sector of the city, a young, East German guard embarks, removing his cap and combing his hand through his hair, before parading down the carriage. He looks bored but the passengers watch him keenly. He stops next to Kitty. She's not surprised. The young ones always pick her out.

"Sie machen ein Urlaub, Fräulein?" he asks, observing her suitcase.

She smiles freely, replying in English. "I'm afraid I don't speak German." Her accent is educated East Coast American, but the confusion in his face suggests this observation is beyond him.

He tries again. "Englisch?"

"American. I've been visiting relatives here." She enjoys the role play. It's good practice for later. To speak in German, holding out her East German passport, would have been no fun at all.

She can tell he hasn't understood because he forces a smile and moves on down the corridor without further questions.

At Parade Strasse she steps out and emerges from the dimly lit station into the Western sector. Already it feels a different city, like a better-looking twin. There are more cars on the road and the building repairs are further advanced. But it doesn't fool her, nor is she envious. She knows America has poured in money just to taunt the East. Petty power play. And war reparations have not been forthcoming, despite the incredible destruction they inflicted on the Eastern sector of the city. She's heard that beyond East Berlin the outer regions of the newly formed German Democratic Republic have suffered even greater deprivations.

Crossing the road, the vast, arc-shaped terminal of Templehof Airport looms before her: an impressive if repugnant reminder of Hitler's Fascist regime, sadly not destroyed by the war. Still, she must enter its portentous departure hall with equanimity if she's to fulfil her assignment. To show any political bias from now on would be extremely foolhardy.

A Pan American DC-4 climbs into the sky above her head and banks away to the north. The strain of the engines seems to vibrate through her chest. Or maybe it's just her adrenalin pumping. In which case she must contain it. Basic intelligence training; remain cool and forensically observant at all times in order to survive. And she promised Ursula this morning that she would.

A handsome young man in a navy, Pan American suit greets her at the check-in desk. Kitty presents her ticket and this time a West German passport. Always confuse the trail. He checks the passport before commending her English. "I'm guessing you must have learnt it back in the good, old US of A with that accent, mam?"

She grins. "I went to Philadelphia a few times."

"Great city. Have a nice trip."

"I hope so."

She thanks him and turns away towards the waiting lounge. Until this brief conversation it hadn't occurred to her that, with her false passports, she could just ditch everything and take a plane from London back to the States if she wanted. Make contact with her parents again. See her childhood house. She brushes the thought aside. For one it's distracting and for two it proves just how far she's travelled in recent years. Once she was weak, unformed, now she's a rising star in East German Intelligence. Trustworthy, dependable and committed to the cause.

2

SEPTEMBER 1954,   LINCOLNSHIRE, ENGLAND

The scrambled eggs have congealed to a dense, yellow mass. Ed replaces the lid on the silver serving dish, instead choosing a slice of toast which he drops with some ostentation onto the bone china plate. His mother looks up from the head of the mahogany table, dabbing her napkin at the corners of her mouth.

"Do try to eat more, darling. It'll settle your stomach." She has a distinguished air about her, aquiline features, grey eyes that match the shade of her cashmere cardigan, a double rope of expensive pearls. Many people are intimidated by her meticulous style but he has long understood it's an effective veil to disguise her shyness. He can't remember when he last saw her lustrous, auburn hair fall out of place, or her lipstick askew. She would feel too exposed. People say he looks like her which he takes as a compliment.

"I'm not a child, mother." He butters his toast, adding a spoon of thick marmalade.

"Of course not, darling, but really it's not enough."

"Even The bloody Times is saying Churchill's sense of occasion has deserted him." His father's voice is assured, but it harbours a flicker of rage. A cup of coffee is poised in his free hand. He, too, is immaculate; a freshly pressed shirt and cravat, a mane of sandy hair which suggests a certain vanity. "Why can't these journalists show some respect instead of banging on about his age and some spurious nonsense about his health?"

"…Have you packed, darling?" His mother's interjection is perfectly timed. Ed smiles sympathetically at her, understanding he must be complicit in her bid for distraction.

"There's just a couple of things to sort."

"I'll have Cleggy collect your cases when you're ready. What time do you need to leave?"

"When I'm ready. I don't need Cleggy to chauffeur me, I'll take the MG." He can see he's upset her but it's really not hard.

"If that's what you want. As long as there's somewhere safe you can leave it."

He's about to remonstrate when a young woman breezes into the dining room, diverting their attention. She is dressed as perfectly as her mother, almost a carbon copy. She has her father's lighter hair and his deep-set, ice blue eyes. "Morning, all. Morning, daddy." She kisses him softly on the top of his head and he reaches for her hand.

"Hello, my darling."

She kisses her mother, too, before perusing the breakfast dishes. Ed lights a cigarette, bored with his toast. His mother has recovered from the distraction. "Well is there?"

"I'll leave it at the station. No one in Cambridge will steal it."

"But then you have to carry all your things to the college. Are you sure Cleggy can't help you?"

"Oh for God's sake, Marian, let him do what he wants." His

father hasn't raised his head from his newspaper. "If he can't appreciate Cleggy, that's his business." A phone rings, distant but intrusive. "Who the hell's that?"

"Don't be so tetchy, daddy." His daughter grins flirtatiously as she settles at the table. "It might be someone fun. A handsome prince come to steal me away."

Her father's face softens. "Then he'll have to secure my permission." Ed wonders how he's so easily beguiled by her. At best she's irritating. He presumes his father's intelligence is outwitted by his egotism. The dining room door opens again and an older woman appears, stouter than the rest with a face worn dry by long servitude. But she is familiar enough not to apologise for her intrusion.

"It's for you, Master Ed. The gentleman says you're expecting his call."

"Thanks, Sam." He inhales a last drag of smoke into his lungs, aware that his palms are suddenly cold, his mouth dry, a quickening of his heartbeat. The phone sits on an occasional table at the foot of the staircase. He waits until she's disappeared to the kitchen before picking up the receiver.

"Edward Grant speaking."

"Your cousin's arrived." The voice is like grains of sand. A heavy smoker.

"Thank you, that's good to know." Ed glances to the dining room, relieved to hear idle chatter.

"She'll have to buy a guidebook while she's here. I thought Morgan's Bookshop would be a good place for you to catch up. I've suggested the 18th at 11 o'clock."

"Excellent. I'll look forward to it."

The phone clicks to silence. He replaces the receiver and steps back to the dining room.

"Well? Who on earth was that?" His father can barely conceal his impatience.

"Someone I knew vaguely at school. He got a place at Emmanuel so we're going to meet up." He flattens his half-smoked cigarette into the ashtray. "If you'll excuse me I'd better finish packing."

Sitting at the writing desk in his bedroom he unlocks the central drawer and removes a buff folder, searching its contents until he finds a small photograph. Black and white, head and shoulders; he assumes a passport photo. It's of a young woman. She stares blankly but the absence of character can't deny her grace.

A sharp rap on his bedroom door breaks his gaze. He slips the folder and photo back into the drawer before opening the door, a smile etched onto the handsome face that greets him. "Hope I'm not disturbing you. I thought maybe we should have a quick chat. Before you go."

They drift into the neat room, his father casting his eye about its contents as if he'd never previously entered. There are some clues to his son's pre-occupations; a map of the world above his desk, a few history books on the bookshelf, chemistry textbooks neatly stacked above them; a framed photograph of Ed captaining the First Eleven school hockey team. Dust motes dance in a band of sunlight streaming through the window.

His father takes a slim, silver cigarette case from the pocket of his jacket and offers the opened case, urging Ed to sit. Taking the desk chair for himself he leaves Ed to perch on the edge of the bed. An empty suitcase lies beside him.

"Not quite as packed as you suggested." His father taps his cigarette on the case.

"It's just moving clothes from A to B. Hardly a complex equation." Ed bends his head forward to reach the flame of his father's cigarette lighter. "Thank you."

"Sam could do it so much better. You'll just crease everything."

"I survived two years in the army perfectly well without Sam." His tone is more sarcastic than he'd intended. But he has a lot to sort out and his father is wasting his time.

A plume of dense smoke drifts lazily from his father's lips "Up to you." He pauses again, letting his words hang in the air. Plainly there's a lecture coming. And there is. "You're an intelligent man, Edward. You'll do well, of course you will, I've no doubt about that. But I'd be disappointed if you didn't take this opportunity more seriously."

If that's the entirety of it then he can cope. He's had far worse. "Thank you for the compliment. I promise I'll do my best."

"Good. I think that would go a long way to – shall we say, putting you on the right road? I've accepted the Navy wasn't your bag. It's a shame but there we are. But don't embarrass me again. I'll tolerate many things but I won't tolerate the family name being dishonoured. Do you understand?"

"Of course."

"Good. In that case I'd just like to wish you good luck."

"Thank you, father, I think I might need it. Now if you'll excuse me I really do need to get on."

"Of course. That's settled then. No more fucking about."

Ed expels the curdled smoke in a thin stream. "None at all."

His father rises from the chair, still an athletic build in his late forties. Ed wonders momentarily how many women have succumbed to his charms. He hesitates at the door. "I'm glad we had a chat. Part of growing up means understanding life isn't a game."

Ed raises a feeble smile. "It seems not."

"I'll be in my office if you want to find me. Before you go."

After his father's left, Ed remains on the bed, staring at the sports team photograph on the wall. The cigarette burns slowly to his fingers. He drops it into the wastepaper bin and walks across to the picture, considering it more closely for a moment before lifting it from the hook. It follows the cigarette stub into the bin.

An hour later Cleggy swings the MG Magnette out of the garages on to the broad, gravel drive fronting the Edwardian mansion. A midday sun flatters the maroon paintwork to a burnished glow. He steps out, brushing any invisible crease from his uniform, and relieves Ed of his suitcase, placing it carefully in the boot of the car before handing him the keys.

"Thanks, Cleggy." Returning to the stone porch, where his family have gathered, Ed kisses his mother and sister on their cheeks and extends his hand to his father. He feels relief more than anything. At last the chance to escape without too much ceremony.

"Goodbye father."

"Goodbye, Edward."

Turning back towards the car, he's aware of the crunch of gravel beneath his shoes; a silence where perhaps other families would shed tears. The interior of his beloved Magnette greets him with the scent of warmed leather. It's both heavenly and comforting. He turns the key and revs the engine, letting it find its throaty breath. Gravel flies. The chrome wheels spin towards the wrought iron gates where he catches a last glimpse of his family in the rear-view mirror. His father is the first to turn back to the house.

The route takes him first east, then south past Peterborough towards Cambridge. He drives fast, oblivious to the unbroken Fenland landscape passing his windscreen. In less than an hour he reaches Cambridge but ambling traffic slows his progress; bickering parents, he imagines, pushing their Daimlers through narrowing streets to unload their innocent offspring. Nearing the station, he drives past a meandering sprawl of fresh students heading towards their chosen colleges. Far more men than women, their earnest expressions and smart tweed jackets belying their still juvenile minds. Some look elated but others are clearly exhausted, impeded by a sleepless night and the dead weight of overstuffed suitcases and golf club caddies. He pities them; more for their shackles of privilege than their ridiculous accoutrements. At the station car park he selects a space towards the far end. A locomotive hisses and belches into the cloudless sky, presumably on its way to King's Lynn. He steps out to watch its passengers disgorge from the station, already deep in conversation, observing them closely, wondering which, if any, will become part of his circle. Perhaps one of them will be his room-mate.

He's seen a photo, knows his name and his family history, but it'd be impossible to distinguish him amongst this herd. An unwelcome apprehension tightens his belly at the thought of his task. Until the phone call this morning it really had seemed a game.

Abandoning the car, he follows the procession towards the colleges. He is steadier again now. It was only a brief moment of doubt. And his mental list is drawing better shape. What were previously sketches, shaded outlines, are finally attaining flesh. Made human.

3

London is not unfamiliar to her; but witnessed through the eyes of a child. She has a vague memory of sitting on her mother's lap on the top of a bus, watching the neatly choreographed dance of umbrellas down the shopping streets; the tarnished Regency facades, dimly lit, their inhabitants no doubt reminiscing on a more glorious epoch. But before long they were on the train to Liverpool, and from there by ship to America, where all of Europe and its messy wars slipped her mind. For a while at least. Not much has changed as far as she can tell. Where New York and West Berlin gorge on excess like two spoilt kids, London seems content to wrap itself in the mantle of its past; cosy, familiar, a little complacent, perhaps still arrogant despite the devastation of war. Whatever the affliction it still dresses for the theatre, oblivious to its terminal decline. Not yet realising that Capitalism has poisoned its drink.

Kitty alights from the bus that has brought her from the airport to King's Cross Station. It is late afternoon. The cool air already predicts shortened days and she promises herself that she'll buy some warmer clothes. A ribbon of dark overcoats and folded newspapers emerges from the escalator onto the concourse. One handsome office type raises his trilby as he passes, which she finds more amusing than flattering. But it won't distract her. Scouting across the main foyer she spots the line of three wooden, telephone kiosks adjacent to the newsagent. They are all occupied so, as instructed, she buys a copy of the Daily Mail and waits patiently until the middle booth is free. Once inside, the phone rings almost immediately. She picks up the receiver and peers through the grimy glass to the concourse.

"Hello?"

"It's Joseph." The voice is flat. Uninviting.

"Hello, Joseph, it's your cousin."

"How was your flight?"

She's rehearsed the line a thousand times. "A little bumpy. But uneventful. We landed safely."

There's a pause. For a moment she fears her contact is unconvinced. Perhaps she got a word wrong. But he resumes the conversation, his tone more urgent. "Take the next train to King's Lynn. It leaves in ten minutes. Find carriage G and sit in the compartment furthest from the engine. There are no reservations, it's full of undergraduates. Ask for a light. Get to know the student with dark hair wearing a green sports jacket and a light brown tie. You will be met at Cambridge."

A click. Then nothing. Kitty replaces the receiver and steps out of the booth. She buys a packet of Senior Service cigarettes from the newsagent before marching to the ticket office. A sallow-faced individual slips her ticket across the counter and barks the platform number. She thanks him and hurries to Platform 5. It's exactly as her contact suggested. Young men hover beside their parents in protracted farewells, others watch from carriage windows as stoic mothers wave gloved hands. She embarks at carriage G and slides open the door to the first compartment, the furthest from the engine. Four of the seats are already occupied; young men, each wearing a greenish or brown sports jacket. She shouldn't find it funny but she does. A window seat is still free, facing the rear of the train. Stepping between knees she lifts her suitcase towards the rack. Immediately a boy in the opposite window seat interjects, insisting he should help. She finds him cute, not bad looking either; grinning helplessly as she accepts his offer. He blushes. Shy she surmises. Inexperienced. Virgin? Bound to be.

As they both sit down another young man steps into the cramped compartment. He looks a bit older. Or at least not as innocent. He throws a battered suitcase onto the rack and claims the seat diagonally opposite Kitty, at the same time pulling a magazine from his jacket coat pocket. Another greenish sports jacket; a tie that could be brown in brighter light but then so could the others. She tries to relax. They have an hour or so before they reach Cambridge.

A distant whistle blows. A curtain of steam drifts past the window. The train creeps forward, gathering speed through a series of tunnels, until suburbs relinquish to mud-tracked fields, which lie stubby and barren since harvest. She gazes from the window, the newspaper open at her lap, trying to assess in the reflection which of the young men is her target. She hadn't expected to feel nervous but she does. Until now everything had been training, a textbook of scenarios, a blackboard of information, bootcamp exercises; but here she is alone, an outsider in a world strangely familiar to her, but one which she no longer admires or countenances. Ironic therefore, almost laughable, to find herself sharing a few cubic metres of air with the future elite of the British establishment.

The older-looking student who arrived last speaks least; his intense concentration reserved for his magazine. On closer inspection it's one she's familiar with. The New Statesman. In the brighter light she can see that his tie is definitely brown but then so is that of the thicker-set individual who sits next to her. From her leather handbag, one of the few American possessions she retains, she removes the Senior Service cigarette packet, opens it and places one to her lips, pretending to search in her bag for a lighter. "Oh, jeepers, I'm such a dim wit." Her Philadelphian accent a touch over-played.

In a breath the thick-set boy next to her is delving in his jacket pocket. Finding it empty he tries the other one but discovers he's already missed the deadline. The magazine reader has an arm outstretched; a match lit. No smile to accompany it. She bends forward to touch the flame with her cigarette then settles back into the mottled upholstery. "Thank you, that's very kind."

He blows out the match and flicks it to the floor, scrutinising her now as much as he scrutinised his beloved magazine. "You're American."

More of a statement than a question. She can't trace a regional accent. Nor is there any strong indication of class. She pushes a plume of smoke to the ceiling and smiles. "Why does that sound like an accusation?"

"Sorry. I was just curious."

Kitty considers for a moment before she answers. "Not a bad trait to have. My parents live in Philadelphia. I was brought up there. But I was born in Germany."

His face softens. "Sie sind weit von zu Hause weg."

His German is both accurate and well pronounced. She tries to veil her surprise, tipping a line of grey ash into the ashtray under the window. "Ihr Deutsch ist gut."

"I studied it for Higher School Certificate. After that I was posted out to Bremen for National Service."

"And now you're at university?"

"Starting. First term."

"Well, I wish you luck with your studies." Kitty inhales on her cigarette, deliberately waiting to see what he does next. Turning her gaze to the passing fields, she catches his reflection. He is still watching her.

"Do you live here now?"

She wonders why he doesn't conduct the conversation in German. It would be more private. Perhaps he's a perfectionist and fears a mistake. Which could be costly, depending on the circumstances. Her gaze returns to his. "I'm on secondment to a school near Cambridge. The headmistress thought it'd be a great idea to teach her pupils some rudimentary German. I guess she hopes it'll do a bit to break down prejudices some of them may've gotten from their parents since the war." She breaks into a smile. "So here I am."

"I hope you enjoy it."

"Thank you. I hope so too."

He exhibits a brief smile before dropping his head back to the magazine. She uses his deflected gaze to assess his potential. Definitely more man than boy. The bone structure strains under the tight, pale skin; his appearance made more intense, even hostile, by the slick, jet black hair and heavy shadow along his jawline. But her impression stretches beyond his physiology. In their brief conversation she'd sensed a current, a flicker of something unresolved and heavily guarded. She hadn't encountered it very often in young people, the majority were usually unwritten palimpsests. But she thinks she can work with it if requested.

Thirty minutes later the train jolts to a halt in Cambridge Station. As if to appease his failing, the thick-set young man grabs her suitcase from the rack. She thanks him, but insists he let her carry it, once they've disembarked. Her interlocutor has already disappeared along the platform into the throng of fresh students. She would have liked a longer conversation but at least she has a morsel to report from her first assignment. She stops to take a breath, a moment to compose herself. Straightening the lapel of her jacket and lifting her chin slightly, she presses on.

It's hard to spot what she should be looking for. The contact gave no clue. But then, amongst the commotion, she sees her name scrawled on a piece of card, *Miss Bernstein,* held aloft above the head of a rather short, young woman. Kitty composes a lipstick smile. "Hi. I'm Kitty. Kitty Bernstein."

The woman drops the card to her side. "Miss Bernstein. Welcome to Cambridge."

"Thank you. But please call me Kitty. Everyone does."

The briefest flicker of doubt crosses the young woman's face. "I'm afraid American informality hasn't quite reached here yet. I'm Jane by the way, but when we're in public I'm Miss Farley and you're still Miss Bernstein."

Kitty smiles again. "Got it."

"Let me take that, the car's not far."

Without remonstrating Kitty relinquishes her suitcase. It feels appropriate. She likes Jane instantly. She's not exactly an English buttercup; her facial features are too small for her round face and her hair is forced into submission by hairclips but she has a cuddly warmth to her. A faithful spaniel.

Jane maintains a patter of words until they reach a sage green Morris Traveller. "The beast. I apologise for its demonic state."

Books and files are strewn on the seats and a sprinkling of sweet wrappers litters the floor. But she's a confident driver as Kitty soon discovers. Driving north at speed through the city centre she's forced to admit that it's as historically impressive as her guidebook had claimed. Untouched by the blight of war, she assumes. How different from her own city.

"Do you teach at the school, Jane?"

Her new companion chucks her head back with mirth. "Oh no. No, I'm the school admin girl, come receptionist, come general dogsbody. Any help you want, or any questions, come to me first. The kids are a lovely bunch but they can get a bit unruly if you're soft on them. Nothing outrageous. The usual thing; boys throwing pencils under your desk so they can retrieve them as an excuse to stare up your skirt. I'm sure you're used to it in Germany."

Kitty finds herself picking an imaginary fleck of dust from the fold of her skirt, surprised at her own prudishness. "I'm not sure I am. But I'll look out for it."

"I'll take you to your lodgings first. There's no point going to the school but I'll drive you past so you can see where you have to be in the morning. It's only a five-minute walk from where you're staying."

The village of Stratham is a forty-minute drive from Cambridge. The conversation remains light and sporadic but she's relieved when they finally enter the village.

"That's our pub on the right." Jane laughs again. "Most important building in a village after the church. Lots of the locals would say I got that the wrong way round."

It's more isolated than Kitty had imagined, a small community surrounded by flat, arable land. According to her companion, the inhabitants are a mixture of farm workers and commuters to Cambridge, but there's no train service, just the regular bus. The Norman church stands at the centre of the village. Beside it, a substantial, Victorian brick building lies in its long shadow. She reads the weather-beaten sign at the gate. "Stratham Primary School for Boys and Girls."

"It's a lovely school. I think you'll be very happy. You're just further along the road."

A minute later they pull in behind another parked car. A tall beech hedge stretches far into the distance.

"That's the Manor House behind there," Jane explains, pointing to the hedge. "It's a beautiful place. The family still own most of the village and they throw a lovely party for everybody at Christmas. I'm sure you'll be invited. Your landlady, Mrs Johnson, is a housekeeper there. She's just across the road."

Jane steps out of the car, retrieving the suitcase from the rear seat. Kitty follows, her eye drawn to a row of cottages, opposite the hedge, perched on a high grass bank. A sheep bleats somewhere. A dog barks in reply. No children playing, no rumble of trains or wrecking balls dismantling bomb-torn tenement blocks. The rebirth of Berlin had become her daily soundtrack. She thinks she will miss it.

A footpath runs along the back of the cottages, framed by low picket fences on one side and open countryside on the other. There's no access for cars; accommodation built originally for labourers at the manor house, she assumes. Jane opens the back gate of the third cottage and walks across a neat, stone yard to the door. Before she can knock, the door is opened.

"Hello, Mrs Johnson, may I introduce Miss Bernstein?"

A plump woman wearing a pinafore stands in the doorway. Her

mousey hair is cut for economy, a tight fringe framing her face. But she has kind eyes and wrinkles around her mouth that suggest a previous life of laughter. "Good afternoon, Miss Bernstein. Welcome to Stratham."

Kitty smiles. "Thank you. Lovely to meet you, Mrs Johnson."

In the narrow kitchen there is little room to manoeuvre. It smells of polish and damp laundry. Her landlady brushes her hands fastidiously on her apron. "Let me show you to your room. I s'pect you'll want to rest before tea. It must've been a long journey."

Kitty expects Jane to follow them into the corridor and is disappointed when she doesn't. "I'll leave you to it, if I may. Thank you, Mrs Johnson. Goodnight, Miss Bernstein, I'll see you tomorrow at school. Eight o'clock. You know where it is."

Before she can reply Jane has gone. She follows her new landlady up a steep set of stairs, bending her head to avoid a low timber above the bedroom door. A single bed nestles under the eaves but it's the view from the dormer window that compels her. Beyond the field a line of elm trees stands like sentinels guarding the border of the village, their silhouettes imposing, as if they'd challenge anyone to cross it.

"The bathroom's the first door on your left. I've put out a towel. Tea'll be ready in an hour."

Once the door is shut and her landlady's footsteps retreat down the stairs, Kitty flops onto the bed. The mattress is thin and uneven. She sighs, not having expected to feel so listless. Or lonely. They didn't mention that at training. Resisting the temptation to close her eyes, she pulls herself up again, opening her suitcase to hang what few clothes she possesses in the corner wardrobe. She's dying for a cigarette but there's no sign of an ashtray. Returning to the edge of the bed, her eye falls to the

27

threadbare carpet. No one had mentioned boredom either. A silent room in a silent village, the only indication of life coming from occasional footsteps on the stone floor below. It will change of course, this temporary displacement, but for now she feels profoundly homesick, longing for the company of Ursula and her comrades at the department. To remind herself of her purpose, she takes a small notebook from her handbag and leafs through to the last entry. *Morgan's Buchhandlung September 18, 11 Uhr.* Until that date she's a teacher at a primary school. She must take this duty seriously; to pursue the guise half-heartedly would not only arouse suspicion but also fail the children. And she must also be an excellent tenant. A companion to Mrs Johnson. An aroma of cooking seeps through the floorboards. Steaming fish. She's surprised at the comfort it fosters.

4

Finding himself with time to kill, Ed walks through the narrow Cambridge alleys, thinking he might use the spare half hour to reconnoitre his rendez-vous. Even the words appeal to him, there's something romantic about the French, which he knows is facile, but it conjures thoughts of the Resistance. Brave men and women fighting the yoke of Fascist oppression. Except the fight isn't yet won. His student eye considers the revered spires and Georgian facades that line his path but he feels impervious to their flirtation. The guidebooks are full of sycophantic eulogies, both nauseous and anachronistic; surely in mid-twentieth century Britain, a modern factory should engender equal praise?

When he'd arrived at Trinity Hall, he'd discovered his room-mate hadn't yet appeared so he'd left his suitcase with the porter, claiming he wanted to explore the city before settling to his quarters. The porter mapped a route for him, to which he listened politely but instantly discarded. It seemed good tactics that his new room-mate should discover their room first, believing it would put him at ease, perhaps even give him a sense of control; anything which might muddy the reality.

Rose Crescent is familiar to him but he's never paid it much attention. It's just another cute, Cambridge lane, housing an array of idiosyncratic stores, like any other in the city. He finds the bookshop, a Dickensian bay-windowed building, in a sorry state of disrepair. The brickwork is etched with streaks of rust from the leaky guttering above; window frames a furrow of splintered wood.

Pushing against the heavy, wooden door he steps into the gloom.

His first impression is one of chaos. There's no order to the array of bookshelves; nor particular way to circumnavigate them. It's quiet as Sunday prayers, despite a few fellow browsers. And crucially there's nowhere to sit. Climbing the stairs to the first floor, he wonders why his contact had chosen such an unsuitable venue. Here the layout is much the same except there's music emanating from the floor above. He climbs toward the sound to find a series of booths, like rail carriage compartments, standing either side of the staircase. Perched on vinyl-clad benches, groups of students, cigarettes dangling from their young mouths, indulge in animated conversation. Wisps of smoke dance under the table lights, as if mimicking the beat of the jazz quartet which radiates from a small, metal speaker in each booth. Straining to catch what the students are saying, he realises he can't; the combination of acoustics and music make it impossible. It's perfect.

Satisfied with the reconnoitre, he makes his way back to the porter's lodge to collect his suitcase. His first impression, as he enters the college grounds, is of an exquisitely manicured front court, dominated by four impeccably mown, rectangular lawns. Late summer roses release their perfume against the soft stone walls to the windows above. Ahead of him a portal in the building leads the eye to another garden at the far side. He walks through, remembering the grand dining room to his left which he'd visited earlier in the year. Stepping out again to the sunlight, he sees students communing in idle groups under the canopies of mature trees. Other newcomers appear more solitary; reading books in quiet contemplation. Perhaps they're too nervous to join in. He has some sympathy. To his right, a nineteenth century, red-brick, resident's hall hugs the length of the lawn. He notices the casement window of his room is open. A silhouette slips out of sight. He hopes his new room-mate appreciates the view. The room had been selected at the beginning of summer; his contact had made the necessary arrangements.

He steals a breath.

Climbing the hallway stairs to the first floor, his fingers trace the flaking, pale cream paintwork. The door to his room is half ajar. He knocks anyway. It's polite. Pushing the door wider, he sees a young man, at least two inches taller than him, standing close to the window.

"Hope I haven't interrupted anything?"

His room-mate turns. Apologetic. More handsome than his photograph. "I was just looking - it's a nice view." He walks over, steady arm outstretched. "You must be Edward."

"Call me Ed, everyone does. Less pompous." He takes the hand; the grip hard and calloused.

"Alec. Alec Carter."

"Delighted to meet you, Alec."

His room-mate retreats, enabling Ed to enter the room. There's a suitcase on the bed underneath the window. Next to it lies an open magazine. He can't tell what sort. Plainly Alec has caught his gaze.

"We could toss a coin for the beds. I just dumped my case..."

"...No at all, if that's the one you want, you should have it. I've got relatives dotted about nearby so I'll probably be away from time to time anyway." He drops his own case onto the far bed in a recess behind the door. It's darker but at least he's hidden if someone crashes in. The room is as he remembers it from his summer viewing. Two small wardrobes by each bed, a couple of tatty easy chairs in front of the fireplace, a sink behind the door, a gas ring and a shelf accommodating a kettle, a toaster and two zinc saucepans. A bit grim but National Service was worse.

"How about you? Have you come far? I'm sure for some Cambridge must seem like a foreign country."

Alec Carter smiles. "Almost. I'm from Wiltshire."

"Oh. Too bad."

"It's not all pigs and fields. We've got the highest cathedral in the country."

"And some of the best beer."

"You've been there?'

"A long time ago. But I don't suppose much has changed."

"I don't s'pose it has. You don't know when tea is, do you? I'm starving."

There's no particular regional accent. He assumes it's because Alexander Carter went to grammar school which will have a wider catchment than the local secondary. It makes him more conscious of his own clipped delivery. Glancing back while his room-mate opens his suitcase he sees a rugged face; pallid skin accentuated by eyes and hair that are blacker than night. There's an almost thuggish quality but also a mournfulness that suggests he'd shed tears while beating the shit out of you. At any rate he knows several women who would bed this man instantly. Dismissing his petty jealousy, he extracts a bottle of Bells Whisky from his case. "The porter told me supper's at seven. There's some sort of tedious welcome by the vice chancellor before we get to throw buns. Anyway, what it all means is that we've got an hour to get pie-eyed. But first we need a glass." On the shelf above the basin he spots a tumbler housing a toothbrush. Alec's Presumably. "Ah. Do you mind?"

"Be my guest."

He removes the toothbrush and fills the tumbler with a large measure, handing it across the room to his room-mate. "Hope you like whisky. I managed to light-finger it from my father's drinks cabinet just before leaving. He'll fly into a rage then demand that Sam brings him another. Poor Sam. She'll hate me too."

"Who's Sam?"

"Our long-suffering housekeeper." He pours again, this time into a silver flask which he's retrieved from his jacket pocket. A little spills to the floor. "Cheers, old boy. Pleasure to meet you." Arching his neck, he presses the flask to his lips. An observer, namely Alec, would assume he's drinking copiously. "Right that's the formalities over. Let's begin the interrogation. Ten questions each. Sit down on your bed. You'll need to concentrate. I'll go first as I provided the booze. Question one. Answer mandatory. Have you got a pretty sister?"

His room-mate laughs as intended. "I'm afraid I don't have a sister."

"That's a bugger." The first objective, to put his room-mate at ease, has been executed; the second is to see how he handles alcohol. He's chosen whisky because it reveals character traits more quickly, particularly those quick to anger, which he's been told could be Alexander Carter's greatest failing. Pouring a second glass for his room-mate he asks routine questions; nothing he doesn't know already, favourite football team, Swindon Town, country, Russia, most-loved book, film, worst hangover etcetera. Tedious stuff. He purposely avoids Imber. Too early. The game switches. His turn. But he's happy to oblige, carefully sketching an impression of class privilege and superficial cares. It's not an inaccurate description of his family but he hopes his humorous anecdotes will entertain more than repulse. The more he presents the irredeemable aristocrat the more Alec will try to convert him. Of course Ed will resist these attempts. Part of the plan. He reaches for the bottle and fills the tumbler for a third time. Alexander Carter can hold his drink. No sign yet of inebriation. "Okay. That's six, you've only got four more."

His room-mate stares into the whisky before pouring another mouthful down his throat. "So unlike me, you have a pretty sister. In that case my next question is, how old is she?"

"Nineteen. Three more."

"Is she at university?"

"Don't be silly, she's a girl. Two left."

"So does she have a job?"

"Yes. Never frame a question that can be answered with a simple yes or no. Bad slip up, old man. Last question."

"Sorry. Alcoholic error. So, if she has a job, what does she do?"

"She's looking for the richest bachelor in Lincolnshire. And when she finds him she'll get herself invited to dinner and slip a dexterous hand around his bollocks while pudding's served." He observes a flicker of shock register on his room-mate's face. The Wiltshire thug obviously does have some sensitivity. But suddenly his head rocks back. They laugh together. The whisky is doing its work. "Come on. One last drop before supper."

His room-mate sips again before handing over the empty tumbler. "I'll be honest, Ed, I'm fucking nervous. I've never eaten in a dining hall."

"Then, my friend, we absolutely have to stick together. I've barely eaten out of one." Raising his flask as a mark of solidarity,

Ed seals his lips across the open neck to feign another gulp. As they finally step out into the courtyard, he finds the evening air cooler than expected. He's grateful for it after a stuffy room. So far his impressions are good ones. Alec Carter, though now understandably quite drunk, hasn't shown any significant character deviation under alcohol; critical for his suitability. He can file a good report.

Trailing their fellow students towards the dining hall, he watches his room-mate suddenly deviate from the gravel to the lawn where he retches in the shadow of a large beech tree. Presumably not the first to abuse the facilities. He observes more with interest than concern. The physical ability to consume alcohol can be improved. It's a minor detail. More importantly how does he recover himself? Waiting patiently for Alec to re-emerge he wonders what they'll be offered for supper. Or tea, as his room-mate put it. He doesn't have to wait long. A moment later his room-mate steps back out of the shadows on to the path; saying nothing, not even an apology. The incident might as well not have occurred. Another good indicator.

The dining hall is exactly as he'd remembered. Four long tables stretch almost the length of the room. Above them a timber framed, vaulted ceiling suggests the authority and order of a Protestant church. Portraits of former masters glare down at them from gilt-framed pictures, bathed in ethereal candlelight, as the chaplain conducts Grace. Ed doesn't close his eyes, aware of the elaborate cutlery laid before him and what, Alec, standing next to him, will make of it. An unwarranted shiver flickers down the length of his spine. At least he thinks it's unwarranted. He's in control of his assignment. Confident of his touch. Perhaps he's not immune to the illustriousness of Cambridge; the ancient history of its traditions. But it's Trinity Hall's recent history that he reveres most. An event the college will undoubtedly try its best to smother once it finally breaks the surface. Which it will. And it is this, he realises, which is turning his fingertips to ice. The excitement of what may yet come. The part he will play in it. An almost unbearable sense of purpose, the like of which he has never felt, is hammering at his door.

5

Kitty enjoys the film more than she'd expected. John Wayne isn't one of her movie heroes but her father adores him. He'd promised that it wasn't another cowboy Western and he was right; the wise cracks between Wayne and Maureen O'Hara make her laugh, the Irish landscape radiates in all its Technicolor glory. Perhaps she and Robert should go there someday; perhaps even for their honeymoon. She thinks this while observing her father's profile. He gazes adoringly at the screen, the smoke dusted rays of light dancing on the edge of his glasses. Kitty's pleased he's enjoying himself. Movies have always been his escape. The more stressed he seems, the more he suggests going to the cinema. And they've been going a lot recently. Her mother doesn't appear to be so enamoured. She watches, solemn faced, as if she's witnessing a different story. But then that's her mother. A warm hand settles around her own; Robert's way of saying pay attention, concentrate, stop worrying about your father. She smiles an apology and returns her thoughts to Irish romance.

Driving back to Clifton Heights they discuss the merits of The Quiet Man. She curls into Robert on the back bench, the bumps in the road smoothed out by the miracle of her father's Chevrolet Deluxe; his latest pride and joy.

Her mother is as forthright as ever. "And why did Kate insist on chasing the money in the first place? She should've let it go, she got the husband she wanted, what else matters?"

37

"It wasn't about the money, mother."

"Of course it was about the money."

"So why do you think she opened the boiler door? It was so Sean could burn it. She didn't care about the money, it was more the principle of the thing. Her brother was being dishonourable."

"But they lied to him."

"Only because he refused to let her marry Sean!"

"Okay, enough already." It's a timely interjection from her father. She glances at Robert. He's smirking. His own family aren't quite so vociferous. Now her father has their attention he continues. "I thought it was a good film. Not Wayne's usual but good anyway. None of the characters are unblemished, who is? But they all showed a bit of contrition. Isn't that right, Robert?"

Kitty catches his glance in the rear-view mirror. Her father always likes to include Robert, sensing that he's not used to fighting for airtime. She doesn't believe anyone is as compassionate as her father, despite his experiences in Berlin.

"I'm not sure, Mr Bernstein. I guess it was funny enough but they should've taken him to court first. Or at least seen an attorney."

Kitty rises to the bait. "It's a film, Robert. Not a legal handbook."

She is even more irritated when he laughs; his pearl white teeth completing the ordered symmetry of American good looks. "All I'm saying, there's no dispute can't be settled by a decent lawyer at a fair price."

Her father pulls the Chevrolet on to the drive of a sizeable, clapboard house. Clifton Heights is an affluent, middle-class suburb, not especially known for an immigrant population. There are doctors and lawyers and academics, and Walter Bernstein is just another of those, except he's a German Jew who's chosen to cohabit with American protestants rather than confine himself to a ghetto; and Kitty is proud of him for that. They step from the car towards the front door, still laughing and negotiating their viewpoints on the film. Candy pink blossom hangs from the cherry trees and she can smell the scent of freshly mown grass lingering in the unusually warm, evening air. She can't quite believe that by the following Spring she and Robert will occupy their own house. They will make their own decisions about which shrubs to plant, and which to remove, and what colour they should paint the front door. Not that she imagines Robert will care. A brushstroke of guilt touches her as she wonders what her childhood friend, Ursula, would think. But the dreams they conjured together all those years ago would not be appropriate now; to survive one must adapt, as her father constantly reminds her. And she has adapted, but she sometimes wishes her father would acknowledge the sacrifices they have made, the sense of loss. She only tried to question him once; 'dear Kitty," he said, "much better we share love than pain.'

"There's a funny thing." Her father hovers at the front door, his house key poised at the lock.

"What is it?" Her mother is already anxious, as if she's been expecting something.

"I swear I shut the door when we came out." He pushes the door open and steps into the house. Almost without realising, Kitty links her arm into Robert's before crossing the threshold. Casting her eye quickly across the living area she sees nothing untoward or out of place.

Her mother's relief is palpable. "You must have forgotten, Walter. Your mind's always too busy on higher things. Maybe you didn't eat enough. I'll make something up, I think we could all do with eating something."

Before anyone has a chance to reply she's disappeared into the kitchen. Kitty catches a complicit smirk from her father; it's a family joke that her mother regards food as the salvation for any number of evils.

"Night cap, Robert." He's hovering over the drinks cabinet.

"Thanks Mr Bernstein. A scotch and soda."

"Kitty?"

"No. I have some schoolwork still to mark."

"You okay?" Robert has settled on the sofa beside her. She's not sure why she feels tense, either the unexplained door, her father losing his memory, or the thought of Ursula and their dreams of greatness.

"Just tired. That's all."

Her father is searching amongst the array of bottles but clearly can't find what he's looking for. He shouts to the kitchen. "Agnes, have you seen the scotch any place?"

"Didn't you have a drink with Bill in your study the other night? Maybe it's there."

"Oh my God, she's right. She's always right, Goddamn it." He turns away towards a door behind the sofas. Kitty's attention is distracted by Robert who's massaging her neck, rubbing her earlobes at the same time. She finds it comforting. If her father weren't in the same room she'd find it arousing.

"Oh, Jesus."

She breaks away. "What is it, Paps?"

"Jesus Christ."

She rushes towards the open door, convinced he's having a heart attack. Instead she finds him surveying the disarray of his office; papers strewn across his desk, drawers wide open or tipped on to the floor, a picture of his parents knocked from the wall. The curtains are billowing in a light breeze; the sash window is lifted; the glass shattered. "Oh my God, Paps, what happened? Shall I call the police? I'll call the PPD."

"No. Wait."

"What? Why?

"Just let me think."

Robert is now with them. "Hell's teeth, you should really call the police, Mr Bernstein. The sooner the better."

"What's going on?" Her mother has arrived from the kitchen, knife still in hand. "Oh my God."

"It's alright, Agnes. It's okay. They obviously got scared by something and ran out. There's nothing missing. Robert, will you help me check upstairs?"

"Sure."

"I'll call the PPD when I know the situation."

"For God's Sake, Paps. Why not call them straight away?" Kitty's finds her father's hesitancy exasperating. She assumes he's in shock.

"It's fine." He already has a foot on the staircase, shadowed by Robert. "You and your mother wait here. Everything's gonna be fine."

As soon as they disappear she lights a cigarette and paces the floor. The knife is still clasped tight in her mother's hand but she has slumped into an armchair, her face drained of colour. Kitty tips a fragment of ash into an ashtray. "Why's he so stubborn?"

"You know what he's like."

"But he could get himself killed."

"There's no point trying to stop him. When you've seen as much as he has you get a little too self-reliant. I'm sure they'll be fine. Shall I make a bed up for Robert?"

"What? Oh, no. No, he has to get back. He's in court in the morning."

"But he'll need something proper to eat before that. Why don't I just make the bed up in case he decides…"

… "There's nothing touched, it's all fine." Her father reappears at the bottom of the stairs, once again trailed by Robert. "They must've gotten themselves in through my study window, then something must have spooked them. I guess they must have rushed out the front door. I knew I shut it when we left for…"

"…Who's they, Paps?" Kitty finds it hard to hide the frustration in her voice. "You're jumping to conclusions already. It could've just been a guy by himself…or even a woman, for God's sake."

"Don't be silly, Kitty." Her mother's face is full of reprimand. "Your father just meant anybody."

Robert steps forward, putting his arm around her shoulder, for which she feels grateful. He'll quell whatever fire has started inside her with his soft words and courteous manner. "I think the main thing is everyone's okay. It was probably just a petty thief but I'm sure the PPD will be able to shed some light on it. I really think it would be the best idea if you made that call now, Mr Bernstein. It should help reassure you and it's best if they get here as soon as possible."

Her father sighs. She watches the air exhale from his body like a sail collapsing without a breeze. "Thank you, Robert, I will. Right away."

"I should be going, anyway. I have court early. I'm really sorry. But I'll come by tomorrow to make sure you're all okay."

Her father finds a smile. Always courteous till the last. "I really appreciate that. And your bravery just now. If you'll excuse me, I'm sure Kitty will see you out."

He gives a wan smile before turning back to his study. Kitty hovers, taking a last drag on her cigarette as her fiancé finds her mother's cheek accompanied by a few last words of solace. Stabbing the butt out into the ashtray she follows him to the front door where he glances both ways along the street, as if searching for clues in the darkness. "Probably just some deadbeat looking for a lucky break. Make sure your dad calls though. But I really don't think there's anything to be frightened of." He kisses her tenderly on the lips before retreating. She wishes he would stay but he's too dedicated to his work. Watching him climb into his car she suddenly feels afraid, despite his reassurance. The car pulls away up the street and rounds the corner on to the main boulevard. She can hear the engine still, until it fades into the quiet emptiness of a late Sunday evening. Stepping back to the house, she's aware of a visceral fear that seems to be multiplying within her. She can't remember feeling as anxious as this since the darkest days; just before they fled Berlin.

6

SEPTEMBER 1954,   LINCOLNSHIRE

She wakes with a start, staring at an unfamiliar lattice of oak beams above her. A chink of light through the curtain catches the edges of her bed before finding a vanity mirror. It's enough to let her make sense of the room; to re-assemble the objects into a space she can recognise.

"Your breakfast's ready, Miss Bernstein. I'd hate it to get cold." The voice behind the door is muffled but firm. Her landlady knocks again on the wooden frame. Presumably it was this that woke her. Glancing at the alarm clock Kitty's worst suspicions are confirmed. She's overslept. "Thank you, Mrs Johnson. I'll be down in a minute."

She's already chosen an outfit for her first day at school so she has time; the grey suit and her white blouse, perhaps more conservative than necessary but she wants to convey the right impression. If it's too hot she can find some summer dresses in Cambridge. The sleep thing is an error but she puts it down to a long journey. It won't happen again. Entering the kitchen she finds her landlady on her knees, washing the tiled steps that lead out to the back yard, a starched apron tied about her waist. She rises stiffly at Kitty's approach, wiping her hands on the apron. "Miss Bernstein, I trust you slept well."

"I did. Thank you. I'm so sorry. That bed's so comfortable, I think I…"

"…No matter. I've made a pot of tea which should still be warm. The egg'll be past its best, I'm afraid. Sit yourself down."

Kitty does as she's told, observing the pot under its thick cosy and a boiled egg, sitting in disconsolate isolation on a pale, yellow plate. "Thank you."

She's aware that she's being watched. Or studied rather, like an animal in a cage. Slipping the cosy off the pot she searches the kitchen for some point of conversation. But nothing presents itself. The walls shimmer under a coat of green gloss paint. There's a row of hooks for mugs, a high shelf for saucepans, and a tall cupboard, presumably a larder, with a calendar hanging on its door. Nothing is written on it for the month of September. She slices the top of her egg with a knife. It's boiled hard. Her own fault. She scoops it with a teaspoon. "It's delicious. Thank you, Mrs Johnson. We never get them so fresh in Berlin. Quite a treat." She offers a smile, aware that she is still under scrutiny.

"You been living there long? The school tells me you're more American really."

"Well I guess I am. It's a bit complicated. I'm an American citizen but I spent my early childhood in Germany. I just felt like going back."

"I can't think why. If I was in America I can't imagine I'd be wanting to return anywhere much."

"I had friends I missed. That and other things."

"I see. Well. Each to their own."

Kitty butters a slice of the cold toast, grateful that Mrs Johnson returns her attention to the tiles of her doorstep. She wonders if this woman has any friends. There's no sense of any other life around her. And yet she was plainly married. Perhaps her husband died fighting in the war, he'd have been the right age, in which case it's remarkably broad-minded of her to welcome a German into her house less than ten years later. Except it's hardly a welcome; there's plainly a reticence, some unease about Kitty's return to Berlin. So it must boil down to one of two things; either Mrs Johnson is lonely and grateful for her company, though nothing in her bearing suggests such a vulnerability; or more likely, she's desperate for the money, her war widow's pension being pretty meagre, and the opportunity to rent out a room, even to an enemy, must seem like a gift from God. Returning upstairs to collect her handbag, she stumbles across the clue she seeks. A framed photograph hangs discreetly in an alcove at the door to Mrs Johnson's bedroom. Smiling back at her is a young man in khaki uniform, perhaps late twenties. Not handsome but a gentle face. Imperfect teeth. Hair lacquered down across his forehead. Perhaps taken before he went to serve. Maybe after the war was over they were thinking they'd start a family. Maybe this is the sadness her landlady has to endure.

She hears the school before she sees it. Children gathered in the playground before morning prayers, their high-pitched squeals assaulting the sleepy village. Ridiculously she realises she's nervous, not having taught for two years; and wondering how she can be more apprehensive about a classroom full of primary school kids than a high-level assignment for the Foreign Intelligence Service. Smiling dutifully at mothers who wave their farewells at the gate, she steels herself to walk across the threshold. The school is a ramshackle affair, an assortment of low buildings in warm, ochre brick that link themselves to a higher central block. Its vaulted roof conveys more the impression of church than school. On either side there are separate entrances for girl and boys and she wonders which to use. She doesn't have the chance to decide. Jane Varley bustles out of the boys' entrance to greet her, her stubby legs working overtime.

"Miss Bernstein, welcome. The children are really looking forward to meeting you."

Kitty finds herself led by the arm towards the school, grateful that this charming woman is putting her at her ease. Stepping into the lobby, crowded with wooden lockers and abandoned shoes, she feels her nerves abate. She knows this world. It's so familiar. The architecture might be more outmoded than her bright, primary school in Philadelphia, but the atmosphere and the smells are identical; a combination of organised chaos and sweaty rubber plimsolls.

Morning prayers are led by the headmistress, a starched figure in her fifties, hair short and grey. Her patent heels clatter across the parquet flooring as she makes her way to the lectern, the entire school collected before her under the high ceiling. There must be eighty or more children, far more than Kitty expected. Jane Varley has found her a seat at the side of the hall where she watches the fingers of a pretty, young woman bounce across the piano keys in accompaniment to hymns of God and Country. When the headmistress extends prayers for the Queen, Kitty lowers her head, but doesn't shut her eyes. It's a petty act of defiance, she knows, but nevertheless she must stand for her principles. Both God and monarchy should be shown the trash can. Before morning assembly is dismissed, she's called to the plinth to be introduced to the school. Jane had warned her; she's prepared a few words. But once the headmistress has listed her credentials, she finds a well-manicured hand placed on her arm, inviting her to return to her seat without further ado.

Jane, efficient as ever, has allocated her a room; it's more a box room than a classroom. A line of chairs hugs together in a tight semi-circle. One thin window, high up the wall, offers a hint of ventilation. There are no artefacts; no maps or globes or pin boards. Her first class is a small collection of nine-year-old boys. Their faces betray some curiosity but hardly enthusiasm. Much as she'd expected. They wait politely for her to make the first overture, reminding her of the turgid atmosphere at some of her Intelligence training meetings. She smiles brightly, hoping to kindle something more inspiring.

"Guten Morgan, Kinder. Meine Name ist Fräulein Bernstein."

Swivelling to the black board on the stand behind her, she picks up the chalk and begins to write in a large, looping hand, repeating the sentence as she does so.

Each boy is asked his name and she transcribes the answer to the board, at once committing it to memory. The only German she imagines they'll be familiar with is Hitler's ranting propaganda on the radio or in newsreels. Hardly an auspicious start. But while she's here, even if under false pretences, she's determined to teach them well. When she switches to English they gasp at her American accent. It doesn't bother her; knowing it'll form part of their bond. Their trust. One boy in particular merits her attention; Tom Gilliam, more alert than the others, and a bold glint that would melt butter instantly.

"Please, Miss, I know a German sentence."

"Yes, Tom Gilliam. I'd be very happy to hear it."

"Ich liebe dich."

His pronunciation is dreadful but he makes her laugh. "Danke Schön, Herr Gilliam, I'm flattered" She turns to the rest of the class. "What Tom has just told me is that he loves me."

The class erupts with laughter. She thinks she will grow fond of Tom Gilliam. Which isn't a good thing. Her training warned specifically against it. By the time the school bell signals the end of their lesson she has a reasonable grasp of the personalities and the psychological make-up of her eleven pupils. And she will have eighteen more etched in her brain by the day's close, categorised and coded like an elaborate sports ladder.

As she follows her last set of pupils out of the box room, Jane Varley is pinning notices to a board. "Ah, Miss Bernstein, I hope they didn't cause you any trouble. Sometimes the boys can get a bit rowdy but at least it's the girls turn tomorrow."

Kitty smiles, grateful that the end of day bell has finally been silenced. "In my experience girls can be equally disruptive."

Jane Varley laughs, but not convincingly. Perhaps it's not the answer she wanted. "You're probably a better judge than me. Was everything alright at Mrs Johnson's?"

"Thank you, it was fine. She's been very kind."

"Only I was just wondering, if you're not doing anything tonight, a few of us meet at the pub. You'd be very welcome."

It's a thin line. If she doesn't go she risks being seen as elitist, or different. If she does, there's a danger of getting embroiled; too open to scrutiny. "That's really sweet but actually I'm quite tired, I still have to unpack properly and sort things." She knows it sounds lame. "But next week would be fun."

"Of course. You're always welcome. Any time."

"Thank you. Goodbye, Miss Varley."

"Goodbye, Miss Bernstein."

Returning to the quiet of her landlady's house and a sobering dinner of steamed haddock and cabbage she wishes she'd accepted the offer of a drink. She hadn't expected to feel so isolated, made worse by Mrs Johnson's lack of conversation. She doesn't want to pry, nor reveal too much of her own life, so she trundles out routine questions about the village, its history and its characters which are answered with polite, but rudimentary responses. For pudding she's served some sort of dry sponge. She eats heartily, not wishing to appear ungrateful, but she's glad when the meal's finally done and she can retire to her room.

The girls, as she'd predicted, are no more angelic than the boys. While they're quicker to learn they're regularly disrupted by one agitator, Rose Thorpe, more thorn than rose, who makes Tom Gilliam look like a saint. Giggling incessantly, she kicks the friends either side of her to maximise disruption. She will be a challenge but that's no bad thing. It'll keep Kitty focused.

"Rose Thorpe, why did your parents call you Rose?"

"Don't know, Miss."

"Because a rose is beautiful. She writes on the board. "*Eine Rose ist schön.*"

After two days she begins to wonder if her Intelligence assignment is merely a figment of her imagination. There's been no communication, though she's not expecting any. But frankly the excitement is waning. Or maybe the reality is more conflicted than she'd imagined; already she's forming precious bonds with her pupils which at some point will have to be severed. To counteract the sentiment, she meticulously plans her rendez-vous at the book shop, checking the timetable for the bus to Cambridge, the duration of the journey and the exact position of Rose Crescent on the school's city map so she can commit it to memory and not look like a hapless tourist.

When Saturday at last arrives she leaves Stratham early. The weather has changed again, as erratic as she'd been led to believe.

Warm sunshine bakes the pavements as she alights from the bus, intent on finding a suitable clothes shop. It doesn't take her long. She has a scent for these things. A light cotton dress, the palest yellow, catches her eye. The shop assistant flatters her ego, which is kind but unnecessary. She knows it looks good. Like an American cousin should. She swaps it for her suit, which the assistant wraps in a bag, and steers a path through the morning tourists to the bookshop, recalling the details of her contact, such as she knows them. He's a Cambridge student, studying chemistry, with contacts in high places; and reasonable looking. She's seen a photo. She also knows that his father served in the Royal Navy; part of the Eastern Fleet that was forced out of Singapore harbour by the Japanese. A very bloody nose for the so-called British Empire. And she knows her contact's name. Edward Grant. She'd been told that codenames wouldn't be required at her level. Which disappointed her.

The bookshop is exactly as had been described. She steps into its darkness, lamenting the loss of warm sunlight. Familiarising herself to its eccentric geography, she spends a few minutes studying the shelves on the ground floor. It's surprisingly busy; a student hangout she guesses. She climbs to the top floor, sliding into one of the booths and choosing the bench that faces the staircase. A trumpet solo squawks from the little table speaker. She thinks it might be Dizzy Gillespie. Robert would know; jazz was his domain. A young waitress in three quarter jeans and tucked-in shirt, probably a student, offers her tea or coffee. She chooses coffee which arrives five minutes later, piping hot in a transparent cup and saucer. Kitty lights a cigarette and sips the coffee. It tastes of nothing. Boiled water.

Ten minutes pass before a slim, well-dressed man ascends the stairs. He wears a tweed jacket and open necked shirt; in the flesh better looking than his slightly gawky photograph. An appealing grin lights his face when she stands to greet him. He plants a dry kiss on her cheek, a faint musty smell seeping from his jacket, cold flesh pressing her palm.

"My dear cousin, how lovely to see you."

"It's been too long, Edward. I'm so sorry."

He laughs. "You're here now, that's what matters. How was your flight?"

"Oh God, so bumpy I thought I was on a fairground ride." Another terrible line but she couldn't argue the case. Procedure is procedure and its safe delivery seems to have relaxed him. He suggests they sit down, ordering two more coffees as soon as the young waitress appears, his eyes shifting fleetingly to the other booths. Two couples, probably romantically involved. And three geeky-looking jazz freaks. Nothing to worry about. Without the mannered charm his face becomes harder again. It's an exquisitely English-looking face, like a character in a Gainsborough painting, but his eyes are the blue of ice rather than sky. Hiding not giving. He asks polite questions about the school and her accommodation. She gives polite answers. Trust has to be built and she has no intention of revealing more than she needs. Vigilance is crucial. She asks nothing of him. It is not her role. And she knows he will quickly turn the conversation to her assignment.

Perhaps sensing her reluctance to elaborate, he offers her a cigarette from a silver case and conjures an ebony carved lighter as if from nowhere. When the volume of the music rises his voice dissolves into its melody; so much so, she has to strain to hear.

He puffs a line of smoke portentously to the ceiling. "Enough of school transgressions. Please listen carefully. There are two people I'd like you to meet while you're here. The first is by far the bigger catch, someone I think you'll get on with very well. He's a high achiever, a chap named James Buchan-Smith, destined for great things at the Ministry of Defence. Very clever, charming man but he has a weakness for attractive women. Married of course, but while his wife's supervising weekend jamborees in the country he's busy at his flat in town, if you understand my meaning. Typical of his class, really."

She notes the disdain in his voice. Though as far as she knows, and by his own manner, she assumes he's a fully paid-up member of the same tribe.

"He and his wife are hosting a party soon. You'll come as my guest and I'll make all the necessary introductions. You're my wealthy American cousin on vacation for a few weeks from Philadelphia. Flatter him and get to know him, it won't be hard. Make no reference to your work in Cambridge. As far as he's concerned none of that exists. You'll use a different name, but only for this assignment."

"Lucky me. I was told I wouldn't get one. What is it?"

"Vanity Adams."

She tries not to smile, pausing to drag on her cigarette. "Nice name. Did you choose it yourself?"

He smiles. Evidently open to flattery. "My mother keeps lots of old copies of Vanity Fair. It was her favourite magazine till it closed. And Adams led the American revolution against the British and was the first president to occupy the White House. I thought they worked well together."

"I'll try and do Vanity justice."

"I can't think that'll be a problem." For a moment she feels him scrutinising her in some way but she's not sure how. Sexually? Competence-wise? Hard to tell.

"Your second assignment you already know something about.

The young man you were instructed to observe on the train to Cambridge."

"Bright boy. I quite liked him."

"He's Alexander Carter, a Cambridge history student, who I'm sharing a first-year room with. He has a lot of potential, political opinions going in the right direction but as yet unformed. It's vital for operations that he doesn't know my role in this. To him I'm just a friendly upper-class toff with little political awareness."

She bites her tongue, desperate not to say what she's thinking.

But he's there already. "Once, I concede that was true, but people change. Even a Philadelphian bride to be."

She forces a smile. "Touché." But it hurt more than she likes to admit.

"I'll introduce him to you, but probably through coincidence. Again you're my cousin; an American of German descent, based in West Berlin, and teaching German at a local school here as part of your training. I want you to befriend him and steer him. Don't push too hard. Let him feel he's found a political ally, someone who he can confide in. Begin to cultivate Marxist sympathies but never reveal your true assignment until my contacts agree he's reached an appropriate stage of development."

"That being?"

"That's for them to decide. You'll report back to me every two weeks. At the moment he's our best potential recruit but he could fail the personality test. And there might be better sources at the university that I haven't managed to tap yet. So don't go in too deep straightaway."

Kitty stubs her cigarette out in the ashtray. A part of her feels irritated for being admonished over a mistake she would never make but she knows it was never Ed's job to charm her. She wants to ask about his own background; natural curiosity, and absolutely contradictory to Intelligence policy. Instead she focuses on Alexander Carter. "I'll do what's necessary. But a bit more background would be useful. Like why's he so ripe for the picking?"

"He harbours a long-held resentment. He was born in a tiny place called Imber on Salisbury Plain; about as remote as you can get in the south, roughly a hundred miles south-west of London. The Ministry of Defence had been buying the land around for many years, then in '43 they suddenly demanded that Imber be evacuated so they could train American troops for D-Day without blowing up the inhabitants. No one was given any warning. The villagers had six weeks to leave. Most did so without complaint, thinking they'd be back as soon as the war ended. Which never happened, despite their protests they were never allowed to return. They had to find a life elsewhere without any compensation. Some never recovered, including his mother; it'd been a tight-knit community with its own way of living. She died a couple of years later. His father looked after her but struggled. He was eventually found dead in a barn. Alec was taken in by one of the teachers at his secondary school. Worked hard. A bright young man but with a burgeoning sense of injustice. And who can blame him?"

"It doesn't sound like he'll present too many problems. Provided, as you say, that he has the appropriate characteristics."

"Your job to assess, dear cousin. Now we should go. Settle yourself at the school and I'll be in contact soon. We'll leave the booth together but I'll stay downstairs to look for a book. Any other questions?"

She smiles. "Only one."

"Which is?"

"Where's the cinema?"

She enjoys the moment of confusion crossing his face. The switch of balance, the disruption of the status quo, can have its uses; sometimes just for play, sometimes to survive.

But her contact has recovered himself with his alluring grin. "You could try the Regal or the Central, they're both in walking distance."

He stands to indicate the meeting is over, guiding her with rehearsed courtesy to the ground floor whilst describing the detailed routes to each cinema. Parting from him with the lightest kiss, she heads out into the piercing sunlight, wincing slightly, and wishing she'd worn sunglasses. The streets are busier now, the candy-striped market alive with sellers of vegetables and cheeses which lend a rich scent of earth and salt to the warming air. It's a strange day to choose a trip to the movies, she admits, but she has a pressing need to feel closer to her father and there can be no better way to achieve it. Following Ed's directions, she finds the grand Art Deco building, exactly as he'd described it. The posters advertise a film called Malaga, starring Maureen O'Hara. A short description makes her smirk. Apparently O'Hara plays some kind of spy. Entering the Regal foyer she hopes Hollywood will provide more exciting espionage tips than those foisted on her by the East German Foreign Intelligence Service.

Cold Road to Imber

7

The telephone kiosk on the corner of Senate Passage is the first he finds that's unoccupied. He dials the London number from memory; his inclination being to give Kitty Bernstein a positive report. She'd impressed him with her cool head; and her identity photograph had not lied. Only the queers would resist her, and even some of them might succumb. The phone picks up at the end of the line and he thrusts a shilling into the slot. "Hello?"

A voice of whisky and fags. Lower register. "Who is this?"

"It's Kitty's cousin."

A pause. "I trust you had a pleasant time."

"It was very enjoyable. We're going to meet again soon." Instinctively he checks the street through the grubby glass. Two students bicycle past, knitted scarves draped from their shoulders. The smug uniform of exclusivity which he quietly detests.

The gravelled monotone continues. "I've had word from her foster parents. They're not willing to pay for a long holiday so they'd like you to introduce her to your London friends straight away."

"There's a party in two weeks, I've arranged…"

"…Sooner than that."

He feels a bead of sweat prick his temple, the sun's late summer rays magnified by the glass. "That might be difficult. The social scene has a strict agenda."

"You'll find something. We don't want her to get bored."

The phone clicks dead. Ed wipes the sweat from his forehead with a handkerchief and steps out into the cooler air to consider his options, free of the school-boy panic which had momentarily gripped him. The chances of contriving an encounter with Buchanan-Smith any earlier will be negligible and anyway applying pressure might make Kitty more vulnerable to suspicion. "Find something," his contact had said. Meaning give East Berlin a morsel, however small, so appetites are wetted; his own position more secure. Failing has only one consequence and he has no intention of succumbing to it. Heading south, towards the market, he contemplates his only option; to bring forward her introduction to his room-mate. Alec Carter might still be a minnow, albeit a very handsome one, but if he can report soon with progress, maybe even exaggerate his suitability, the APN might show more patience waiting for the big fish. And how could Buchanan-Smith fail to bite? Kitty Bernstein is quite the prettiest grub he's seen.

As the awnings of the market square come into view a pleasant aroma of salty cheeses fills his nostrils. From the French stall, elaborately decked with Tricolore bunting and woven bunches of garlic, he selects a generous portion of ripening Reblochon, a baguette and a bottle of the pinkest Rosé, still chilled from hibernation in a cooling box.

The boxing club is a five-minute walk. He knows of it but has never had reason to visit. It's housed in one of the deserted back alleys, where the arse ends of high street shops present a featureless wall of Victorian brickwork. With a suitable fog, he thinks he could well stumble on Jack the Ripper, such is its gloominess. The entrance presents a black door with no sign of its purpose. It yields to his touch and he enters, finding himself in a dingy corridor, lacquered with flaky paint. A baize noticeboard is covered with calling cards for pawn brokers and prostitutes. There's an overpowering stench of sweat mixed with bleach. His gut instinct is to retreat but instead he follows the growing cacophony of barked commands and pummelled flesh. No one takes much notice of him as he enters the cramped training room. Three young men pound relentlessly at punch bags, supervised by a stocky, razor-faced coach. Beyond them, in the ring, he spots Alec, boxing gloves raised close to his chest, shadowing his opponent under the sharp light of a single bulb, his face contorted with violent intention. He's stripped to the waist, sweat dripping from his forehead as he ducks and weaves, finding undefended flesh that buckles under his throw. Ed watches from the doorway, transfixed. He'd been informed of Alexander Carter's brutal qualities, described as 'a young man of easy anger and impulse', but witnessing this spectacle of unbounded savagery he feels his own thrill, aware of hairs lifting at the nape of his neck.

Perhaps fearing for the opponent, the coach calls Alec out and the two boxers retreat, panting hard. Ed still says nothing, hoping his room-mate might notice him, which he does once he's mopped his face with a towel. "What the hell are you doing here?" His face barely flickers a muscle of recognition; his body succumbing to exhaustion.

"Discovering the world's a darker place than I thought." Ed takes a tentative step forward, his vowels more finely clipped than ever. Intentionally.

"If it offends you, you can bugger off. It's not the sort of place your lot are supposed to see anyway." Alec drops his face back to the towel, presumably hoping Ed will go. But his desire is thwarted. "Please don't tell me you want to join."

"Nothing so foolhardy. I don't know if you've noticed but it's a beautiful day." He holds aloft the bottle of Rosé. "I thought lunch on the riverbank avec mon ami. The sun shines so infrequently in this country I feel there's a moral obligation to picnic."

He's aware he's drawn the attention of the room. A murmur of contempt. It's not a comfortable feeling, yet he needs to maintain this parody of himself, at least until he's certain Alec is convinced of his class-bound vacuity. He keeps the bottle raised; grinning through his discomfort, waiting for a response.

But it's Alec's coach who comes to his rescue. "Same time, Thursday. We can't keep your picnic pal waiting."

Ed smiles benignly. "Excellent. Ten minutes, South Paddock." Turning to the door he wills himself to continue his performance; reminded of the loathsome school plays he always felt compelled to sabotage. "Sorry to interrupt, chaps. As you were."

Stepping back into the alleyway he breathes more freely. If he gets beaten up it's no bad thing. Collateral damage. Provided it's minor bruises. He pushes an unconscious hand through his mane of hair, glad to touch busier streets again, his eye cast to the river for a suitable spot where he can watch the punters drift by on a lazy current. Several groups of students have had the same idea. If the weather stays fair in September the meadows bordering the river remain more manicured lawns than paddocks. It's an idyllic scene, he can't deny, wondering briefly what all his subterfuge is designed to achieve, when his life could be so easy if he chose. It's a thought he instantly rejects, as if chastised by those who've led the way before him, still fighting in the shadows at their mission, despite the ever-present danger. Who is he to hinder the cause, when political revolution, even perhaps his own distinguished notoriety, could lie within reach? As if on cue, batting his doubt to the long grass, he sees Alec walking towards the spot he's chosen. His tweed jacket is hooked over his shoulder, his face sullen and brooding, a purple weal under his left eye. Ed rehearses his intentions; the desired outcome of their little picnic. A tremor, not unpleasant, flickers down his spine, as it had in the boxing club. For better or worse he's in deep now; the path back to respectability too full of minefields.

He pops the cork from the bottle as Alec throws his jacket to the ground. A wounded gladiator. "Don't ever bloody embarrass me like that again."

Ed mimics his room-mate's surliness. "Thanks for the picnic, Edward. Not at all, Alec, glad you could come."

"I mean it. Those guys would string you up if they could."

"They won't get the chance. I have absolutely no intention of re-visiting that sweat pit in my entire lifetime. Now drink up, it's no fun having a picnic with someone so truculent."

He hands the bottle of wine across, Alec accepting it with obvious reluctance. "It's not poison. If you're going to study at Cambridge I need to teach you the rules of being a gentleman."

"Not interested."

"You're being a bore, Alec. And nobody likes a bore. Even a clever one. Now take a slug or I absolutely won't be your best friend anymore."

A reluctant smile breaks across his room-mate's face, no doubt bemused by the intended audacity. Ed watches Alec arch his neck, slurping from the bottle before a sudden splutter, forcing him to wipe his mouth with the back of his hand. "Wine's not like beer, you have to take it more gently."

"You said a slug."

"Did I?" He smiles, enjoying himself now. "My mistake. Now sit down. I thought you'd probably be hungry after all that mindless violence."

"It's called boxing. It's a sport."

"So's ripping foxes apart and I don't approve of that either." Ignoring the comment Alec slumps his aching frame to the grass. "I bought cheese and bread from the market. A much more civilised way to waste one's time."

"Hooray for the toffs. Where would man be without picnics and Henley Regatta and straw hats."

"Now you're just being venemous. And anyway, they're called boaters." His room-mate has closed his eyes to the sunlight, his bruised chin jutting to the sky like a ragged mountain peak. Kneeling on the grass, Ed begins to unwrap the cheese and break the baguette in to smaller pieces, which suddenly reminds him of countless, tedious Communions.

"What the hell's that? It stinks."

"It's delicious. Called Reblochon. French. Try some. You can eat the rind as well. Just pat a bit onto the bread and slurp down with a bit of rosé.

Alec opens his eyes again, pulling his frame up to rest on his elbows. "It looks more like custard."

"That's just because it's melting in the heat. Come on, don't be such a baby." He hands a piece of bread across, the Reblochon oozing either side. "Pop the whole thing in."

His room-mate accepts the offering, considering it briefly before dropping it into his mouth.

"Well?"

"D'you think all French girls smell like this?"

"Oh for God's Sake, Alec, are you really so uncultivated?"

"Well you wouldn't want to kiss one, would you? Not if they smelt like that."

"They don't."

"So you have kissed one."

"No, I haven't."

"Then how would you know?"

"I don't know."

"My point exactly. Until we find a French girl to kiss we'll never know. Pass the bottle. I'm unbelievably, bloody thirsty."

Ed passes the wine across, observing his friend who slurps easily this time before slipping back to the grass. "She'd probably kiss you first. You're better looking."

"But you're the one she'd want to marry. The posh toff with the easy charm and the country estate."

"How would she know?"

Alec opens his eyes. "Look at you, I've seen rougher hands on bridesmaids."

He laughs, amused by his friend's observation but somehow also, slightly offended. Swigging from the bottle himself, he lies back on to the cool grass, his feet not far from Alec's head; two sardines in a tin. He wonders if his own degree of hurt, though admittedly minor, has been caused by a feeling that he's lost control of the conversation, aware that Alec has manipulated the debate to his own advantage. Instead of teasing out his room-mate's politics and background, they're debating halitosis and

French girls. But his contact had put him on edge, pushing harder than he wanted. He should ignore it and work the scene slowly. Relax. Nothing had to happen immediately. Not today anyway. He shuts his eyes, enjoying the luminous flare that dances from the shadow of a tree. "I might have bridesmaids' hands but at least I don't reek like a carthorse."

"Your point being?"

"Downwind from you any girl would be bound to turn lesbian, such is the aroma of fetid sweat and dank articles of clothing."

"Sorry to offend. Maybe this'll help."

A sudden sensation of something landing on his face forces Ed to open his eyes. Binding tape, presumably for Alec's boxing gloves. The stench is foul.

Alec laughs. "You should hear yourself, you're so fucking pompous. Why would any girl want to snog someone with a rod up his arse!"

Whether it's the wine, or the heat, or just the ephemeral moment of lightness, Ed finds himself launching at his friend, fists flaying in mock indignation, a scuffle which he is bound to lose but which he can't help but enjoy, fleeting and ridiculous, such a moment the like of which he can barely recall, until Alec pushes him fairly and squarely on to his back, his heart pumping, ready to accept defeat, knowing there was never an option.

His room-mate beams. The glorious smile of a victor. "Take up boxing and I wouldn't find it so easy," before he collapses on the grass again, this time beside Ed, both staring at the sky; Ed aware that he is more breathless.

"Touché. Pass the bottle."

Alec levers the wine across with his arm. Ed drinks, not

bothering to lift his head, dabbing at the trickle that run downs his cheek. The tape lies close to his fingers. He shoves it into his trouser pocket, unwilling to render it part of their conversation again. For a few moments he's content to enjoy the silence, or at least the sounds of others enjoying themselves; hapless punters emitting cries of mirth on the river, or the hubbub of other students around them; they as content, he assumes, as he is. Though he knows it can't last.

His breathing begins to ease, but he remains prone, his eyelids still firmly shut. "Talking of girls, is there anyone? You know, a sweetheart or whatever?"

"Not really. There was one in Salisbury. Rosaline. She worked in Woolworths on Saturdays. But I knew I was going to university."

"Were you in love?"

Alec laughs. "I'm not sure what that means. How about you?"

"What?"

"Is there a special girl? Someone you've fallen in love with?"

"There were times when I thought I was in love. But now I think I really wasn't."

He pauses. It's time to resume charge, his hedonistic moment over. There are plans to be made. He rolls over, opening his eyes. "Why don't we do something fun at the weekend?"

"Like what?"

"I don't know, see a band or something. There's a jazz trio called The Quiet Three playing at the Red Cow this Thursday. They're supposed to be really good. It could be a blast."

"A jazz trio?'

"Don't sound so sceptical. Jazz is the thing. It'll just never reach Wiltshire. Anyway, don't try my patience. Straight yes or no."

"Can we drink cider while we watch?"

"We're in Cambridge, you bonehead, not prohibition America."

"Then I suppose it's a yes."

"Excellent. Step two in your route to education. Have some more Reblochon."

He could telephone Kitty Bernstein at the school but it would be a difficult conversation for her to have in some public arena. Far better to drive out there. It would be useful to see a little of her cover world, just in case something untoward should happen and he needed to scatter the trace of her footsteps. Late on Monday morning, after attending a chemistry lecture on twentieth century developments in organic synthesis, he hurries to the station car park where he discovers to his annoyance that a fine layer of dust has settled on to the maroon paintwork. Too bad Cleggy isn't on call. Though he knows such thoughts are antediluvian if not heretical. Heading north, through Cambridge towards the Fen villages, he presses his foot hard on the accelerator, calculating he should reach Stratham by quarter to one when hopefully she'll be on her lunch break.

Thirty-five minutes later, according to his Omega watch, he pulls the Magnette up outside the school. Cacophonous screams fill his ears with shocking familiarity, returning him to sombre memories of prep school. He takes a breath, steps out of the car, a rigid smile fixed to his face, as if he might be attending some ghastly but necessary school re-union. A football spins towards him and he kicks it back with unintended strength. It arcs out to

the street. A teacher runs to the rescue and he slips gratefully out
of the playground into the quieter lobby where he finds a door
marked "Office" and knocks twice. A youngish woman bids him
enter. She's tapping slowly on a typewriter with one hand and
holding a half-eaten sandwich with the other, looking friendly
enough; a little overweight but her face has an open, almost
innocent quality.

He hovers, his manner intentionally obsequious. "Good
afternoon, I'm so sorry to disturb your lunch."

She drops the sandwich to her desk, evidently surprised by an
unfamiliar guest. "Do excuse me, I wasn't expecting – anyway,
how may I help you, sir?"

 "I've come to see Miss Bernstein. I thought she might be on her
lunch break."

"Oh. Yes. I think she's in the staffroom. Who shall I say…?"

Better to use some sort of pseudonym. "…Edward Grainger.
We're cousins." He plays it meek still.

"Of course. She mentioned she has a cousin nearby. Do take a
seat in the lobby, Mr Grainger. I'll just see if I can find her for
you."

He follows Jane Farley back into the lobby and watches her
clamber up the narrow set of wooden stairs before settling
himself on a chair. Finding nothing much to distract him, his eye
falls on the array of plimsoll-filled wooden lockers, until light
footsteps turn his gaze back to the landing where an elegant,
patent shoe descends; the unmistakeable panache of Kitty
Bernstein. Despite the orthodox suit of school mistresses
everywhere, he finds her radiance a little unsettling again. She
smiles as she draws near, turning up her face so that he might
kiss her cheek. "Edward, what a lovely surprise. How are you?"

She plays it beautifully he thinks. And she smells intoxicating. "I'm very well. And yourself?"

"Happier for seeing you of course. What on earth brings you here?"

"I was just passing by on my way to Cambridge. You're probably far too busy but I wondered if you'd like a walk. It's such a lovely day and there's masses of family gossip to tell."

"In that case I can't wait." Jane Farley has crept up behind them. "I won't be gone long, Miss Farley.

"No. of course. You go and enjoy yourself."

Strolling up the hill, away from the centre of the village, he sees a Norman church, surrounded by a graveyard. There's a well-trodden pathway leading towards what looks like open countryside. Steering her past the moss-ridden tombstones, he immediately drops his patter of small-talk, though aware he'd enjoyed their conceit in front of Miss Farley. It seems he and Kitty Bernstein have professional chemistry.

"I'm afraid the plan's changed. We're going to have to speed things up a bit." He smiles lightly. He doesn't want to rattle her. "Because you're untested in the field they want to make sure they've made a good investment. So we need some results fast."

"What do you propose? A dinner date with Anthony Eden? At least he's more pleasing on the eye than Churchill. And a hundred times more beddable." Her limpid brown eyes are full of mischief. He chastises himself for feeling aroused.

"Nothing so elevated, I'm afraid. I can't change the meeting with Buchanan-Smith. It's vital for credibility that you meet him by chance at the party first. After that I know he spends every Wednesday evening at his club then stays at his London apartment. It's a cosy little arrangement he has with his wife. The usual thing, he professes too much work, she doesn't ask any awkward questions."

"Why would she? She's only a wife after all."

He ignores her jibe. "In the meantime I want you to see what you can do with Alec Carter. I'm taking him to a pub in Cambridge on Thursday evening. There's a jazz band playing. It attracts quite a crowd, all sorts of young, avant garde types. Not the sought of place a young woman would go by herself but we'll bump into you first. I'll tell him I need to pick up a book on the way, at Morgan's, where we met. You'll be browsing there by chance and we'll invite you along. After that it's up to you. While I'm buying drinks get him to ask if he can meet you again. As soon as possible. We need to know what he's really worth."

"I'll do my best."

"I can't imagine you'll fail."

She smiles. "My ex-fiancé loved jazz. If he'd loved me quite as much as he loved Charlie Parker I don't think I'd be standing here now. I guess I should be grateful to him."

"Perhaps you should. To my mind love is a dangerous game best avoided."

"So speaks the mind of a typical English gentlemen."

He smiles, genuinely enjoying her mockery. "You don't agree?'

"I'd like to think there's the possibility of a fairy tale ending. If we're receptive enough."

"And are you?"

Kitty Bernstein stops, presumably to admire the view. Stems of ripening corn march to the distant horizon, halted only by a low hill, dotted with oak trees. Turning back to him, a rueful smile touches her lips.

"That's information which will always remain classified, Mr Grant. Now what time do you want me to be at the bookshop?"

"Make sure you're there by twenty past five. I'll aim to bring him in at half past."

"I'll look forward to it."

Turning back to the school, he finds it harder to maintain a patter of conversation. There are no more arrangements to be made, for now at least, and he knows he's overstepped the mark with such a personal question. He got carried away; after all that's her job, to lure, but to slip into the trap so easily was a primitive error. He won't let it happen again. With a gentle kiss of the cheek, he leaves her at the school gate, anxious to restore his professionalism and most importantly his superiority. They're a team, and Kitty Bernstein promises to be a highly efficient seductress, but it's imperative she dances to his tune. She's the pipe, and he the Piper. Speeding back to Cambridge he watches the Magnette's speedometer edge past ninety. He winds the window down; a howl of air, brushing away his doubts into the slipstream behind him.

Apart from brief, late-night exchanges, he hardly sees Alec Carter in the ensuing days. His room-mate's joined the rowing club as well; slipping out early in the morning onto the River Cam and telling Ed that he breakfasts in the dining hall before heading on to lectures. It sounds impossibly smug but at least he's motivated. For his part he rises an hour later, completing whatever the chemistry syllabus demands of him, which isn't much, before choosing which pub to frequent in the evening. So far no one other than Alexander Carter has struck him as a potential candidate. They all seem too lame, or unbothered. Or obsessed by cricket scores. Hardly budding radicals. He might have to look further, in darker establishments, aware that the emergent cell of revolutionary zeal is rarely born of an idyllic childhood. He needs those who will bite rather than fester. Who will linger in shadows and work by night. These are the people he seeks.

By mid-afternoon on Thursday he is lying on his bed, waiting for his room-mate to return, his eye drifting across a textbook but absorbing nothing. The heavy footsteps he eventually hears in the corridor are undoubtedly Alec's but they're even weightier than normal, and the crash of the door as it flies back on its hinges presents a sombre and recalcitrant individual, furrowed brow and eyes that could shoot poison. Not promising. Hopefully Kitty Bernstein will change that. He waits for an explanation but none is forthcoming.

"You haven't forgotten, have you? About the Red Cow?"

"No. Why?"

Ed throws his chemistry book to the end of his bed. "Nothing really. You just don't seem in the best mood."

He watches as Alec throws off his shirt and selects another from the cupboard. "I wasn't selected for the rowing team. Any other questions?"

"Not till you come down from your crucifix."

"Good. Shall we go?"

Stepping out of the porter's lodge, Ed turns left, up Trinity Street, his room-mate pushing his arms at the holes in his tweed jacket as if it's the most irksome job in the world, trying Ed's patience. "If it's that difficult leave the bloody thing behind. No one wears that sort of thing there anyway."

"It's all I've got. Where are we going? I thought you said it was in Benet Street."

"I need to pick up a book from Morgan's. We're a bit early anyway. Doors won't be open for another twenty minutes."

"Now you tell me."

Casting a reproachful glance back at his room-mate's petulance, he wonders exactly what Kitty Bernstein will make of Alec Carter. Whether she'll see what he can see. Although on present form it might require a little imagination. Still, she said he'd made a good impression on the train up to Cambridge, so hopefully her presence will stir Mr Carter from his pathetic indulgence. He pushes at the brass handle of the book shop. A brass bell tingles above his head; something he hadn't noticed before. Perhaps it's been newly repaired. He's aware of a few bodies lingering in the aisles, of Alec's sulky footsteps behind him, but no immediate sign of Kitty. Pressing further into its depths he finds a grey-bearded individual sitting at a counter, his face partially lit by the band of light emanating from an angle poise lamp. He's writing out small cards, squinting behind a smeared pair of gold-rimmed spectacles, only looking up when Ed requests, without much solicitousness, whether the book he's ordered has yet arrived. Without speaking the man searches a row of shelves behind him, eventually finding a leather-bound volume. He wraps it slowly in brown paper and requests a shilling and sixpence, for which Ed fishes in his pocket.

"Why d'you want to read Shakespeare?" His room-mate's tone suggests impatience more than genuine enquiry.

"Because his sonnets are more compelling than first term chemistry." He turns away from the counter, at once confronted by the delectable form of Kitty Bernstein.

"Edward?" She holds a book in her hand, as if she's just picked it off the shelf. Her smile radiant.

"Kitty? What are you doing here?"

A cute chuckle. "Looking for books, I guess."

He has to admit, she plays it better than him. And she's dressed for the part. A light summer dress, flowing like a breeze from her slim waist, honeyed arms and lustrous hair; not like any schoolteacher he remembers. He kisses her and turns to his room-mate, who looks baffled but suddenly vital. "Alec, this is my cousin Kitty, from America. She's teaching in one of the local villages. Kitty this is Alec, my college room-mate.

His room-mate straightens his gait. "Yes, I believe we met…"

Kitty holds out her hand. "…Of course we did. On the train. We had a nice chat. How do you do…again?"

He takes her hand.

"I remember you speak excellent German."

"Well, of a sort…"

Ed chips in where Alec breaks off. "…He's good at lots of things which can be quite irritating."

"That's not true…"

"…But he doesn't know a thing about jazz so I'm taking him to a club tonight to rectify his appalling ignorance."

She laughs, as he had hoped, her eyes turning to Alec who he notes is showing promising signs of leaving his surly past. "Do you like jazz, Miss…?"

"…Bernstein. But please call me Kitty. I like hearing it played but I can't say I'm an expert. So I guess I'm reliant on others to guide me."

His room-mate smiles for the first time. "That makes two of us."

She smiles back. All lipstick and pearl white teeth. "I suppose it does."

The exchange gratifies Ed, at least on a professional level. But he hadn't expected to feel jealous. Again, he knows it's her job, and she needs to find intimacy. He presses his fingernails into his palms; a short cut to restore his equanimity.

To his surprise, Alec poses the next question, before he has a chance. "Why don't you come along? There's bound to be tickets available."

Another smile, demure this time. Bashful even. "No, that's kind, but don't let me impose. I wouldn't want to interfere with your evening…"

"…Please. We'd be delighted. Wouldn't we, Ed?"

Right there. Alec Carter's fallen into their pocket. Ed beams. "Of course we would. In fact, I insist."

She grins in return. Like playing tennis. "Well, I suppose even schoolteachers should have some fun once in while."

Sliding out of the bookshop, they walk three abreast until they come to the narrower lanes where Alec drops behind them, deferring presumably to their blood ties. Ed keeps the mood light, asking after the work at her school and watching with professional admiration as she fields Alec Carter if he slips out of range.

The pub is already busy, despite the early hour. They climb the stairs to find the Quiet Three already working the room with their easy riffs; a black pianist setting the score accompanied by a trumpeter and drum player. It's exactly what Ed wanted. An intimate setting, less overtly masculine than most of the local pubs and a perfect melting pot in which to foster intimate alliances. Guiding his guests to an assortment of battered lounge chairs, grouped at the far end of the room, they pass fashionably self-conscious young couples, arms draped about each other, cigarettes hanging in the air; dotted amongst them bearded men nod their heads in quiet appreciation, sipping from pint mugs. The piece ends with a light tap of the cymbals and Ed and his guests applaud while others choose to whistle.

He turns back to face them. "What d'you think?"

Alec Carter is already at hand with a match for Kitty Bernstein's cigarette. She pushes the smoke away in an elegant plume. "It's fun. I didn't think places like this would exist in England."

His room-mate protests with a warm smile. "We're not all stiff-lipped toffs in bowler hats."

She laughs at the joke. "I'm glad to hear it."

It's flirtatious, but light. Just as Ed had hoped. He wonders why he ever doubted the match. Both have film star looks, one just needs a bit more refining. And Kitty Bernstein will be good at that. He stands up, sensing a suitable moment to leave them alone. "Let me get some drinks in. What'll you have?"

She asks for a martini, his room-mate, a pint of Merrydown cider. Popping himself on to a stool at the end of the small bar he secures himself a vantage point from which he can observe his matchmaking. They have their backs to him, watching the trio, occasionally sharing a comment with forced intimacy due to the pitch of the music. Although it hardly seems forced. He orders a Bells Scotch with water to drink first and downs it quickly, aware of feeling a little maudlin despite the apparent success of his mission. He'll be able to file a positive report to his contact; one which will at least guarantee his and Kitty Bernstein's continued operation before they net Buchanan-Smith, which he's confident they will. There's an overwhelming urge to order a second scotch before he returns with their drinks, but he resists, knowing it would be unprofessional. Predecessors have fallen into that trap, unnerved by the stress of covert lives. His mind turns to Donald Maclean, wondering whether he ever came to the Red Cow to hatch plans while at Cambridge. And whether after his public defection he and Guy Burgess will turn up anywhere soon. Moscow presumably. The bar tender gives him a tray for the drinks and he retraces his steps to his guests. The not so Quiet Three are reaching a peak of rhythm, repeated notes which thread down his spine. It's hard to ignore the thrill. And at the same moment, seeing the intense concentration etched on Alec Carter's face, he can't help wondering, indulgently, if he's found the next man in waiting.

8

After the robbery Kitty wonders where her father has gone. Not literally. It's just that in the subsequent weeks she can't quite reach him. As if a part of him has shut down; the family part, the kind, fun-loving man who loves to go to the cinema and watch ridiculously romantic stories, despite his extraordinarily keen intellect.

At her mother's insistence he had called the police that evening. About an hour later two policemen knocked on the door. Kitty remembered one was chewing gum and grinned at her as if nothing much was the problem. The other, older one, was more helpful. He walked around the outside of the house and then examined her father's study, taking a few notes with a stubby pencil.

The younger one just seemed like he wanted to get home, which Kitty would have preferred, because she didn't like the way he kept looking at her. While his colleague was examining the shattered window and searching the carpet for footprints, he stood on the threshold between the study and the living room, watching Kitty's father as he paced uneasily from his armchair to the hallway. Whatever calm he'd sourced earlier, while Robert was still here, had now deserted him and was painful for Kitty and her mother to watch.

"Was anything actually stolen, Mr Bernstein? That you can tell me for sure?" The younger policeman is losing patience, perhaps disappointed, Kitty thinks, that it wasn't a homicide.

"No. No. I don't think so. But like I told you, I haven't checked everything yet. My study's a busy place. And most of it's still on the floor like they told me to leave it when I called."

"You got your wallet, right. Cos you came back from the cinema."

"Yeah, sure."

"No money stolen, no pictures, furniture, jewellery?"

"No, nothing like that."

The older policemen steps out from the study. "They did a good job. No obvious footprints or fingerprints. I guess it was a professional thief, someone who knows the area. Lucky you scared them off."

Her father says nothing, leaving the older policeman to fill the space while his colleague shoves his notebook back into his shirt pocket. "We'll file a report, Mr Bernstein. See if there've been any similar incidents in the neighbourhood. I'd get your window fixed soon as you can. Maybe check all the downstairs locks while you're at it."

When they leave her father appears rooted to the spot, unable to ameliorate for the dip in the road, which would be his usual way. It leaves Kitty perplexed. It's not pleasant knowing someone's broken in but at least nothing was stolen and no one got hurt. Her father had encountered far worse in his life so why did he seem so defeated?

Her instinct is to comfort him. "Don't worry, Paps. I'm sure they'll solve it."

"Since when did the PDP solve anything?" His tone is uncharacteristically aggressive. As if sensing his own misjudgement he turns and retreats to his study.

Her lessons finish early so she decides to come home and catch up on some marking. Her students in Grad 8 have been badgering her for the results to their English test. As she turns in to the driveway she notices that her father's Chevrolet is already parked at the edge of the lawn. He's never usually home before seven; it surprises her, even disturbs her, a reaction which she tries to beat away. It's irrational.

Walking into the house she dumps the pile of exercise books on the bottom stair and heads for the kitchen. Most days her mother would be making headway on the newspaper crossword whilst waiting for a pie to bake, or darning socks beside the wireless, but today she is sitting opposite her husband at the breakfast table, a cup of coffee hanging in the air, which she neither drinks nor lets drop to the table. They both look up as Kitty enters.

Her father finds a meagre smile. "Hello, darling, how was school?"

Kitty is instantly on her guard. Even her father's impeccable manners can't hide his empty heart. "Is something wrong Paps? You're never home this early."

Her mother drops the cup. She is looking at her husband, not Kitty. Interpreting the glance that passes between them, Kitty knows instantly that they have shared some pact, and whatever it is or whatever it refers to, they will have been discussing whether, or how to share it with her.

As if seeking more distraction her mother asks if she wants coffee; there's a little more in the pot. Kitty declines. She imagines one of them is terminally ill. Which one? Which should it be? Ridiculous thoughts that she cannot resolve in the split second before she demands to know what the problem is.

Her father sighs. He picks up a letter from the table which Kitty hadn't noticed. She reprimands herself for the oversight. "I got this letter today," he says, holding it between the tips of his long, bony fingers. "It's not exactly a love letter…"

"…In God's name, just tell her, Walter."

The weighted smile drops from his face. He folds the letter up and sighs. "It's from the House Committee on Un-American Activities. I've been subpoenaed to appear before them next week."

"Come and sit with us, darling."

Kitty ignores her mother's interjection. She remains standing, her mind exploding. "What for? What are you talking about?"

"It's nothing to worry about."

"Don't be ridiculous, Paps. Don't say that. Why the hell do they want anything from you?"

"They're alleging I've been involved in Communist activities."

"What? But you haven't."

"No I haven't. Which is why it's gonna be fine." He lifts the smile again. "So how about we order some pizza this evening. Your mom's been so wrapped up in her crossword she's forgotten to cook already. How about that? In my book that's a much more salty crime worth stewing over. Am I right or what?"

Kitty can't help herself. Despite everything she now knows, despite the axe man's blow, she finds herself laughing with him. She will eat pizza, and curl on the sofa with him and watch The Ed Sullivan show, laughing as her father laughs; knowing not to mention the letter again this evening, because she knows tomorrow their life will change.

Two days later she meets Robert in a downtown diner, their regular haunt, nothing fancy; they are saving to buy a house. She hasn't told him over the phone, knowing the news would be too shocking. Robert is genuinely fond of her father, almost the son, she likes to think, that Walter never had. Robert is already in their usual cubicle, studying the menu though she knows he'll have a coffee and a donut. She kisses him fondly, trying to look casual, deciding to wait for an opportunity to slip the information in between anecdotes of his day and her own share of students' linguistic follies. They laugh, he more freely than her. She can delay no longer.

"Robert, there's something I need to tell you."

"God, really. You've saved the breaking up spiel for now?"

"I mean it."

"Ok, sorry. I'm listening."

She tells him what she knows. It is no more than her father told her at the kitchen table. Since then they've barely discussed it.

Robert's face is a blank. She can't read it. "Say something."

"Why didn't you tell me before?'

"I didn't want to worry you on the phone. I guess I thought it'd be better…"

"…You should have told me straight away, Kitty. Jesus. When's he got to testify?"

"Next Tuesday afternoon. Can you be there? Or talk with him before, or something? You know how stubborn he is, any coaching you can give him will help."

She waits for him to reply but instead he stares down at his coffee, stirring in more sugar despite the fact he's already added some. "Robert?"

"I'm a lawyer, Kitty, I have to remain impartial. Otherwise - well, otherwise my reputation's blown."

"What the fuck does that mean?"

"It means even if I wanted to advise him I can't."

"For God's sake, no one would know. He's your father-in-law. Or will be. Surely you want to help him."

"I'm sorry. Please don't ask me to do what I can't. There's boundaries I can't cross."

"You mean you're not on his side."

"I didn't say that. You're putting words in my mouth. All I'm saying is, in this instance, I can't help. It's too public. You must have a family lawyer. Someone who can help."

"I assumed that would be you."

"I'm sorry. You assumed wrong."

Somewhere in her heart she thinks she understands but still she can't quite forgive him. "Well at least can you be there, right? Mom and I are going even though he insisted we shouldn't."

"I have a court session next Tuesday afternoon."

"Well shift it."

"We're not talking some two-bit speeding offence. It's a serious case."

"More serious than being labelled a traitor?" Her tone is sharper, sharper than she's ever been with him.

"I can't change it, Kitty. How would it look if I dropped my client's day in court to support my father-in-law? I'd lose my job."

"So…that's it? You can't help at all?"

"Even if I wanted to."

"Wanted to?"

"Jesus, Kitty, don't make this hard. You know what I'm saying."

She knows but his tone is patronising and she wonders if he is lying to her. Finding nothing more to say, she stares out of the window; cars passing in the street, shoppers drifting in and out of the hardware store as the spring sun beats down on the sidewalk. Nothing seems to have changed.

He stands up, slurping the dregs of his coffee. "I gotta go. I've got a load of paperwork to catch up on. I'll call later this week. Send your parents my best. Tell your dad – well tell him I'm very sorry."

He leans down to kiss her but she turns her lips away. She is not sure what has just happened. "Please don't be mad, Kitty. I'll call."

He disappears behind her out of the door. She doesn't bother watching him walk to his car, instead ordering another coffee.

By Friday she hasn't heard from him and as the weekend draws nearer she resigns herself to spending it alone with her parents. They plainly need her more than Robert. The house has wrapped itself in an alternative reality; there are no whispers or weighty silences, just the usual easy jokes and clockwork exits and entrances; her father still goes to work, Kitty marks schoolbooks and her mother bakes pies. But it is a mirage. And she knows they are all colluding to maintain its fragile form. When on Saturday morning over breakfast, her father asks casually if Robert will be coming over, he does it while reading the paper, half a toasted bagel falling from his mouth.

"He's out in Charleston, Paps," she lies. "Some case that's taking more time than he thought. He says hi and sorry he won't see you this weekend." She leaves it at that. Her father's no fool.

"If you speak to him, tell him I hope his firm's paying good overtime."

She smiles. "I will."

She dreads the day arriving but it comes mercifully quickly. She's heard nothing from Robert and wonders whether to call. While her parents are dressing upstairs she hovers by the phone. It is early. He'll be at his apartment. She realises she's twisting her engagement ring around her slender finger, wondering what to say. But before the chance arrives she hears her father's footsteps descending to the hall and she is somehow grateful for his interruption. She calls the school, telling the secretary that she is sick and will be back tomorrow. She presumes that after today everybody will know the truth of her absence but she has a steadfast conviction that by then the ridiculous charges will have been dropped and her father can continue to be an upstanding and loyal American citizen.

Very little is said in the car on the way to the district courthouse. When they step outside he is swiftly consumed by a wave of officials and press and she doesn't see him again until she walks into the viewing area of the panelled gallery. His back is towards her so she cannot make contact. Beyond him on a plinth a long table stretches almost the width of the courtroom, on which microphones are placed at regular intervals. Behind the plinth a Stars and Stripes flag has been erected. The courthouse is surprisingly full. Suited men huddle in deep discussion, officials of some kind she assumes, clerks sitting with typewriters just short of the plinth, a full press gallery, already scribbling in notebooks and an even larger number in the viewing gallery. Though she hopes most are there out of sympathy, she can't help wondering whether in truth they've just come to gawp.

When the court's told to rise she and her mother rise with them. A line of middle-aged men enter through the side door and take their places behind the microphones. When the senior judge invites the court to sit he waits portentously for silence to fall before asking her father to step before them and give his name and profession. She hears the scrape of his chair on the floor, like chalk on a board. His short statement echoes around the chamber, the delivery steady and measured. No trace of nervousness. There follow a few more procedural questions but she remains more focused on the cadence of his voice; the hint of anything that suggests guilt or doubt, or a tremble of his hand, though half-hidden because she notices his suit is now a touch too big for him. But his composure doesn't falter. She feels her mother's clammy palm reach out for hers and she holds it tight, like a talisman. Satisfied with her father's responses the senior judge invites the man sitting next to him to proceed. She misses his name; he looks like any other father on the edge of a football pitch; grey, sallow face, slightly overweight, his athletic days a mile behind him. She imagines he will ask his father to give an account of himself. She's never been at a court proceeding before and realises with a pang of regret that she had never fully listened to Robert's tales of his court appearances. How pathetically innocent she'd been. A shift of weight, from one leg to the other, draws her attention back to her father's composure. His gait appears to have stiffened slightly; it could just be tiredness. Or maybe it's fear.

The sallow-faced man leans heavily towards his microphone; almost a theatrical gesture. The men grouped either side lean towards him. It feels so staged, she thinks, like a macabre version of Michelangelo's Last Supper.

"Mr Bernstein, are you now or have you ever been a member of the Communist Party of the United States?"

The question shocks her, so direct, outright. She'd seen trials like it on television but they were for film stars and dubious public personalities, all done for show surely, not for university professors.

"Mr Bernstein?"

Her father straightens himself. 'No, sir, I have never been a member of the Communist Party of the United States."

"What about in Germany? Were you a Communist Party member before the war?"

"I was against the Fascists, I believe that…"

"…Answer the question please, Mr Bernstein."

"I think if you'd experienced what I saw in Berlin, sir, you might have wanted to do all you could to protect those around you."

"You don't deny back then you were a member of the Communist Party?"

"I didn't say that."

"Mr Bernstein, if you're not prepared to admit it, or even deny that you were ever a member of the Communist Party, perhaps for the protection of the security of the United States and the democratic principles that this great country cherishes, principles that you accepted and the freedoms that were gifted to you when you arrived on our shores in '38, perhaps you'd be prepared to name others within your university who are Communists and testify against them."

Kitty waits for her father to reply but he hesitates. Her mother's hand feels leaden. Like dead flesh.

"I don't know any Communists, sir. So it wouldn't be possible to…"

"…Mr Bernstein, these men beside me are all very busy. They haven't got time for lies. They have a country to protect from people like you. I'm going to make it easy. Do you or do you not own a copy of The Economic and Philosophical manuscripts of 1844 by Karl Marx, first published in the Soviet Union in 1932?"

Murmurs ripple through the court. Kitty feels her heart shiver.

"How did you…?"

"…Please answer the question, Mr Bernstein."

"Yes, but I'm a Philosophy tutor. What do you expect?"

"You have several such books, Mr Bernstein. Some are in German, bought before you left Berlin, others you have purchased that are not on your university syllabus. Acquired for personal reading to enjoy with your Communist friends. So I ask you again, Mr Bernstein, are you or have you ever been a member of the Communist Party of the United States?"

She hears her father clear his throat. The first indication of discomfort. When he speaks his voice is almost unrecognisable, as if he's been physically wounded. "I do not wish to waste anyone's time, sir. Each one of us has precious time to lose. I request to claim Fifth Amendment protection."

The chamber erupts as Kitty drops her head to her lap. She takes in little more, a call to order, sporadic shouts which make no sense. Aware that the court has adjourned she takes her mother's arm and leads her out of the chamber. The viewing public are decent enough to clear a path but press photographer's fill the void, bulbs flashing in Kitty's face like an electrical storm. She tries to protect her father as they head for the car lot, taking the keys from him and pressing him into the passenger seat, her mother scrambling in behind them. She presses hard on the gas, photographers still clinging to the car.

"Are you alright, Paps?"

"I'm fine, honey."

But after that, as the courthouse recedes behind them, their silence is as impenetrable as lead.

She makes her father and mother a cup of coffee, watching over them as they collapse onto the sofa without changing out of their formal clothes. Her father at least undoes his tie and settles to stare at the fireplace. She adds sugar to each cup and brings cookies on a tray, setting them down on the table between the two sofas. She wants to find words of comfort but none come to her. It's her father who eventually breaks the silence.

"That's what they were doing when they broke in."

"What? Who are you taking about, Paps?"

"The FBI. They were looking through my personal library in the office. That's why nothing was stolen."

"Are you sure, Walter?"

"I've heard a lot of similar stories."

"Why didn't you say something, Paps? That's outrageous!"

"My word against theirs. Who's the court gonna believe?"

"You should fight it! So what if you were a Communist in Germany. You're a decent, kind, intelligent human being, Paps. You've done more for this country than any of those assholes."

"Kitty.."

"It's true, Ma." She feels her blood boil. She's not used to it, as if she's always suppressed it somehow, but by the look on her father's face she knows it's not helping him. He looks exhausted. "What'll you do, Paps?'

He conjures a ridiculous laugh. "Nothing. Wait for my letter of dismissal. Find some manual work if I can."

"Dismissal?" She's becoming aware that her parents must have talked the whole situation through. That they knew this would be the outcome. Her mother wears a look of resignation rather than bitterness.

"I'll be fired, honey, sure as eggs is eggs. By claiming the Fifth Amendment in the court's eyes I'm declaring that I'm a Communist without actually saying so. It's the only way I can get out of naming other people they want to accuse of being traitors. Only trouble is it's guaranteed to lose me my job. McCarthy and his cronies have got me by the balls. There's no university or any other goddamn place where they can afford to be seen working with supposed Communists. Hand me another cookie, will you?"

She takes the plate of cookies from the table and places it beside him. Outside she can hear a car drive up. Immediately she's on alert, anticipating some danger or trouble, but quickly realises that it's only their neighbour, Tony, returning from work.

She hears nothing from Robert but a couple of days later a letter arrives in the mailbox. She recognises the handwriting. She barely wants to open it but forces herself too, if only to confirm what she already knows. She takes it to her bedroom.

My dear Kitty,

I hope you and your parents are doing okay in the circumstances. I have taken some time to think this through, so apologies for not being in touch sooner, but I think it would be inadvisable for us to marry now. Much as I loved you I have to consider my career and my future and if we were to stay together I fear my ambitions, and consequently our life together, would be thwarted…

She skips the rest of the page, picking up on the last lines.

…I'd be very grateful if you could return the ring by post or drop it at my office. I doubt you want to keep it in the light of what's happened. I wish you and your family well for the future and am sorry it had to end this way.

Best regards,

Robert

She tears the letter up and throws it in the bin. In a way she's glad to have the confirmation. Ever since meeting him at the diner she'd felt cast adrift. Her parents are still in bed so she breakfast's alone, determined to eat properly for once before the drive to school. She makes herself scrambled eggs on toast and sits at the counter, staring into space as she eats. It seems so unreal. She can't fathom how a good man like her father, a brilliant professor and pillar of the community can suddenly be so vilified. It doesn't make any sense. After being hounded out of Germany by the Fascists he'd put his trust in America and that trust had been rewarded, for which he'd been eternally grateful. But now? Now, despite all his best efforts, he's a pawn again, thrown at the mercy of those who abuse their power. And just as happened in Germany, they've proven themselves short of tolerance and basic, human decency.

Her thoughts drift to Berlin; her innocent childhood playing in the streets before she noticed the stars daubed in yellow paint on friends' houses and the looming danger to her own family. She wonders what Berlin's like now, particularly the East, where she grew up. The worst is over, thank God. She's seen the images of re-building on television and can't imagine the Eastern bloc can be as evil as McCarthy makes out. She knew those people. They were her kinsman. A part of her wants to return, to restore those connections and prove that the propaganda about the East is unfounded. That McCarthy is nothing more than a heinous agitator. Maybe it's a knee-jerk reaction, but she doesn't care. The main thing is she must never allow herself to be dependent on someone again, never trust a person and see that trust eviscerated. To be vulnerable to others is suicide, especially in affairs of the heart.

Cold Road to Imber

9

Stepping out onto the forecourt at King's Cross Station, she hails a taxi, as Ed Grant had instructed, and asks to be taken to Chanel in Bond Street. A woman in a tailored, burgundy suit greets her at the entrance, her hair swept high into a platinum blonde bun. She ushers Kitty to a Regency chair while a young model parades a series of outfits from which she's invited to choose. Kitty selects two; a strapless evening gown in plum satin and an alternative in emerald-green that emphasises her breasts. Having spent two years in East Berlin she's horrified by the price but the quality's better than anything she'd find in Friedrichstrasse. A second taxi delivers her to the Dorchester Hotel in Park Lane where a liveried doorman steps forward to open the cab door. She frames a grateful smile, speculating on how it must feel to lead this charmed life. Vacuous, she imagines. She feels no jealousy, private wealth never bred empathy or manners, but she is not immune to the frivolity of her circumstance. To dress up is fun; a game that children understand better than anyone; but to believe it signifies your superior status, well that fallacy should have been routed by the horrors of the First World War.

The doorman carries her bags across the lobby to the reception desk. A sleek décor of gold and black art deco reminds her of hotels she visited in New York but never had the chance to stay in. If they were lucky, Paps would order them a glass of wine in the handsome bar, before hastily retreating round the corner to one of his favourite Polish diners, always complaining his pockets were on fire because the bar had charged so damned much. The memory touches her. She dismisses it.

"Welcome to the Dorchester, Miss Adams, we trust you'll have a delightful stay."

"I'm sure I will." A different porter carries her bags to the lift and guides her down the thickly, carpeted corridor to her room. She tips him well; everything should suggest she's just another wealthy American. The room is furnished in the same Déco style with a picture window overlooking Hyde Park. Late afternoon sunlight burns early, autumnal leaves to gold. She has an hour to spare. Ed Grant said to be ready for six thirty, so she takes a long bath and rehearses the details of her fictional American upbringing. Vanity Adams. It sounds phoney but she still likes it. And she's added a bit of flesh. Too wealthy to bother with work, but she dabbles with paint at her home in Connecticut. Her father's a stockbroker. But she doubts Mr James Buchanan-Smith will be interested in such detail.

At precisely six thirty there's a knock on her door. She checks the keyhole view. Her collaborator is holding a bottle of champagne wrapped in a cloth. She thinks he looks remarkably handsome in his dinner jacket, but not her type; too refined, like a figurine. She eases open the door.

"I thought you might need a little Dutch courage."

"Very thoughtful." Turning back into her sumptuous existence she selects two flute glasses from the Japanese, lacquered cabinet.

"You look fabulous."

She grins, warming to her part. "I meant to." A single twirl shows off the curvaceous folds of the emerald-green dress. "I hope you like it."

"Impossible not to."

"I thought the slight shimmer would be good to catch a fish."

From his pocket he produces a slim, rectangular box. "May I suggest one more thing? Just to add temptation. Open it."

Uncertain of his intention she takes the box anyway, lifting the lid to reveal a Cartier wrist watch. Silver, glistening and oozing entitlement.

"Here, let me." His nimble fingers attach the watch her wrist. "It's only a loan but I thought it would help complete the identity. "There. Perfect."

"Yours?"

"My mother's. I stole it the other day. She won't miss it and I'll put it back."

She's unsure what to say, amazed by his casualness. Though it's only property. She admires its effect on her wrist, barely able to lift her eyes as he begins to open the champagne; which it's clear he's mastered since birth. Dexterous, flamboyant, barely a drop spilt. He hands her the flute and raises his own glass to meet hers. The sparkling chime of crystal.

"Here's to a successful fishing trip, Vanity Adams."

She laughs. Deliberately coquettish. "And here's to a big fish spilling his guts."

Sipping the champagne, she suddenly feels grateful for its kick. Everything prior to this has been a rehearsal; classroom psychology lessons, attack and defence training, weapons, code interpretation, but now, the metamorphosis complete, she is simply bait, waiting to be preyed upon. As if sensing her ambivalence, Ed smiles reassuringly.

"And here's to you, Vanity. You've already scored a one hundred percent success rate. Alexander Carter's asked for your address. I couldn't see the harm. But I told him he's on no account to visit as your landlady disapproves of visitors."

"Lucky me." Edward Grant's approbation, though she's grateful, does little to reassure her. Her task is only sanctionable through her unfaltering belief in the cause. An innocent bystander would simply see it as prostitution. Which it is in a way. How can she deny it? The only difference being her price; information rather than a grubby hand of bank notes. Either way her body is for sale. She needs a moment before they go. "I think I left my lipstick in the bathroom. I won't be a minute."

Closing the door behind her she pulls the light switch and steps toward the large, gilded mirror above the basin. What she sees she barely recognises. An apparition of sorts. Someone from an American magazine cover staring back at her. Though shocking it's a useful tool, a device which gives her the permission to continue, like a prop for an actor. She's playing her part, that's all. A Shakespearean player of seductive intent. More Cleopatra than Lady Macbeth, she hopes. It's a florid analogy, she knows, but the champagne has already affected her imagination, presumably due to first-time nerves. She dabs her neck and wrists with a new perfume. Femme de Rochas. Importantly not one she's used before; draws a long breath and returns to her handsome chaperone. "Shall we?"

They take a taxi, pulling up outside the classical façade of a Georgian town house. A welcoming light emanates from the symmetry of long windows. A parody of a child's doll house. Passing the iron railing gates Ed guides her into the vestibule where a doorman takes their coats. She feels Ed's arm pressed softly at the back of her waist, leading her into an elegant drawing room, its contours lost in the haze; an excited hubbub of chatter swirling through the density of bodies, bare shouldered young women in satin frocks, the men, nearly all middle-aged, attentive and tactile. Two glasses of champagne are plucked from a passing waitress by her chaperone. She drinks quicker than she wanted, wondering still whether she really has the guts for this.

Again Ed Grant comes to her rescue, whispering softly into her ear. "Remember, cousin, it's for the cause. Let's go fishing."

They pass through to another more intimate room where a young black girl sings blues ballads accompanied by a guitarist. No one is paying them much attention. Ed conjures two more glasses from another waiter but she will only sip now. She has to be vigilant.

"Edward, my darling, how lovely that you could come."

An immaculate woman stands before them, blonde hair neatly permed, pale skin and vermillion lips. In her early forties, Kitty guesses.

He kisses her on both cheeks. "Hello Caroline, how lovely to be here. Can I introduce you to my American cousin, Vanity? Vanity Adams this is Caroline Buchanan-Smith, our charming hostess."

Kitty detects an almost imperceptible hesitation before her hostess proffers a welcoming smile. "Ed never told me he has a cousin in the States. Delighted to meet you, Vanity."

"Likewise. You're very kind to invite me." The alcohol has made it easier. She's resumed her Philadelphian vowels which had diminished a degree since her two years in Germany. "And it's great to be back in England. You have so much fascinating history."

Her hostess smiles approvingly. "Well we can't deny that, can we, Edward? Are you here on holiday?"

"I'm calling it an educational tour. I wanted to see a bit more of Europe. Ed promised to show me some of the sights while I'm in London. Beyond that, I've not yet made any specific plans."

"No better hands to be in while you're here, I assure you. You'll take care of Vanity, won't you, darling?"

"It'll be my pleasure."

A glass shatters at the far end of the room which distracts Caroline Buchanan-Smith's attention. "Please excuse me, unfortunately the staff come with the venue. I'd rather have hired my own." She emits a small, complicit chuckle. "Go and say hello to James. I think he's in what they call the music room."

They watch her disappear into the crowd. Kitty takes her chaperone's arm. "She seems nice."

"She's a monster. I can't say I blame her husband for being such a philanderer."

"Maybe he turned her into a monster. But maybe you never thought of that."

She can see her comment has taken him aback slightly. A moment later she feels the press of his hand again at her lower back again, guiding her to yet another cavernous room. He's playing a role, she knows he is, or at least she assumes he is. But still, suddenly she resents the manipulation of her puppeteer.

The music room is ironically the quietest. And also the darkest. Embossed, velvet wallpaper lines the walls; the curtains onto the courtyard garden are half drawn, allowing a thin stream of light to partition the space, like a dividing wall. A circle of men line the contours of a grand piano, their elbows pressed to the varnish. Two others stand at the mantel piece, deep in conversation. Plainly this is the more serious room, but serious about what, she wonders. Politics or promiscuity? Ed takes her hand and leads her across the floor to the mantelpiece, showing no hesitancy at interrupting the conversation.

"James, dear chap, Caroline said you'd be in here."

The taller man answers. Clipped vowels, like razor wire. "Edward, how lovely to see you. Shouldn't you be eating baked beans in your digs?" His accomplice laughs. The tone is vaguely condescending but Ed seems unbothered.

"I've taken the weekend off to entertain my American cousin. May I introduce Miss Vanity Adams. Vanity this is our charming host, James Buchanan-Smith."

To her surprise he takes her hand, pressing his lips deftly to her skin. "A great pleasure to meet you. This is my friend, Robert Woolcott."

She turns briefly to acknowledge the colleague before reverting her full attention to her host. "Thank you so much for inviting me. It's a wonderful party."

"All my wife's work. I'm afraid I can't take any credit. But we're always delighted to welcome our friends from across the pond, aren't we Robert?"

Robert nods before making his excuses and departing.

"So, how long are we blessed with your company, Miss Adams, before you take flight back to the modern land?"

His eyes, she can't help notice, have already assessed her vital statistics and cup size. "Oh, please call me, Vanity."

"A very pretty name, if I may say so." His smile is unmistakably predatorial.

"Thank you. You may. And I guess the answer is I'm not sure yet. It depends how things pan out."

"We'll have to make sure Edward does a good job of keeping you here. Won't we Edward?"

"I've promised Caroline I'll take care of her."

"Good." Though a slight cooling suggests Buchanan-Smith isn't too impressed by the reference to his wife again. But he recovers quickly. "Now be a sport, Edward and get me a top up of Scotch. And another glass for Vanity."

When Ed leaves she returns her gaze to her host, waiting for him to lead their dance. She wonders if his wife ever found him physically attractive. Undoubtedly he has a superficial charm, and a voice as rich as sugar mollases, but his face already bears the hallmarks of over indulgence, not helped by a receding hairline. The eyes hide under a heavy brow and thin lips evaporate under tucks at the corners of his mouth. None of which seems to diminish his bearing. He reminds her a bit of a younger Truman. A comparison she doesn't think he'd much enjoy.

"Smoke?" He offers her a cigarette from a slim case and lights it with a match struck on the mantelpiece. "What does a delightful young American do when she's staying in London. Apart from sight-seeing."

She exhales a thin whisp of smoke, summoning her best Lauren Bacall. "Oh this and that. I paint so I thought I might go to a few galleries, maybe even look for an agent to represent me."

"Excellent. And where are you staying?"

"The Dorchester. But if I stay much longer I might take an

apartment. Ed said he'd help me which is sweet of him."

"I can't think why he's never mentioned you before. If I had such a charming cousin I'd be very keen to show her off."

"Perhaps he didn't want to." She leans a little closer. "Between you and me I think he finds Americans a touch vulgar."

He laughs. Which pleases her. "I think you know your cousin very well. Personally, I find the priggishness of the English very depressing. There was a time, probably around when this house was built, when vulgarity was all the rage. As depicted by our wonderful painter, Hogarth. Maybe you know of him?"

"I've heard the name but I have to confess I'm an American innocent. Perhaps you'd enlighten me."

He smiles. "I'd be delighted. And maybe in exchange you could introduce me to some American art. I'm afraid in that area I, too, am guilty of indecent innocence."

"It sounds like we have a deal." She thinks of artists she can name. Precious few. A little research might be necessary. Though from his gaze she deduces that art is hardly the point. She looks bashfully at the floor then back to his face, resisting a more compelling urge to wipe out his unctuous grin; instead surrendering to his next move which comes quicker than she'd expected.

"I have a little soiree on Wednesday evenings. Nothing as elaborate as this, just a few close friends. It relieves the tedium of having to be in Whitehall all week. Ed should bring you along. Or if he's busy just come along by yourself. Here." He scribbles an address hastily on a scrap of paper from his jacket pocket.

She takes it. "Thank you. That'd be fun."

"Don't mention it. By which I mean, in the literal sense. If you understand me."

"I can't wait."

Driving back to Cambridge along the Great North Road, she watches the cats' eyes slither under the bonnet, each one like a beacon, each making her feel less soiled as they escape from London. She had drunk more than she meant to; hardly surprising but she won't make the same mistake again; and she'd happily drift into sleep if it weren't for Ed Grant's obsession with reviewing every word at the party. She tries to hide her irritation. She feels she's worked hard enough for one day. Maybe he's just trying to stay wake. She glances at the Cartier watch, still attached to her wrist. Just gone two in the morning. She takes it off, intending to drop it into the glove compartment, but it's locked.

"Just leave it on the back seat."

"Isn't that a bit reckless with something so valuable?"

"It's only a watch. I presume you've got a house key."

She searches in her handbag, lifting the key to his view, annoyed that he needs to ask.

"If your landlady says anything about being late, tell her one of the family offered to drive you home. If she's asks more tell her they live north of here. Swaffham will do. It's a charming place. And try and get some decent sleep in the next couple of days. We can't let anything slip."

His tone is petulant, a nervousness she hasn't seen before. She wonders if this is his first serious call of duty. A test. But she can't ask him. Never seek information on a fellow operator. It may compromise the operation, an order drummed into her at the Belzig training camp. And tested in their dormitories with hidden microphones. Most pupils failed the test and were dumped unceremoniously at the train station. And they knew they would now be watched forever. So instead she chides him. "Thanks for the concern. Maybe you'd like to tell me which nightie I should wear."

He turns briefly to her, a wry smile touching his shadowed face. She's glad she's strayed into unofficial territory. It's a breath of oxygen. They both need it. "That's outside my domain."

"Too bad, Mr Grant. Then it'll remain my little secret."

At breakfast the following morning, as he had predicted, Mrs Johnson wastes no time. "You were very late in, Miss Bernstein."

"I'm so sorry if I disturbed you. My family love to party so I was too late to catch a train. Luckily one of my distant relatives lives in Swaffham so he offered to drop me on the way."

"That's kind of him."

"Yes. I was very grateful."

"I know Swaffham quite well. Does he live in the centre of the town?"

Kitty slices the top off her egg and places it neatly on to the plate. "No, he mentioned a farm on its outskirts. But don't ask me where, I was too tired to take it in."

Her landlady looks unconvinced but mercifully lets it drop, returning her attention to a colander of apple peelings whilst Kitty prepares for school.

To her surprise, her teaching day provides some welcome distraction; it's a simpler and in many ways, more pleasant task. The children are warming to her informal style, some even showing progress in their linguistic skills. Tom Gilliam, with his cheeky interruptions, is fast becoming her favourite, which she knows she should resist; and even the stony façade of Rose Thorpe betrays a hint of crumbling. But steering a course between good teaching practice and emotional detachment is already proving a harder task than she'd imagined.

By the close of school on Friday she's heard no sound of Edward Grant and wonders whether he's submitted an unflattering report. Perhaps she drank too much with Buchanan-Smith, or she was over familiar about the nightie. There is something about him that she can't fathom. Returning to her landlady's house, doubt tightening her stomach, she finds Mrs Johnson holding out a letter in her calloused hand, plainly expecting Kitty to open it before her. She glances at the handwriting. It's unfamiliar. But she's guessed its provenance. Avoiding her landlady's expectant gaze, she opens the envelope in her bedroom; a one-sided page from a hand that is almost child-like in its pedantic assembly.

Dear Kitty,

It was a pleasure to meet you last week. I'm very glad we bumped into you by chance. I hope you don't mind but Ed gave me your address and I wondered whether you might like to meet for a walk or a trip to the cinema? I'm free on Sunday. I will be in the market square at eleven o'clock if you would like to join me. If not, I apologise for troubling you.

Best wishes,

Alec Grant

She finds the note quite charming in a very British sort of way.
An invitation countered by an apology. It wouldn't be
impossible to deliver a response through Ed Grant but she
chooses not to; it'd be more dramatic to keep him guessing.
Folding the letter in to her diary, she's reminded of her early
days courting Robert. She played much the same game then,
arriving ten minutes late just to tease him; cruel really, but in the
end she paid the price.

On Saturday she marks the tests she'd set the children. More
games than tests but it passes a day which otherwise she'd find
tedious. Stratham's orbit seems defined by the pub or the
church, or both, neither of which appeal. Either the workers are
unusually content, which she finds hard to accept given the
feudalistic perversion of their world, or they're sleep-walking to
their graves, resigned to a political system which subjugates their
worth. By the amount of beer they imbibe, she suspects the
latter. Even Mrs Johnson, a bright, capable woman, tethers
herself to needless, menial tasks and exudes dismay, when, on
Sunday morning, Kitty had mentioned that she wouldn't be in
for lunch. "Suit yourself," she'd said, "Sunday roast's obviously
not for foreign tastes," before making a point of slamming the
oven door. Kitty had tried to make amends by offering to help
with the housework later, but the look of disdain etched across
her landlady's face spoke for itself. Only as she walked down the
lane did she understand her mistake; Sunday being God's day.
Housework strictly forbidden.

Three villagers are already waiting at the bus stop, two elderly
women in raincoats and a young man in his best Sunday suit, a
paper bag clasped tight in his hand. Sandwiches she assumes.
She greets them measuredly, aware that the news of an American
German arriving in their midst has caused a flutter of
disapproval; nothing overt, but she occasionally clocks a local
crossing the street before they're forced to greet her. She doesn't
blame them; there must be many like Mrs Johnson who have

lost loved ones because of Hitler and his Fascist thugs. When the bus arrives, she chooses a seat at the back, her thoughts turning to Alec Carter. She has to admit, she's looking forward to their little rendezvous. Though there's deceit in her intention, she'd genuinely liked him and thought he'd shown all the hallmarks of a potential recruit. And almost more importantly, for her own well-being, he wasn't Buchanan-Smith, who was lurking like a dark cloud in her brain. Ready to piss on her from on high whenever he chose. The bus passes the outskirts of Cambridge. She extracts a vanity mirror from her handbag and applies a layer of lipstick. It seems ridiculous to feel nervous, but she can't ignore the flutter in her stomach.

She arrives in the market square five minutes early, disappointed to find that Alec Carter isn't waiting for her. Being the first is inappropriate so she retires down the back streets for a little window shopping before returning at three minutes past eleven, according to the town clock. She spots him standing at the centre of the square, as if to give himself the broadest viewpoint, a raincoat draped over his arm, his spare hand ruffling through his dark hair, dropping quickly to his side once he sees her. He is undeniably handsome. She smiles encouragingly, waiting for him to approach, his hand rising again as if for a handshake, before he evidently rejects the idea.

"I wasn't sure you'd get my letter."

She sets her eyes on his. "It was very charming. Very British."

"Whatever that means."

"It means I'm here."

Her comment appears to relax him. "Would you like a coffee? Or a walk? Or there's a film I think you might like which starts in half an hour."

Sensing that he'd be more comfortable in the cinema she opts for the latter. "I'm a sucker for the movies. My dad always took me as a kid so I got hooked."

"Me too. Not with my dad though, I just liked them anyway. A temporary escape."

"Nothing wrong with that."

He smiles at her affirmation. "I hope you like it. It's one I saw it when it was released earlier this year but on Sundays this cinema always shows films people might have missed. There's even some American characters so hopefully you'll feel at home."

"That's very thoughtful of you. Just don't tell me what it is. I like surprises."

'This way." Stepping away from the square, she asks him simple questions about his studies which he answers without elaboration, seemingly more interested in her work as a teacher. To lighten the mood she tells him about Tom Gilliam's comment that she couldn't be German because she has dark hair and brown eyes.

He smiles. "Und was haben sie gesagt?"

She's momentarily thrown by his switch of language, not least because his accent is impeccable. Precise, Hanoverian Deutsch.

"Ich sagte ihm, in Deutschland gibt es mehr als nur hubsche blonde Madchen; er sollte mal dort Urlaub machen, um selber zu sehen." *I told him that there's more than pretty blonde girls in Germany and he ought to go on holiday there to find out for himself.* He laughs which pleases her but she doesn't want to speak any more German with him. Not in public at least. "Anyway, hopefully his curiosity will be aroused if nothing else."

"He might even explain to Germans that not all Englishmen

wear bowler hats."

"It is kind of disappointing."

"I'll remember it next time."

Next time. So there's confidence, if not a certain arrogance.

The cinema is a shadow of the grand Regal where she'd watched Malaga. It's set back from the street, a two-storey building, almost bullied by the larger properties on either side. There's a small queue at the box office window, mostly student types. Alec insists on buying the tickets and she accepts gracefully, but on condition she can buy him coffee afterwards. A single aisle rakes down the side of the auditorium to the screen. There's no usherette to greet them, just the occasional flare of a match struck amongst the rows of seats. As her eyes adjust, she understands the lack of light; long strips of wallpaper fall from the walls and the fabric on her seat is worn to thread, frayed at the corners. He grins at her as they sit down. "It looks a lot better once the film starts."

As if on cue, the dim light dips to darkness. She turns her focus back to the screen. A white title fills the black screen. "The Good Die Young." She has a sense that she'll enjoy it.

Through the haze of lit cigarettes, she watches the plot unfold, undisturbed by her companion. And she hadn't really expected it. Too much of a gentleman. Unlike Buchanan-Smith. She sinks down into her seat and finds herself relaxing, enjoying the twists and turns until the credits roll, when they adjourn to the small café upstairs. Formica chairs and tables line the wall, occupied by many who were in the audience with them. It's functional rather than cosy but on a Sunday afternoon she doesn't suppose there are many other places to go.

He accepts the mug of coffee she brings to the table, stirring in two sugars. She settles opposite, her back to the counter, hands clasped around her own mug. Usually she'd sit facing into the room but today she's happy to bend the rules, studying her assignment against the glossed wall behind him.

"What did you think?"

She sips before responding. Coffee insipid as ever. She's getting used to it. "Three men down on their luck fall under the spell of a wealthy charlatan. He promises redemption but instead they get shafted. It's not the first time I'd heard that story. But it was still a great film."

"You mean it was derivative?"

His gaze is intense. She's reminded of the first time they met on the train. "I mean it was depressingly accurate. Working class people being exploited and abused. Look around you, it's hardly fiction, is it?" By the look of surprise on his face she wonders if she's gone too far. "Sorry, it just upsets me sometimes."

"No, it's fine. I'm glad you came to see it."

She smiles. "So am I. Sorry. My big mouth getting me in to trouble again." She plays it with a smile, tantamount to seduction. Make yourself look innocent, don't press too hard. Remember your training.

"Honestly. Don't' apologise. I feel the same."

Ignoring his confession, she grins conspiratorially. "You remind me a little bit of the Stanley Baker character. Not his story, I mean. I guess that'd be a bit tragic, just the way he looks."

"What, dark and angry? I'm not sure if that's a compliment."

"It is. Kind of."

"Ed says I look like a perpetual thunderstorm."

She laughs. "He has a way with words."

"Too many usually. So how are you two related? I don't want to be caught bad-mouthing your favourite cousin."

"Oh no, we hardly see each other." She slides easily into the lie. "It's complicated and boring really. But somehow he's a cousin. Anyway, when I left America and went back to Berlin I got in touch. You know how we Americans brag about our European credentials. And I had a cousin at Cambridge University, for God's sake. No way was my family going to let that little nugget pass by."

He smiles. "I'm pleased you didn't."

"Me too." She senses a moment to probe. "So how about you? Ed told me you come from some abandoned village?"

"I do. A place called Imber."

"That sounds kind of romantic. Like something out of a smuggler movie."

"Except it was real. Abandoned only because we were kicked out by the army."

"I'm sorry, that was crass."

"Why should you know?"

She holds his gaze. "Actually I'd love to know. If you're willing to tell me."

She listens patiently to the story that she's already heard. There are no signs of self-pity, as he describes the final occupation of the village by the US Army, in preparation for D-Day. No hint of emotion when he recounts his mother and father packing their belongings into two suitcases and loading it, along with the furniture, on to a trailer pulled by carthorse and finding shelter with relatives. In a way she finds his coolness more astounding than the story itself.

"That's rough. Really. But the way you talk about it, it sounds like some else's story."

"Maybe I have to."

Again she chooses to hold back. Hold the tension between them. Form a bond. "Have you ever been back?"

"Officially it's out of bounds. But when my mother died we were allowed to bury her there. I've been back twice since. Once legitimately, once just for the hell of it."

She knows the answer to the next question but she'll ask it anyway. Complete the story. "What about your father? Where's he now?"

"Deep underground next to my mother." He smiles unexpectedly. "That was the legitimate visit. I think he's happier there."

She remembers Ed Grant had mentioned suicide but again she's not going to probe. She chooses to push for the next link, while there's a chink of vulnerability, mindful of her collaborator's instruction to speed things up. "You can say if this is way out of order, I won't be offended, but I'd love to visit the village, if you'd be willing to take me there."

He looks up from the coffee mug. Surprised, obviously, but not offended. "You really mean that?"

She smiles. "I'm German, remember. I mean what I say."

He returns the smile. "It's highly illegal. We'd have to choose the right moment and we'd need a car. But I'd like that very much. I haven't met many people who can be bothered to listen."

"I guess all of us have a story to tell. Finding someone to listen's the hard bit."

He grins again. "What's yours?"

"Oh, nothing as intriguing. But it'll have to wait. I've got homework to mark. And a bus to catch."

"I'll walk you to the bus stop. I'm rather hoping it'll be delayed."

She smiles. "And risk getting me into trouble with the headmistress."

"Some risks are worth taking."

10

Spits of rain speckle the window, drawing his attention away from a game of Patience, which he fails to resolve despite cheating. A distant roll of thunder threatens a gathering storm. He pushes the cards aside, wondering if Alec Carter and Kitty Bernstein kissed on their first date, and what that felt like; instantly scooping the cards off his bedspread and back to their packet to settle his mind. The thunder drifts closer. He never liked it. As the rumble subsides it's replaced by a heavy tread on the staircase in the hallway. Unmistakeably Alec Carter's. His footsteps have a uniquely impatient quality, like someone stamping on a nest of ants. Slumping his head back to the pillow his hand reaches to the floor for one of his discarded textbooks. He resists the temptation to look up as the door opens, despite Alec Carter's curses.

"Fucking rain. I'm soaked through."

At the periphery of his vision Ed's aware of his room-mate hanging his raincoat on the back of the door, an angry hand sweeping through tousled hair as he strips to his underwear.

"I hate this fucking country. You can't do anything without getting pissed on."

"Literally or metaphorically?"

"I thought you'd be out somewhere."

"Meaning that you wish I were?"

"Meaning you could at least be sympathetic."

Ed lifts his eyes from the page. His room-mate is searching through the drawers for a shirt, throwing to the floor those he deems unsuitable. He feigns a yawn. 'Alright, I'm sorry you got wet. I had some work to catch up on. I was engrossed."

"I thought you disapproved of studying, especially at the weekend."

He lowers the textbook, dropping it back to the floor, assuming his ambivalence about Alec's date should have registered by now. "I disapprove of unnecessary study. But my tutor had the temerity to suggest I'm falling behind and will fail to achieve my Nobel prize unless I buck my ideas up." He throws the silver hip flask from his bedside table across to his room mate's bed. "You look like a dog from Battersea."

"At last. Sympathy."

"Only because I like dogs."

His room-mate spread eagles himself across his own mattress, limbs falling to the floor; taking a swig from the flask. He closes his eyes, soaking hair resting against the pillow. "You could forget the Nobel Prize and just be a wealthy nob."

"Try telling that to my father."

"He'd disapprove?"

"He'd cut off my balls."

"Better stick to the Nobel Prize, then. Not much point in being a castrated millionaire. You've got no heir to pass it on to."

"My turn for the sympathy."

Alec smiles, eyes still closed. "Nothing better than mocking the rich."

"So did you get to a film?" He throws it in casually, as if he doesn't really care.

The eyes open again, his room-mate propping himself on his elbow, as if caught alight by the change of topic. "We did. I think Kitty really enjoyed it. Only the Good Die Young with Stanley Baker. He's very good. Have you seen it?"

"God no, sounds far too depressing. I hope you didn't bore her. How is she, by the way?"

Alec Carter grins, which irritates him. "She's charming. She thinks I look a bit like Stanley Baker."

"Myopia runs in the family."

"If you don't have any objection, I'd like to meet her again."

He can hardly say no. That Alec Carter would fall for her, was precisely the intention. Aware that he's sounding rather petulant while his room-mate presents a model of courteousness, he tries to moderate his tone, raising a fractured smile which he hopes will prove convincing. "I'm hardly her keeper, dear boy. But I'm flattered you ask for my sanction."

"Which in layman's speak means yes?"

"Just remember she's not here for that long."

"The ridiculous thing is I'm not allowed to visit. Or even ring the school. How mad is that?!"

"Village life, old chap. You of all people should know what it's like."

"I don't remember being told not to visit the school."

"They would if you'd been a German."

"For fuck's sake, Ed. I'm serious!"

His loss of temper takes Ed aback for a moment. But then he'd been warned about the boiling anger, the childish sense of injustice. "Look, you'll just have to be patient. I'm sure she'll get in touch." He feels some sympathy, more than he'd expected to in a professional capacity. The fear of unrequited love perhaps.

Alec flops back to his pillow, the anger abated. "I'm terrible at being patient. People wait for things and then they never come. I'd rather run after them. At least you feel you're got a chance then." He closes his eyes again, looking like he might fall asleep.

Finding nothing better to do, Ed lights a cigarette and stares back at the purple clouds assembling at their window. The air is heavy and thick. He feels a headache building, wondering why he feels ill at ease. The chemistry between Kitty Bernstein and Alec is obviously potent. For that he can congratulate himself. She's undoubtedly beguiling and it's clear that she can look after herself. But Alec. He might appear something of a bull but in truth he's an innocent; utterly unaware of the strings that are beginning to manipulate him. Perhaps he's growing too fond of him. He'd been warned by Jim Atherton and he needs to take heed. In the business of espionage friendship is an unpredictable enemy.

On the Monday morning he rings the school, leaving a message with Jane Farley to suggest that he and Kitty meet in the Stratham pub the following evening. It's useful to have a friendly chat with the school office again, just to establish his credentials; the lack of threat he poses. Although Buchanan-Smith will be having one of his soirees on Wednesday evening, he calculates they've made enough progress to satisfy Berlin, so Vanity Adams can decline his first invitation. The disappointment should make her even more alluring. Buchanan will bite harder.

Stepping into the lounge bar of the village pub at seven thirty the following evening, he orders a pint and settles into a deep inglenook beside the fireplace, where he assumes any vital exchanges will be swallowed by the walls. There's enough hubbub from the locals to help his task, but the moment Kitty Bernstein enters through the glazed door, he witnesses a perceptible lull in the conversation. Something of her beauty steals the room, drawing the energy like a fire draws oxygen. He stands, taking a breath himself, and welcomes her to the table with a light kiss on her cheek.

"How are you, Kitty, darling? Sit down. Let me get you a drink."

She smiles demurely "A bitter lemon and soda would be great."

Returning with her order, he's aware that they're still the subject of attention. It doesn't matter provided they establish the familial nature of the relationship. He knows they'll have to meet here for convenience; the more natural it appears, the less they're a subject of interest. But more than that, he has to admit it feels good to be seen in her company. For a moment the trophy is his. There's no reason he shouldn't enjoy it. A perk of the trade. She smiles again as he places the drink before her; the lightest of smiles, so different to the woman he met last at the Dorchester. This adaptation seems so incredibly casual, so unaware of her own beauty.

"How's the teaching going? All under control?" It's a lame question but she'll warm to his casual intent.

She takes a sip of the bitter lemon. "I'm not so sure about the control but I'm really enjoying it. The kids are great. Although I've been easy on them so far. Nest week I'm thinking about introducing some German grammar which'll probably make them run for the hills."

He smiles. "I can't say I'd blame them. When our schoolmaster said it was a bit like Latin, the whole class let out a collective groan. Except for the class swot."

She chuckles freely. Playing her part. "It doesn't sound a great line to use with unenthusiastic nine-year olds."

"Not unless you want a revolution." Instinctively, maybe because they're in public, he wants to flirt with her, enjoying her knowing smile at his little joke. "I'm sure they all adore you. Particularly the boys. In the wilds of Cambridgehire attractive school mistresses are probably a rare sighting."

She drops her eyes to her glass, breaking the flow; perhaps some kind of professional admonishment. He sups from his beer, grateful for the liquid in an overheated room; aware that he's maybe strayed too far and should change the subject. "So presumably you haven't had much chance to do much else since you arrived. No trips to Cambridge or anything like that?"

Her eyes lift again, smiling once more. "I did. On Sunday. I went to the movies which was great. The Good Die Young. Have you seen it? I found the main character very interesting. Quite complex but worth investing in. I might go again if I get a chance."

A shadow passes across their table before he has a chance to reply to her coded description of the date with Alec Carter.

"Kitty, how lovely to find you enjoying our little pub."

Jane Farley is hovering over them, her face flushed, either from the heat of the room or, as he suspects, she's been drinking a while.

Kitty Bernstein offers her sweetest smile. "You told me how cosy it is so I thought I'd bring my cousin. You've met, Edward, haven't you?"

He stands up to shake her warm, clammy hand.

Jane Farley beams. "Yes of course." But her attention is quickly redirected towards Kitty. "I'm just over there, with a few local friends. We'd love you to join us, I could introduce you to a few more locals."

His heart sinks. Absurd, he knows, but it feels too bloody soon to have his moment of fun with Kitty Bernstein hijacked. Glancing through the fug of tobacco fumes to where Jane Farley is pointing, he recognises a clan of local farmers, the indigenous tribe of every country pub. Easy swilling habits. Weathered faces. Raucous.

Kitty Bernstein beats him to the snub. "That's really kind, Jane, but we were just about to go. Ed has to get back to Cambridge and I still have some work to mark. Another time maybe."

"Of course. Another time." Jane Farley's smile withers from summer to autumn as she retires.

Ed sits down again, throwing the beer down his throat as fast as possible. His moment of pleasure has been stolen. He could curse Jane Farley. Tapping his fingers on the beermat, he waits impatiently for Kitty Bernstein to finish her bitter lemon. "We can talk in the car."

Outside a cool wind begins to clear his thoughts. He holds the Magnette's passenger door ajar, like any decent cousin would; stepping round the bonnet to the driver's side with a quick glance to the pub windows to check if they're being watched.

Apparently not. It's only two minutes' drive to her lodgings so he wastes no more time with chivalry. If she wants a cigarette she can light her own. "You should accept a drink with her this week. She's either lonely or a lesbian so keep her on your side. If she feels rejected she might turn nasty."

"Or perhaps she's just being friendly. Or a friendly lesbian."

He finds her smile annoying now. As if she's got the better of him. "I'll leave it to you to find out." Swinging the car out on to the deserted main road he deems it time to talk detail. "What did you get out of Alec?"

"Quite a bit. He wants to see me again."

"So he tells me."

"He's really quite cute."

"Forgive me if I omit that from my report. What else?"

"He told me a bit more about Imber. I sympathised and told him I'd really like to see the village if he felt up to it. He seemed to fall for that but said we'd need a car."

"You would. But it's a good idea. It'll give you some emotional lever."

"You mean let him weep on my shoulder."

"He doesn't strike me as the weeping kind."

"Everyone weeps if pushed hard enough, Ed. Even a cold fish like you."

"Is that your assessment?"

"I haven't filed my report yet, if that's what you mean." She grins. "You were flirting with me earlier. Why the sudden change of tone?"

He grips the steering wheel tighter, frustrated that she's pushed him again. "The pub was theatre. Public consumption. Now it's business. I imagine they taught you that in your training."

"That and the perils of jealousy. It happens to everyone in the field. Nothing to be ashamed of."

He casts her a glance. "First rule, Miss Bernstein, give nothing away. Which I assume you're applying."

She chuckles. "Okay, you got me. Bam. I was just testing you. You're doing the same."

He chooses not to answer, drawing the car up opposite the cottage where a light shines in the upstairs window. "Your landlady's waiting for your safe return."

"I like her. I think she's had a rough time."

Her sympathy throws him. It doesn't suit his mood to agree, though he knows he should. "There's thousands of widows like her since the war. Husbands lost to honourable combat and they're left with some pointless medals and a telegram and a hollow pride that their men did their duty. Rule bloody Britannia. Imber's a good idea. I could drive you both down. Make a day of it."

"So long as you're okay being the gooseberry."

He deliberately ignores the question. "Remember to keep Jane Farley sweet and unless you hear otherwise I'll meet you in Cambridge station car park at five thirty next Wednesday. After that Buchanan-Smith's yours for the baiting. Don't mess it up."

He observes her ruby varnished fingernails clasp the chrome

door handle, then soften as she turns back to face him. "I'm going to admit something, strictly against rules but, hey, I'm guessing you've got a heart beating there somewhere."

"Again. Classified information."

"What you need me to do, with Buchanan-Smith, I've never done before. Professionally speaking. In training I only began to grasp what they wanted of me when I was way down the road. I know it's for the cause but in the baiting ranks, I'm a virgin. I'm asking you not to expect too much too soon."

He can't afford any bourgeois sensibilities now. She knew the job. "One piece of advice. Make him wear a sheath. You'll be no use to the service up the duff."

"Thanks for putting it so sweetly."

"This isn't a game, Kitty. We're on the front line, fighting for a just cause. If I smell doubt you'll be pulled straight back to East Berlin. And no one there likes a traitor."

"In that case thanks for the pep talk, comrade." To his surprise she reaches over to kiss him lightly on the cheek before opening the car door. "I'll see you next Wednesday."

Watching her cross the road in the narrow beam of his headlights, vanishing into the night, he realises that their exchange has aroused him. But then she's a beautiful woman. And he's only human. He spins the Magnette round, the balmy scent of her perfume lingering in the car like latent heat on a summer's night.

On the Saturday night he arranges a pub crawl with the motley crew of drinking companions he and Alec have picked up in the first term. He exudes generosity at the bar, buying more rounds than necessary, his reputation for bonhomie and magnanimous gestures having secured his position as one of the good timers; not too earnest, entertaining, occasionally unpredictable. After the second pint he pours all his subsequent drinks into the urinal. His intention is to get Alec Carter talking about Imber. His opportunity arises when a swell of latecomers separates the two of them from their peers.

"Why are you looking so miserable?" It's not especially true but he wants to start on a combative note. Alec is clearly drunk so he knows he'll react.

"What? I'm not miserable!"

"Yes, you are. You've been like it all evening."

His room-mate tips his beer down his throat. "You're talking bollocks. As always."

"The others might not notice but I have. You've been behaving like this since you saw Kitty."

Alec Carter wipes the spilt beer from his mouth, as if assessing his friend's comments. "What if I have? How would you feel if you liked someone but can't bloody speak to them? It's ridiculous. I hate this country."

"Of course you do. I take it she hasn't been in touch."

"She said she'd ring or send a note. I've checked every bloody day with the porter but bugger all. I don't get it. At the cinema she seemed desperate to meet again. She even said she wanted me to show her Imber."

"Crikey. What did you say?"

"I said I'd love to."

"Was that a good idea?"

"Why the fuck not?"

"I don't know. Old ghosts and all that."

"It's not about bloody ghosts."

"I just thought it might be upsetting…"

"…it probably would be – look you're a charming room-mate, Edward, but you're hardly sensitive to the plight of the underdog."

"Meaning what exactly?"

"Cleggy the chauffeur, daddy a Navy Commander…"

"…Captain…"

"Exactly. The whole bloody boat of toffs who keep us in our place and tell us not to complain. What we need is a fucking revolution! Kitty understands. She gets it. I can just tell. So I want her to come and see what they did to my village, the havoc they caused, without so much as an apology or a single penny of compensation."

Ed sups his beer, noting the vein throb in his room-mate's sweaty forehead. It doesn't take much to rile Alec Carter. "Thank you for the thoughtful speech. And you're right, I'm nothing more than the product of my upbringing. So, in small way, to make amends, I'd like to offer to drive you and Kitty down to Imber. Seeing as you haven't learnt to drive yourself yet."

"Really? You'd be willing to do that?"

"If it helps my revolutionary credentials."

A faint smile brushes Alec Carter's face. "Sorry about that. Too much to drink. Same old record."

"Don't apologise. Better a poor man with a soul than a toff with a chauffeur. Now do your duty and grab another pint. It's nearly closing time."

When he sees Kitty approach in the station car park on the Wednesday evening, it's evident her aura of silky confidence has returned. Though she's still in her work suit, she carries herself as elegantly as a model on the catwalk. Climbing in to the Magnette, her perfume reclaims the air. "How was school?' He asks to make conversation, not because he particularly cares at this moment.

"The introduction to grammar wasn't well received."

"They have my sympathy." He pulls out into the rush hour traffic on the main road.

"But Jane Farley sends her best wishes. I think she quite likes you."

He turns to see she's smiling, presumably enjoying the tease. "Not my type."

"Pity."

Ridiculously he feels the need to justify himself. "She's hardly a potential spy so why would I bother to sleep with her?"

"We all get lonely. No one's infallible."

"Talking of sleep you should probably get some. The seat tilts back. The lever's at the side. But have a look through this first."

He hands her a dossier with all the information on Buchanan-Smith. Photos, press cuttings, academic background. Nothing outstanding but she should familiarise herself.

On the journey down he avoids looking at her. He tells himself she's a commodity; she has a use. He can't care about her welfare, despite her little confession. She'll have been made aware of the dangers as much as he has; aware too that her physical assets are a weapon as much as anything. He's not her nanny. After she's searched through the reports she closes her eyes and drops her seat back. An hour passes before she wakes, without his prompting, just as they reach the outer suburbs to the north-east of London. He glances across, framing a smile, when she sits up to check her face in the vanity mirror. "Do you always sleep so well in cars?"

"Training. Sleep when you're safe or die when you're not. I trust you."

Now he has her attention he repeats the fundamentals of the evening. "Don't push him for information. Get to know him. Get to know what he likes. They always finish at twelve. I'll be at the end of the street at eleven. The latest you should leave is half past." He pulls the Magnette into the forecourt of the Dorchester. A porter is instantly at the door. "Good luck, Vanity."

"Thank you. What a lucky girl I am." She steps out of the car without looking back and he lingers for a moment, watching her traverse to the foyer; primary school teacher reborn a wealthy heiress. It's nothing but a sway of the hips, an elegant hand floating in air. He is startled by her grace.

Driving back up Park Lane he turns west, heading for Bayswater and parks the car in Salem Road, a narrow residential street of London town houses. A five storey, Edwardian brick building stands at the corner with Moscow Road. Ed presses one of the bells and waits.

"Hello?" A croaky, smoker's voice cuts through the dusk.

"I'm in London with my cousin."

The front door buzzes open and he steps into a dimly lit
entrance hall. Wooden letterboxes line the cream wall; a tall
stand contains three umbrellas and a walking stick. He climbs
the wooden stairs to the top floor where a trace of moonlight
sifts through the skylight. The single door on the landing opens
to his touch. He walks into a narrow hallway. A kitchenette
occupies a windowless space opposite him. He turns left into a
thick, carpeted room, once presumably a bedroom, where a
silhouetted figure draws the curtains before switching on a
standard lamp in the corner of the room. An electric fire glows
in front of the chimney breast. Two large armchairs, both frayed
and limp, face a small, ring-stained, coffee table. Opposite the
window a telephone sits on a trestle table, next to a wooden-
cased, valve wireless. A headset rests nearby on the surface, its
roped cable linked to a grey metal case. Hinged doors opened to
reveal an array of dials and switches.

"Do you want coffee or will whisky do?"

"Whisky's fine."

"Sit down. Water?"

"Just a drop." Ed watches the man move away from the curtains
to a small trolley sitting in the recess of the chimney breast. He
selects a bottle and pours, adding the water from a jug.

"Is it cold out?"

"Damp more than cold." The man settles in the empty armchair,
pushing the whisky across the table towards Ed. A small anchor
tattoo is visible amongst the dark hairs on his forearm as his

129

shirt cuff catches the table edge. He lifts his own glass.

"Good health."

Ed lets the whisky slip down his throat. Its heat comforts him. He is on edge, as always when he comes here.

"Are you confident?"

"I think so. Her taxi should be arriving any minute. It's all arranged."

"She can't stay at the Dorchester again. They won't fund it."

"I'll motor her back to Cambridge tonight. It's just a cover. The more they see her there, the better her story looks."

"How does she look?"

"Perfect. Her photograph doesn't really prepare you. She dazzles."

"Buchanan's in for a treat. Lucky him." His companion emits a light chuckle. He's a tall man, at least six feet two, and broad as well. Wiry hair clipped short, greying at the temples. Most noticeably a large strawberry birth mark covers his left cheek. Yet for all the rugged threat, he dresses like a second-rate academic, cord trousers, loose beige cardigan over a crumpled check shirt, a pair of gold-rimmed glasses, too delicate for the bone of his brow. "Has your father ever met him?"

The question is unexpected. But he's used to Jimmy Atherton throwing him off balance, as if always trying to test him, specifically his loyalty. "Not to my knowledge. But I suppose you could argue they inhabit much the same stable."

"How is he, by the way?" Atherton smiles through stained teeth. "Still throwing Christians to the lions?"

"He's been sent on a tour of the Eastern Med, now the government's fretting about Nasser's burgeoning power base. Of course, my father thinks he should be shot and the Egyptian monarchy restored."

"Nasser won't be intimidated by western bullying. It'll just build him more support. He can see colonial rule's doomed even if the British elite can't recognise it." He sips the dregs of his whisky. "Another?"

Ed hands over his glass and watches him retreat to the trolley. There's the merest hint of a limp in his gait which Ed's not noticed before. Unkindly he thinks it might be gout, though it could as easily be the remnant of a war wound. There are thousands of men his sort of age, up and down the country, limping prematurely.

Atherton returns with the two tumblers of whisky. "Tell me about Alexander Carter. How's he shaping up?"

"I think he's going to be very useful. He's obviously still searching for a route to vent his sense of injustice but I think she'll be the perfect source to channel him."

"Is she sleeping with him?"

He feels thrown again. There's something oddly distasteful about the question. Or perhaps it's simply his jealousy. "I have no evidence of that. But she's asked him to show her Imber and he's jumped at it."

He watches Atherton swirls the whisky in his glass, as if he might find inspiration there. "Make it soon."

"I told him I could drive them. Three new friends on an illegal adventure. What could be more bonding?"

"Just don't get caught. Go on a Sunday, late afternoon before it gets dark. They don't usually patrol then. The signs and the barriers are more of a deterrent than anything else. But be careful."

"Even if they stopped us what's the worst they could do? A little, condescending lecture to two silly undergraduates and their American pal. It would probably make their day."

Atherton doesn't laugh which disappoints him. Instead he pulls a packet of cigarettes from his shirt pocket. "Want one?"

"No thanks."

He hunts for a box of matches around the cushion of his armchair, eventually lighting the cigarette between his lips. "I want you to give Carter the idea that he should introduce me to you. Ask him a bit about his tutors at school. If you come over to Salisbury afterwards, between five and six, then I could meet Kitty Bernstein properly. But it's vital she doesn't know. I'd only be Alec's old history teacher. If she's as good an agent as you say, it'd be useful to meet her in person."

"You won't be disappointed." He wonders if it really would be useful for Atherton to meet her, or whether he just wants what he can't have.

"Make it this Sunday if you can. And make sure she sees Carter again beforehand. We need to get him trained up as soon as we can. Berlin's invested a lot in Kitty Bernstein so they're anxious for results. If she can make Buchanan-Smith stain his ministerial trousers tonight she'll have proved her investment."

Ed lets the last mouthful of whisky sit on his tongue, as if hiding the distaste which he feels but tries to combat. It had seemed easy to begin with, following his ardent belief that the system must change, that the abusers of power should be brought to justice, but sitting with Atherton in his shabby Bayswater flat, he suddenly feels seedy, a spectator at a pornographic peep show. He drains his glass, knowing that Atherton will not want to indulge in small talk.

Realising that the whisky's made him hungry, he buys fish and chips from a takeaway on the high street and drives the short distance toMayfair, parking at the end of the mews, out of sight of Buchanan-Smith's flat. He waits for an hour, wondering if Kitty will leave earlier than he's suggested. In a way he hopes she does. It's a cold night and he's grateful for the warmth of the food. The streets are empty, most lights in the apartment blocks already switched off. A fine rain shimmers like a pool of amber in the sodium street lights. At quarter past eleven he notices a familiar figure heading towards him down the mews. He opens the passenger door and she steps in quickly beside him. She appears composed, untarnished at least.

"God, it stinks in here."

"Sorry, I was hungry." He drives away quickly. It'll take them at least two hours to get back to Stratham. "Have you eaten?" He thinks it sounds ridiculously maternal.

"There were sausages on sticks with pineapple and something called Scotch eggs. But I wasn't very hungry."

He deliberately doesn't ask any more for a moment. In case she volunteers the information herself. Turning on to the North Circular he puts his foot down. There's unlikely to be a police car lurking at this time. Glancing at Kitty he realises she's closed her eyes. But he doesn't want her to sleep. Here, in the darkness, staring at the road ahead, it'll be easier to ask the questions he knows he has to.

"How did it go?"

She opens her eyes. "Very well." Then closes them again.

He must ignore her obvious intention to sleep. "What happened?"

"Much as I expected. There were ten of us, five men, five women. We had cocktails, the men talked, the women laughed. At some point Buchanan-Smith said he had a book of Hogarth's paintings up on the mezzanine floor. Which of course was his bedroom, but it's open-plan and the others were still down in the living area, so I stalled him. He's asked me to go again next Wednesday."

"You didn't sleep with him?"

"Is that level of detail necessary at this stage?

"If you want to survive, yes. I have to report. They'll want to know everything."

She sighs, the distaste evident in her face. "What fun for them."

"You can save your outrage for another day. But now I need to know exactly what happened, and why you didn't sleep with him."

"Like I said, it was open-plan. There were other people there for God's sake. Just make something up for me. And if you want the details I let him fondle both breasts under my bra. But when his hand slipped to my knickers I held him back. He was polite enough to except my wishes. Satisfied now?"

"Sleep with him next time."

11

AUTUMN 1953,   LINCOLNSHIRE

The fleshy hands assessing the contours of his neck are cool and dry. They convey a reassurance he's cherished since earliest childhood; his first visits to Dr Treacher, who'd been practising his balm of soft words and sympathetic nods for a generation. The doctor removes the stethoscope from his ears and retires to the other side of a large mahogany desk, settling into the leather chair before addressing his patient.

"You've got glandular fever, Edward."

"Well that's a relief at least."

The doctor chuckles. "What did you think it was?"

"I don't know. Maybe something horrid I picked up in the jungle."

"Not unless you had sexual intercourse. Did you?"

"Of course not." It's easier to lie.

"I'm afraid the remedy is nothing but rest and more rest."

"But what about Cambridge?"

"You'll have to postpone until next year. I'm sorry."

Returning to the Rover, parked on the driveway at the front of the house, he's dimly aware of the scent of jasmine cutting through his befuddled mind. Cleggy opens the door from the inside. He hates the chauffeur making a fuss. The plum leather has heated in the sunlight, conjuring an oppressive fug after the airiness of Dr Treacher's surgery. He winds down the window.

Cleggy turns the key in the ignition. "Do you need anything from the chemist?"

Typical of him to be discreet. In others it might appear rude but with Cleggy he knows the lack of enquiry about his diagnosis is born of a deeply ingrained servitude; personal questions are not within his remit. But he'll tell him anyway. "Just home, Cleggy, please. It's glandular fever. Apparently there's bugger all I can do about it. The worst thing's that I can't go to Cambridge this year."

"I'm sorry to hear that. Perhaps you can…"

"…Perhaps it's a fucking balls up, is what it is! Another year stuck here with father harping on about me not wanting to join the Royal bloody Navy!" He takes a breath, aware that he's perhaps been a little insensitive to his father's employee. "Sorry, Cleggy. It's just a bit of a shock. I'm sure I'll find something to occupy my mind."

The chauffeur guides the car effortlessly on to the main road, the engine purring to his touch. "I know it's not quite the same as university, Master Edward, but I could teach you to drive. That way you could be independent and your father might even buy you a car rather than you having to drive around in this. Something more suitable for a young man." He smiles discreetly. "I'm sure if you told him you needed a motor car to do some scholarly research in Cambridge he'd come round."

"That, Cleggy, is quite brilliant. I'd love you to teach me. Let's start as soon as I'm feeling better."

"If I may, I'll leave it to you to tell your father. There's no rush, just as soon as you're up to it. We could start by driving around the estate."

Ed settles back into the warm leather, a welcome breeze now curling through his window. He's surprised how deeply enthralling he finds this little conspiracy, wondering whether Cleggy would have been a more empathetic father. As far as he knows, Cleggy has no children, but then he knows very little about this man. Despite twenty years of service, interrupted only by the war. Quite shameful really.

Back home, his mother fusses, as he knew she would, so he's tempted to play the afflicted, even though his symptoms aren't too bad in the morning; puffy eyes and a fever will probably reassert themselves by evening. His sister is less impressed; obsessed only by whom he might have kissed to spark the infection and whether she knows her. He refuses to oblige her curiosity. Thank God she'll be back at school soon.

Despite a cool morning, the day has grown humid. To avoid the stuffiness of his bedroom his mother suggests lying on the divan outside the French windows, where a large cherry tree provides welcome shade. Listening to the wood pigeons and the occasional bad-tempered crow, he drifts in and out of sleep, realising that some hours must have passed before he wakes more fully. Sam, the housekeeper has arrived with a glass of lemonade which he drinks quickly to quell his sore throat. He enquires about his father, aware that he hasn't yet come to visit. According to Sam he's culling the dead trees in the wood. It doesn't surprise him. When his father's on leave he never appears to settle, as if life outside the Royal Navy is only bearable if it's productive and timetabled.

After the lemonade he drifts to sleep again for a while. When he wakes he finds his father standing beside the divan. Ed guesses it's early evening because his father's hair is wet, the blonde mane swept back from his forehead, from a shower presumably, after his efforts in the woods. He's dressed in a white shirt and cravat; impeccable as ever. Drawing up a wicker lounge chair, his father lights his cigarette, a long gin placed on the table beside him.

Ed rubs his eyes. "What's the time?"

"Just after six. Your mother says you've been sleeping all afternoon. How are you?"

"I've been better."

"Glandular fever's a bugger. I had it at much the same age, a bit of rest and you'll be up and about in no time."

"Dr Treacher says I can't go to Cambridge this year."

"Your mother told me. He's a good doctor, Treacher, but like all GPs he can be a bit of a bloody nanny. Anyway, we'll have to make the best of it; see if we can find you something to do. At least it explains why you ballsed up your last month in Malaya."

"Can we talk about it some other time? I feel pretty bushed."

He lies back again, aware of his father sipping at his gin and tonic; observing, assessing. Right now he really couldn't care.

A month passes before he feels strong enough to take short walks around the estate. In that time he's barely seen Cleggy but he remembers their last conversation. In the long days without much to occupy him but puzzles and card games, he's given considerable thought to their long-serving chauffeur, not least his shameful lack of knowledge of his life, for which he wishes to make amends.

He discovers Cleggy outside the garage, polishing his father's Bentley. His shirt sleeves are rolled up; his trousers a shabbier version of the pair he wears for duty. Under the crisp, golden light of early autumn he breathes heavily on the chrome headlights, polishing them with a chamois cloth. Ed walks slowly across the gravel, startled by his sense of pleasure at seeing this unassuming man.

"Master Edward. I'm glad to see you're up and about."

"Please Cleggy, we're both adults now. Call me Ed or Edward. I'm nobody's master."

Cleggy's face hosts a paradigm of perplexity. "As you wish. I can't say it won't take some adjustment."

He smiles. "I might forgive you the occasional lapse." He's aware that Cleggy wouldn't usually expect him to arrive outside the garage. The floor above is his living quarters, his home; it feels like he's breached an etiquette, as if it's incumbent on the poor man to entertain him. But he has no intention of forcing their chauffeur to tidy in his honour. "I don't think I've seen more lavished headlamps."

"They're not done quite yet."

He watches in awe. "Cleggy, you remember, when you took me to the doctor, you offered to teach me to drive."

Cleggy rises from the chrome, stretching out his back, his expression not exactly one of delight; perhaps just irritated that his polishing routine has been interrupted. "You're well enough now, are you? Your parents think?"

"They both think it'd be an excellent idea. We'd do separate payment terms and all that of course." The lie comes easily. He hasn't told either of them. His father's set sail on his ship again and his mother will just be happy that he's doing something. He'll pay cash. No questions asked. Their own contract. Still the chauffeur looks uncertain.

"Only if you'd still agree to?"

Cleggy drops the chamois into his trouser pocket, the glint of a smile breaking across his face. "I suppose a break won't hurt. Give me five minutes and we'll try you in the Rover. Unless you've other plans, master…Edward?"

"None at all, Cleggy."

He learns the basic mechanics quickly. Cleggy's a patient and focused teacher. On the first drive he encourages Ed to accelerate the car to thirty miles an hour along the long section of narrow lane between the poplar trees. He's exhilarated by the speed after a month of slothfulness, unable to refrain from hollering out profanities which Cleggy tactfully ignores. But slowing down proves more complex, the Rover shuddering to a graceless halt when he mistimes his gear change. Slumping lower in the seat, he realises the concentration has left him frustratingly tired. Cleggy offers to take over. He doesn't object, happy to be driven back to the house and delivered into the bewildered arms of his mother.

Three days pass before he finds the energy to try again. He's less proficient than the first time but he still enjoys it, particularly the brief moments of exchange when he gathers fragments of Cleggy's life, slowly building a vague picture, but one far more satisfying than the dreary landscape puzzles scattered on his bed. Over the shortening days of October his driving improves considerably, parallel to the fortunes of his health, and the conversations extend in topic and length until he feels they could talk about pretty much anything. It's apparent that Cleggy enjoys it too, and why wouldn't he, seemingly spending the rest of his day doing God knows what in his lair above the garage. It'd be an added pleasure to step inside the makeshift home, his curiosity stirred, but he'd never ask and senses that Cleggy will not invite him. It would cross some arbitrary but symbolic line.

Towards the end of November, after a day when they've driven for twenty miles across the Lincolnshire landscape under a foreboding sky, Cleggy pronounces that he's convinced his protégé is ready for his driving test. Ed has swung the car into the garage, pulling the Rover up neatly at the hay bales, stacked at the far end. "Do you really think so, Cleggy?"

"I wouldn't say if not."

"Thank you. It's been an honour."

"Pleasure's all mine, Edward. Just pass first go if you can see me to that."

"I'll do my best."

Alighting from the car, the rain has finally started to fall; a sudden and impatient deluge. He glances up at the gun metal sky. It's obvious there will be no let up soon. He'll just have to get wet. He couldn't possibly ask Cleggy to drive him back to the house. For a moment he hesitates at the garage doors, searching for a remedy.

"Why don't I make a cup of tea? It'll be a while before this blows over."

Turning around, he's delighted at the unexpected invitation. "That would be lovely. Thank you."

A narrow set of stairs leads from the back of the garage up to a door which Cleggy unlocks. They enter a small kitchenette, tiled and gleaming under the light, with little sign of food or cooking utensils. It's ridiculously ordered. "I'll put the fire on. It's a bit damp." They enter a larger room with a window looking out over the courtyard; the window Ed's always noticed from below. A single bed lines the wall at the back of the room, two armchairs sit at the window, an electric fire in between which Cleggy switches on before offering his guest a seat. "Sit yourself down now, it'll warm up in a bit."

Falling into the armchair he surveys the room once Cleggy's disappeared. There's disappointingly little to go on. No pictures on the wall. No ornaments or knick-knacks. The only object of interest is a small bookcase nearer the window, all hardbacks, some car mechanic manuals but also weighty volumes of history with faded titles; History of Europe, the English Reformation, the War of the Roses. On the top of the case black and white photographs stand in wooden frames. A middle-aged couple on a windswept beach; his parents perhaps, but long ago. Another of a young soldier. Presumably Cleggy during the Great War. He'd have been about the right age. A gaunt young man wearing the stiffest smile.

When Cleggy returns with a tray he attempts to help by searching for a table to support it but Cleggy insists he remain seated, using his spare hand to unlock a trestle table standing against the wall. He pours tea surprisingly elegantly, as if, over years, he's established his own ritual, which is not to be hurried. For ten minutes they talk about cars; which make would be suitable for Ed once he's passed his test. They settle for an MG Magnette. Cleggy thinks it the best choice; fun and fast but not flashy.

"If you book a test you might pass before your father's back from leave. It'll be a lovely surprise for him, then you just need to persuade him you can't study without your own car."

"You make it sound so simple, Cleggy."

He smiles. "I'm just a chauffeur. I don't worry myself too much about the way the world works."

To Ed his shelf of books suggests otherwise but he refrains from commenting. A lull falls in their conversation having discussed all they can about cars, at least from Ed's point of view. He has an assailable urge to learn more deeply about Cleggy, sensing this might be his only opportunity; reluctant to leave without some attempt. He places his teacup back on the saucer. "Would you mind if I ask you a question, Cleggy?"

Cleggy chuckles. "You've already asked me several over the last few weeks."

"More personal, I mean."

"As long as I can choose whether to answer."

"Of course."

"Fire away then."

He takes a breath, praying that he's not about to destroy all he's created. "I was wondering why you never married."

His new companion places the empty cup on to the tray, his fingers then pressed together, as if in prayer. A trace of oil imprints his fingertips, presumably evolved over decades of maintenance. "I never intended not to. It's just one of those things. I was sure as a young man I was going to marry some lovely girl but when I got back to England after the war I found it wasn't that easy. Don't get me wrong, there were plenty of pretty girls but I just didn't seem to be in the right frame of mind to find one."

"What did you do in the war? If you don't mind telling me?"

"I looked after cavalry horses. I was posted out to Egypt. I was a blacksmith by trade. We were stuck out there for months. It was so bloody hot, everyone was desperate for action and then to get home but we had to wait forever. Eventually we were mobilised to fight the Turks in Palestine. It was a bloody mess. Machine guns do terrible damage. Those poor horses, young men trapped beneath them. I shan't forget it. The worst was I couldn't understand what we were doing there. It was so far from home. So pointless."

"It must have been awful."

"When I got back to Blighty we were heroes for a minute. I thought everything would change. The old rules swept aside. I found myself scratching around for work. There wasn't much. I found I couldn't really talk to girls. I didn't know how. I channelled my energies to politics, attending rallies for working men's rights. I was quite a shouter, I can tell you. In between I found odd jobs travelling around the country as a blacksmith but then I realised the motor car was the future. If I'd been cleverer I would've borrowed some money and become a car salesman. Instead I became a chauffeur. Would you like more tea?"

"No, that was lovely. Thank you. I just wonder, whether now you – well how you cope with being – well, effectively a servant, Cleggy, after what you just said. I mean surely it must hurt somehow, after everything you did."

Cleggy smiles kindly. "In the end I learnt to keep my mouth shut. It got me further. And now I'm older I don't have much to shout about. I've had a good life. Your father's looked after me."

"But you call him 'sir'."

"It's just a title. It doesn't mean much."

"It means everything, Cleggy." He smiles, feeling the relationship is strong enough to be a touch disrespectful. "I think you're just too stubborn to recognise it."

His new friend laughs loudly. "Or too comfortable."

A silence falls; perhaps a natural time to leave but he feels reluctant; their conversation unfinished. He feels a need to unburden himself, to confess, the opportunity having always evaded him.

Clegg rescues him, somehow alert to his state of mind. "Your father told me your service in Malaya was a bit troubled."

He smiles. "Not his words, I'm sure."

"Not exactly."

"My father was trained to believe anyone who doesn't hold iron discipline is a traitor. When I was in Malaya I couldn't help expressing my doubts about our position there. He got to hear about it and took me to task. In some ways he was right of course; a soldier breaking ranks is dangerous for the morale of everyone, but the more I saw the more convinced I was that we shouldn't be out there."

"There'd be many who thought the same way as you. They'd just learn to hold their mouth shut."

"It just didn't seem right. Malayan-Chinese who'd been trained by the British to fight the Japanese, now taking up arms against us because we wouldn't give them their independence. From what I saw I couldn't help being sympathetic to their cause. The poverty was awful, they had no rights, no chance to vote and yet it was my job to suppress them. By whatever brutal means necessary."

'You can't bear responsibility for that. South-east Asia's a stick of dynamite since the war. It's too complicated for one man to worry about."

"Maybe not when you're talking maps and flags. But on a personal level. May I be frank with you, Cleggy?"

"Nothing you say will ever pass these walls."

"Thank you. There was one night, a group of us were off duty. So we went for some beers in the local town. A bunch of unruly eighteen-year-olds let loose amongst the natives. One chap, Peters, was our ringleader. He thought we should finish our evening by finding a prostitute. We'd all drunk a lot. I was a virgin and it seemed the least scary opportunity. We followed him like dozy sheep till he found somewhere. It wasn't a brothel. Just a hut on the edge of the town where a woman was beckoning us to come in. She wanted to sell her daughter to us, so they could eat. We took it in turns. This beautiful girl, who never spoke, probably no more than fourteen. She didn't even cry. I feel so guilty about it, I can never quite put it out of my mind."

"I saw similar things, it's not uncommon. It's not your fault, Edward. War let's all the worst out. You musn't feel responsible."

"Thank you, Cleggy."

"I'm afraid I took the easy road. Put it all to the back of my mind because I didn't have the stomach for a fight. You mustn't let it fester, Edward. If you can't forget about it, then do something about it." He smiles. "But only if you're willing to sacrifice a life of comfort."

Two weeks before Christmas his father returns home on leave. His sister isn't yet home from boarding school but his mother regards the event as the official start of celebrations and has arranged a sumptuous, candle-lit dinner. Over a course of beef wellington and a bottle of Pauillac, his father regales them with the stories of his travels; the training in the western Mediterranean before what he imagines will be a posting to the mouth of the Suez Canal to sort out Nasser. He opens a second bottle, Ed and his mother having barely spoken a word, and pours freely into the crystal glasses. "Oh, God, another thing I discovered, that bloody Bolshevik Atherton's teaching history again. God knows what warped propaganda he'll be spreading."

He remembers the story of Atherton, told by his father on so many occasions since its origin, as if somehow with each telling his father seeks to shake his nemesis, though apparently never quite achieving it. He feigns interest, and if he's honest he quite enjoys the opportunity to needle his father. "Where's he teaching?"

"I don't know, I didn't ask. Some God forsaken school in Wiltshire. Poor buggers."

Catching the sullen expression of his mother's otherwise elegant face, he knows he should let it lie but the wine and his regular conversations with Cleggy have brought him new courage. "Maybe he's a very good teacher. Just because he disobeyed your orders in Singapore doesn't mean he can't teach history."

"Thank you, Edward, I don't need your opinion about something of which you know nothing."

"I only said he might be able to teach."

"You were insinuating that his Court Martial was somehow a minor transgression."

"I was trying to suggest that the military doesn't have a moral code it can simply impose on civil life."

"Atherton was a traitor! He should not be allowed to impose his poisonous opinions on unformed minds."

"Oh for God's sake, father, have you any idea how pompous you sound?!"

"I stand for what I believe in. If that sounds pompous then I apologise. But at least I'm not a coward!"

He has no answer. It's an argument his father will always win while he has no crusade of his own. Or one which is not yet fully formed. He glances to his mother, a sultry apology of sorts. He knows he has spoilt the home-coming dinner. A situation he could so easily have avoided by keeping his mouth shut.

A moment of silence ensues but no-one leaves the table. The dinner might yet be salvaged. Cutting through the scrape of cutlery on near empty plates, his mother's voice is warm, conciliatory, heaven-sent. "Did Edward tell you he's passed his driving test?"

His father looks up from his cradled glass, aware, Ed presumes, as much as himself, that they have been sent a lifeline and it's up to them both to prevent the evening from drowning. "No. No he didn't. Well done. When did this happen?"

He attempts to smile, find the right tone, agreeable but not compromised. "About a month ago. Cleggy offered to teach me and I thought it would be a good way to use the time at home. He was a wonderful teacher. Very patient."

"I'm sure he was. Well done, Cleggy."

A lapse in conversation recurs, once more bridged by his mother. "Cleggy and Edward have been talking about what sort of car he should have?"

"Oh yes?" His father sounds sceptical. In Ed's opinion his mother raised the subject too soon but then she had her reasons. He might as well put his case.

"I thought I could use this year by travelling to Cambridge to do some research. So that I'm ready for the first term next autumn. If I had a motor car it would make things a lot easier for everyone."

"I see. Let me have a chat with Cleggy. I think he's the chap to talk to."

"Thank you, father." He sips freely from the Pauillac, sensing his argument is won.

With the consent of Dr Treacher, he travels three days later by train to London, to visit the British Museum Library. There he enquires about any records concerning historical articles written by a Mr James Atherton. He doesn't hold much hope but to his surprise is directed to a file containing studies on the final expedition of Captain Cook, 1776-1779, one of which is hand-written by a J. Atherton. For the next fourteen days he retires to his bedroom after breakfast and writes a letter. Each is identical in content but the delivery address changes. Using an Ordnance Survey map of Wiltshire he begins with schools based in the city of Salisbury and fans his way out to Warminster, Malmesbury and Swindon. He only selects senior schools, recalling from his father's accounts that Atherton taught Higher School Certificate History before he was drafted into the Navy at the start of the war. He has scant expectation of a reply, prepared to concede defeat after the last letter elicits no response.

Borrowing his mother's car he makes excursions to other towns, in part just to get away, but also to fuel a blossoming curiosity. He deliberately tours the industrial areas, searching for the heart of the working communities. In Peterborough he spots men entering a local hall. A noticeboard on the pavement states that it's a meeting of the Communist Party. All are welcome. He stops the car. But as soon as he enters he's aware he's regarded with suspicion. It doesn't surprise him. The jacket and shirt and brown brogues mark him as more alien than from Mars. Persevering, he buys a pint of beer and sits down amongst the packed audience to listen to the speaker; a sinewy union man, preaching an invective which spreads like a virus through the smog-filled room. He thinks it lacks any intellectual zeal or optimism. At worst it's divisionary and exclusionary. It's not the Brave New World he's looking for.

"What are you going to do today?" His father is peeling fragments of shell from a boiled egg.

"I thought I might take the dogs for a walk along the river."

"I talked to Cleggy by the way. He gave you a very favourable report. I'm not promising anything but I'll think about the car."

"Thank you."

"There's a letter for you on the plate. I don't know if you saw it. It's addressed to Mr E Gant. You'd think with a name like Grant you couldn't really get the spelling wrong."

His heartbeat quickens but he continues at his task, adding marmalade to the buttered toast. Taking a bite, he rises from the table, picking up the envelope from the silver platter, which nestles next to the dish of drying, scrambled eggs.

His mother can barely conceal her curiosity. "Do you recognise the writing, darling?"

He turns the envelope in his hand. "I made an enquiry about some chemistry books. It's probably just about that."

She looks crestfallen, and he swallows the toast to assuage his sense of guilt, knowing he has both lied and disappointed her.

In his bedroom he slices the envelope open with a small, hunting knife. His hand is shaking and he lights a cigarette to steady himself. He notices the letter is addressed from Bishop Wordsworth's School, one of the first he wrote to.

Dear Mr Gant,

Thank you for your letter. I apologise for not replying sooner but the autumn term is a busy time as there are always many tasks to complete regarding the new influx of pupils. I read with interest that you are planning to write a book which explores aspects of Cook's expeditions to the South Pacific and am flattered that you consider me a source worth tapping. My knowledge, if I can call it that, relates most specifically to the conditions on board ship and the consequences for the crew, as well as the circumstances that led to the murder of Cook on the island of Hawaii.

I would of course be delighted to meet you. Perhaps you could make your way to Salisbury at your convenience?

Yours sincerely,

James Atherton.

He replies immediately, writing so fast that twice he has to crumple the paper and start again.

A week later he boards the train up to London and from there to Salisbury, using the journey to rehearse his words; telling himself he can always step back from the brink if Atherton doesn't show interest. Alighting at the sleepy platform of the main station he hastens down the hill to the main road and follows Atherton's instructions to find the café. A cool wind blows through the town. He shivers. He didn't bring a coat. When he reaches the café it's somehow not what he expected; surprisingly quaint; an Elizabethan parody of timber and tresses, the dark, dusty windows revealing no hint of the interior.

Atherton had described himself in his subsequent letter as dark haired, of medium to heavy build with a distinctive strawberry birth mark on his left cheek. At first, in the dim light, he fails to pick out anyone responding to the description. The majority of patrons are women. But as he walks deeper into the building he sees a man hunched over a text book, his pen hovering then scratching furiously, like a pecking hen. When he lifts his face the birthmark is bigger than he'd imagined. It spreads both to his mouth and left ear, like some grotesque map.

"Mr Atherton?"

"Mr Gant. I apologise for hiding in the shadows but it was almost full when I got here. How was your trip down?"

"Long. But uneventful at least."

"Sit down, sit down. Will you have a coffee?"

"Thank you."

At Atherton's wave of his hand, the waitress takes their order and retires down a set of steps to the kitchen. "I've no idea why they have to wear those stupid headbands. It makes them look like Victorian servants."

Ed smiles. "Maybe that's the idea." He is nervous, feeling his way, uncertain where this might lead him.

"I dare say. How's the book coming along?" Atherton is remarkably affable. Not what he'd expected.

"Slowly I'm afraid. I'm reaching a dead end with some of my research. Which is why I took the liberty of approaching you. I thought you might have some pointers for a novice."

Atherton laughs. "There's only one rule. And that's to persevere. If someone tells you something's not on record, ask again or ask someone different. Or when someone tells you you're not authorised to make an enquiry, fake your authorisation. It's not hard. Most of the time a letter written on high quality stationary will do. What exact aspect of Cooke's expeditions are you finding difficult to uncover?"

The conversation is interrupted by their waitress who makes an elaborate show of shifting two cups of coffee from her tray to the tablecloth.

"Thank you." Atherton shifts his glance back to Ed, plainly seeking an answer. He'd hoped to keep the conversation on a general level for a while longer but Atherton clearly has neither time nor inclination for small talk. He places his hands on the table, seeking the best way to phrase the true nature of his visit.

"I'm afraid, Mr Atherton, I've been rather underhand. I am genuinely interested in Cooke's expeditions and I have read and thoroughly enjoyed your book. But I'm not writing one myself. My wish to meet you is for other reasons."

He pauses, waiting for some sort of rebuke. But Atherton merely places his cup back in its saucer. Ed notes his eyes flick to the door. As if escape might be the best option. He wouldn't blame him. He takes a cigarette from the packet in his breast pocket. "D'you mind?"

"No, not at all."

Atherton proffers the packet but Ed refuses. Worried his fingers might shake.

Atherton breathes the smoke out through his nostrils. "So now I'm intrigued. To what do I owe the pleasure?"

"My surname isn't Gant, it's Grant. I'm Edward Grant, the son of Michael Grant."

The schoolteacher's eyes widen slightly. "He sent you? To find me?"

"He knows nothing about it. I came because I wanted to meet you."

He waits for a response. Atherton's eyes upon him. Then the barely smoked cigarette quickly stubbed out in the ashtray. "I suggest we go our separate ways. Mr Grant. I'm not interested in dredging through the past." He rises from his seat.

"Please. It's not the past I'm interested in. I've come to you looking for help."

His words have the effect he'd hoped. He just needs to hold his nerve. Atherton has settled again, the avuncular posture superseded by guarded restraint. "Help?"

"My father and I don't share the same opinions. I find aspects of his behaviour…"

"…Mr Grant, if this is some personal vendetta against your father you can forget about…"

"…No. That's not why I came." He looks around. None of the ladies seem much interested in them. Nevertheless he lowers his voice. "From what my father told me and from what I've read in your book, I think we might share similar views. Political views. I mean about the direction this country should go in. I've tried going to local workers' meetings but it wasn't what I was looking for. And I didn't get the impression they'd much trust me. I don't blame them. I come from a very privileged background. But mine's not a world where I meet people with similar views. So I thought of you. Naïve as that might sound. I have no idea where to start. I'm sincerely sorry for the subterfuge. I just didn't know what else to do."

He sees no point in pleading further. If Atherton wants to walk away he's quite entitled to do so. Looking at this ordinary man, save the extraordinary mark on his face, Ed wonders if he's guilty of building up a ridiculous fantasy while he's been recovering from glandular fever. Which Atherton, a humble Salisbury teacher, is in no position to fulfil.

As he'd half expected, Atherton closes the textbook in front of him and reaches for an overcoat, slung over the back of his chair. "As you've come all the way down here the least I can do is give you a tour of the cathedral. It's only five minutes' walk away."

Outside he feels the cold less than earlier. Perhaps it's the coffee or more likely the faster beat of his heart. Atherton leads him past the shops to the outer perimeter of Salisbury Cathedral. It triggers a vague memory of visiting with his parents when he was a small child, his mother pointing excitedly at the Magna Carta, which at the time meant nothing to him. They take the outer paths, framed by neatly trimmed lawns on one side, and hedges on the other. An occasional dog walker passes by but otherwise they remain undisturbed; a distant hubbub of city traffic mixing with the excitement of children playing somewhere, presumably at the local school.

"It's a stunning achievement, don't you think?" Atherton is directing his gaze above to the long spire which pierces a brooding sky. "Such an extraordinary feat of architecture which they had the capability to build over six hundred years ago. All those men who gave the best of themselves to construct it. Doubtless many losing their lives. Quite humbling."

"I never thought of it quite like that." Glancing to the tip of the spire he has the feeling of being watched, though there's no justification for it. He puts it down to nerves, aware he's out of his depth and could easily still drown.

"So you're Captain Grant's son?"

"I apologise again for my deceit."

"What's he up to these days?"

"He's about to take his ship to the Eastern Med. Ready to attend to any trouble in Cairo."

"Not so much trouble as justified resistance."

"That's not how my father sees it."

"I doubt he does."

He settles into Atherton's pace, feeling emboldened by their preliminary exchange. "You didn't much like him, did you?"

"He was the captain. Liking him wasn't a requirement."

"Perhaps not. But respecting a senior officer is."

Atherton grins briefly in response. "Let's sit down and take in the view." He indicates a bench under a large oak tree, facing the cathedral. "What's your father told you about me?"

"That you were discharged from the navy for misconduct."

"That's all?"

Ed searches for the right response. He doesn't want to anger Atherton but lying also seems pointless. "He said you were trouble, that you had a problem with accepting orders from your superiors. He called you an agitator."

Atherton smiles. "Perhaps he's right. At least the Royal Navy seemed to think so. I served under three different commanders during the war. Each had their own way of maintaining discipline. A ship under fire is a febrile place and no one wants the order of command to break down, it's vital for survival. Serving under your father in Singapore was one of the most difficult times. He took the sinking of the Prince of Wales and Repulse by the Japanese very badly and was obviously deeply humiliated by our retreat to Java. But he began to turn his anger on his own men. We were all shocked by what had happened, we were young, some barely out of school. One man in particular starting wetting himself in his hammock. Crying out in his sleep. I reported it, hoping he might be sent home on sick leave, but instead your father thought it better to put him in solitary confinement. I requested to speak to him about it. He warned me not to interfere or I'd be disciplined in the same way. I'm afraid I lost my temper. I shouted at him. Told him he wasn't fit to be a captain. Next thing I knew I was in Navy jail for three months then booted out without pay. Luckily the headmaster who'd supervised my teacher training thought I was worth a second chance."

"My father told the story quite differently."

"We each have our own view of the world. It just depends how high we're standing."

"When I was a small boy my father used to punish bad behaviour by putting me in the cupboard under the stairs. I often wonder if his parents used to do the same thing to him."

"Probably. It's hard to break patterns of behaviour. It takes a huge amount of discipline. You'll never make the world a better place by goodwill alone. It demands great sacrifice." Atherton is gazing at the cathedral, his thoughts impossible to read. "What do you want from me, Mr Grant?"

He stares up at the spire, finding it easier to make his confession without eye contact. "I want to prick the shiny balloon of complacency. I want to shatter the establishment's smug belief that it's the rich men who shall inherit the earth. The ones who pray for the poor on Sunday before shagging their mistresses on Monday."

He's aware of Atherton turning his face towards him, a broad smile revealing stained teeth. "I'd offer you the role of saviour, Mr Grant. But sadly Jesus Christ already bagged that."

A week later he meets Atherton again; this time at the bridge spanning the Serpentine in Hyde Park. Atherton has an afternoon free once a week, when he likes to visit relatives in London. Ed has arrived early, watching nannies wheel prams around the lake's perimeter under a pewter sky. He lights a cigarette, trying to calm the nerves in his gut, desperate to impress, understanding that the invitation to a second meeting is potentially a door to his purpose. He smiles at Atherton's analogy of Christ; perhaps this is his equivalent of passing through the eye of a needle, not as a rich man seeking eternal life, but as an agitator seeking justice.

The figure striding towards him wears a black, peaked cap; the collar of his duffel coat collar raised up against the cold. They do not shake hands. Intuitively he senses it inappropriate. Atherton suggests they head to the café. "It's too cold for a stroll."

He tries to hide his disappointment. Chatting over a coffee seems oddly domestic, the refuge for nannies and mothers and their noisy offspring. Atherton chooses a table set apart from the rest with a view back to the bridge. He insists that Ed faces into the café, ordering two white coffees without consultation.

He removes his cap, placing it on the table; his hand drifting through his stubby hair. "Have you had a good week?"

"It's been rather dull to be honest. "I've either walked the dog or fed my sister's pony. She's at boarding school."

"By choice or by command?"

"By circumstance of background. There is no choice. At least she's happy there."

"How old is she?"

"Seventeen. The apple of my father's eye. Do you have children?"

"My wife wasn't able to."

"I'm sorry. It's really none of my business."

The waitress brings the coffee to the table and leaves. Atherton smiles again. "At least they don't wear ridiculous head bands here." He stirs two heaped teaspoons of sugar into his cup, seemingly transfixed by the process. "Do you like games, Edward?"

"Games? What sort do you mean?"

"Any games. Football, rugby, hockey, tiddlywinks?"

"I wasn't bad at hockey. But I didn't love it."

"So what do you do…in your spare time?"

"Read, go for walks, like I said. I suppose I ask myself a lot of questions and see if I can find some answers."

"In other words you're a loner…and a bit of a narcissist?"

"I wouldn't put it like that."

"How would you put it?'

"I don't waste time on things that are spurious."

Atherton smiles but it quickly evaporates. "I don't like games either. I think they're a sop. Designed to keep the working man entertained and distracted so that he doesn't think too much. We all dance to the tune of the establishment and they watch us and laugh. We can only change that by force; refusing to play the games they want us to play. But to do that you have to be tough. You have to be prepared to do things that you find run counter to your instincts."

He hesitates before answering. Under Atherton's intense gaze he feels his palms turn clammy. "If that means the world will change for the benefit of all rather than the few, then I'm ready to adjust my principles. But it's quite an irony, isn't it? To improve the lives of working people you're asking me to be less scrupulous."

"It's a means to an end. That's all." Atherton takes a sip of coffee. "Behind me there's a man in a navy overcoat sitting with his wife and small child. He's smoking a cigarette and his wallet is on the edge of the table. There's also a glass of water beside his wife. Do you see them?"

He looks over Atherton's shoulder, seeing the family exactly as described.

"I want you to go over and ask him for a light. In the process you knock the glass of water onto the child. The mother will be distraught. You'll apologise, and in the commotion, slip the man's wallet from the table."

"I'm not a thief."

"But if you work for me you will be under orders. If you question them everybody's vulnerable. I need to know if I can trust you. In any circumstance. If you don't think you can do it we go our separate ways and never meet again. I'll wait for you at the Albert Memorial. Ten minutes. Then I'll be gone."

Atherton drains his cup and leaves without further comment. Watching him slip out of the café, Ed feels his throat constrict, his breathing shallow and fast; daylight pulsing in his eyes. He could be back on a train to Lincolnshire in twenty minutes. He can still walk away. No trace. A waitress approaches, asking if he'd like another coffee. He declines politely. He watches the mother kiss the child's head, slicking down a stray curl while the father looks on like a proud lion. He thinks of Cleggy, wondering what he would make of his circumstance. But then, Cleggy, by his own admission, failed to pursue the fight, choosing a life of servitude instead. Perhaps his new-found friend would admire him. Perhaps he should do this for Cleggy.

The mother begins to gather the crumbs around her child's plate. It's obvious they're about to leave. He stands up, an unlit cigarette held between his fingers, and wanders across to their table, a magnanimous smile framing his face. "Excuse me, I wonder if I could possibly trouble you for a light?"

The father lifts his head, examining Ed's appearance in a single glance before searching for a lighter in his pocket. "Of course."

Bending down to accept the flame he brushes against the water glass, knocking it safely into the child's lap.

Cold Road to Imber

12

OCTOBER 1954, CAMBRIDGE

A persistent drizzle smatters her gabardine trench coat, as she makes her way through the streets of Cambridge to the station car park, where the Magnette is waiting for her. She steps into the passenger seat and removes her headscarf, grateful to be in the warm fug of the car.

"How did it go?" Ed barely glances at her, which she can't help finding impolite, wondering if he's still brooding about her indiscreet comments when he dropped her back after the pub.

"The porter was sweet. He said he'd deliver it personally."

"You must have charmed him."

She smiles. "I did my best." Fine droplets of water fill the windscreen, cocooning them from the outside world. She imagines they could be illicit lovers although if anything Ed exudes less courteousness than he did before.

"What did you write?"

"How much I enjoyed our trip to the movies. And that I'd really like to visit Imber if he's up for it. I suggested he might persuade you to drive us."

"He won't like the idea but he doesn't have much option."

"I'm sure you'll make a very discreet chaperone."

He ignores her provocation. "Let's aim for Sunday. He'll want to visit his old school master as well; he and his wife are the couple Alec lived with after his father died. I'll pick you up at at one. If your landlady asks questions tell her where we're going. Moderate doses of truth are a useful weapon."

"And too much poisons you." She hadn't meant to be so sharp, annoyed that she's displayed a chink of vulnerability. But what the hell? Some things are too personal.

He turns towards her. "Your own circumstance might make you think that but when the establishment's brought to trial…"

"Oh, screw the establishment. They'll find a way to hide no matter what. Unlike my father. He was crucified for telling the truth."

"At least it woke you from political slumber. You owe it to your father. Don't fail him now."

She knows he's right. And his minor display of sympathy has surprised her. She sighs. Maybe she's just tired. "Sometimes I think I've nothing to offer but a cauldron of rage."

He smiles. "You've obviously read your training assessment. Don't fool yourself you're employed for intellectual gravitas, Kitty. You've got a job to do, in the field, use your talents to that end. I spoke to Buchanan-Smith yesterday. He'd like you to go over again next week. I told him you'd be delighted."

"Which is the biggest lie of all."

"Understood. But I'm not sure I care."

"Very professional. But I'm not sure I believe you."

"I'd offer to drive you back to Stratham but I have a tutorial in half an hour."

She wants to trip him up in some way. To prick his self-assurance. "And I guess that's a moderate use of the truth;" her tone, sarcastic.

"If you're as good as East German Intelligence claim, you'll figure it out."

"You flatter yourself that I'm that interested. See you Sunday."

She steps out of the car back into the rain. It's falling faster now. Turning her collar up and tying her headscarf tight under her chin, she heads north back to the bus stop. The bus arrives mercifully quickly. She chooses a window seat, wiping the condensation from the glass, chastising herself for her conduct. The notion of sleeping with Buchanan-Smith makes her nauseous to say the least but she shouldn't have reacted so pettily. She'd brought it upon herself. She'd besmirched her father's name. Drawn him in to her own world of subterfuge and expected what exactly? She doesn't imagine Ed Grant will tolerate much more outpouring of emotion. He seems impervious to sentiment, which is precisely why he's suited to his job. But she can't help feeling compelled to test him. To see what lies underneath. There's something she can't quite read.

By Sunday the weather has turned brighter but colder. She waits under a pale-washed sky for Ed's car to appear, promising herself to adopt a charming but professional tone; a purposeful stance of neutrality. The Magnette draws up precisely at one and she steps inside. He greets her pleasantly enough before moving to the subject of Alec Carter. Her note had apparently been greeted with rapture, which she dismisses lightly as an objective achieved. Yet somehow it means more. At the very least Alec

Carter has the power to erase the sordidness of Buchanan-Smith from her consciousness, if only temporarily.

As they draw up outside Trinity College, she spots him leaning against the wall. He stamps out the butt end of a cigarette when he sees them, lifting his arm in acknowledgement; a sheepish smile stretched across his face. She feels touched somehow, and steps out of the passenger seat.

"Hello, Kitty."

"I thought I'd let you boys ride up front."

"There's no need."

"It's your day, not mine. I insist."

"Very well.' He holds open the rear door of the Magnette and she climbs back in.

She smiles. "It's nice to see you again." He shuts the door behind her.

She imagines that visiting Imber might feel like walking on his own grave, a traumatic event which he'll be forced to endure as part of an awkward threesome. Still, she mustn't be swayed from her objective. Today she'll be operating under Ed Grant's direct gaze. More errors of judgement will cost her dearly.

It takes them over three hours to reach Wiltshire. She dozes occasionally then wakes at a jolt in the road camber to see that the landscape now stretches to the horizon, clusters of oak turning to copper in the afternoon sunlight, the contours of harvested fields exaggerated by the low angle of light. She watches entranced, almost mesmerised, until Alec interjects.

"As soon as we reach the top of this hill you'll see Stonehenge. The road takes us straight past."

She sits forward, curious to see the famous stones through the windscreen. "Can we stop there? I'd love to take a walk around."

Alec spins round, plainly delighted by her interest. "Of course. Turn right at that fork ahead. There's a layby where you can pull in."

Ed swings the car up a narrower road to the right of the henge, pulling in where Alec had suggested. Stepping out into the clear air she follows him up a scraggy bank of grass. The view that greets her does not disappoint. A monumental ring of sarsen stones stands in battered union, their long shadows spread across the field like the regimented infantry of ancient gods. There are no other visitors. She feels surprisingly intimidated. But Alec presses on to its centre, apparently undaunted by its scale, as if he's amongst old friends.

"You're lucky to see it like this. It's not quite so majestic when you get a coach load of tourists spreading out their picnics."

She smiles, compelled to touch each stone that she passes, aware that Alec is watching her. In the distance Ed is taking pictures; business or pleasure, she wonders.

"I used to try and carve my name in them as a kid but the stone was too hard."

"What a very bad boy you were."

He smiles, lighting a cigarette and casually tossing the match to the ground.

She walks around the two massive stones that stand together at the henge's heart. "It's funny how you want to touch them. They're only stones."

"The men who dragged them here might feel a bit offended by that.

"Who says they were men?" She enjoys teasing him, though his only response is a wry smile. Leaning against one of the stones she feels the last comforting touch of autumn sunlight on her face. She shuts her eyes, basking in the warmth. But immediately a shadow blocks the light and she opens them again to find Alec standing before her; his face a breath away from hers.

"Thanks for the note. It meant a lot."

She smiles. "My pleasure."

His hand reaches out to her hair, holding a solitary curl between his fingers. "Come away with me."

She has no hesitation in replying. "I'd like that."

He smiles. "Somewhere without Ed."

Before she can answer their escort steps forward from behind one of the key stones. "I hate to interrupt the party but we should get going if we want to see the village in daylight."

She turns back to Alec. "Let's see Imber first."

The road dips and undulates across the Plain for several miles, passing through two villages before he instructs Ed to turn up a narrower lane, leading to higher ground. A track to the right eventually brings them to a barrier impeding their path, a large sign next to it warning trespassers to keep out. At the side of the road a sentry box stands abandoned. Ed cuts the engine. "What now?"

Without answering Alec leaps out, lifting the barrier and

signalling that Ed should drive through. Kitty notices he's grinning when he climbs back in. "It's them against us. So long as we keep coming here they'll never win."

She returns his smile. Ed was right, he's an obvious candidate. The job of re-education shouldn't be hard. Provided she keeps her head. And provided he keeps his.

The track begins a long winding descent into a valley. She sees a decapitated tree standing near the road, a shard of split wood stabbing at the empty sky. Slowly they become more commonplace until the trees with full canopies are an exception, standing defiantly like the last participants in a marathon dance. Between the decimated trunks, craters pock the fields. Turning right at the bottom of the valley she glimpses the first sign of habitation. A substantial, well-built farmhouse stands back from the road, its walls covered by a creeper that's obscured the windows and threaded itself across the main entrance. Further along she sees what look like a series of allotments, dishevelled and rotting, autumn raspberry canes growing wild and tall but bearing no fruit.

"You can pull in here."

Ed follows Alec's instructions, stopping the car past the abandoned allotments. As Kitty steps out she can barely comprehend the devastation. Every one of the houses has been wounded; windows shattered, tiles missing from roofs, several gaping open to the elements. Some have sunk on their foundations, their doorways listing precariously. Others stand like shells; ghosts of homes now forgotten. She watches rabbits sprint from one doorway to the next, their territory reclaimed. A lane leads up through the village towards a small, Norman church standing at the top of the hill; its square, stone tower reaching up to the darkening sky. At first sight it appears surprisingly undamaged apart from cracks in the stained-glass windows. But as she draws closer she sees the entrance is boarded up; the graveyard beyond surrounded by thick barbed wire.

"Wait for me here." With casual ease Alec steps through a vulnerable part of the wire, presumably a feat he's completed many times before. Kitty glances to Ed who waits as requested. She lingers beside him, not having expected to feel so powerless; or so sombre. Her gaze follows Alec's march across the overgrown graveyard until he crouches at one of the farthest graves. Beyond him the grassland stretches to the crest of the hill. What lies beyond? More of the same, she imagines, not quite comprehending how anyone could have lived so happily in such isolation. She watches him wrench handfuls of wet grass from around the grave, wiping them across the face of the headstone, before discarding them.

Ed steps closer, his breath a cloud of vapour. "I took quite a good photo of you both at Stonehenge. You make a very handsome couple."

His tone grates. Something personal. Inappropriate. She can't help but react. "And I'm guessing he'd be more fun in bed than Buchanan-Smith." She can tell by his face the comment shocks him.

"Was that what he was suggesting, when I interrupted?"

She resents the enquiry but there's no choice. She at least is professional. "He said he'd like to go away with me for a weekend."

He displays no sign of emotion, nothing she can ascertain. Perhaps he's not jealous after all. Perhaps she misread it. But it would be unusual.

"Stall him for a while. Buchanan-Smith is more important." His gaze shifts across the field. "I assume that's his parents he's attending."

"I guess it must be."

"How sweet."

She doesn't bother to reply. When Alec returns he leads them along a path running above the main road; a vantage point that shows the destruction is even greater than she first assumed. She concludes that Imber must have been deliberately targeted in several raids, one pointless bomb after another. He points out the old vicarage, once obviously a grand, Victorian house. The multiple chimneys have tumbled to the ground; an outer wall collapsed in clumps of jagged stone.

Further down he indicates another ruin. "That was my school. It's where they held the meeting about the evacuation." The brick building has shed its tiles, the windows blown out, a skeleton amongst the graves of many others. They reach the road again.

Alec turns his face to the sky. "We've still got about half an hour of light. I'll show you the Dring, where I lived."

She already feels she's seen enough; its effect more depressing than she'd imagined, dispelling any romantic notion she might have had. Walking in Alec's wake she searches for something to say but finds no words and anyway, it seems almost disrespectful to break the eerie silence. Ed is equally withdrawn; she wonders if the whole mission has backfired, instead of drawing her closer to Alec it's only exposed his potential vulnerability. Across the road, behind a small copse, her attention is drawn by another house, the grandest yet.

"That's Imber Court. My mother used to do some washing for them. We used to have village parties there."

The road leads them to what must have once been the village

pub; its sign, The Bell Inn, drifting in the strengthening breeze. Beyond, a row of terraced cottages lines the side of the road.

"It'll be easier to get in round the back." She follows him down a muddy track adjacent to the cottages, their route soon blocked by an ugly, municipal fence which acts as a barricade around the perimeter of a small chapel. A hand-painted notice proclaims it "Consecrated Ground."

"Where my mother worshipped. Just round here." He breaks off on to another field which takes them past the backyards of the cottages. Brambles and hawthorn make a mockery of the once neatly defined rectangles. A fence has been battered to the ground, presumably by the wind. Alec steps over into the yard, stooping to pick up an old washing line which has threaded itself through clumps of grass. He begins to wind it into a neat loop then sensing perhaps the folly, drops it back to the ground. She follows him through into the house, the rotted back door ripped from its hinges. The rancid air of putrefaction instantly fills her lungs. A dead rabbit, eyes gouged out, lies on the tiled floor. Glancing around she begins to make sense of what once must have been a kitchen. There's no sink or pipes, just an absence of green gloss paint where the sink must have stood. He says nothing. She finds no words of comfort, nothing that wouldn't seem wholly insufficient. He leads them to the front room; wallpaper peels like rotting skin, there's a gaping, black hole instead of a fireplace, a dead blackbird spread across the ashes of the last fire. Rabbit droppings everywhere.

"I'll show you my bedroom." The narrow flight of wooden stairs leads them to two doors which face each other off a strip of landing. He opens the door to the left and she follows though there's barely enough room for them both. Ed hovers at the doorway. There's nothing to discern except darker squares of cream paint where pictures must have hung. She wonders what they were.

"I used to sit in that window watching the trees sway when there was a storm." His smile is one of apology. Misplaced she thinks.

Peering out of the grime encrusted window she sees the yard below and the coil of washing line where he had left it. Further up the hill ancient oaks allow their most vulnerable branches to dance in the steady breeze. Flesh pink tentacles of light cling to the ridge above.

"I knew straight away something was wrong. The day my father came back from the school."

"It must have been awful." She instantly regrets her comment; so trite yet she meant it, the circumstance beyond anything she can sum up in words. Empathy wasn't exactly a big part of her training.

But Ed interrupts her thoughts. "Sorry to spoil the party again but we should go if want to visit your old tutor as well."

She winces inwardly; his crassness far outweighing hers. Though it's probably deliberate. And Alec seems unoffended, nodding to his room-mate.

"Well at least I've shown you Imber."

His obedience surprises her. She'd expected a flash of anger at some point on their tour rather than this strange humility. But then she realises she'd probably be the same. Anger would reveal vulnerability. Perhaps he's not ready for that. Descending the stairs her mind turns to the idea of a weekend away with him. How it might play out. Maybe they'd go to the seaside, some tin pot hotel in Scarborough. Walking on the beach with the wind in their hair, fish and chips for supper by the fire. She draws back the thought instantly. She allowed it too long a leash.

By the time they reach the car, the plain is shrouded in darkness. The headlights barely find their path as they begin the ascent out

173

of the valley. She can't remember experiencing such an absence of light, not on this scale at least. Its feels acutely claustrophobic, a weight pressing on all of them, forcing a respectful silence. Stuffing her hand in to the pocket of her coat she finds the soft, comforting lining between her fingers and waits patiently for the return of civilisation. But she's startled by a sudden beam of light, or several lights, which bear down on them from along the road. So blinding Ed shields his eyes, drawing the Magnette to an abrupt halt. "What the hell's that?"

Alec seems surprisingly unperplexed. "Army convoy. They often move at night."

"What do we do?"

"We wait and see. Just do as I tell you. If it's squaddies they might let you pass. If they've got an officer with them we're in trouble."

She sits forward, her mind alert now, as if the piercing light has startled her to professional wakefulness. The convoy has stopped not far short of them. In an instant a human silhouette is looming out of the harsh, truck headlights.

"How's your reversing?"

"Not much in the dark."

"If it's an officer don't wait for him to reach us. There's a track off to the right about twenty yards back. It's rougher but it still gets us out."

Ed glances momentarily over his shoulder, addressing Kitty. "You'll need to duck."

"Shit. It's an officer. Go!"

She lurches forward as Ed throws the car into reverse, ducking into the footwell as best she can. The officer's shouting but she can tell there's already distance between them. The car screeches to a halt. She's thrown again, clinging to the arm strap for balance. Ed accelerates up the track, wheels spinning for traction. Her heart beats wildly as the car bounces across the uneven surface. She scans the rear windscreen. Nothing but a distant halo. The darkness has reclaimed them. An overwhelming sense of elation suddenly envelopes her. A childish defiance but thrilling nonetheless. Even Alec's mood has lifted. He's laughing.

"You did it! You fucking did it!"

"Mind your language but thank you. I had an excellent driving instructor."

"Sorry Kitty. I forgot for a moment."

She laughs. "No apology required."

"You can slow down now. They won't bother pursuing us. Not worth their while."

She leans forward, wanting to see his face. "How can you be sure?"

"I've been playing this game since they chucked us out." He grins back at her, charming and boyish.

"Your rules or theirs?"

"Theirs. I don't have any."

She sits back again, content this time to let the darkness envelop her. There's no point in quizzing him any more about Imber until they next meet. She tries to imagine what it must feel like, to be given six weeks to pack up your home with no possibility of ever returning. But then she thinks of her parents, how they

175

must have felt abandoning Berlin in '38. She was too young to know. It occurs to her she'd never thought to ask them. Or maybe she just knew that the wounds were too sore to pick at.

Thirty minutes later streetlamps on the outskirts of Salisbury throw hazy pools of amber light. A fine mist exaggerates their arc. Ed drives under a railway bridge, turning off the main road into a residential street of terraced, Victorian houses, at Alec's instruction. Coal smoke dips and weaves from the line of chimneys. Most of the houses have curtains drawn. She can't help wondering what happens behind each one; why the British are so private.

The car draws up outside a home which is virtually indistinguishable from its neighbours. A low privet hedge lines the front wall, a tiled path leads to a navy-blue front door. She waits for Alec to step out but he appears to hesitate for a moment, staring toward the house. "Promise me you'll both be on your best behaviour. They mean a lot to me."

Kitty smiles. "You're safe with us. I promise."

"Thank you."

She tries to ignore the pang of guilt. Meeting his surrogate parents under a cloud of deception feels dirty but it's the end result that counts. Alec opens the car door and heads up the path. She follows with Ed, stepping back a discreet distance as he presses the doorbell. She hears footsteps then a woman stands before them, partially silhouetted by the hall light. She's quite petite, in her fifties, Kitty guesses. A radiant smile lights her face as she sees Alec.

"Hello Molly."

"Alec, darling, how are you? I'm so happy you thought to come."

"These are my friends from Cambridge. Kitty and Ed."

"Come in, come in." She takes Kitty's hand in hers; surprisingly soft and warm. In the light Kitty's struck by her piercingly blue eyes, like a cloudless day; the crow's feet around them suggesting laughter and a hint of mischief. She guides them out of the narrow hallway into the front room where a bottle green sofa and two matching armchairs huddle around a warming fire.

"I made your favourite apple pie for tea. I couldn't help myself and made three which Jim and I can't possibly eat so you'll have to take them with you. Sit down, sit down. I don't know where he's got to. He had some marking to do. I'll go and find him and put the kettle on. It's so lovely to see you."

"You too, Molly."

Kitty returns Alec's smile as their hostess leaves the room. Without specific intention she has sat next to him on the sofa while Ed chooses to perch on the edge of the armchair by the window. She wonders why he looks so strained; this is the easy bit, something to eat and drink, innocent chatter with a charming couple. But perhaps Ed isn't really the family kind. Nothing she's observed in his psyche suggests a desire for intimacy.

A heavy and slow tread on the stairs precedes a man entering the room, a beaming smile furrowing his cheeks. Alec leaps to greet him, arm thrust out to shake his hand. "Dear boy, how marvellous to see you." A bear-sized pat on Alec's back. "And your friends. Welcome. Welcome."

"This is Kitty, she's a German teacher in a village outside Cambridge."

Kitty feels the big man's gaze fall upon her. It's hard not to stare at the strawberry mark which covers his left cheek. She also observes a small tattoo at his wrist. A hangover from war service perhaps.

"Jim Atherton. Delighted to meet you."

"Thank you. It's really kind of you to invite us."

He smiles. "Ah, so you're one of our American friends?"

"Yes and no. I'm German by birth. We moved to the States before the war."

"Difficult times for you, I'm sure. But you're very welcome here."

Alec throws his hand towards Ed. "And this is Ed. My room-mate."

Ed steps forward. "Mr Atherton, very pleased to meet you."

"Please, everyone calls me Jim." He chuckles. "You're surviving alright living with Alec?"

"He's a terrific room-mate."

"Good. Good. He never caused us much trouble. So long as he was fed. Please. Sit down." He settles into the free armchair. For a moment the conversation falters which prior to her training Kitty would have felt bound to fill, but now she uses it for observation. A waiting game. She casts another glance at Ed who is staring at an ornament hanging above the mantelpiece. A flying duck. She wonders why he finds it so fascinating; his usual ebullient manner seeming to have faltered. Despite all his Marxist credentials she imagines it's hard for an Englishman to throw the yoke of class snobbery.

"How was Imber?" Jim Atherton reaches forward to stoke the coal embers in the fire. More than necessary, she thinks.

"We got stopped by a convoy as we were leaving but I managed to steer us out of it. Or rather Ed did."

Atherton laughs again. "Well done."

"Thank you."

"I think the villagers will be a thorn in their side for some time yet. You're not going to give up without a fight, are you Alec? It's an injustice that still needs resolving. Never give up hope, no matter how hard the fight."

His flow is interrupted by the arrival of a tea trolley, pushed by Molly into the centre of the room. "You're not boring them with your sermonising are you, Jim? He does go on sometimes."

Kitty can't help but laugh. The domestic trivia of life has escaped her since she left the States. She finds it quite touching.

Molly directs her summer gaze towards her. "Will you take a slice of apple pie, dear? Though I'm sure it's not as good as your American ones. They're famous, aren't they?"

Kitty smiles again, charmed. "Yours looks a picture." Meeting Molly had not been on the agenda. Alec had not mentioned her. And seeing this kind, generous woman standing before her, she laments the absence of her own mother. She can't help marvel at the way Molly steers the line of conversation so effortlessly. Where it falters she finds another track, when Jim veers to riskier terrain she guides them back to unchallenging meadows. It's an art which she remembers so well. Like empathy, small talk had not featured in her training. Perhaps it should have. Getting what you want need not always be heavy-handed. Perhaps espionage training needs someone like Molly.

After several slices of apple pie have been devoured and the embers turn to ashes in the grate, Alec announces that they should leave. She feels almost sorry to go.

Back in the car they wait patiently while Ed fumbles in his pockets. "Bugger. I must've left the keys on the table." Before Alec can respond he leaps out and disappears up the path. She settles quietly on the back seat, waiting to see if Alec will say anything. He doesn't. But she needs to press him, reasoning the dark intimacy of the car's interior will help.

She begins quietly. "Molly's lovely. Thank you for bringing me."

He doesn't turn around. "You didn't answer my question."

"Which one?"

"Don't play games, Kitty. You know which one."

His directness surprises her. "I rather thought I had."

"You said Imber comes first." He turns around to face her.

"But before that I said I'd love too."

"I wasn't sure if you were just playing."

"I don't play, Alec. I never play at anything."

"When can we spend some time together?" There's no suggestion of warmth, no hint of a smile or glint in his eye. It feels like a formal request, a contract to be honoured.

"When have you got in mind?"

"Next weekend. We could take the train to King's Lynn. It's a lovely seaside town."

She smiles "That sounds nice." She turns to look out of the window. "How long do you think Ed needs to find a set of keys?

"He's probably got caught talking to Molly. Why?"

"If I knew I had time, I'd kiss you."

His eyes flick to the window. Ed's heading towards them. "Shit."

"Too bad indeed. I guess we'll just have to wait till next weekend."

The driver's door swings open and Ed clambers back inside.

"Sorry about that. Help yourself to some more apple pie." He throws the wrapped pie onto the back seat.

She watches Alec redirect his attention to his room-mate, impressively composed. "Was Molly holding you up?"

"And your friend, Jim." The engine emits a throaty roar as Ed pulls away from the kerb. "I could hardly get away. Nice chap."

She settles back again, watching the streetlights pass, and thinking that Ed and Jim Atherton couldn't possibly have much in common to talk about. Perhaps Ed was just trying to please Alec. Strengthen their bond. At any rate, her task is achieved. She'll let Ed know in due course about the plan to go to King's Lynn. Professionally he should be as delighted as she is. She wonders whether there'll be a cosy pub on the seafront where the two of them can eat fish and chips. Then tries to dismiss the thought again.

Cold Road to Imber

13

OCTOBER 1953, WEST/EAST GERMAN BORDER

The train shudders to a halt at the platform of Schwanheide border station. It is late afternoon. Soldiers in grey uniform board the carriage and demand that passengers prepare their passports for inspection. A German Shepherd dog barks at the window. Kitty fumbles in her handbag, her heart beating a little faster. The gracelessness of these soldiers makes her uncomfortable. The border is new; between West Germany and the newly-founded German Democratic Republic, or East Germany as the West calls it, within which West Berlin is now an island, a symbol of Western defiance. She knows little about the GDR except what's she's heard through negative Western propaganda; a Communist enclave now sharing its soul with the mighty Russian bear. Her own feelings are ambivalent. She still considers East Berlin her true home; growing up there until Kristallnacht forced them to flee. And she knows there will be painful reminders of her aunt's family who stayed put, believing Hitler would be assassinated, and who were never heard from again. But she's determined their fate will not dictate her attitude to the future. The GDR is at an embryonic stage and with it comes hope and opportunity. This is her manifest belief as the guard scrutinises her American passport, returning it without a word.

She looks out of the window to the platform. The three border guards have stepped down from the train, the German Shepherd dog straining on its leash. As the train steams away towards Berlin she can't help feeling a sense of relief mixed with expectation. Watching the countryside slip by in the autumn light, she wonders what she'll see. Some sign of Soviet presence? Portraits of Stalin nailed to trees, Hammer and Sickle flags? But there's nothing more than remote farmhouses, rusty tractors abandoned in fields; hardly an indication of Communist revolution. She closes her eyes. It'll be another couple of hours before they reach Berlin. It's already been four days since she waved farewell to her parents at the quayside in New York, aware her father would never return to Germany to visit her. But he had understood and respected her decision. She had tried to resist tears as the ship drifted away from the dock. An old lady on the deck beside her had donated a lace handkerchief from her handbag. Frau Hummel was her name; a widowed Jew who regaled her with stories on the crossing. She never spoke of the war, only of skating on the Rhine with her brother in winter and stealing grapes from the vines in late summer. When they'd disembarked from the ship at Hamburg she'd embraced Kitty and wished her well. "Make the most of your life," were her final words before disappearing into the throng of porters and baggage. Kitty had taken a taxi straight to the main station. She had no desire to see the city, knowing how badly it had been bombed by the British. There'd be enough destruction to cope with in Berlin, why walk on more graves than she needed to? It almost felt disrespectful. Voyeuristic.

She's woken by the screech of iron. The train has come to a standstill but there's no sign of a station. Just a rudimentary, wooden platform. It's already dark. Several guards strut about in pools of amber light thrown by tall lamps. She realises they must have arrived at another border, from the Socialist GDR into Capitalist West Berlin. She checks her watch. Seven thirty. She should make Ursula's by eight fifteen. In time for food she hopes. She's desperately hungry, hoping her friend might have cooked something special as a welcome. Though she's no idea whether Ursula's a decent cook. It occurs to her how little she knows of her once, best friend. In her regular correspondence over the years, she'd told Ursula all about her life, even the break-up with Robert, but the replies had always been paltry, lacking in much detail.

Swapping trains in West Berlin at Spandau she takes the overground S Bahn, her excitement mounting as the train travels east towards her childhood haunts. The carriages snake across the city, roughly following the path of the Spree River, but despite pressing her face to the window, she has little real sense of the city. Rivulets of water glide across the panes of glass, lit by the glow of carriage lights. A glimmer of dancing reflections suggests they're crossing the river again. Moments later the train pulls into a grand, nineteenth century station. Friedrichstrasse. Having studied maps of the newly-divided sectors of the city she realises they must have crossed into East Berlin but nothing on the station platform indicates the transition. It surprises her. She'd heard it was difficult to cross between East and West but perhaps that was only rumours. She counts away the stations to Alexanderplatz where she alights, climbing down the stairs from the concourse to the lobby. It's raining hard. Other passengers skittle away into the darkness but she hesitates inside the shelter of the building, removing a folded piece of paper from her purse. On it are scribbled Ursula's address and the directions. It's almost too dark to make sense of them.

"Katja? Kann es wirklich du sein?"

She lifts her head to find the source of the voice. A woman stands in a shadowed corner. She steps forward into the dim light so that Kitty can study her more easily. Her hair is tucked under a black, woollen beret and an over-sized raincoat hides any sense of shape.

"Ursula?"

The woman slips the beret from her head and holds it before her. The gesture seems respectful, almost submissive. Her hair falls flatly to her cheeks which are pale and puffy. She looks exhausted. But the eyes, still as green as Baltic seawater, are definitely Ursula's.

Kitty's unsure whether to hug her or remain absurdly polite. "Mein Gott, Ursula. Ich hab' gedacht…"

German comes to her surprisingly easily. As if she'd never left.

Her friend takes another step forward, plainly encouraged that they can converse in her native tongue. "…I walk past the station on my way home from work. I thought I might wait a while, just in case."

Kitty feels the tears well up. It surprises her. Even when Robert wrote his cowardly letter she hadn't cried. Then tears turn to laughter. "Oh God, you were always so loyal, I've missed you so much." She can't contain herself any longer, running into the arms of her friend, wrapped in the ridiculously over-sized raincoat.

Ursula folds her arm around her waist. "Come. We'll get a tram. It's too wet to walk."

"Why don't we get a cab? I'll pay."

Her friend smiles. "You've spent too long in America, darling. Here everyone takes trams." She grabs Kitty's over-large suitcase. "It's not far, just across the square."

Walking out into the city she feels torn between the draw of Ursula and a lust to absorb the scene around her. She has fragmented memories; snapshots rather than geographical knowledge, but on first glances East Berlin seems quieter than she remembered. There are people on the street but not many, walkers rather than idlers. A few, sputtering cars speed around the square. Nobody's window shopping, no lovers drifting through the streets. Presumably it's the rain.

They don't have long to wait. Their tram glides to a halt in the centre of the windswept square and Ursula pushes her aboard. She's glad to be out of the cold. Sitting on the bench, she feels the warmth of Ursula's body radiate to hers but the conversation suddenly falters, and she forms the impression that her friend is uncomfortable to maintain a flow of words while others around them remain silent. But ten minutes later, when they alight, the veil lifts.

"Not far now, my darling. You must be exhausted."

She smiles at her friend's obvious concern. "Exhausted but happy."

"I'm afraid it's not much. If you want to stay in Berlin longer we'll have to sort something else out."

She'd made it plain in her letters that she wanted to return to Berlin for good, but she can understand if Ursula doesn't want her to stay. They've been a long time apart. She follows her up the deserted street. On either side, the familiar five storey tenement buildings remind her of her family's old apartment. Except all the buildings are pocked and scarred and where once they stood in neat rows, many are now reduced to rubble, cascades of bricks fallen in ragged piles. It's what she'd prepared for; she'd seen enough damage in the newsreels at the cinema, but it's still shocking.

"You can see there's much to do. The last weeks of fighting were particularly brutal on the city and there's not much money for repairs. America's happy to pour funds into West Germany but not here. And because the Soviets suffered such terrible losses trying to save us from Hitler's Fascist thugs we owe them the debt. So East Germany remains very poor." She stops outside one of the tenement blocks; a plague of craters scarring its façade. Ursula smiles. "I think there's more holes than concrete. But at least it stays cool in summer."

She leads Kitty up three flights of stairs. The interior is equally damaged, blocks of plaster dangling from walls, long cracks in the brickwork; wounds hiding in the darkness. A long corridor guides them towards Ursula's apartment. She flicks the switch, the bare light bulb revealing a single, narrow room; much smaller than anything Kitty had imagined. A window at the far end looks towards the lighted windows of a block opposite. Below the window there's a sink, a draining board and a small cooker. A divan lines the longer wall, rugs draped across it like something from an artist's studio. Kitty guesses it doubles as a bed.

"Let me take your coat."

"Thank you." She unfastens her belt, feeling oddly self-conscious, and watches Ursula hang the coat on the back of the door.

"Sit. I'll make some tea."

There's nowhere to sit but the divan so she settles herself and smiles at her friend, desperate to hide the shock at the lack of space, and realising just how American she'd become. Ursula places a kettle on the stove and lifts a hinged flap from the wall to form a small table. A single chair stands beside it. Kitty searches for something appropriate to say. "It's very cosy."

"It'll be better when you have some hot tea inside you. The bombing shook the building so much the windows no longer fit. Here, you can see the gap. Like I said, great in summer but when winter comes…"

She places a porcelain tea warmer on the table, lighting the small candle inside it. Once the kettle's boiled she pours the water into a pot and sits it on the warmer.

"Ursula, darling, I can stay in a hotel nearby. I'm sure there's somewhere. I hadn't realised you had such - limited space, you should have said."

Her friend hands her a cup of black tea. "No, you must stay with me, I insist. We can take turns with the divan, I've got blankets for the floor. And another body makes it warmer. Now move up, we have lots to catch up on."

The display of warmth relaxes her. She slides along the divan, just about making room for the two of them. "I can't quite believe I'm here. It's been so long."

"Too long. Tell me about America."

"Hard to know where to start. Young lawyers are spineless, well one in particular, and the judges are bastards." She makes Ursula laugh. "Anyway, it isn't the dream everyone makes out. I can't forgive them for what they did to my father."

"Why doesn't he come home too?"

"Too many horrible memories, I guess. What happened to his sister's family. He says at least in America he's not haunted by the past. It's his choice."

"It's a different country now, Katya. In the German Democratic Republic everybody's looked after and treated equally. We even have women driving the trams, I bet you don't see that in America!"

She smiles. "Mostly they're supposed to stay at home and make cherry pie for their husbands to grow fat on." Again she makes her friend laugh. "Do you have a job?"

"Of course. I work at a printing factory. We make big banners for events. We're always busy. The government likes lots of them around the city to remind everybody of our mission. But we do smaller things too. Official documents, birth and death certificates, marriages. These fingers tell the story best." She holds out her hands to show the deep imprint of dark ink around her fingertips.

Kitty laughs. "I remember when my bicycle chain used to come off you always put it back on for me. You were only six but already so practical. And always with smudges of oil on your face and hands."

"I wanted to be the greatest engineer of the twentieth century. Somewhere I still have the plans I made for an aeroplane that flaps its wings like a bird." Her smile evaporates. "But that was the time of dreams."

Kitty sips from the tea, sensing a moment to move their conversation to more delicate subjects. "You never mentioned your parents in your letters. I wondered."

"They were killed in one of the first British raids on Berlin. My sister too. It was a stray bomb, dumped, probably because they missed the target zone. The wardens said mother must have tripped rushing down the lobby stairs, after the air raid siren. They think Sonja and father ran back to help. You never know exactly. I was staying with a friend. A sleepover birthday party."

"I'm so sorry, darling."

"It's the past. Now you're here. And that is its own miracle. I want to hear all about your plans. Maybe I can help you in some way."

"Nothing too formulated yet. Get a job if I can. I thought maybe I could work as a teacher, teaching English. I've got all my certificates but I don't know if they'd be accepted here."

"More tea first." Ursula takes the cup from her hands and returns to the table to pour the tea. "You must understand it's difficult here at the moment. It'll take time for the country to settle. You might have heard there was an uprising in summer, a lot of people were angry because the Party demanded a ten percent increase in output without increasing people's wages, to help the economic situation. They've rescinded that now but there are still frustrations. I have some sympathy for the Party. It's hard to create economic security and greater equality when the country's so poor. A lot of people are fleeing to the West with the impression life will be better and they will be taken care of. I tell them only the rich will be taken care of, the poor will be left to fight for themselves. What sort of society is that?"

She sits down again. "I'm sorry Katja, I've told you our problems rather than saying how I could help you."

"Don't worry. It's better to know. It must be hard."

"Everyone has to play their part. I'm not sure whether you'll get work as a teacher but I know someone you can ask. In the current situation you'll probably have to accept any work you can get. Do you have all your identification papers?"

"I brought my birth certificate, my American passport and my old German one, even though it's out of date."

"Good. The woman I'm thinking of knows official procedure better than me. She runs a primary school just up the road. You can go and see her in the morning." She smiles. "Now let's eat, you must be starving."

Kitty had forgotten her fantasies of supper but a sudden pang of hunger grips at the mention of food. She watches as Ursula heats a saucepan on the stove before ladling out two bowls of a thin, green soup, peppered with slices of sausage. She places them on a tray, adding two slabs of dark rye bread, and returns to the divan. Kitty sits the bowl on her knees and eats quickly, mopping the last dregs of soup with some bread. When she finishes the exhaustion of her journey suddenly overwhelms her, and as if sensing her plight, Ursula begins to sort the sleeping arrangements, insisting Kitty takes the divan while she sleeps on the floor. She must leave early for her shift so it's better that way. Kitty finds no strength to object. Before they settle Ursula leads her to the shared bathroom and toilet out in the main corridor. Kitty goes first, changing into her nightie; glad she thought to pack a dressing gown. Brushing her teeth she ignores the mirror above the cracked tiles. Tomorrow she'll be happier to look at herself. Fifteen minutes later Ursula has switched out the light.

When Kitty wakes she finds that Ursula has already gone. She pulls back the thin duvet and stumbles to the window. There's a sombre sky, still full of rain. The tenement block opposite is so close she imagines she could almost touch it. Shadows move past the windows. A woman stares at her from a floor above. She turns away. A scrap of paper has been left on the drainer; the handwriting scribbled, like a doctor's.

Make yourself coffee and eat whatever you can find. I'll be back at lunchtime with some shopping. Frau Lehman runs the school at the top of our street. Take your documents and explain that I sent you. After you see her come straight back here. You can sort official things tomorrow but I think it's safer to stay here in the meantime.

A house key sits beside the note. She wonders why Ursula is being so cautious. As far as she knows there are no restrictions on Westerners travelling to East Berlin. So why shouldn't she be safe? After a cup of strong, bitter, coffee she sets out along the street to look for the school. The clouds have surrendered to a forensic sunlight, casting the scale of devastation into sharp relief but this morning it doesn't dint her optimism. Her return is more emotional than she'd imagined. As if the city smells of her childhood. Like home. Perhaps she should be grateful to Robert for his timely rejection; without it she might never have found her purpose. In the fragility of East Berlin she's convinced she will.

The school stands on a corner, two blocks up the street. Like every other building it bears the scars of war, traces of machine gun fire splattered along the concrete walls, windows distorted within their frames, as if hit by an earthquake. She thinks of the primary school she taught at in Philadelphia; a modern, airy building surrounded by grass lawns and a large playground. It's hard not to be shocked by the level of poverty.

Knocking on splintered, double doors she finds herself opposite a woman about ten years her senior. Her face is impossible to read; blank and ungiving.

Kitty smiles despite it. "I'm sorry to trouble you madam, I was hoping to speak to Frau Lehman. If she's not too busy."

"And you are?"

"Katja Bernstein. My friend, Ursula, suggested I come." She remembers American informality is inappropriate here. "I mean Fräulein Meyer. She lives up the road. I'm a teacher. I'd be extremely grateful."

The woman seems to consider her story before opening the door wider. "Sit down in here please. I will consult Frau Lehman."

"That's very kind." She watches the woman approach a door across the dingy, empty lobby, knocking before entering. Her hand searches in her bag again for her documents, though she knows she put them in there. The woman takes her time. Kitty listens for the children but there's no sense of them. Either they're incredibly well behaved or they're out doing sports somewhere. But she's seen no field to play in. Just bomb sites.

Eventually the woman returns. "Frau Lehman will see you. You have ten minutes." She leads Kitty back to the door, knocking and waiting again for a reply before entering. "Frau Lehman, may I introduce Fräulein Bernstein?"

Entering the office, Kitty's first impression is of sparseness. Nothing greets the eye except the absolute necessities; a desk, two chairs and a filing cabinet. The only concession to the wall is a paper calendar and a framed photograph of a baldish man with a goatee beard. She assumes it's Walther Ubricht, the First Secretary of the Central Committee. A thin woman in a cheap, ill-fitting flannel suit stands up to greet her, arm thrust out. Her face is deeply lined but the neat bone structure gives her the glamour of an ageing film star.

"Fräulein Bernstein. Welcome. Please sit down. How may I help you?"

Kitty settles in the chair indicated on the opposite side of the bureau desk. Woodworm riddles its stout legs. She attempts to smile.

"You're very kind to see me, Frau Lehman. I won't keep you. Where to start? I've just returned to the GDR from America. I was born here but my family fled before the war. My father was Jewish. I'm an English teacher by profession and my great friend, Fräulein Meyer, suggested I get in touch with you. To see if you could help me in any way. She said you'd be better at official processes than her."

"I see. Fräulein Meyer is a very good comrade. We have worked together in certain capacities to guide our young people. I assume you have documents to prove your identity?

"Yes, of course." She removes the two passports from her bag and hands them across the table. "The German one's expired but I thought I'd bring it anyway."

Frau Lehman reaches for a pair of glasses that hang on a thin, gold chain around her neck, studying the documents in more detail than Kitty imagines necessary. Eventually she lifts her face. "Tell me Fräulein Bernstein, why would a beautiful American lady want to live here, amongst all the rubble and carnage that has been our suffering? If it's to make amends then I suggest you ask President Eisenhower to write us a cheque. Then I can build a proper school with running water and a playground."

The note of bitterness, almost accusation, takes her by surprise. "I understand your circumstances must be extremely difficult. But America, like all the Allies, was fighting for a just cause. I realise Berlin was a terrible casualty of the war but wasn't the damage in this sector of the city caused mainly by the Russian offensive?"

"Do you have any idea how many people Russia lost trying to defeat Hitler? Over fifteen million. And do you suppose as a result they have many resources to help us? It was the Americans who stole our scientists and technicians. They bled us for our intellectual wealth and left us to suffer. I'm sorry, Fräulein, but it's hard to feel much empathy for them."

"Where I lived, it was seen a bit differently."

"Of that I have no doubt. But tell me, you haven't answered my question. Why are you here?"

"I suppose I'd have to say disillusion. My father was put on trial by McCarthy for his Socialist beliefs. He lost his job as a professor. It made me realise America wasn't what I'd hoped it would be. And I was homesick. I wanted to come back to where I belong."

"I'm sorry for your father. And I confess I find your thinking admirable. But in my experience people are rarely motivated by elevated principles alone. Something more personal usually lights the fuse first."

"More personal than your own father branded an outcast?" She finds herself shifting uncomfortably under this woman's intense gaze.

"It's his story. You don't strike me as a natural political agitator."

She wonders if Ursula could possibly have already told this woman about Robert. They hadn't talked about him over supper but she'd mentioned the break-up in a letter. Though surely Ursula wouldn't confide this to a total stranger? Still, keeping it secret now seems futile. The revelation might even help her, sordid as it feels. She sighs, barely able to look Frau Lehman in the eye. "The piece you're so clearly missing is that my fiancé dumped me when he found out about my father. He couldn't possibly marry a woman whose father had been branded a Communist traitor. At the time it seemed the worst thing ever. Now, if you can help me, I think it might be the best thing."

Frau Lehman returns her eye to the documents in her hand. "I commend your honesty. There will necessarily be certain procedures but I'll see what I can do. You are staying with Fräulein Meyer?"

"Yes. For now."

"Please remain there. Someone will contact you. Now if you'll excuse me I'm very busy."

"Yes, of course. Thank you." Kitty raises herself from the chair, wondering whether she should shake hands again. But Frau Lehman fails to lift her head. "Thank you for your help."

She turns towards the door, feeling heavy-hearted, the euphoria spun out of her.

"Fräulein Bernstein?"

Kitty turns around. The creases at the edge of Frau Lehman's mouth have lifted. There's almost the hint of a smile. And to Kitty's surprise she suddenly addresses her in English. "The pursuit of love is always fraught with danger. But as an English teacher I imagine you've read enough Shakespeare to know that."

"Auf wiedersehen, Frau Lehman."

Returning to Ursula's apartment she wonders whether she should buy some provisions, something at least to express her gratitude. But she sees no evidence of a corner shop and straying off her course would be contrary to her friend's advice. The few pedestrians she encounters avoid her gaze. It's eerily quiet apart from the occasional two-stroke rattle of a passing car, trails of oily fumes hovering in its wake. The poverty of which Ursula spoke is papable, not only in the dilapidated state of the buildings, but also in the demeanour of the residents. Those she sees have a waxy, pale complexion; a tale of exhaustion not helped by ill-fitting clothes.

Closing the door of the apartment behind her she collapses on to the divan and begins to weep, a wave of panic and misgiving so acute she's compelled to rush to the sink and retch. Scooping mouthfuls of water from the tap she remonstrates with herself. It's her family she misses, not their Philadelphian suburb. Here she's surrounded by the pitiful consequences of war, its painful reality, but to witness it first-hand is an honour; a privilege she must not shy away from. Hopefully she can do her bit, even if Frau Lehman had seemed a little overly officious. She wipes away the last evidence of tear stains at the sound of approaching footsteps in the corridor, standing with her back to the sink to greet her friend's return from work. Ursula smiles wearily, black rings circling her eyes which appear to repeat themselves in dark patches of ink on her overalls. In her hand she holds a string bag which she brings to the kitchen drainer.

"Thank God. I thought you might've gone."

Kitty make space for her as best she can, finding the greeting oddly terse. "Why would I go? I've only just arrived."

"I just felt as I walked along the corridor -" From the bag she produces a lump of cheese and another small loaf of dark bread. " - I don't know, I'd got used to the idea that I'd never see you again."

"Ursula, darling, I can go if it's difficult. If you want me too."

"No, no. I mean, it is, in so many ways. We don't live in the same world anymore. The place you thought is home has gone - I'm sorry, Katja, I'm tired. Let's have some lunch then I must sleep. I have an evening shift."

Kitty attempts to help her friend prepare their lunch but the confines of the narrow room make it impossible. She retreats to the divan at her friend's instruction, grateful to be presented with the plate of bread and cheese and a tin of some sort of meat paste. It smells vaguely of liver, though the taste is less definable. But spread thickly on the bread it cures her hunger. Conversation is sporadic; clearly Ursula is desperate to rest her head. Her friend eats at the pace of a starving dog and Kitty struggles to keep up, not wanting to deny Ursula sleep any longer than necessary. But a sharp rap on the door interrupts her best intentions. Ursula appears unsurprised. Perhaps she's expecting a friend. She shifts around Kitty's legs to reach the door, opening it just enough to permit Kitty a view of two men waiting outside. The thicker set one produces some sort of ID.

To Kitty he looks like a sleazy, private detective, the sort you use to hasten a divorce; grubby, faux leather jacket tied about the waist, badly tailored slacks, scuffed shoes. His younger friend is thinner, creased shirt too loose round his neck, tie slipped from its moorings. In a brief, low-key exchange Kitty hears her own name spoken and almost immediately Ursula steps aside to let them through.

The older one addresses her, his words crackling in his throat. Plainly a man with a serious smoking habit. He addresses her in German. "Fräulein Bernstein, you're to accompany us, please. Bring your passport. You don't need anything else."

"Excuse me?" She glances at Ursula for reassurance or explanation. But her friend says nothing.

"Please hurry. Our car is downstairs."

"But where to? Who are you?"

Ursula breaks her silence. "Don't be alarmed, Katja. It's routine. They...the police just have to make enquiries. Like I said, these are difficult times, we can't be too careful."

"But who do they think I am? I'm not a spy for God's sake. I'm German."

The leather jacketed one takes her arm. "Where do you keep your passport?"

She shakes off his arm. "Hey. I can manage."

"Bring it please."

Realising she has no choice, she collects her coat and handbag from the back of the door, throwing a pleading glance to her friend, hoping against hope that she might save her yet.

"I'm sorry, Katja, darling. If you do as they ask it'll be best for you."

Stepping out into the corridor, she hears the door drawn closed behind her. The older one retrieves her arm but this time she doesn't resist, attempting to calm her breath as they descend the concrete staircase. A brief sting of cold rain slaps her face before she's shoved unceremoniously into the back of an oil-fumed car, the seat littered with empty cigarette packets and discarded apple cores.

She sweeps them away with her hand. "Perhaps you could at least tell me where we're going?"

The younger one speaks for the first time, turning to look over his shoulder from the passenger seat. "Headquarters, Fräulein."

"Headquarters of what?"

He doesn't answer, turning instead to his accomplice. "She looks like an American movie star."

"Forget it, she won't open her legs for your skinny pay cheque."

Kitty ignores their laughter, turning her attention to their route, frantically attempting to gain her bearings. The roads are unfamiliar but she realises from the shadows cast on the buildings that they're heading east, away from the border. She reaches for the soft lining of her pockets, determined to show no fear. The car turns fast onto a wide boulevard. A gleaming, modernist cube structure rises incongruously from a bomb site between the crumbling classical facades. But there are still acres of mud. Of emptiness. A moment later they drive around another vast square and head south. She catches a glimpse of two soldiers, grey coats with red epaulettes, parading in front of a building, rifles pressed to their shoulders. The leather-jacketed driver switches direction again. She wonders if he's deliberately trying to confuse her. Passing under a railway bridge the car finds narrower lanes until they bear right onto a quiet road which runs the length of the river. West again, she thinks. He slows down. The buildings facing the river are unremarkable, nothing about their municipal exterior would suggest a specific function. She's surprised to see a tank parked in one of the shadowed streets between them. A young soldier stands at the opened hatch. His uniform suggests an officer; a dark green jacket and a scarlet sash wrapped around his peaked cap. She can't help thinking how handsome he looks, which is a ridiculous thought to have, but somehow it makes her less scared.

Her assailant brings the car to a halt in a small car park outside one of the bland, two storey buildings. His colleague leaps out and opens the door for Kitty. "Follow me, please, Fräulein."

She holds her head high, mirroring the deportment she was taught at school. She will not be intimidated. Flanked by her officials, they climb two steps into a vestibule. Footsteps echo on the stairs above them. Two swing doors, left and right, lead to corridors. It reminds her of a local hospital. They take the left one, passing a row of identical windows facing the car park. Sitting at the far end, a clerk shuffles paper at a narrow desk and stamps a document with a seal. She's instructed by the younger one to sit on one of the metal chairs beside the desk. He plainly enjoys his role. His colleague gives the clerk her name and her residing address then turns to leave without a glance to his captive.

She will not let him off so lightly. She calls out, "Wiedersehen und vielen Dank, meinen Herren," grinning at him when he turns around and waving her hand delicately in the air. She despises him.

Minutes pass but the clerk ignores her. If only to make conversation she asks him if he minds if she smokes. And it will give her something to do.

"Yes, of course." His tone is flat. Unengaged. But as she draws the cigarette from its case he steps from his desk and produces a lighter, bowing down with almost elaborate courtesy.

"Thank you." She blows a trail of smoke along the corridor, watching as he proceeds to find an ashtray in the top drawer which he places on the window ledge beside her. A phone buzzes on his desk as he returns to his chair. He reaches, listening rather than speaking, his eyes never leaving Kitty.

"This way please, Fräulein."

She holds the cigarette aloft, wanting to make an impression. She thinks instinctively it will serve her well. He escorts her to the door, the last in the corridor. With the same formality he steps aside to let her enter. Immediately she sees her cigarette is of no significance. The room is already dense with smoke.

A man stands in silhouette by the window. "Fräulein Bernstein, thank you for coming." He holds out his hand and she takes it with a degree of reluctance.

"I didn't have much choice."

He smiles. "They are only precautions. I'm sorry if you were alarmed. Please take a seat."

She settles in the chair opposite his desk, glancing about the room. There's a large map of Berlin on the wall, some sort of metal trophy on the filing cabinet, a couple of photos on his desk but angled away so she can't see them.

"You are of course wondering who I am and why you're here."

She wants to say as little as possible. To listen first. He appears more educated than his colleagues, and sharper. Silver-grey hair clipped neatly to his skull; a long, sculptured face under hooded grey eyes.

"Allow me to introduce myself. My name is Herr Ehrmann. I run the language department of our national college of education. Your name was given to me by Frau Lehman."

She feels a moment of relief but still requires more explanation.

"You went to her looking for a job as an English teacher. That's correct?"

"My friend suggested it. Do you think you might have work for me?"

He leans back in his chair. "I must say, Fräulein Bernstein, your German is excellent. The tiniest hint of American vowels but nothing that can't be addressed. May I see your American passport, please?"

She reaches in her handbag, handing it across the table.

"If you don't mind we'll keep it to note down some details."

"Is that strictly necessary?"

"If you wish to obtain a work permit I'm afraid it will be. You'll get it back in due course I assure you."

"So, forgive me Herr Ehrmann, are you saying you have teaching work for me?"

"Perhaps. We need to establish your credentials first."

"I can list you all my teaching qualifications, if you want I can have all the certificates posted over."

"Fräulein Bernstein, I'm sure you're a very good teacher. You are clearly intelligent and as I say your German is excellent. But there are other considerations. I appreciate you were born here but you've been in America a long time. Your values might not be the same as ours."

"I enjoy teaching, Herr Ehrmann. In that respect I believe our values will be compatible. I foster excellent relations with my pupils and I try to help them if they falter. They trust me."

"Your father's a philosophy tutor?"

"How do you know that?"

"And he was brought before the McCarthy senate committee for un-American activities?"

"It was a witch hunt, nothing more. How do you know this?"

"A witch hunt?"

"Reds under the bed, a paranoid fear of Communist spies in high places."

"Were you sympathetic?"

"To my father? Of course."

"But he's a Communist."

"A socialist. As you may be aware that doesn't exactly make you the belle of the ball in the States."

He smiles briefly. "You see Miss Bernstein, we have to be very careful. We know the Americans and their Western partners despise our progressive ideas. They feel threatened by us because we are implementing a system that takes power out of the hands of the few and gives it to the many. We believe in equality and respect, not in wealth and extortion. A factory worker is as important as a politician. One man may be brighter than another but he doesn't use his brain to fatten his wallet and his own belly, he uses it to make enough food for everyone so that when he sits at the table with them his heart is warm. And they are all well fed."

"You make this man sound like Jesus Christ. And that didn't end well."

"Exactly. Worshipping false gods and living in fear of their wrath has caused nothing but destruction. This is the twentieth century. Mankind must be reliant on his own virtues for salvation. We must learn from our mistakes. We must be scouts for peace."

She finds his delivery portentous but really her father had said much the same thing. An ordinary man hounded by the Fascists for being a Jew. A Jew who wasn't very Jewish at all.

Ehrmann fixes his grey eyes on hers. "I would like to know why you left America."

The answer that Frau Lehman forced out of her, about Robert, seems pathetic now. She straightens a little; aware that she is on trial, seeking redemption for her father; a second chance. "My father's a bright man, and very wise. But above all else he is a kind man who would never choose to hurt anyone. He was done a terrible injustice and I can't live somewhere where politicians boast of the land of the free while condemning innocent people to oblivion."

"Fine words. But your father and mother chose not to come with you. Which makes me wonder whether your actions were truly noble or just a petulant display of defiance. Like a jilted lover."

She taps her cigarette into the ashtray that he pushes across the desk. It helps quell her anger and shock. Or perhaps he's just guessing about Robert. "My parents decided they were too old to start a new life again. But they were fully behind me coming here. So I'd like to ask again, if I may, what do I have to do to teach here?"

She holds his eyes, waiting as he relaxes back to his chair, studying her as if she were his muse. Which she won't countenance.

"I think we may have work for you, Fräulein Bernstein, but you will have to be patient while we consider your application. In the meantime I would like you to return to your friend's apartment and remain there until we have verified your documents. You may leave to go to the local shops, but no further, and on no account must you cross to the Western sector."

"You make it sound horribly like I'm a prisoner."

"Like I said, in these uncertain times we have to be careful. You'll be escorted back to your apartment." He stands to shake her hand. "I bid you good day, Fraulein, perhaps we shall see each other again."

Reluctantly she takes his cold hand and turns to the door. "Auf Wiedersehen."

In the corridor she's surprised to find her old accomplices waiting for her. Their evident indifference encourages a moment of sarcastic relish. "We meet again, boys. How delightful."

On the journey back she doesn't bother to engage with them, watching the ravaged city pass by, attempting to straighten her thoughts. She wonders what Ursula might have said; what betrayal of confidences. Turning the key in the door of her friend's apartment she rehearses her lines. She doesn't want to be confrontational, their relationship is fragile, and Ursula has been kind to her. Her friend is sitting at the fold-down table, scooping a thin soup from her spoon. She's wearing the same dark overalls, presumably ready for night shift.

"Katja, I'm so glad. I was getting worried."

Kitty hangs her coat onto the back of the door; despite everything she's glad to be back in this temporary home.

"What happened? Did they give you a job?"

"Maybe. I don't know yet. They just wanted some details." She doesn't elaborate, not sure yet how she should respond to Ursula's enquiry. But she's aware that her reticence has been noted.

Ursula prods a dumpling with her fork and thrusts it into her mouth. It's the first time Kitty's noticed her rather crude eating habits. "The bureaucracy takes time. You must be patient. Everybody needs good teachers."

She flops onto the divan, deciding to eat after Ursula has gone, despite the pangs of hunger. "They want me to stay with you until they decide. I'm only allowed to go to the local shops. He didn't call it a house arrest but I'm not exactly a welcome guest."

"Katja, my darling, what do you expect? In their eyes you're an American. They might well be thinking you're a spy."

She's unsure whether to laugh or cry. "For God's sake, Ursula. I came here because I couldn't bear what America did to my father! Why would I be spying for them?!"

She bites her lip, worried that her emotions might overwhelm her; breathing deeply as her friend turns away to the sink to rinse her bowl. The seconds gather and stretch before Ursula swings around again.

"It's more complicated here. People you want to trust, you learn not to. People you don't trust, you pretend are your friends. There's no black and white, no moral high ground, our world has been shattered, war destroyed our homes, our families, and inside we're all still full of splinters. Thousands of little wounds, some of which have gone septic and poisoned our relationships with one another. It's spread distrust like a disease. It will take a long time to heal. Now if you'll excuse me I need to get to work."

Kitty draws her feet back to let Ursula pass; watching as she puts her coat over her overalls. She knows it would be better to remain silent, respectful; but she can't help herself. "Did you tell them about Robert?"

Ursula pauses at the door, releasing the handle from her grasp. "You sent me many letters from Philadelphia, Katja. Which was lovely. But the postman noticed the American stamps and presumably considered it his duty to inform the authorities. There are such people. They came to visit me before you arrived."

"They? Who are they?"

"The Stasi. The secret police, in charge of state security. They asked me to tell them everything you'd written about. If I'd withheld any information, and they'd found out, life could have become very difficult - for both of us. You see, the scars haven't healed yet, so if you really want to help this country recover, do as you're asked and don't complain. Hard work will bring its reward, there's no room for self-pity."

In the days that follow Kitty behaves exactly as she's been requested. She buys bread and some vegetables from the local shop, adapting her cooking skills to the limited choice available. As a treat she buys fatty pork to make a casserole; she still has some money left and wants to spoil Ursula who evidently works all hours for little remuneration. They don't speak again of the visit from the Stasi; what conversation they have is limited in scope. She has learnt not to say too much. But she finds slowly that they can laugh again, like the children they were, finding humour in the intimacy of their circumstance. And despite the fact that for many hours of the day Ursula sleeps, while Kitty passes the time reading the newspaper, Neues Deutschland, to understand the plight of East Germany, she notices in the precious time they share together that a softness has returned, a glimmer in her friend's eye, reminding Kitty of the girl she loved.

Five days pass before their domestic serenity evaporates. A lunch of rye bread and hard cheese is interrupted by another knock on the door. Ursula answers but they know it can only mean one thing. Kitty has already reached for her coat by the time her two familiar drivers have crossed the threshold into the room and requested she accompany them. Their sullen attitude spikes her brazenness. "I hope you cleaned your car this time."

She traces the route with a keen eye, mapping this part of the city in the belief that it might somehow be useful, and quickly realising that they are bound for the same location. But this time she doesn't have to wait in the corridor. The clerk guides her directly into Herr Ehrmann's office. To her surprise he is flanked by a shorter, balding man in his forties, a little overweight, a rim of sweat gathering at the edge of his thick glasses. Ehrmann offers his hand. "Fräulein Bernstein, thank you for coming."

"Again, a little courtesy from your stooges might have made the trip more enjoyable."

He gestures to his colleague who sits down without a greeting. "May I introduce Herr Kirsch. He has been informed of your credentials and expressed an interest to meet you."

Kitty glances at the rounded face but it conveys nothing.

"I'm pleased to say all our checks are in order and we'd like to offer you an opportunity of employment."

"That's finally some good news. May I ask in what role?"

"You'll have to go on a course first. Just a little way outside Berlin.."

"What course? I said I could get all my teaching qualifications posted if you…"

"…Fräulein Bernstein, we are not offering you a job as a teacher. This is something far more important. A position where you will be taught thoroughly and learn to put your skills into practice."

"I'm sorry, Herr Ehrmann, I don't understand. Taught what?"

"How to elicit information that might be beneficial to the state. It's a six-month course, in a small town called Belzig. Once completed you will begin your duties in whichever role is assigned to you. Of course, the better you perform, the more illustrious your duties will be."

She tries to conceal her horror, wondering if they, too, can hear the beating of her heart. "Are you asking me to be an informer?"

"You will be an unofficial employee, a contact person. I think the word informer has rather negative connotations. Of course informers are necessary but someone of your intelligence and flare I would hope would rise far above that level."

"I'm not charmed by your flattery, Herr Ehrmann. And anyway, I thank you for the offer but I'm afraid I must refuse."

She sees Ehrmann hesitate before glancing around at his

colleague. Herr Kirsch leans forward. When he speaks Kitty's surprised by the shrillness of his voice. "Fräulein Bernstein, I believe you came to the German Democratic Republic wanting to be of service. Well, this is how you can serve us. We all have a duty to protect and nurture the state. It is in all our best interests. I'm afraid an act of refusal would not be well received. I'm not saying it would come to this but in court it might well be considered an act of treason."

His gaze is intense and unsettling. She does not imagine he has many friends. Not wanting to appear unnerved she answers as confidently as she can. "Well, thank you for painting such a vivid picture of my position, Herr Kirsch. It seems I have been coerced."

Ehrmann resumes his authority. "Not coerced at all, Fräulein Bernstein. If I may, you will be educated, your eyes opened to the inadequacies of our current world which I think will serve you well. Now if you'll excuse us, you'll be escorted back to your apartment to pack your things. And from there you'll be taken to Belzig. Good luck. I have no doubt you'll prove an outstanding candidate."

She's aware of the door opening behind her. She assumes Ehrmann must have activated some kind of buzzer under his desk. She rises from her chair.

"Thank you, gentlemen, this has been most informative. But before I leave I'd very much appreciate the return of my American passport."

Ehrmann smiles. "That won't be necessary, Fräulein. You are now a welcome citizen of the German Democratic Republic. Of which I hope you'll be very proud. Your new passport will be presented to you by my assistant."

She doesn't bother to reply, turning around to find his assistant waiting at the door. For the first time she sees him smile, a sympathetic face spoilt by a rotten incisor. Whether his smile is a gesture of welcome or the satisfaction of conquest she cannot tell. She will ask him to light her cigarette. He did it so courteously last time and she senses the small gestures might be worth cherishing.

14

AUTUMN 1954, CAMBRIDGESHIRE

After the trip to Imber Kitty finds her mind distracted. Usually she would look forward to her Monday morning class but instead she finds the children's antics frustrating; rebuking them where previously she would have laughed. It's clear the two, main protagonists are unsettled by her change of temperament. Tom Gilliam proclaims in his best German that he doesn't love her anymore, sulking at his desk. Rose Thorpe starts to giggle; a predictable reaction to Kitty's admonishment. A part of her feels guilty. She has grown fond of these kids. But she knows at some point she'll have to break the bond, so a deliberately unkind word, or quick rebuff, might dampen their affections; ease the inevitable uncoupling. She scratches more chalky verbs on the blackboard while fleeting images of Imber flood her brain, most vivid the details of Alec's cottage; the eyeless rabbit in the kitchen, the discarded washing line.

At break time she finds herself alone with Jane Farley in the staff room. She's not sure whether by accident or design. But it irritates her. She should have known better and gone for a walk. She needs the space to ponder Alec and his suggestion they go away for a dirty weekend.

"How was your weekend? We thought we might see you in the

pub, yesterday." Jane is nursing a mug of coffee and slumps in to the threadbare armchair next to her.

"Sorry. I had a batch of work to catch up on."

"But not the whole weekend, surely? All work and no play's not good for anyone."

"I like working." She's aware she's been a bit sharp. But Jane Varley seems to register no hurt; still watching her. Kitty wishes she'd just bury her head in a newspaper, or smoke a fag, like all the other staff.

"You'll exhaust yourself, if you're not careful. Tell you what, why don't I drive us around somewhere after school? I could show you some English countryside. We could have tea and scones somewhere. There are some beautiful villages, much prettier than this one."

"That's kind, Miss Varley, but I have to go into Cambridge. I'm meeting my cousin again. The one you met. Who came out here."

"That'll be nice at least. Please give him my best."

Kitty returns her attention to the textbook. The lie at least has helped her formulate a plan. She'll visit Cambridge but not to meet Ed. He can wait. The trip will be a fleeting one but it will serve its purpose. She knows Buchanan-Smith is the main fish to catch but Ed had told her to pursue Alec Carter as well. It's a situation she can handle and this assignment will be far more agreeable than the other. After the meeting she'll report back to Ed; and hopefully she'll have more titbits to feed his contacts.

At the end of the school day, she collects her coat and hurries to the bus stop, clutching an envelope in her pocket. She'd

scribbled the note in her lunch break. Rain threatens as she steps
off the bus in the city centre hastening her walk through the
empty passages to the lodge at Trinity Hall. The porter
recognises her immediately, which isn't great, but the risk is
worth it. He takes the creased envelope with a wry smile and she
leaves abruptly. She's tempted to browse about the city but a
light drizzle has started to fall and anyway, she has school work
to mark, having let it slip due to Ed's demands. There's no one
waiting at the bus stop; she must have just missed one, so she
retreats to the shelter of a shop awning. To pass the time she
decides to add up the prices of all the items displayed in the
shop window. It will take a while being a hardware store, but
who knows when the next bus might arrive.

"Kitty?" Kitty!"

She recognises the voice instantly. But Alec Carter has reached
her side before she has a chance to prepare herself. She smiles.
Not yet sure how to handle this unexpected development. "How
did you know I'd be here?"

"I didn't. But the porter said you'd only just left. I ran a circuit of
all the local bus stops." He wipes the drips of water from his
forehead.

She laughs instinctively. "Full marks for persistence."

"Thank you. And thanks for the note."

"My pleasure. I didn't want you to think we Americans are an
anti-social bunch."

"Far from it."

She enjoys his abashed grin. "So what does a teacher pack for a
weekend in King's Lynn? Bucket and spade or her best ball
gown?"

"It's East Anglia, unfortunately. The poorest cousin of California. Probably an umbrella and hot water bottle."

Again she smiles mischievously. What's the harm in a little puerile pleasure? Behind him she sees the bus approach. "There's my carriage."

His eyes flick to the road before returning to hold her gaze. "Come for a walk. The rain will ease off. What harm can it do?"

A lot, she thinks. She knows she shouldn't be seen around with him. But the rain's kept the streets quiet. And one walk can't do any harm. "I promised my landlady I'd be back for tea."

He smiles again. She realises how it must sound. "I won't let her down."

She's aware of relinquishing control, allowing him to guide their direction, steering her to the grey meadows, beyond the Cam, where no one is venturing. Witnessing this playful side, she feels the draw more acutely. Though she must be on her guard. Every intimate moment is a gift; an opportunity. She should concentrate on Imber; test his responses to ascertain whether his trauma can be radicalised. She must not let attraction dent her aptitude for character assessment. A shimmer of rain drops teases the grass. As they walk towards the heart of the meadow she feels she's entered a No Man's Land, a void between the university buildings and the distant, perimeter road.

The veil of rain drifts away towards the city, as he'd promised. A glimmer of sunlight emerges before it's obscured again by cloud. She rehearses her opening sentences before speaking. "Thank you for yesterday. It was more shocking than I'd expected. People often say, oh I can imagine how that must have felt. But I really can't."

He sweeps the wet fringe from his forehead. "Sometimes Imber feels like a pet dog. I love it but it's got an insatiable hunger. It fills my head so much sometimes I want to kill it. But you don't kill the thing you love." He stops to look at her, half smiling. "I bet you're sorry you asked."

"Most people would have told me they felt a bit sad. But then I wouldn't be standing in this field with most people." Kitty doesn't back away as he leans towards her; his lips dry and surprisingly cool. She feels his arms clasp around her waist, his tongue pushing harder and further into her mouth. She doesn't resist. Robert wasn't the last man she'd kissed but the intensity of the thrill surprises her and she feels cheated when he breaks away. Though she knows he must. For both their sakes.

She's the first to break the silence. "Your jacket's soaking. Maybe you should change before you catch pneumonia."

He smiles in response. "There's a bench under those trees. We can dry off there for a bit."

"You sure you don't want to go back?"

"Why would I?"

She steps in beside him, thinking hard now. How to best manipulate the situation? Convincing herself that she still has the means to control the outcome. He leads her along a well-trodden grass path towards a sheltering copse of chestnut trees. "I thought we should meet at the station on Saturday morning. There's a ten o'clock train, leaving from platform one. We could board separately. I know a place we can stay. It's right by the harbour. Quite discreet."

He's rushing the information. A sure sign of nerves which pleases her. It helps restore the balance in her favour. She smiles. "I hope you do your history research this thoroughly."

"I'm sorry. You're probably thinking I'm…"

"...I've never seen the English seaside If a train takes me there I promise I'll be on it."

He smiles again. "Don't expect too much. I imagine it's like a poor man's Coney Island. Without all the fun bits."

"We'll see what we can do about that."

Taking her hand he guides her to the bench, wiping it dry with his jacket sleeve before inviting her to sit. "Chestnut trees are nature's best umbrella. I sometimes come and read here when I know no one else will be around."

She settles on to the bench, checking discreetly that they're not in anyone's direct line of view. He was right; it's well hidden. He sits beside her but there's an awkward formality in his pose. She finds it charming; reminded of her trips to the movies with traumatised teenage boys. He touches her thigh lightly with his long fingers. Her skin flushes hot under her dress and she wonders whether she's kidding herself about her ability to maintain control. In training she was told to trust her judgement. But the assumption was that any seduction would be mechanical, an expedient requirement. Not a volatile, almost adolescent yearning. "Do you have a cigarette?" It's a stall of sorts, but it might relax her.

"Of course." He fishes in the top pocket of his jacket for the packet, drawing one out for her to select, then taking another for himself.

She hovers close, so that he might light it. But Alec is searching his other pockets. "Christ. Must have left them in my room."

She reaches in her bag to find her lighter. "Modern girls always keep a lighter for emergencies."

Alec smiles, bending his face towards the small flame before she lights her own. She becomes aware he's reading the fine gold print embossed on the black lighter. "Dorchester, London. Lucky you. When was that?"

She returns it to her bag. It's a small mistake. But she's cross with herself. It means a lie that she didn't need to tell. Still, what else could she have done in the circumstance? "It's where I met my cousins when I was in London."

"Not a bad place to meet. Do they stay there?"

She can tell he's a little perplexed. "Once in a while. When they're over from the States. They're only distant relations."

"But very rich ones."

"I never really thought about it. I suppose they must be." She can't shake off the mistake. It irritates her; such a stupid error. Kindergarten level. The sun finally breaks free again, it's late Spring warmth penetrating the tree canopy in fine shards of light. She feels Alec's breath on her neck, pressing closer. Her sense is to step away. "I really think we should go. I need to get some work done."

He follows her as she steps away from the bench; plainly bemused by her change of tone. She wants to make light of it. To reassure him that all will be well. Just a stupid little error. She finds what she hopes is a smile of encouragement. "Everyone'll be getting out now the sun's shining. And I have my reputation to look after."

"But you'll be there. On Saturday?" He looks awkward again, school boyish. She wonders if he's a virgin. Probably not. The thought of Saturday shoots another flush of blood across her skin. Not because she hasn't had sex for quite a long time. Because it's Alec Carter.

"I'll be on the first carriage behind the engine."

It's his turn to fall in line beside her, back towards the river, his body language more reserved now. careful not to appear too intimate. "When you get off the train you'll see a newspaper stand on your left. I'll meet you there."

"No flowers please. I really need to be discreet." He laughs. She's grateful. The awkwardness has evaporated; their exchanges charged by playful banter, which she has to admit, is delicious foreplay.

They part at the river's edge. She has no desire to be accompanied to the bus stop, mindful that they should keep their public appearances to a minimum. He makes no attempt to kiss her either. Learning fast.

Stepping off the bus one hour later she contemplates a quiet evening of indulgence. Perhaps she'll paint her nails, listen to the comedy hour, although she's finding the shows too class-obsessed, always posh bloke meets Cockney geezer. Maybe she'll just read a book. Walking back up the road she spots a maroon car parked up a track, a little way short of her cottage. Her heart sinks. The car's facing the road. Ed flashes the headlights. It's not what she'd wanted. But she must be professional; at all times.

The interior reeks of ash; the ashtray overflowing with cigarette butts. She wonders how long he's been waiting. But his demeanour suggests a good mood. "Your landlady was very helpful. She told me you'd gone into Cambridge and I could wait for you if I wanted. Apparently you went to buy a book called Emil and the Detectives."

"By Erich Kastner. I loved it. I think the children would too."

"But they didn't have it in stock?"

"That'll be my story. I was seeing Alec. I've moved things on a bit, as you requested." She instinctively wants to play it down. "He's a smart boy. I think with a bit of time and persuasion he could be an excellent candidate. He's got all the anger, and the brain."

Ed smiles. "And the charm."

"You don't always need charm to make a decent agent." She regrets her response instantly. Wondering whether Ed will take this as a slight. But if he has, his face doesn't show it.

"What should I report back?"

"The truth. I'm going to King's Lynn with him for that dirty weekend." She notices the muscles around Ed's mouth tighten, almost imperceptibly, and a part of her feels delighted to have shocked him. "I know you told me to stall when we were at Imber but it seemed the perfect opportunity. We hatched a plan today. So just like you wanted I've dangled some bait."

She waits for Ed to respond. He stubs out another cigarette, this time tossing it out of the window before speaking. "This weekend?"

"Yes."

"You should have consulted me first."

"I thought you'd approve."

"You'll have to cancel."

"Oh Jesus. Why?"

"I drove out here to tell you that Buchanan-Smith's in London this weekend. Whether it's genuine business or another insidious lie I have no idea, but he's asked to see you. I said you'd be delighted."

"Tell him I'm busy. Next week or the weekend after."

"For Christ's sake, this isn't someone you turn down, comrade. It's not your choice to make. You do exactly as I tell you. And you won't disappoint me."

For the first time she feels genuinely frightened, not by his physical strength, he's a delicate Englishman, but by his amorphous power. All she knows is that he's her contact; she has no idea how deep his roots run. 'Fine. We'll do it your way. I'll tell Alec I've got a better offer."

"Tell him nothing. Just change the date. He'll hang on like an adoring puppy."

"Perhaps."

"Trust me."

"Trust no one, you said." She can tell by his pinched expression that she's exasperating him. And she knows it's unprofessional but she can't help it. The disappointment is hard to contain.

Ed shifts his eyes to the windscreen. "Buchanan-Smith is having another of his little soirees at his mews flat. The idea is everyone else buggers off and you stay."

"And suck his dick to shreds, or whatever schoolboy fantasy his nanny induced."

Clearly she's shocked him. As she meant to. But it's worth it just to burst his bubble of privilege.

"You make it sound like you're being forced to do something you didn't sign up to."

"At least Alec Carter shows me a little respect rather than treating me like his sex toy."

"Respect doesn't play a part in any of it. You're doing it to bring Buchanan down. And his elitist clan with him. We're as complicit as they are, we just happen to be on the right side."

She knows he's right, of course; feeling disappointed by her own vulnerability, a remnant of her old self which she thought she'd banished for good. Treat it as a warning. Be vigilant. Let nothing in. "So what's the plan?"

"I'll pick you up from here on Saturday. Be ready at one. We'll drive down to the Dorchester. You can get ready in my room. On Sunday I'll be waiting at the end of the mews at seven am. I'll need to find you a cocktail dress. Have you got any sexy lingerie?"

"I sleep naked. Define sexy."

"I'll find something appropriate. Okay, time to go. I need to get back to Cambridge."

She opens the car door, aware that some professional point has been crossed, but she's not sure exactly what. Ed is an enigma. Perhaps it's deliberate on his part. But there's a personal element spiking his attitude. Does he want her himself? The thought provides some welcome light relief. If he does, she can see his job must be hell. She slams the door shut, setting out for the cottage without turning back. But she's aware of the Magnette stealing away into the night, making more noise than necessary.

The aroma of boiling cabbage lingers in her landlady's kitchen. She's minced some lamb and added boiled potatoes to create a greying pulp. But Kitty's grateful for food. Her stomach needs soothing. Sitting together at the table Mrs Johnson regales her with every detail of her conversation with Ed. Evidently he was charm itself and this brief encounter has, for a moment, refreshed the mundane reality of her war widow's lifestyle. Perhaps espionage has the power to touch hearts beyond its remit.

After pudding Kitty retires to her room. She paints her nails, lingering over each one with more care than she would usually muster, wondering how to break the news to Alec; unsure whether to send him a note as soon as possible or leave it till Saturday, so it seems like a last minute, unavoidable cancellation. Perhaps the decision can wait till morning. Her nails finished, as scarlet as the dying embers of a fire, she turns her thoughts, reluctantly, to Buchanan-Smith. She unlocks the chest of drawers to withdraw the dossier Ed gave her on him. In training at Belzig she'd begun to develop a scent for the lucrative detail; it had provided its own tantalising thrill. But sifting through the photos and documents again she feels no such thing; just the dread of a child on a Sunday night who has yet to start her homework.

15

After leaving Kitty, Ed pushes the Magnette hard towards the next village, hoping to find a public pay phone. It's a sleepy place, more of a hamlet. A red telephone box bathes under a light opposite the pub; beyond it the black canvas of night. There's no one about; no danger of being overheard. When the receiver picks up, he thrusts the coins into the slot, instantly recognising Molly's emollient tones.

"It's Ed."

"Hello, Ed. How are you?"

He senses his breathing slow, some alchemy doing its work. "Is Jim there? I need a word."

"I'm afraid he's gone to the pub, dear. It's skittles night. Can I leave a message for him or help in anyway?"

"It's my cousin. I don't think she's very well. I need some advice."

There's a momentary pause which he finds reassuring. Molly's brain has set to work. He can trust her to do the right thing. In her quiet, unassuming way she always does. "I'm sorry to hear that, dear. Why don't I tell him you'll pop by his office on Wednesday evening? His diary's pretty full before then. How ill is she?"

"She'll live till then. Tell him I'll be there at seven."

"I will. Take care, dear."

He replaces the receiver and slips back into the car, resisting a quick gin at the pub though he's sorely tempted. Kitty's ambivalence has rattled him. He'd been told she was the best; achieving the highest grade of professional conduct at Belzig, but ranking Alec Carter above Buchanan-Smith was a serious flaw. Her protestation had all the ugly hallmarks of adolescent capriciousness, the kind of behaviour he'd locked away years ago.

Thirty minutes later, when he arrives back at Trinity Hall, he finds Alec Carter lying on his bed, a cigarette dangling from his hand. A hardback book lies open on his chest; no doubt something worthy from the library. He barely looks up as Ed throws his sports jacket across the chair and reaches for the silver flask of whisky in his bedside cabinet.

"Where were you?"

"I went for a drive in the country."

"In the dark?"

"Sometimes it's more appealing that way. Want some?" He hands the flask across to his room-mate. He won't mention Kitty; preferring to wait. "As a matter of fact, all those boring views of dreary fields cleared my head. I decided I haven't been studying enough."

"You don't say."

"Studying isn't just about shoving your head in a textbook. Though maybe it is for a history scholar." He takes another sip from the returned flask, flinging his other arm behind him on to the pillow. "I can't really understand the obsession with everything that's dead and past. You must wonder what you're doing sometimes? What the point of it is?"

"Not really. It interests me."

"What interests you, exactly?"

"Finding the reason for things."

"Cause and effect. The subject of a thousand tedious school essays up and down the land. It's only interesting if the effect has a seismic effect. A release of controlled energy. Which is why chemistry's more interesting than history."

"Like the atom bomb."

"Oh, spare me your proselytizing, Alec."

"History teaches us about mistakes. It helps guard against dangerous ideas. And dangerous men."

Ed thinks of Kitty Bernstein. "And women. But it doesn't tell us what we should strive for."

To his surprise his room-mate suddenly grins. "I know what I want. It's just a question of getting it."

He closes his eyes, tempted to ask Alec exactly what he means. Though he knows. But an indirect approach might be more revealing. "I hope you haven't spent all day cooped up here. It does make you horribly earnest."

"I went for a walk across the meadows. But it started to rain so I came back."

"So apart from me, you've not spoken to anyone all day?"

"It's not a crime. I'm used to my own company You saw what Imber was like."

Too defensive. He knows Alec's lying anyway but his technique will have to improve if he's to prove useful. Propping himself up on his elbow he turns towards him, unable to resist a second crack. "Just because life in Imber was horribly dull doesn't mean it has to stay that way."

"It wasn't. And what the hell would you know? Fast cars and fancy hotels are all well and fucking good but they don't define a life well led."

The aggression is undisguised. It's not the first time Ed's felt the intensity of his room-mate's glare, but it always has the power to shock; like a tamed dog suddenly baring its teeth. He wonders where the reference to the hotel came from. He can't remember mentioning any. Presumably an assumption. At any rate it's obvious Alec Carter harbours class resentment; a useful asset, though the evident disdain compels him to apologise. "I'm sorry. What I said about your childhood was crass. I'll buy you several rounds in the pub as a token of apology." He holds his hand to his heart; a touch theatrical but he feels the gesture is sincere.

"Did anyone ever tell you you're a cunt?"

"Only my father."

At least he's made his room-mate smile again. "Like father, like son."

He grips his chest tighter. "Now you burn me at the stake."

Late afternoon on Wednesday he hurries from his chemistry seminar to collect the Magnette at Cambridge Station. The road to London is quieter than usual and he reaches Bayswater in perfect time for a soothing scotch. He knows Jim Atherton always drinks Bells, half whisky, half water, and always on the dot of six thirty. He's not disappointed. Atherton is pouring two glasses as he enters the room. A faint smell of damp blends with the alcohol; presumably the landlord's more interested in rent than upkeep, which must suit Atherton as well. The older man turns away from the cabinet and places a cheap tumbler into Ed's hand. The light from the window is beginning to fade but he shows no interest in switching lights on, preferring to sit in the half dark. Only the glow of the valve wireless penetrates this world, and the dulcet tones of the BBC Overseas Service.

"How was the drive?"

"Eventless. Which has its own pleasures."

Atherton smiles, sipping his whisky quietly, whilst studying Ed like he might a sculpture. "Molly tells me you might have a problem."

"I thought I did. Driving down I found myself questioning whether I over-reacted."

"I can't say I've noticed you're susceptible to that. But we all have a tipping point. Tell me what happened."

Ed accepts a cigarette from the opened, silver case that Atherton pushes towards him. It strikes him as a rather bourgeois affectation; perhaps his mentor has more of a taste for the finer points of life than he'd imagined. He uses the moment to compose himself. Although Atherton is his mentor, perhaps even a friend, he's aware the relationship could be terminated at any moment should he fuck up. He sits back into the chair's curdled stuffing. "I told her about Buchanan-Smith's latest get together. I made it clear the opportunity to spend the night with him would present itself. She told me she'd already booked a dirty weekend with Alec Carter; without informing me first. She said Buchanan could wait. She was very reluctant to change her plan, even though she knows Buchanan's a much bigger fish. I'd say there was a worrying degree of petulance."

He waits for Atherton's response. Longer than makes him feel comfortable. Then the man laughs in his face, a hearty cackle, like he'd just heard a line in a Noel Coward play.

"For Christ's sake, she's made you jealous. I can't say I blame you, even Molly thought she was a stunner and she's never commented on an agent's physical attributes before. Jesus, if I were a younger man."

Atherton slugs deeply from his tumbler while Ed attempts to disguise his disgust. He's never heard Atherton express any sexual desire. Nor has he wanted to. "What do you suggest I do?"

Stained teeth slip back behind tight lips. As if the cackle never happened. "Watch her more closely. Impose your authority, even if you have to threaten her. She's an intelligent girl, I know her talent stood out at training. But perhaps our comrades in Berlin weren't as attuned to her easy, American charm. I liked her. I confess, probably too much. And not just because she's a looker. Which means, despite the training, she must still have a lingering weakness for sentiment. Affairs of the heart. I'm afraid you must be ruthless, my friend. Her body's no temple. Just a vessel to capture information, and hearts if necessary, but not to surrender her own. Do what you have to. We can't afford to lose Buchanan-Smith."

As Wednesday surrenders to Thursday he waits for some sort of note or message from Kitty Bernstein. But none is forthcoming. Do what you have to, Atherton had said. Sitting in his car, the only place he can guarantee his isolation, he runs over the facts, a cigarette hanging from his lips. She had a moment of petulance, it's true, but she'd promised she'd see Buchanan. The only reason she might send a note were if she were backing out. But then that would be tantamount to suicide. Even if she wanted to abscond with Alec Carter she wouldn't get very far. So why worry? But he can't help himself. He spends Friday closer to his room-mate than usual, but not so suffocating that Alec Carter would question it. His first idea is a punt on the Cam, to soften their hangovers from the night before. Though surprised, his room-mate agrees. But after an aimless hour on the river Alec fails to mention anything about weekend plans. The same thing happens after an afternoon studying together in the library, and a subsequent pub crawl with their friends, despite Ed's surgical explorations. Either Kitty Bernstein hasn't yet told Alec that she's cancelling, or they're taking flight. Perhaps she's told him everything. In which case he needs to contact Atherton. Urgently.

But he delays. He has his reasons. This is what he tells himself. Nothing need happen until it's confirmed that she's absconded. To panic would jeopardise everything.

He wakes up early Saturday morning and turns abruptly to see if his room-mate is still in his bed. His heartbeat instantly slows. The familiar, black waves of hair spread like ink across the pillow. From the rhythmic breathing he assumes he's still sleeping. Hardly surprising. They'd ended up drunk last night at the dance hall. At least, Alec had. He'd disguised his own sobriety; too big a day dawned. He climbs out of bed and boils the kettle for morning tea, knowing it will wake him. The routine has become risibly domestic. Alec will now struggle from his lair, slip straight in to shorts and a sweatshirt without a word, and stumble from the room for a twenty-minute run to clear his head. On his return he will buy four lemon curd tarts from the bakery. Two each. Only then will they exchange greetings.

As soon as Alec's left Ed gulps the last slops of tea, dresses quickly, and steps out to the courtyard. No students disrupt his path towards the porter's lodge. It's far too early. The nearest phone box is just up the narrow lane, beyond the college gate. Until now he's delayed booking at the Dorchester, just in case plans changed, but this morning his gut tells him the Buchanan plan will proceed so he reserves a suite under his usual pseudonym. By the time Alec returns, Ed is back on his bed, happy to receive the lemon tarts. He bites into the soft pastry and lights his first cigarette of the day, watching Alec strip a sweat-drenched vest from his torso, which he throws to the floor, followed by his shorts. As they land an envelope, hand-written without a stamp, slips from the pocket.

"You've dropped something." It's hard to make it sound nonchalant.

His room-mate turns his back on him, washing himself down at the basin. The muscles in his shoulders ripple like cables. "It's a letter." His tone is petulant.

Ed stifles a wave of jealousy. His own physique is less honed. "I can see that."

"The porter told me an attractive, American woman brought it. I'm guessing it wasn't Lauren bloody Bacall." His tone is terse, exaggerated by the contemptuous throw of his towel to the chair.

Ed maintains his breezy air despite the crabbiness. "How nice for you. Why don't you open it?"

"Because no one delivers a letter to someone on the day they're going to meet. So it means bad news." He grabs a clean shirt from the wardrobe and slips on a pair of trousers. But suddenly he has a change of heart, abandoning his shirt to the floor and grabbing the envelope instead. "We're supposed to be going away this weekend. I wasn't going to tell you because…well she's your cousin. My apologies for my deceit." He flops onto the bed and rips through the envelope, his eyes darting across the page before crumpling it in his hand. "She's seeing cousins in London. Again. So sorry to cancel. How many fucking cousins have you two got for Christ's sake?!"

"I've lost count. We're a big family."

"And you're going too, I take it? Part of this happy family, sipping cocktails at the Dorchester, which each cost more than the barman's wages?"

"It's not what you think…"

"…Is that where you always go when you're not here? Drinking champers with your posh chums when you're not playing at being a poor student?"

"Don't be ridiculous. And no, it's not where I always go. I do have other friends." It feels lame as he says it. Defensive. But he's reeling from the mention of the Dorchester. "And where the hell did you get the idea we always go to the Dorchester?"

Alec visibly softens for a moment. "Kitty has a lighter with its name embossed in gold. I put two and two together."

"And came up with five. Kitty likes to fantasise a bit, it's part of her charm." He inhales deeply from the cigarette, having to think fast. She's made an error. A basic one, suggesting her thought process is compromised. Atherton's right, she's still susceptible to emotion. Which endangers all of them. He pushes the plume to the ceiling. "Look, old boy, I understand you're disappointed. Christ, who wouldn't be? She's a beautiful girl. But it's only a family re-union. And it's in one of those Italian restaurants full of Chianti bottles for candles where you can barely see the spaghetti. Definitely not the Dorchester. Maybe you could see her another weekend."

Though acutely aware of his room-mate's gaze, he hopes he's diffused the situation. But Alec Carter springs from his bed, thrusting his arms into the sleeves of his shirt.

"Where the hell are you going now?" Almost impossible to disguise the alarm in his voice.

"Stratham. I'm going to find her, rules or not."

He rises from his bed. "Alec, don't be a prick. You'll do more damage by going to the school. Think of it from her point of view."

His room-mate grabs his jacket from the hook on the back of the door. "I don't know what to think. Except I keep feeling I'm being fed a lie."

"Wait!" The urgency in his voice makes Alec turn. "Close the door a second, will you?" His room-mate complies. So far so good. But there's damage to be sorted. "Sit down a second. You're right. I haven't been entirely honest with you." To his surprise Alec walks slowly back to his bed. Ed settles opposite him, knees almost locked. "You might want a drop. And don't tell me it's too early." He hands across the silver whisky flask.

"Now you're worrying me."

"Drink up." He watches Alec swig then repeats the gesture himself with the returned flask. "Kitty and I are cousins. That much is true. The reason she's here is to get over being dumped rather unceremoniously by her lawyer fiancé after her father was blacklisted by McCarthy. I have taken her to London to meet up with a couple of relatives, just to make her feel at home, and once we had tea at the Dorchester which is where she must've got the lighter. But the way she's reacted to the break-up has been a bit unpredictable." He focuses on his room-mate's eyes, which are alert and keen. Like a hunter. "I'm afraid you're not the only one, old man. She's thrown herself into a number of affairs. And I don't blame her. She doesn't trust anyone anymore so she's enjoying the ride. I didn't tell you because I thought the whole thing would blow over, but everyone can see you're infatuated. But she's a dangerous game to play, Alec. And to be frank, you're not in her class." He hopes this last comment bites more than anything. By the expression of disgust on his room-mate's face he's right. "If you want to keep sane give up now. Go any deeper and you'll suffer for it."

A part of him is relieved he's cut the lifeline. He's been as charmed by Alec Carter as she has. But Kitty Bernstein is an unpredictable source of errors. Now he just needs to sit tight, pull his room-mate back from the brink, and let Berlin decide her fate. He watches his friend's face for some sign of capitulation; but there's nothing discernible, just the same intense gaze. Shock, he assumes.

But when Alec Carter finally replies, his tone is hardly submissive. "Do you know any of these other people?"

"None of them are particularly savoury characters but she wasn't looking for Prince Charming. Which is why she made a mistake with you."

"Did she tell you that?"

"She realised she'd crossed her own boundary. She's not totally amoral. That's why we arranged a cousins get together in London tonight. So she could let you down gently. I'm sorry we had to spin a lie. But of course you're a bright chap, so you didn't buy it. Sometimes it's better to tell the truth, even if it's ugly."

He raises a half smile from Alec and hopes the job's done. There'll be questions to come in the next few days at the pub;

drunken laments over a late-night scotch, but nothing he can't prepare for. "Why don't you go and get smashed with the boys tonight? There's another dance on at the Dorothy Ballroom. You might find a nice local tart to drown your sorrows. Tomorrow we'll go punting again but this time we'll pop a few corks."

"And drown happy."

"I'd forgotten how tedious punting is without bubbles. It's like eating snails without garlic." Finally he succeeds in making his room-mate smile. "Come the revolution they'll shoot wankers like you."

"Nothing I can do to save myself. It's simply in the blood." He pushes himself up; the interview over, and slips over to the wardrobe, retrieving a bottle of gin from the top shelf. "I have to go and get some petrol. Why don't you find someone to share this?" He chucks the bottle at his friend. "It'll help get you over the shock. Have an afternoon snooze on the riverbank, Mole and Ratty style."

He steps quickly from the college, heading for a different phone box. Atherton answers directly this time; the exchange as brief as possible. Ed confirms that his cousin's unwell, but not so sick that they should cancel her evening engagement. Stepping back into the chilled air, he has no intention of returning to his room; best to leave Alec Carter alone now; hopefully he'll be pissed by mid-afternoon. He heads for a smart boutique in the city centre and charms the sales assistant with an easy patter. He's looking for a stunning cocktail dress for his fiancée. It's quite a party. One of the elegant shop models poses in three separate dresses, of which he chooses the second; a tightly contoured, black, velvet top, sleeveless and cut low to a V at the breast, separating at the waist to a flared skirt of black chiffon. He acquires lingerie to match. Something sexy, he'd said, and the assistant blushed. Kitty Bernstein will look irresistible. At the station carpark he lays the boxed dress carefully on the back seat and heads north, out of town, stopping at a roadside café for sausage and chips washed down with a milky tea. It settles a nervous stomach. Pushing the plate aside, he lights a cigarette and scrutinises the headlines of an abandoned newspaper; guerrillas have attacked targets in Algeria in protest against French rule. He reads on, transfixed. The revolution is coming.

Kitty Bernstein is standing at the layby opposite the row of the cottages, just as she'd promised. He breathes more easily. She's nicely turned out, a short jacket and pleated skirt, nothing too fancy, appropriate for a re-union with relatives. He steps out to take her vanity case, dropping it next to his in the boot of the car. He'd packed the day before when Alec was out, just in case the revelation to his room-mate had been more volatile. Swinging the car back towards the main road he feels like driving fast. Maybe he just wants to show off. But what of it? He's had enough to deal with, covering for her mistakes. Kitty Bernstein can put up with a little speed.

"How are you?" His tone is flat, as if the answer doesn't interest him much.

"How do you think?"

He chooses not to answer, grateful when she fills the void.

"My landlady wants to chat all the time so it's hard to walk away. She must be very lonely. Do you have to drive so fast?"

He ignores the question. "Try to get some sleep."

"Not easy when you're rolling in a tin can."

"We can talk when we get there."

Reluctantly he slows down. It's the professional thing to do. If she's going to perform it seems fair she gets some beauty sleep.

"I assume Alec got my note."

Her tone is nonchalant but he's not going to discuss her errors, not before Buchanan-Smith. "He wasn't exactly pleased. I told him to go and get drunk with the boys. He'll be okay but we might have to review that operation."

"No need for pretty euphemisms, comrade. If you mean terminate, just say it."

"I said it's under review. Now get some sleep. Buchanan-Smith won't want a dullard."

"I was under the impression all he wants is a pound of flesh. Or make that two if he nuzzles both tits."

She's tried to shock him again. Which he assumes is what she wanted. But he won't react. He lights another cigarette and throws the lighter back on to the dashboard. "It's a straight road from here. Perfect for a nap."

In his peripheral vision he sees her sit back a little, turning her head away from him towards the passenger window. His stomach is tense. A part of him feels sorry for her, it's a hell of an ask, but he can't afford to let it show. Tonight's a big night, the biggest yet, and despite the hiccup with Alec he has to keep his sight on the prize. Toppling Buchanan-Smith could bring down the whole establishment like a pack of cards. The beginning of the end. Whatever spats he might have had with Kitty Bernstein, whatever erroneous tasks they may each be assigned, they're minor scratches compared to the wounds they can inflict. He might not fully trust her now; might not even like her for reasons he chooses not to explore, but they're both on the side of justice. Either Atherton or Berlin will decide her fate. It's out of his hands. He throws the cigarette butt out of the window, feeling calmer for rationalising his thoughts.

In the distance a band of low sunlight light turns a wet field to a sparkling lake. A mirage. Unreachable. He wonders if his desires have much the same quality.

Cold Road to Imber

16

She wakes with a start at the cut of the engine, realising that she must have slept for most of the journey. Beyond the windscreen she sees a quiet, high class, London street. Somewhere in Mayfair, she guesses, presumably one of the smart streets behind the Dorchester. Without a word, Ed climbs out of the Magnette and removes the two cases from the boot. She checks her make-up in the vanity mirror and steps out beside him, fully awake now, and with an aching dread at the demands of the next few hours.

"You look better for some rest. Quite a transformation."

He seems more conciliatory than before, the almost hostile tone replaced by an avuncular decency. Perhaps he cares after all.

She takes a breath of stale, London air. "Let's hope our fish feels the same."

He allows himself a smile at her wisecrack. It helps. She wants to cloak herself again, to prepare for what's coming; to push Alec Carter to the back of her brain. It's the only way to survive; the immunisation against emotion which was core to her training. She falls in beside her faux husband, a smart London couple, beating a path to the hotel where a doorman attempts to take their bags. But Ed bats him away with a courteous stroke and heads straight for the gilded reception desk.

"Wait here, darling."

She settles on an art deco chaise longue beneath a potted palm and contemplates the polished sheen of black and white marble. Glancing back to the desk she marvels at his ease. In this elaborate setting he seems older than his years. She wonders how he pays for such luxury; surely the GDR wouldn't tolerate such extravagance? Nor should it. Which suggests it must come out of his own pocket, in which case she's happy to accept. It's a small compensation for her sexual sacrifice. Her thoughts return to Buchanan-Smith until Ed takes her hand, her knight in shining armour, to guide her to the lift.

They're in the same suite as last time; her husband is obviously a creature of habit, except this time he'll slumber in silky sheets, while she fakes an orgasm in a mews flat, or whatever sex act a wealthy politician demands. Still, the room in its familiarity, provides some comfort. She takes a long bath, sips from the champagne that he's thoughtfully brought to her. She has no compunction now about letting him see her naked, enjoying how he attempts to look without looking. Look but don't touch. She wonders what demons clash inside his head. Feeling more relaxed for the soak, she cocoons herself in towels softer than mink and dabs richly scented perfume in places not usually for sale.

She approves of the outfit Ed has purchased for her. She suspects she would have chosen much the same. Her breasts are not large but the combination of bra and plunging neckline accentuates her cleavage. Not in a vulgar way, more Elizabeth Taylor than Jane Russell. She's pleased with the result. Sitting on the sofa with a view to Hyde Park she feels bizarrely closer to Ed than she has at any point. He remains courteous, encouraging and not without sympathy for her task. Together they sip more champagne as the late sunlight shifts shadows along the walls.

He runs over the plan and objectives several times, what to tell Buchanan-Smith of her American past, how to flatter him, how to earn his trust and later his confidence. Whatever it takes she must become his mistress of choice. Tapping him for defence information will follow. He highlights three, key areas for her to target; the purpose of British troop operations on the Rhine; the terms under which West Germany will be accepted into NATO; and the Cabinet's response to an offer by the Soviet Union to join the North Atlantic alliance to preserve peace in Europe. The last of these is news to her, but he doesn't want to elaborate. Just catch the fish. Tomorrow morning he'll be waiting at the end of the mews.

"Don't be late, seven am exactly." He smiles. "Otherwise my car turns into a pumpkin."

She laughs. It's a lame joke but she's grateful at his attempts to alleviate the tension. A clink of glasses. The last sip of champagne cools her throat.

She takes his arm as they leave the hotel, nodding playfully at the doorman. It's a mild evening, Buchanan-Smith's mews is only a minute away, but Ed insists on driving.

There's no time for reflection. The car draws up with indecent haste at the end of the mews, beyond the search of the sodium street lamps. In the space of fifteen minutes three taxis enter the cobbled lane and stop outside Buchanan-Smith's flat. Ed takes a pair of binoculars from the glove compartment. His action is swift, he doesn't even need to look down, but in that moment she's sure she glimpsed the dull metal of a small pistol. But it was just a glimpse. He holds the binoculars to his eyes and watches two men descend from the first cab, one from the second, and three giggling women from a third. He knows them all; a big wig in the aeronautics industry, a Swedish politician, a civil servant and three local tarts. She takes in the details, totally focused now. It's an assignment like any other.

Apparently satisfied, he drops the binoculars to his lap. "Over to you, Vanity Adams. Time to haul in the catch."

She smiles. "I hope there's a nice treat waiting for me when I'm finished."

"Not an unreasonable request in the circumstances."

"How about a buttery croissant, and some strong coffee?"

"How about you catch the prize first?"

From the back seat she gathers her handbag, large enough to hide a toothbrush and a wash bag but still discreet. It doesn't look like she's intending to spend the night. She presses the car door closed and walks slowly towards the flat. Her stilettos clip and skip across the cobbles. She could break a leg, she thinks, and then where would they be? The sound of the Magnette departing is her cue to ring the doorbell. She doesn't have long to wait. She can hear someone hurrying down the stairs amongst much raucous laughter. Buchanan-Smith opens the door, open shirt, casual trousers, for some reason bare feet. He looks younger than she remembered, greeting her like a puppy and ushering her up the stairs in front of him, his hand lightly brushing her bottom, as if she were in danger of falling without him. Such a gentleman. His guests are gathered in the room she recalls from her last visit. Two windows overlook the mews. At the opposite end the Swedish guy is opening yet more champagne in a small kitchenette. A door beside it opens to a bathroom. Along the main wall an open staircase leads to the mezzanine floor; the bedroom she managed to avoid last time. There's no handshaking, just air kisses with the girls, Rita, Tara and Bunny, and a peck on the cheek from the men. Bizarrely Buchanan-Smith hasn't kissed her at all yet. The one called Tara starts sifting through the record collection on the floor. She finds something that delights her and slaps it on to the record player. Dean Martin croons "That's Amore".

At first Buchanan-Smith, or Jim, as she remembers to call him,
shows her little attention and she wonders whether Ed Grant
has over-egged her marketability. Why might he want her when
there's three perfectly attractive tarts in the room? Perhaps she
should pursue one of the others but what would they know of
NATO and cabinet meetings? She accepts a glass overflowing
with bubbles and joins the girls, mimicking their willingness to
dance and parade while the men look on, still relatively sober.
She's reminded of a high school dance. Spotty boys ogling pretty
girls. At least the Swedish politician looks like he wants to
partake. Tara turns the volume up and begins to swig from the
bottle. Her friends pass the champagne as they dance but Kitty
declines the offer, still clutching the glass in her hand. She's
realised Buchanan-Smith's gaze tracks her exclusively. Not in a
malicious way, more that he appreciates her difference, so she
will play to that difference, distancing herself almost
imperceptibly from the girls, both physically and behaviourally.

Soon the Swede throws himself into the throng, drinking heavily,
no longer able to resist his aching libido. Tara is his obvious
goal. The aeronautical wizard, all limbs and bony chin, follows
suit, grabbing Bunny's hand. But the civil servant bides his time,
standing awkwardly by the kitchen door until even he can no
longer ignore the seductive call of Rita's scarlet-nailed finger.
She's the least ebullient, but to Kitty's mind, the prettiest. She
leaves them to dance, meandering across to the G-Plan sofa
where Buchanan-Smith has settled, cigarette and champagne
glass in hand, clearly enjoying the view. She sits down beside him
and observes the scene, wondering if his arm will rest around her
which it doesn't. Watching the newly formed partnerships at
work, they seem extraordinarily successful. Some alchemy at
work. More likely the girls have been fastidiously selected. She
wonders if this is Ed Grant's work. If so, he's very good at his
job. But she knew that.

A brush of warm flesh against her bare arm redirects her

thoughts. He's smiling at her. Jim. Not leery. Almost paternal. "I'm glad you came."

"You've got some interesting friends."

He laughs. "I never met the girls before. But I thought it might be a little presumptive to invite you without company."

She smiles. Deliberately coquettish. "How thoughtful. Quite the gent."

"Except I'm not sure you believe that."

"I guess it would depend on your intentions."

For a moment he seems lost for words. It's a moment to relish but it doesn't last long. "I hope you've been treated courteously since you came to Britain. A beautiful American girl in London. Single. Artistic. Some of those arty chaps have disreputable reputations."

"Like I say, all you Brits seem perfect gentlemen."

"I'm pleased to hear it. But don't be deceived by the veneer."

She smiles. "Oh? Something I should know?"

"English gentlemen are often prone to psychological weakness, the consequence of being ripped from their mothers' arms and packed off to some frightful, Dickensian boarding school. Once married they take their anger out on their wives, treating them with callous indifference at best, abusing them at worst. Then there are those who worship their spouses like gods. But they seek their gratification elsewhere."

"Sounds a little gloomy, but I guess handy to know. And which of those are you?" But of course, she knows already.

Buchanan-Smith's attention is distracted by the approach of his civil servant friend, who meekly explains that he and Rita are heading off to find a bite to eat. Buchanan-Smith grins. "Enjoy yourselves," waving them away like some benevolent king. It seems the cue for the other courtiers to follow suit, gathering jackets and ties and coats to step out into the night. Above Frank Sinatra's melodious phrasing, she hears laughter outside, car doors shutting, one, maybe two cars. Chauffeurs or arranged taxis? She has no idea which. It doesn't matter. She's alone with Jim now. There's business to be done. To her surprise he pulls his uncoiled body from the sofa and crosses the parquet floor to the record player, lifting the needle to replace Sinatra with a sudden silence. "I don't think we need old blue eyes to entertain us anymore."

She smiles, adjusting to the change in tone, following her breath to relax her diaphragm. "I'm sure he won't take offence."

She watches him move to the kitchen, pulling open the door of the fridge to fish for another bottle of champagne. "I wish I could say that of my department. I'm always briefed not to say this or that for fear of offending some trumped up little leader in a third world state. I sometimes wonder if we'll get to a point where you're forbidden to say anything except vacuous comments about a bowler's throw or the chance of showers tomorrow. And even then someone will argue about how you define shower. And I'll be thrown to the scrapheap. Anyway, now's not the time for despair, and certainly not when I'm in the delightful company of such a beautiful woman. I saved some vintage champers for us. Should be rather good."

He cracks open the bottle with artificial ceremony. She laughs as the cork shoots to the ceiling, wondering quite what to make of him. She hadn't expected the hint of doubt. It doesn't exactly endear her to him but she can see he's more complex than she'd anticipated. Perhaps he really was trying to tell her something with his little speech about boarding school, rather than just a well-worn route to foreplay. With two fresh champagne goblets in one hand and the bottle in the other, he settles back down beside her, clasping the stems so tightly that he can pour from one to the other without spilling a drop. Despite the flicker of vulnerability he's still a peacock then.

"You've obviously done this before."

He hands her the glass, his face closer than ever so that she smells his skin, a combination of aftershave and pressed linen. "My father taught me. The one skill he passed on. Your health."

She sips from the glass, aware of the richness and depth of taste. She's never drunk champagne like it.

"What do you think?"

He seems genuinely to care for her opinion. It's oddly touching, despite everything. She smiles. "It beats Pepsi."

He laughs, a delighted guttural splurge. "Spoken like a true American."

"I guess you'd say we lack sophistication."

"Not at all. As a matter of fact I'm rather fond of the Americans."

She smiles, again, her top-level seduction smile. All kittenish and doughy-eyed. "But I'm guessing you're not very fond of our tastes. Rock n roll, drive in restaurants, Lucille Ball. Aren't they a little too cheap for an Englishman of your rank?" She finds it hard to believe that she's defending American commercialism, but if it's a way in, it's easy to play.

She's amused him again but from the more muted response she can tell he hasn't taken it entirely as a face value quip. He fills her glass and then his. "I think you and I might have some very interesting conversations. I sincerely hope so at least." He reaches out to her hair, tucking it gently behind her ear. "But they're after dinner conversations. For later."

She lets him kiss her, which isn't unpleasant. She's had worse. His hand lingers around her face and she waits for the other to reach for her breast, or scurry, like a rat, up her dress. But instead he draws back, his nose touching hers, a breath between them. "Let's do this properly, like two consenting adults. One an American beauty, the other an admiring Englishman."

He takes her hand and encourages her to stand. "Bring your glass." Taking the bottle with him he leads her up the open staircase to the mezzanine floor. The bed, low and wide, is lined up against a brick wall. Opposite, a low wooden balcony looks over the sitting area. Three books lie on the floor, there's a shelf with an alarm clock. Nothing else of personal effect, just a G-Plan wardrobe on the far side of the bed. All this she takes in before he puts the bottle down on the shelf.

She takes a sip from her glass, aware that she's consumed enough to ease her inhibitions but not enough to lose control. Everything must be on her terms.

He smiles, half apologetic. "I hope you don't mind but I get a lot of satisfaction from seeing a woman undress."

"Is that another schoolboy thing?"

"Very astute."

"In that case I'm happy to comply. Provided you undress first."

She's delighted by the surprise on his face. "You American girls really are quite something."

She smiles, standing a distance away. Happy to see him squirm.

"We're just very modern."

For a moment he hesitates, his hand running across his shirt as if searching for another option. But it doesn't last. Seconds later he stands naked before her, a hairy, broad chest, impressively defined, but more pressingly an engorged penis that bobs and points at her in a way she'd find comic if she could just walk away.

She empties her head of any thought except mechanical objectives. Reaching for the zip at the side of her dress she pulls it down slowly until it reaches the end of its travel at the top of her hip. She slides the satin fabric from her shoulders, pulling it over her waist until the dress falls to the floor at her feet. She holds his gaze. His face is remarkably passive. Her bra unfastens with one deft move and drops between her fingers. She slides her pants off with two hands either side and then stands straight, her breathing shallower than she'd like, but he will interpret it as sexual arousal, which works in her favour.

"Come over here."

She walks towards him, but just distant enough that his penis doesn't touch her. He reaches his hand out to touch her breast. It's dry and warm, not unpleasant. Does it arouse her? She's not sure, such a confliction of emotions. No one's touched her with quite such tenderness since Robert. Who really was a schoolboy by comparison. Buchanan-Smith lifts his hands to her face, pressing his thumbs across her eyes and down to the lobes of her ears. Cupping her neck, pulling him towards her so that she feels his warmth against her, pressing his tongue hard into her mouth. She responds to his touch, falling against the back of his hand as he lowers her on to the bed, feeling his other hand reach across her breasts and down to her navel. And still he keeps travelling, fingers reaching her pubic hair but she is dry; it's too quick. She has to stall him.

"Hey." She tries to sound cute but firm. It works. His fingers hover then return to her breasts.

"Don't tell me this is your first."

Cute grin. "Let's just say I'm not planning on having your babies. So unless you've got something handy from the barber shop – then I guess we're back to basics."

She doesn't bother to tell him she has condoms in her bag. If he goes a bit slower she might yet respond. If it's all in the cause she might as well enjoy herself. For a moment he lingers over her face, smiling. She's terrified he's going to force her anyway and tries to suppress a rising panic. But he turns to the shelf, which now she sees, has a drawer underneath. Sitting up and turning away from her, she guesses what he's doing. She strokes his back sympathetically, quite grateful that he's not the type who'd ask her to slip it on for him. Too soon almost he's spun around again and she falls back, feeling his lips curl around her nipples as his hand slips to caress her upper thigh. She relinquishes to the moment. It's work. And she enjoys working.

But the separate part of her brain, the rational, objective part, thinks she hears something downstairs, a low thud, imprecise, it could be anything. She tries to dismiss it. Buchanan-Smith seems oblivious. She imagined he'd be a quick wham, bam, thank you mam, but he's gentle. Experienced. She hears a similar sound again. Nearer. And then a word, at first softly spoken, coming from the sitting room. It freezes her.

"Kitty?"

She recognises Alec Carter's voice. Buchanan-Smith lifts his head. Instantly alert.

"Oh, Jesus." She leaps from the bed, desperate to pull something around her.

"Kitty?" Louder this time. He's ascending the stairs. She sees his face, it's obvious from his eyes that he's been drinking. But he takes it all in at a glance.

Before she can reason, ameliorate, do anything, Buchanan-Smith launches himself down the stairs. "Who the fuck are you?!" She watches him thrust his hands at Alec, so hard that the younger man falls backward, crashing to a heap on the floor. "What the fuck are you doing in my house?!" She tries to reason with Buchanan-Smith but she can't stop him. He begins to kick, hard as he can. "Get up, you little piece of shit." She remonstrates again but he's deaf to her. Kicks again then convinced his man is down, turns to Kitty. "Who the fuck is this?!"

But before she can answer Alec has grabbed his leg, pulling him down in one solid move so that his back hits the floor. Winded. Fighting. Desperate for breath.

She pleads to Alec. "You've got to go. Now. I'll explain later."

He meets her eye. Blooded face. Deranged. Like a wild animal, she thinks. "Go now. It's dangerous. For both of us."

His breathing is hard and fast. Still he doesn't speak. For a moment he hovers, she thinks she's persuaded him. A little more coaxing. "Please, my darling. You have to trust me."

At that he bows his head, almost as if in prayer. Perhaps his rage has passed. Then suddenly he falls on Buchanan-Smith, pummelling his head till he's a bloody wreck; slipping off to the floor beside him, exhausted.

Watching from above, it transcends to theatre. She has withdrawn from the stage and can now put her critical faculties to action. Unsure whether Buchanan-Smith is alive or dead, she assumes the latter, her first consideration is to deal with Alec Carter. She dresses quickly, unbothered whether he sees her, and descends the stairs with barely a glance at the splayed body of her short-term lover. "We need to clean you up, Alec."

He follows her to the bathroom. She grasps a flannel from the side of the bath to wash his face. He only has minor cuts. Once she's cleaned the blood he doesn't look too bad. "How much have you had to drink?"

"Not enough to forget that it hurts."

"You'll hurt a lot more tomorrow. Are you sober enough to follow instructions?"

"Is he dead? Who is he?"

"None of that matters. Listen to me. I don't know how you got here but you have to get out now."

His face contorts, numb shock shifting to fear. "Oh Christ, he's dead. They'll hang me for that."

"No they won't. I'm not going to let them. But you have to do as I tell you. Okay?"

"Jesus, Kitty, who the hell is he? And who are you? What's the hell's going on here? Christ, Kitty. Jesus Christ, we can't leave him there."

He makes for the bathroom door but she blocks him. "No, listen. Leave him to me. This is bigger than just you and me. Much bigger. Please trust me, Alec. I'll explain everything but you have to go now. No questions. Just do it. For me. Please, Alec. If you want us to be together I can make it happen. Everything can be okay."

"Jesus, what have I done?"

"You're drunk. Let me deal with it. I can solve this."

"Solve it how? How am I supposed to believe anything you say?"

"At this moment you don't have a choice."

He hesitates. She prays he'll do as she asks.

"Where? Where can I go, for fuck's sake? They'll find us sooner or later."

She brings her arm down and crosses the sitting room to her bag, still nestled on the sofa. Before Alec has a chance to examine Buchanan-Smith she thrusts an envelope of notes into his hand. "Where's your passport?"

"In my room at college."

"Get the next train. There should still be a late one tonight. Take a cab to the station but wait to pick it up till you're a few blocks away from here. You'll have to ring for the porter when you're back at Cambridge. Tell him you had a drunken night. Get your passport, pack a bag and leave by the back entrance. Climb over the wall if you have to. Get the first train from Cambridge to Ipswich where you change for Harwich. Only ask for directions if you have to. Play the smart gentleman about town. At Harwich you'll take the boat to Hamburg and from there another train to Berlin. Now tell me you've taken that in.

"Who are you, Kitty? What were you doing here?"

"There's no time to explain now, Alec. Just trust me." She scribbles on to a scrap of paper. "Go to this address in East Berlin. It's just under a mile into the Soviet sector, north-east of Alexanderplatz. My friend Ursula lives there. When you cross into the East, tell them you're just a tourist, if they ask. Tell her that I sent you and I'll be there the same day. Tell her you're a friend, a political one. You're there because you have Marxist sympathies. But no more. Don't mention this. Have you got that?"

He looks down at the piece of paper.

"This money should be enough to cover you. Give some to Ursula so she can feed you. Now go. Now."

She can see he's hesitating. "I'll see you in Berlin, my darling." She forces a smile, reaching up to kiss his cut lip. Tasting blood. "I promise you it'll be worth the wait."

He returns her smile. She sees a confused child. It only confirms what she already knew. She's fallen in love with him. And now they're paying the price.

"I won't leave without you."

She kisses him again. "If you wait for me, it'll end up too late for both of us. This is our only hope, Alec. Now go, please, for both our sakes."

She waits for his response, breathing hard. Finally he turns, descending the stairs. The door shuts behind him. She peeps out from the corner of the curtain to witness him disappear into the darkness.

Returning to Buchanan-Smith she finds no imminent sign of recovery. His body hasn't moved, still splayed across the floor, a trickle of blood slipping across the contours of his chin to collect in a sticky pool. She checks his pulse. It's weak but steady. But lifting his eyelids there's no sign of reflex in the pupils so she calculates she has sufficient time to sort the flat first. Starting on the mezzanine floor, she removes the spent condom and gathers Buchanan-Smith's clothes to stack them in a neat pile on his G-Plan chair which she moves to the top of the staircase. In the reception area she washes up all remnants of the party, including her own glass, and slips Sinatra back in his cover sleeve beside the record player. It takes her forty minutes.

Buchanan-Smith still lies in the middle of the room. He has stopped bleeding but a pool of blood congeals on the parquet. She wipes it up, grateful the floor is so well sealed so no traces can seep through the cracks. He doesn't stir. In the bathroom she opens the mirrored cabinet and explores its contents; razors, tweezers, after shave, and at the back, as she'd hoped, a bottle of Aspirin. She fills the toothbrush mug with water, takes his flannel and crouches back beside her patient. As she'd suspected he's begun to revive. She wipes his face with cool water. There's only one serious cut, the rest is bruising or grazes. Fuelled by alcohol, Alec hadn't been quite as efficient as he might have liked. Buchanan-Smith stirs, moaning at first before his words begin to gain some coherence.

"Here, rest a minute." She wipes the blood from his face, cradling his head in her lap.

He begins to test his limbs, at once searching around him.

"It's ok. He's gone." Her words are emollient, tender. He touches her hand.

"Thank you."

"We need to get you upstairs to bed. Then I'll call a doctor."

"No. No need. Just help me up."

It's the answer she'd anticipated. Otherwise she wouldn't have suggested it. He seems unaware of his nakedness. To Kitty he looks like a baby, or a Buddha. A helpless bundle of flesh. Slowly she eases him up to a sitting position. No broken bones as far as she can tell. The ascent of the stairs takes huge effort. She wonders if they'll ever reach the top.

"Rest for a moment while I make your bed." She eases him on to the chair. "Take these, you'll need them." She places two Aspirin into his opened mouth and helps him to a sip of water.

"You're bleeding a little again." She wipes the blood from his face, dropping the crimson tissue on to the shelf. "Maybe you ought to take two more. It'll help you sleep." He complies with her wish, too weak and vulnerable to protest, groaning at the increased realisation of intense pain. She smiles sympathetically. "Better make that one more. You need some serious recuperation. When's your wife expecting you back?"

"Tomorrow evening."

"Good. The longer you sleep the better." Instead of one Aspirin she gives him two but he shows no sign of protesting. "Okay, stay there. No jumping on me."

He attempts to smile at her joke. She turns her back to him and begins to draw the disordered sheets back across the bed. Her work rate is deliberately slow, as if she wants him to see that she's taking great care, stroking the folds out of the sheets as she places them; the action repetitive, almost hypnotic.

"Who was he? And who's Kitty?"

She doesn't turn around, attending to the corners of the blanket. "Someone I once knew. It was my nickname. He bears a grudge that's all. Not anybody you need worry about." Immediately she spins around, thrusting her full weight at the chair, releasing as it topples back, dipping and spinning, crashing over the stairs on to the parquet floor below. There wasn't even time for him to squeal. His head, crooked at an acute angle, lies trapped under the broken chair; the side of his face flattened against the floor, one eye open like a dead fish at a stall. She cleans her fingerprints from the Aspirin bottle and places it next to his cocktail glass on the bedroom shelf. Descending the stairs she checks his pulse again. There is none. There's time to grab some rest before Ed Grant arrives so she lies on the sofa, collecting her thoughts, and as calmly as her mind will allow, considers her options.

By six thirty in the morning she feels tired but remarkably clear headed. Dabbing her face with cold water and applying a swift layer of lipstick she collects her bag and her coat and slips down the stairs to the front door. The sash window next to it is still raised so she closes it. Presumably how Alec Carter made his spectacular entrance. The mews is quiet except for a tabby cat which curls itself around her feet. She'd like to stroke it but resists the temptation, walking quickly beyond the locked and broken garage doors to the end of the street. The burgundy Magnette is parked discreetly across the road beneath a row of lime trees. She wishes it made her feel safe but instead she's filled with a deep sense of foreboding.

She flattens her coat, takes a breath of air and climbs into the car. He smiles, a deep blue pool of charm. "It was quite a search this time of the morning. I hope you appreciate it." He throws a paper bag on to her lap. The rich smell of fresh croissant.

"Thanks." She wonders which way to tell him what's happened. But there's no good way. The car surges away from the curb, her stomach left behind. Still in Buchanan-Smith's sitting room.

"Aren't you going to eat it?" He's looking at her. She wishes he'd keep his eyes on the road.

"I'm not hungry. There's been an accident."

"What sort of accident?" He swings the car round Marble Arch, heading north.

"It went wrong. Buchanan-Smith's dead. I tried to make it look like suicide but…"

"…Christ! What the hell happened?" He veers away from the curb.

"Carter turned up. He must have found out where we were, I don't know how. He broke in, obviously drunk. I tried to reason with him but he wouldn't listen. He punched Buchanan-Smith to within an inch of his life. Afterwards I managed to get rid of him. Then I had to do the rest."

"You're sure he's dead?"

"I know my job. He broke his neck."

"Your job was to fuck him, not kill him."

"My job was to seduce him. Which I did very successfully."

He doesn't answer for a moment. She resists looking at his face though she's desperate to know what he's thinking.

"Where's Alec now?"

She's already formulated a reply, knowing the question would be asked. If Ed gets to him she can't predict what will happen. She needs to tread carefully. "I sent him back to Cambridge. He doesn't know whether Buchanan-Smith's dead or not. It gives up some scope."

"But he must know something. What have you told him?"

"I didn't tell him anything. He probably had no idea who Buchanan-Smith is."

"So he knows nothing about you? You're just an American whore as far as he's concerned."

"I guess I am." She doesn't want to elaborate though her comrade's word sting. Her one hope is that Alec makes it to Berlin and they can appease for their misdemeanours. At least they'll be together. She waits for Ed to say something but he's gone quiet. Which is the worst. Her instinct is to appear conciliatory. A team. "What do you think we should do?"

He glances across at her, contempt replacing the easy charm of minutes ago. "Head back to Cambridge. Pretend this never happened. There might be a way out. I just need to consult with Berlin."

He races up the awakening streets. Her mind spins. If he drops her back at Stratham she can make a quick escape before he realises. But suddenly the car slows abruptly, pulling up at the kerb beside a telephone box. "I thought we were going straight back." The alarm in her voice is barely disguised.

"This is a big problem. I need to let them know first. Wait here." He steps out, slipping around the front of the bonnet to the kiosk. She watches him dial a number, his face turning away from view once he's connected. Assessing the surroundings, she sees they're parked on a long, straight road. No bends, virtually no side roads, just a dusty street lined with soot black terraced houses. No pedestrians either, not even a milkman doing his rounds. She knows the deal. Ed will be reviewing her situation with Berlin. A failed agent. She knows what happens to them. She considers running but she's in heels for Christ's sake. Even if she whipped them off, how far would she get? Ed still has his back to her in the phone box. She reaches out, pressing on the cool, polished wood of the glove box. It yields to her touch. Behind the binoculars she finds confirmation of her momentary glimpse. A small, grey pistol. Curling her fingers around its cold handle, she immediately recognises the model. Makarov semi-automatic. To her relief it's loaded. She drops it to her lap, concealed beneath the line of her coat.

His face is impossible to read when he returns to the car. He might as well have popped out for a newspaper. She hasn't yet made her mind up how to play it. She needs clues. But Ed is giving away none. It irritates her that he's being so professional. She wonders where his heart really lies, it's buried so deep she contemplates whether it exists at all. He replaces the keys in the ignition. Had he left them would she have driven off? Yes, if she could drive. Why hadn't they taught her that at Belzig? She should mention it when she gets back. If she gets back. Controlling her breath she struggles to sound calm. Professional.

"So?"

He casts her a desultory glance. "We drive home." He pulls away, hands rigid on the steering wheel.

"And that's it?"

"My contact wants to interview you. So we can review the situation."

Now she knows he's lying. Nobody introduces their contact, it's like giving your boyfriend's phone number to your best friend. "He's in town I guess." She knows he must operate from somewhere in London, otherwise why's Ed always rushing down from Cambridge.

"Not tonight. He's got a place on our way back. We'll meet him there."

Her skin turns cold, her hands clammy, every sense working overtime. A place on our way back. Euphemism. Most likely a wood. A ditch. The end. They're heading north, the tight city dwellings surrendering to semi-detached houses. Acres of them. The British love affair. A traffic light turns red as they approach a main junction. She needs to head west, the rest Ed will have to figure out. "I think you'll want to make a left turn here."

His eyes are still on the lights. "Cambridge is straight on." Red turns to amber.

"Nevertheless, I'd like you to turn left." She lifts the pistol from her coat, pointing at his neck.

261

He doesn't flinch. "Am I allowed to know why?"

"I don't want to miss my plane."

As the light switches back from green to amber he revs the car and swings round west on to the main road. "Big mistake, comrade. Running won't help."

"It's called preservation. I'm sure you'd do the same."

"Except I wouldn't have made errors in the first place. The petty theft of a Dorchester lighter which you showed to Carter. Your schoolgirl mistakes have pitched us all into the fire, comrade. They'll find you, wherever you go."

"Maybe. But if you don't mind, I haven't slept and I'm incredibly tired. Let's not talk anymore until we say goodbye." To her relief he seems to comply. Perhaps he's sick of the whole thing himself. She keeps the pistol aimed at his head, pressing herself against the door of the car. He never asks her to lower it, maybe hoping a stray police patrol car will spot them. Unlikely and what would he say? Perhaps he's quietly shitting himself. Praying for mummy to rescue him. She remembers he told her it wasn't a game. Maybe for Edward Grant, until now, it's been just that. She never did quite get him. What's his motive? Posh boy rails against the injustices of the world. Bring on the champagne.

The Magnette speeds away from the cresting sun towards London airport. A circus of municipal, single storey buildings lines the edge of the runway; beside them a group of large canvas tents, outside which the names of airlines are displayed on makeshift boards. He pulls the car up outside the main building and cuts the engine. A BOAC Stratocruiser lumbers past beyond the rail fencing. She wonders how to say goodbye. She doesn't want to be unfriendly. He hasn't tried to trick her again. Still the remnants of an English gent. But she doesn't lower the gun. "Thank you, comrade. I'm sorry it didn't work out the way we hoped. It was my error, I accept that, but it wasn't a big enough mistake to die for."

He tries to smile. But it bears more the hallmarks of a grimace. "It wasn't personal. In this business if you don't do what you're told, you don't survive."

"Well, we'll see about that. It was nice working with you."

"It was a pleasure to be seen with a beautiful woman."

She steps out of the car. "Maybe we'll meet again one day. In happier times."

I'll look forward to that."

She closes the door, not moving until the car has vanished from sight and she can drop her raised arm back to her side. Turning towards the airport buildings she's starkly aware of her choices. She could buy a ticket at the BOAC hut and fly back to Philadelphia. Her mother and father would be delighted. And it's unlikely anyone would hunt her down that far away. She might even persuade herself that her life could resume its former path. Or she could take a BEA flight to Berlin. If she shows contrition the East German government might just incarcerate her for a short period. It's a risk. But afterwards she could be re-united with Alec. They could live together in East Berlin, grow old together, two model citizens in a blossoming Socialist state. Perhaps it's a fantasy. She's too tired to think straight. A black cab draws up at the curb. An elegant woman steps out, swaddled in a long fur coat, her head tilted to the sky in recognition of her standing. She insists the driver carries her numerous cases to the terminal, or at the very least, finds her a porter. To Kitty's dismay he complies. Once the commotion is over, and the black cab has scuttled back towards the city, she takes the pistol from her pocket and drops it to the bottom of the nearest litter bin. Reaching in the other pocket, she fishes for a packet of cigarettes. Her hand is trembling. She wasn't lying when she told Ed Grant she felt overwhelmed with fatigue. A cigarette might help.

17

Watching Kitty wave farewell in the rear-view mirror feels uglier than the pistol she pointed at his head. He tries to convince himself it's the professional ignominy. His monstrous cock up. In truth he's not so sure. It's another claw at his disfigured heart.

On the drive back from the airport Ed mulls over what happened, second guessing what Atherton may throw at him. Should he have wrestled the pistol from her grasp? At best he'd have lost control of the car; an accident would involve the police. If he'd asked where she was going, she'd have refused to say, or lied. So what option was there? Pulling the Magnette up at the corner of the sleepy, Bayswater street there's one thought that nags him, eating away at his conscience. He knows Atherton has always thought of him as an amateur, a bit player who's ultimately expendable. He's aware he's not a top-class recruit, not a bigwig in the foreign office, not a Donald Maclean or Burgess. In Atherton's eyes he's not much more interesting than a kid who resents his father. Maybe he's right. He's glad that Kitty Bernstein found the gun. It was a stupid error, leaving the glove box unlocked; worse than hers. But the alternative, his orders, were too grim to contemplate. Making her dig a hole in a wood. Asking her politely to turn around. The back of her skull exploding. A cold-blooded execution.

He's surprised to find Molly at the door. She beckons him in without a word but still he feels a pang of relief, as if, like a dutiful mother, she might see his side of the story. Atherton is at the desk, his attention consumed by a bank of radios. The valves spread a warm, amber glow on to the wall behind. Seeing Ed he slips the headphones from his ears. "Well?

Ed remains by the door. It seems prudent. "She found the Makarov when I called you from the phone box. She waited till I was driving before she pulled it on me. I'm sorry."

Atherton sighs. "Where did you take her?"

"London Airport. She didn't say where she was going. With a pistol at my head I wasn't in a position to ask."

"Unlocked gloved compartment. My fuck up."

"We all make mistakes under pressure." But he knows he doesn't sound convincing.

In the corner of his vision he sees Molly move to the cabinet by the fireplace. "I'll make some tea." There's a small camping stove on which she places a kettle, lighting the stove with a match before pouring a drop of milk in to three, identical cups. It's all so ridiculously domestic, he thinks. If only it were.

Atherton watches his wife too. Thinking time. When he speaks his voice is flat, unreadable. "She'll probably run back to the States for safety. I'll tell Berlin but there's nothing we can do about her. For now. You said on the phone she told Carter to go back to Cambridge."

"Yes." He takes the tea from Molly's hand and drinks in gulps. It's sweeter than he'd normally take it but he's grateful for the hit.

"Sit down, Edward" she says. "There's no point in rushing this through. That way more mistakes are made."

But Atherton show less generosity. "The biggest has already happened. We need to shut this down as quickly as possible."

Molly's still indicating the armchair which he settles in to reluctantly. The chair beside him, the one Atherton usually sits in, remains empty. He hasn't moved from the radio. "First you head back to Cambridge, check if he's there. What does he know about her?"

"Nothing. At least that's what she claims."

"Let's hope it's the truth. For all our sakes. Especially yours. He won't know yet that Buchanan-Smith's dead but he'll see it in the papers on Monday. Find out what state he's in and stop him from going to the police if he's feeling too fucking moral about his part in it. Tell him he might swing on a rope. Molly, you go too. Find a cheap hotel to stay then go to the school first thing tomorrow; tell the headmistress you're sorry to say Miss Bernstein suffered a burst appendix and died before they got her to hospital, or whatever the hell you want, and that she'll be flown back to her parents in the States. Go and see the kids if you must but make it credible and final. Ed's her cousin so that makes you her aunt. They'll take it better coming from you."

Molly drops her cup back on to the cabinet. "Give me ten minutes."

She disappears into another room. One that Ed's never seen. Presumably a bedroom. He can't imagine they ever have sex; it doesn't seem that kind of marriage. He wonders how his mind can deviate so inappropriately. But then he's a sordid deviant. Answer right there.

Atherton drains his cup, reviewing the tea leaves as if to divine his future. "You know this changes everything."

"The thought had crossed my mind."

"I'll do my best to save you. Sometimes we let the small fish swim away. The minnows. But only if we're sure they'll swim out to sea and either drown or never swim to shore again. Doing that would be fatal."

Ed lights a cigarette, not offering one to Atherton, desperate to show some composure, no matter how manufactured. A trail of exhaled smoke twists to the ceiling. He fakes a laugh. "I'd never thought of myself as a minnow. I suppose I was too arrogant, assuming bigger things lay ahead of me. My crime isn't the mistake I made. Anyone could have done that. It's that I'm neither part of the establishment nor the proletariat. I'm bourgeois. The biggest crime of all."

Atherton barely flinches. "Your crime, as you put it, is that you think too much about yourself. And if you're a bourgeois, like you say, then I think, in the circumstances, you should be very grateful nobody notices you."

Molly re-emerges with a small, leather travel case. "Try to remember to switch it off when you go to bed. We don't want the place going up in flames."

Atherton rises from his stool, kissing his wife, and herding them towards the door. He holds out his hand which Ed reluctantly accepts. "Drive carefully."

He doesn't reply.

As soon as they're inside the car Molly lays her palm across his bony fingers. He realises his hand is shaking. "If you do as Jim requested, you'll be fine." Her voice is a tonic. Soothing. Barely more than a whisper. "Don't let your mind wander, just execute the plan. And remember, the sacrifice will be worth it."

He tries to smile. Thank God for Molly. But her display of kindness leaves him vulnerable to self-pity, which he can't countenance. The dam would burst.

He drives off at speed, aware of a sudden, crushing fatigue which plays havoc with his road judgement. Wisely she doesn't reproach him when he skips a red light; shouting just once when his eyes drift from the A1 and the car swerves towards the fields. His knuckles are rapped. A child contained.

He drops her at the nearest hotel to Cambridge station. It seems a pragmatic choice, if not the smartest place in town.

She pats his hand. More like patting a dog this time, he thinks. "Pretend you know nothing. Just keep him calm till tomorrow morning. I'll be outside at 7.30."

He leaves the car at the station and walks back to college, heart slaying his chest, his breathing snatched, pulse racing.

"Late night, sir?" The porter is beaming. "You and Mr Carter are quite a double act."

A key drops into his open palm. Cold metal. "Did he get back very late?"

"Not back at all yet, sir. Unless he snuck over the wall, of course."

Ed conjures another laugh. "Wouldn't be surprised."

'Nor me, sir."

He hurries across the front court, passing through the arch towards Thornton Buildings. Reaching the narrow landing he sees straightaway that the door has been forced upon. Splinters of wood lie on the floor. His room-mate's bed is untouched, the blanket pristine. The wardrobe door swings on its hinges; inside nothing but an empty rail where Alec Carter's clothes once hung. What had he expected? Retrieving the hip flask from his bedside cabinet he sips till his belly warms. A panacea of sorts. Emergency medication. He draws back the covers of his room-mate's bed. The familiar, blue-striped pyjamas are stacked beneath his pillow. There's no note. Just a few strands of jet-black hair. It was a vain hope. Lying down on the bed he can smell hair tonic on the pillow.

He thinks of rushing back to Molly. But that's just cowardice; clinging to apron strings. Instead, he steps back outside, climbing over the back wall to avoid the porter, and slips into the nearest telephone box.

Atherton answers promptly. "Yes?"

"He's not here. Must've decided it's too uncomfortable."

There's a pause. "He'll turn up somewhere. Anything else?"

"No."

"Hang around the college. Be seen. If anyone asks about him feign ignorance. Play it down."

He needs more but the phone hangs up at the other end. Just the dialling tone to talk to.

Climbing back over the wall, he returns to his room, slumping onto the bed. He needs to collect his thoughts but sleep beckons him first; a fevered sleep, spoiled by dreams that both disturb and arouse. It's mid-afternoon by the time he finally wakes, a warm sunlight touching his eyelids. The gentle chatter of carefree students emanates from the courtyard below. Reluctantly, he knows he must join them, seeking out those acquaintances who hang out with Alec; battering away any curiosity at his room-mate's absence with his usual bonhomie. Though it all now seems in vain. A hollow and pointless mask. Still, in an hour or so he'll march with them to the pub and feign his drinking, as he always does, before retiring again to his room.

Except by nightfall sleep eludes him. Hours tick by, the clarity of his fragile state fuelled by the silence; fear gripping his heart so tight he barely dares to breathe.

At 7.30 the next morning he pulls the Magnette round to the forecourt of the station hotel. Molly steps from the foyer, her bearing somehow even more matronly than usual. Instead of the usual sweater and slacks she's chosen a high collared, cream blouse under a short jacket, with a pleated, flannel skirt. Slipping in beside him he's aware of a vaguely familiar lavender scent. The sort his old aunts would wear.

She wastes no time with polite greetings. "Jim says there's no news."

He pushes the Magnette out to the main road. "He broke in. God knows where he is now."

As they head north Molly's gaze remains fixed at some indeterminate point beyond the windscreen. He wonders if she's anticipating more of his careless driving. More likely she's ashamed of him; the Prodigal Son, returning empty handed. She checks her face in the vanity mirror. Again, quite unlike her. But at last she turns towards him. "He's either panicked and run for the hills or Kitty Bernstein was lying to you when you picked her up. Jim's convinced she didn't tell you the truth. His instinct is usually pretty accurate. He's very good at smelling rats."

He doesn't answer, wondering if she was issuing some kind of veiled threat. The words of sympathy only eight hours ago replaced by a steely edge. Perhaps Atherton rebuked her for being too soft or maybe he's just never seen Molly in a professional guise before. The baking thing was always so homely. Maybe he fell for it too readily.

"How far?" she asks, after they've been driving for twenty minutes.

271

"We turn off at the next village. Then it's another three miles. There's a couple of other villages we pass through first."

She stares out at the bare fields. "I never understood why anyone would want to live in the country. Nothing changes except the seasons. And they're so predictable."

He wants to laugh but it feels inappropriate. So alien to his circumstance.

Plainly bored by what she sees, she returns her attention to the task. "You should do most of the talking when we arrive. I'll play the grieving aunt. But if a suitable opportunity presents itself I'll stretch it a bit, a few noble words on fortitude at times of tragedy."

He wonders at her callousness. It's children they're dealing with. But then Molly never had children, if that makes any difference. "The headmistress is a bit of a cool cucumber. She should be fine. But her secretary, Jane Farley, she could be a bit messy."

"Messy?"

"I think she had a crush on Bernstein."

"Who doesn't?" Eyes cast to the vanity mirror, she applies a thin line of lipstick across puckered lips. "We'll deal with whatever comes. I think Jim's idea of the ruptured appendix is good but let's avoid details. It shouldn't be hard. The British are always too polite to press for the gore. By the way, if asked I'm Mrs Anderson. I assume you have a cover name?"

"Grainger."

"Edward?"

"Yes."

"How boring."

He draws the car up outside the school as the bell peels for assembly. In an instant the playground rinses itself of all children except for three older boys who continue to kick a football at the brick wall. A school master admonishes them with a shrill whistle. Once the evacuation is complete, Ed steps out into the damp chilled air, opening the passenger door with exaggerated formality. A ritual. He leads Molly through the playground to the school office. Jane Farley, late for assembly, almost collides with him, her face registering surprise but instantly composing itself when she recognises Kitty Bernstein's cousin.

"Oh, Mr…Grainger. How nice to see you? I'm afraid Miss Bernstein's not here yet. Is there anything I can do? I'm afraid I'm late for assembly so if…"

He steps forward, blocking her path. "…I'm afraid I have some news, about my cousin. May I introduce Kitty's aunt, Mrs Anderson, her mother's sister?"

Molly bows her head instead of extending her hand. Sensing their earnestness, life drains from Jane Farley's face. Pale as school milk.

He continues, voice low, sombre. Appropriate. "I'm afraid it's a terrible shock. She suffered a ruptured appendix. By the time they got her to hospital it was too late. I'm terribly sorry to bring you such awful news but we thought we should drive up here to tell you in person. Mrs Anderson insisted. We were having such a lovely time. It really doesn't quite seem true."

"Miss Bernstein? Surely not?"

"I'm so very sorry I…" He sees Jane Farley start to crumble and wonders how to play it. But Molly has already stepped ahead of him, gathering the distraught woman to her arms, stroking her

273

hair, containing the tremors that spill from within her. She produces a lace handkerchief from her pocket and pats it into the young woman's hand, encouraging her to wipe her eyes; an emollient flow of empathy nursing her patient to composure.

Jane Farley dabs her eyes. "How awful. I'm so sorry. I can't quite…If you don't mind, I think I should get the headmistress out of assembly. I'm sure she'd like to speak to you, but only if you feel you could…"

"…Of course, my dear." Molly delivers a reassuring smile. "We'll wait here."

They exchange no words while Jane Farley is gone. He observes Molly tapping her fingers on the tan handbag, as if she might be waiting for the dentist. He has no desire to fill the space, desperate to convince himself all the deceit is necessary. In years to come these children will thank them for it. Come the revolutionary dawn.

The headmistress arrives wearing a tweed suit, barely a shade different to her short, mousy hair. Her face is arranged in sympathy, her hand, when he shakes it, drier than sand. "Mr Grainger, Mrs Anderson, I'm so terribly sorry, may I express my condolences to you both. She was such a vital young lady. The children adored her. Such a terrible shock."

Molly smiles beatifically. "She was extremely fond of them. She spoke so much about them."

"It won't be easy for them, I must confess. They'll be gathering now, poor things. She always gave the first class on Monday morning."

He wonders what to say. But Molly intervenes again, biting her lower lip in what he supposes is feigned humility. "I wonder whether it might be an idea if I speak with them. I'm a trained primary school teacher, retired now, but I do have some understanding of children. It might help if I have a few words."

It's not a move he'd expected and clearly the headmistress is equally surprised. But something in Molly's compassionate and intelligent face prevents a rebuff. Perhaps this woman is delighted to pass the buck. He can't imagine her hollow personality providing much of a cushion when the children fall.

"That's very good of you, Mrs Anderson, if you're sure you feel up to it. They might find it easier to accept, coming from her family. Miss Farley and I will accompany you. One's mind goes back to the war when so many children had difficulties coming to terms with the loss of their parents, particularly if they'd been evacuated to the countryside."

She leads them, crocodile fashion, down the corridor. Passing frosted glass panels, he absorbs the amorphous shape of children settling to their desks, a teacher issuing short commands, tapping the wooden blackboard eraser to gain attention. Kitty Bernstein's class is at the farthest end of the corridor. He lets the others enter before him, halting at the doorway to witness the expectant gaze of twelve or more children, all somewhere between nine and eleven, he guesses. He imagines they only chose to study German because Kitty Bernstein was younger, and probably more fun, than the other teachers.

The headmistress hushes the room with outstretched arms. All eyes fall on her with collective obedience. She lowers her arms to her side. "Good morning, everybody. I have something to impart to you which I'm afraid is not very agreeable. This is Mrs Anderson, Miss Bernstein's aunt and her cousin, Mr Grainger. They motored here specially to speak with you this morning but the news they bring is, I'm afraid, most unfortunate. Mrs Anderson will speak with you directly

Ed watches Molly tiptoe to the front of the class, aware that some of the children already hold their bodies for a blow; fists clenched, mouths fallen. She holds her empathy with the skill of an accomplished funeral director. "Good morning, girls and boys. My name's Molly, I'm Miss Bernstein's aunt. But let's call Miss Bernstein, 'Kitty', today because I'm sure some of you probably think of her as a friend."

A couple of nervous smiles break to the surface, as if barely able to comprehend this informality. "Many of us will have had friends who've moved away, or even friends who don't want to be friends any more, for some silly reason best known to themselves. And that can be very sad. But it's not their fault, they can't always control the things that happen to them; sometimes difficult things that we don't understand. We musn't judge them or blame them. I'm afraid it's the same with poor Kitty. Yesterday, while we were together with her at a party, she suddenly fell ill. We tried to help but it was clear that she needed to go to hospital so we called an ambulance. She was still cheerful and joked that she wouldn't be able to test your German vocabulary today. But in the ambulance she fell asleep. And then when they got her to hospital, the doctors didn't manage to wake her up. So I'm so sorry to tell you that Kitty won't be here today. Or ever again. I'm so sorry. But you were in her heart. And you always will be."

Only the muffled words of the teacher in the neighbouring classroom break the spell that Molly has cast. He sees children glancing at one another. Some suppressing twitches, others like stone. The first to raise her hand is an older girl, her frown bullish, almost hostile. "D'you mean she's dead, miss?"

The headmistress steps forward. "Rose Thorpe, we don't talk like that…"

But Molly interrupts "…Yes, Rose, I'm afraid I do."

The girl stares at her for a moment. He thinks she might cry or hurl abuse, but instead she drops her eyes to her desk, her face now hidden by hair. A boy blows his nose with his handkerchief. Again the headmistress intervenes. "Now, now, there's no need for tears, Tom."

He pulls the handkerchief from his face. Thrusts it to his pocket. Scrabbles from his desk to the door.

The headmistress glances apologetically at Molly. "Tom Gilliam. One of our more challenging boys."

Returning to the car, Ed lingers by the opened door while Molly offers a final caring hand to Jane Farley, before turning, head reverently bowed, to abandon the school forever. As they leave Stratham she delves into her handbag for another handkerchief and dabs at her eyes. "Drop me off at Cambridge station please, Edward." There's no hint of vulnerability in her voice. "No need to report this to Jim. I'll tell him what happened."

He feels his senses misaligning, unable to fathom the forensic detail of their visit. "Couldn't we have just told Jane Farley that Kitty was ill and left it at that? Those kids."

She drops the handkerchief to her lap, spinning it between her fingers. "That's the point, Edward. They're children. As far as the Roses and the Toms know their heroine, Kitty Bernstein's, dead. It'll stay with them forever. They deserve to be treated with some respect." Her eyes turn back to the barren fields. "Sometimes, amongst all the deceits and whispers, and tragic casualties, it's easy to forget what we're doing this for. Perhaps we're a bit old school. We want to make the world safer for everyone yet we destroy lives along the way. Sacrifice of the few for the greater good, and all that. There's nothing new about it. But at least we can be certain our war is a just one. It's worth the fight. Please remember that next time you lie for your country."

There is no reply. He knows he's not supposed to give one. He feels admonished and a little ashamed. She's right of course, but more than that he feels ridiculously hurt that it's Molly who's chastised him; someone whom he's always revered as a model of humanity. Quite unlike his own mother whose easy grace and smooth charm disguise a more brittle heart.

He finds his hands gripping the steering wheel a little tighter as they reach the outskirts of Cambridge. Probably the howling need of a ciggie. They haven't spoken for twenty minutes. It compounds his sense of foreboding, wondering how they'll part; what her last words to him will be. What he might decipher from them. Guiding the Magnette through the morning traffic he takes the route back to the station car park.

She slips her handkerchief, until now clutched between her fingers, back into the handbag. "No need to park, just drop me at the main entrance."

He has so many questions but to ask would show weakness. He needs to re-assess, to smarten his act. Find words that reassure her.

But she breaks his thought. "This is what I want you to do after you've dropped me. Walk back to the college, greet your porter and have a joke with him about Carter's disappearance. He won't have returned. Read the paper about Buchanan-Smith's death with as much speculation as anyone else. Meet with your college friends regularly, study hard and once it's obvious Alec Carter isn't coming back, which he won't, accept the sympathies of your fellow students and encourage all speculation. You can even jest that he might be a spy. Coming from your college, no one would be much surprised. Word's out that Maclean will emerge in Moscow pretty soon."

He draws up at the entrance. "Burgess too, I suppose?"

"If he hasn't already drowned himself in vodka." She clips her handbag shut and smiles "Goodbye, Edward, dear. Should we need any further information we'll contact you. I wish you a very successful career, whichever industry you choose."

She doesn't glance back when she slips away to the station concourse. No last wave or hesitant step. After she's evaporated within the building he hesitates, convinced somehow that she'll return, oblivious to the sporadic car horns which pierce the November air behind him.

A policeman wraps on his window, urging him to move on. He smiles apologetically, easing the Magnette out towards the road. Unsure which direction he should turn.

Cold Road to Imber

18

NOVEMBER 1954, WEST GERMANY

Alec disembarks onto the waking quayside at Hamburg exhausted and bilious. The crossing had been rough. His head is not yet adjusted to terra firma so he reaches for a cigarette to calm himself before asking the way to the main station. For the first hour of the train journey to Berlin he sleeps; the compartment is warm and airless, as soporific as a lullaby, but as the border between West and East Germany draws nearer his anxiety returns. At Schwanheide border guards step on to the train from the platform. The compartment door draws open and passports are demanded. Alec reaches for the English passport inside his coat and hands it to the guard, who glances at it, saying nothing before returning it to its keeper.

He has been lucky. At the next hurdle, the border between East Germany and the Allied enclave of West Berlin, some two hours away, he doesn't expect his luck to continue. Most likely he will be arrested by the West German authorities, a murderer on the run, wanted by the British Police who will have doubtless informed border controls. His shirt clings wet and cold to his back, the nausea returning, while his train travels relentlessly through a silent, forested landscape to reach the second border. But his fears are unfounded. The young East German border guard shows little curiosity, perhaps he slept badly too, and ten minutes later, having been similarly dismissed by West German guards, Alec steps from the carriage at Spandau into West Berlin. An unremarkable British tourist.

He takes the U-Bahn train to Kurfurstendamm; it's the one name he recognises, the Oxford Street of West Berlin. He has two objectives before heading on towards the Eastern sector, one to fill his jittery belly, the second to scour the English newspaper headlines.

Stepping out from the underground into the crisp morning light he observes a city remarkably at ease with itself. Lovers drift along the avenue arm in arm. Canary yellow trams glide by stores flaunting the latest trends; everything's for sale, from stainless steel electric kettles to fur coats and leather handbags. There's an upmarket gloss that surprises; perhaps more Regent Street than Oxford Street. He pauses at the nearest kiosk to scan the papers. The Times and the Daily Mail are two days out of date.

At a bustling café he orders pork schnitzel with boiled potatoes and coffee. The coffee arrives first, richer and stronger than anything he's tasted before. It clears his suffocated mind. When the waiter brings the meal, he eats like a starved dog, grateful for its soothing effect on his stomach. Pushing the plate aside he lights another cigarette and watches the world amble, untroubled, past the café window. A patchwork of images teases his mind; a bloodied jaw, a crumpled body, helpless as a beached whale. It was an accident. He'd drunk too much. Way too much. Either way, he's finished, despite Kitty's promises. He stabs the last of the cigarette into the ashtray, surprised at his command of German when he summons the waiter. Jim Atherton would be pleased. He'd always said he had a gift for languages.

From the same kiosk he buys a tourist map and chooses his route to the Brandenburg Gate. He heads north, his eye immediately drawn by an image he's seen so often in news reels it's somehow reassuring; the ruins of the Kaiser Wilhelm church, still standing in defiance of all that the war had flung at it, the tarnished bronze spire severed like a shattered limb, the rubble of bricks piled at its feet. A symbol of West Berlin's heroic survival.

The rumble of traffic dissolves as he reaches the gardens of the city zoo, and beyond it, a wooded parkland. Cyclists ride past him on well-tended paths, somehow incompatible with the aerial footage of slaughtered tenement blocks he'd seen in the cinema. Eventually the canopy of trees gives way to a broad boulevard, stretching in a precise line from west to east; recently renamed the Strasse des 17. Juni, to commemorate the uprising of workers in the Communist sector. To the east, about a mile away, he recognises the Brandenburg Gate, the neo-classical monument that now splits two opposing ideologies. The boulevard is surprisingly deserted except for an occasional car speeding west, as if in a hurry to leave. He turns east and begins the long walk towards the Gate. Drawing nearer, the burnt out remains of the Reichstag dominate the skyline. Once a seat of democratic parliament, now more famously the last post of Nazi resistance; its dome contorted to a skeleton of twisted metal, a former symbol of might weakened to a carcass in a field of weeds and wire. To his right, in contrast, a fresh, new memorial stands tall and proud; its grand, elliptical form flanked at either end by two Russian tanks standing on plinths. Two soldiers in great coats patrol its boundaries. As the sun strikes its face Alec's forced to squint. Its bright stone fascia is unrelenting.

The six, neoclassical columns of the Brandenburg Gate loom closer. A black and white sign stands before it in the centre of the boulevard. The exclamation marks do little to alleviate his trepidation.

Achtung! Sie verlassen jetzt West Berlin.

Attention! You are now leaving West Berlin.

He walks on towards the central arch; cold, clammy hands thrust in his pockets. Kitty said he needn't worry but there's nothing casual about the transition from West to East. It's a blatant symbol of division, as blunt as a wall. Passing under the pockmarked columns, he can see the boulevard stretches still further east, saplings newly planted along its length. But the buildings flanking its sides bear no recognisable form, a powdery monument of bombed out carnage. A border guard stands in the shadow of the Gate, in the Eastern sector. A cigarette hangs from his mouth. His eyes are trained on Alec, who walks on, as he'd been told to. But the guard looks bored, flicking the butt to the ground.

"Wo gehen sie?" The East German uniform is redolent of the Nazis. Perhaps it's been adapted. Times are hard.

Instinctively Alec pretends not to understand. "English, Tourist. I don't speak…"

The guard holds out his hand. "…Ihre Reisepass. Passport."

Alec removes the passport from his jacket pocket and drops it into the guard's hand. It's scrutinised. Excessively, he thinks. Eventually the guard returns it.

"Welcome to East Germany, Englishman." His English is heavily accented, barely decipherable. He waves Alec away.

Close up the scale of devastation is brutal. Former homes exposed to the elements; strips of wallpaper, the splintered remains of beds, trapped above the city, beyond rescue. Old photographs still cling to walls, never to be claimed. Block after block of rubble.

He drops his eyes to the map, heading north-east, roughly following the border between the two halves of the city. Guards linger near most of the crossing points, more guards than pedestrians; some Russian, he supposes, judging by their scarlet epaulettes. Unlike in West Berlin he sees no obvious sign of re-birth, no modernist structures arising from the ruins, just endless rows of wounded tenement blocks, one street as forlorn as the next. The aerial images he'd seen now look depressingly familiar. By the time he reaches Fehrbelliner Strasse his limbs drag reluctantly, his mood despondent. He has no notion of what to expect when he turns up at the apartment, nor any idea of how long he'll stay. He's entirely at Kitty's mercy. He should have reasoned with her, instead of fleeing; stayed put and faced the consequences of his actions. Yet he concedes this rational perspective ignores one undeniable truth. He's infatuated with her. His sense of reason has been hijacked.

Pressing on the bell of the tenement block he attempts to compose his thoughts. He's not sure what he should say to this friend called Ursula, nor how she'll react in response. He presses the bell again but the door remains closed. Looking back to the street, he searches for an alternative plan, knowing he's too dog-tired to formulate anything worthwhile. He could head back to West Berlin but he's spent virtually everything Kitty gave him on his crossing and the train journey. The meal was a last extravagance. Desperate for some sleep, he steps to the side of the entrance and slumps down into a corner of the building, protected from the wind by a low wall. He rests his head against the cold concrete, aware he shouldn't stay there for long. Just long enough to think. A car sputters by, noxious clouds spilling from its exhaust. He closes his eyes.

"Was machen sie? Aufwachen! Sie Müssen los…"

He blinks. No idea how long he's slept. A young woman hovers above him, her glare a study of abhorrence. He picks himself up, dusting his jacket.

"Entschuldigung, Fräulein. Ich suche eine Freundin von mir. Ich glaube sie wohnt hier aber…"

Her face relaxes a little at his polite apology and explanation of his search for a friend.

"...Englisch?"

"Yes."

"Sie sprechen gut Deutsch, mein Herr."

He offers a conciliatory smile. "Danke, Fräulein."

She glimpses across the street, before turning back to him. "Wen suchen sie?"

Her German is more heavily accented than Kitty's, harder on the ear, but he can still understand her. And his German seems to flow more readily with each sentence. "Her name's Ursula. She's a friend of Kitty Bernstein. Perhaps you know her?"

Her eyes flick back to the road again; more nervous, he thinks, than necessary. "You better come in."

She turns her key in the shabby, wooden door. The hallway is dingy and unwelcoming. Walls of chipped concrete. Entirely functional. Climbing the stairs he's aware of the clatter of their feet on wooden treads, a narrow window onto the street at each level, spreading the remnants of daylight. The sets of stairs seem endless. But eventually she turns from the vestibule along a corridor, darker still; a regimented line of dark brown doors only distinguishable by the number attached to them. She hasn't spoken again; he senses she'd prefer he did the same. At the far end of the corridor she produces another key, beckoning him to enter and flicking on a dim, central light before closing the door behind them. She doesn't speak, instead heading for a wireless against the wall. When it warms to life he hears a military band in full crescendo; louder than seems comfortable.

He hovers uncertainly as she drops a shopping bag beside a sink at the back of the narrow room. It's a kitchenette of sorts with a casement window staring at identical windows across a narrow courtyard. Most of the living area is taken up by two uncomfortable-looking armchairs and a cumbersome, wood-burning boiler in the corner.

"How do you know Fräulein Bernstein?" She doesn't offer him anything. He's desperate for a glass of water but fears to ask.

"I met her at Cambridge. I'm a student there. You know her?"

"You were lucky I found you. I'm Ursula, we share this apartment."

The relief is overwhelming. He could hug her. But he senses he must contain himself. "She sent me to you. Thank God. How do you do? I'm Alec Carter."

He holds out his hand but she shows no inclination to accept it. "Fräulein Bernstein...Katja...is well?"

"Yes. But she calls herself Kitty. Do you think I might have a glass of water?" He wants to collapse, close his eyes. He must beg for a bed. If she has one. She fills a glass from the tap. He gulps so quickly a drizzle of water trickles down his chin.

"Another?"

He returns the glass. "Thank you." The second he sips more slowly, conscious that she's scrutinising his appearance.

"She doesn't tell me much about her life now. But you obviously left England in a hurry because you're unshaven and you have no suitcase. So tell me please why she sent you to me."

"May I sit down?"

The chair is harder than he'd anticipated but at least he gets to rest his weary legs. His hostess remains at the sink with her back to the window, almost a silhouette. He wonders how she and Kitty know each other. At first meeting they seem unlikely friends. Perhaps the brief instructions she gave him at the flat might help. Taking the envelope from his pocket he drops the remaining coins onto a small coffee table. "She said to give you these. There would've been more but I'm afraid I had to spend most of it."

Ursula eyes the rolling coins. "West German Deutschmarks?"

"Yes."

Immediately she crosses the room, gathering them into her hand like a child with penny treats.

"Since East and West Germany were separated our currency here isn't worth so much. This will be useful. She drops the coins in to her pocket and settles in the armchair adjacent to his. "But you haven't answered my question."

He has to think fast, his brain finding clarity again as his body rehydrates. Kitty pleaded with him not to mention anything except his political beliefs. But he'd never claimed to be a Marxist, despite his abhorrence of Churchill and his throwback government. Maybe she'd hoped to persuade him. The thought of her that night fills his heart with both longing and raging desperation. But for now he must park it. "Kitty and I talked a lot about the world. We found we had similar views so she suggested I came here for a while to see how your country works."

He can see her thinking. "That doesn't explain your lack of suitcase."

"I left it on the train. The crossing over to Hamburg was so rough I was sick all night. That's why I'm unshaven. My apologies again. And why I was stupid enough to leave the suitcase."

He wonders if she'll buy it. But she still regards him critically, her hands crossed in her lap, blotches of paint and grease almost ingrained into the flesh. He assumes she's back from some sort of work judging by the dirty blue overalls.

"Perhaps they'll find your suitcase and send it on."

"Unlikely. It had no label on."

"How unfortunate. You made quite a journey. Not many Westerners choose to come to East Berlin."

He understands she's testing him and that he'll have to elaborate. "If they're as repulsed as me by the state of my country I think they might. I had great hopes for Britain after the war under the Labour government, but the ruling elite have regained control. Churchill is eighty and runs a cabinet full of yesterday's men. They carve up the profits of industry to line their own pockets while the workers suffer from malnutrition and squalid housing. It's not the modern Britain I'd imagined."

"Your German really is very good."

He smiles. "My history teacher, Mr Atherton, believed the German language should be re-embraced after the Nazis. He taught me himself. And I suppose his politics rubbed off a bit too. But I also did my National Service in Bremen."

"You are a Socialist?"

He remembers Kitty's instructions. "I suppose you'd say I have Marxist sympathies."

"Is that a crime in England?"

"If you admit it, you have to learn to deal with your enemies."

"We know that here too. The West calls us an enemy simply because we want to create a fairer world. I ask you, is not Capitalism far worse? What sort of despair and anguish do you create when wealth is created by exploitation. History shows us it leads only to bloodshed." Her face softens perceptibly. She rises from the chair. "I'm sorry, you are tired. Can I make you something to eat?"

Despite his meal at the café, he eats greedily when she produces a plate of food. It's nothing extravagant; black bread, a lump of hard cheese and two pickled gherkins but he's grateful nonetheless. He notices she consumes a much more modest amount, appearing to savour each mouthful as if it might be her last.

The cheese is surprisingly salty. He drains his glass of water. "That's very kind. Thank you."

She allows herself a smile. "An English gentleman. I have heard of them."

But now he is too exhausted to reply. He wonders if she'll ever switch off the wireless marching band and offer him shelter for the night. As if sensing his state, she stands up, taking both plates to the sink. "My shift starts in six hours so I must get some rest. You can sleep in Katja's bedroom. Tomorrow when I return from work I'll accompany you to the relevant authorities so they can attend to you. Through here."

She leads him down a narrow corridor, past a tiny bedroom and a toilet, to a second room at the end. "I hope you find it comfortable."

There is no space to maintain a courteous distance. Close up she smells vaguely chemical, like a science lab. "Thank you."

"When Katja got her teaching job we were allocated a larger apartment, but now she's hardly ever here. It would be impolite to refuse hospitality to one of her friends."

"You're very kind."

"You must promise me that you won't go outdoors alone. There will be questions. For the bathroom you turn left down the corridor. The last door. It's marked. I think Katja has towels in her cupboard. You'll find coffee and some bread in the kitchen. So, goodnight. Till tomorrow."

He thanks her again, finding it odd that she asked nothing more of Kitty. Casting his eye about the bedroom there's little sense of the woman he's smitten with. A simple chest of drawers squeezes in the gap beside the bed. A hairbrush, a vanity mirror and a framed photograph of a middle-aged couple, he assumes her parents, stand on its surface. The top drawer is locked. In the second he finds some ironed blouses. He brushes his hand against the soft fabrics then quickly shuts the drawer. In the third he finds a towel. It smells of carbolic. He lays it across the chair and removes his shirt and trousers, wishing all thoughts to pass as he slumps onto the bed, willing sleep to envelop him. But a sharp scraping noise from the adjoining apartment steals his mind from slumber. Like the scrape of a chair. His thoughts race again, his body wired by a rush of adrenalin. He sits up, willing his stubborn heart to slow. Reaching for the second drawer of the chest, he picks out a cotton blouse with lace edging and presses it to his face. The trace of perfume is familiar to him. Immediately his breathing deepens, his head falling back to the pillow.

When he wakes the dread returns. He must get up, despite exhaustion, if only to quell his thoughts. He can hear children playing in the courtyard. Looking out of the window there's a thin line of sky visible above the tenements opposite, a brush of light, all colour bled out. Dressing quickly, he looks to see if there's any sign of Ursula but then remembers she was going to work. In some ways he's glad. It gives him time to think. A shower might help; he probably stinks anyway, suddenly embarrassed that he hadn't bothered to wash before he went to bed. He finds the bathroom as Ursula had instructed, washing in a cold shower of brown water. Returning to the kitchen he searches for breakfast. More black bread and salty cheese. He checks his watch. It's nearly nine. He lights a cigarette, falling onto the armchair, wondering when Kitty will turn up. In the corridor he hears occasional footsteps but no voices. Finding the silence too oppressive, he turns on the wireless; sombre music, not anything with which he's familiar, a military dirge. He scours the cupboard again, unsure exactly what he's looking for, until his eyes fall on a dusty bottle of schnapps tucked behind the tins. Taking one of the small glasses from the drainer he pours himself a modest tipple. His gullet burns before the heat spreads to his belly. He pours another, larger this time. But the anaesthetising balm he sought eludes him. Instead his memory replays the image of Kitty naked beneath another body. But who?

Returning to the armchair with the bottle he promises himself he'll buy Ursula another. The cushion's hard and unforgiving. He shuts his eyes, hoping to obliterate his surroundings and find some sense of calm. There's no inkling of the city beyond his walls; he could be anywhere. Stay here, Ursula had said; an animal caught in a trap.

The rattle of a key in the door jolts him from slumber. He must have drifted off. He springs from the chair, preparing his excuses for Ursula. Kitty Bernstein walks in.

"Thank God." She looks drawn, deprived of sleep, yet he's still elated by her presence. She accepts his embrace but her body is stiff and unyielding. He wants to kiss her but chooses not to. He doesn't know her as he'd thought.

"Alec, we don't have much time. I have to explain. Where's Ursula?"

He steps back. "At work. What's happened, Kitty? Is he dead?"

She makes no move to take off her coat. "I was picked up when I got off the plane last night. They're waiting for us outside. They said they'd give us ten minutes."

"They? Who's they?"

"Alec, you must listen to…"

"…He's dead, isn't he? I killed him."

"It wasn't you. Alec…"

"What?…"

"…It was me. I killed him."

"That's not true. Christ, Kitty, now you're really scaring me."

"Sit down a minute. We have to stay calm. It's vital I explain, to save both of us. And keep your voice down."

Reluctantly he slumps back to the chair. She settles beside him. Her exquisite face looks paler than moonlight; a fragility he's never encountered. Like a porcelain doll.

Her eyes bid him to compliance. "You left him in a pretty bad state but you were too drunk to deliver any fatal blow. So I did it."

"What? I don't believe you. Who was he? Why were you even…?"

"…Trust me, Alec, darling. What I'm about to tell you even Ursula doesn't know. You have to listen and not judge. It's the only way we might survive."

He takes a breath, confusion and fear clouding his mind. Yet Kitty Bernstein is sitting beside him. He still aches to kiss her but for now her presence will suffice. "Whatever it is, I won't let anyone take you."

"Nor me you, if I can possibly help it. But you must do as I say. The truth is, Alec, I'm what's euphemistically called an unofficial employee. A contact person."

"You're still not making any sense."

"I work for the East German government. I'm trained to recover information that might be useful."

"Jesus Christ. You're a spy?"

"I believed what I was doing was right. The East needs help to survive. We can talk about it later but right now we need to get our stories straight. They'll interview us separately so I have to make sure you say the right thing."

"They, again. Who the fuck is they?"

"The Stasi, the secret police. I was working in one of their departments. They enrolled me when I returned to Germany but I wasn't given much choice. Look, I know this country isn't perfect but I still believe Marxism will create a fairer society. The German Democratic Republic will support and nurture all of its people. No one will suffer."

"Nice speech, when you've just killed someone."

"I had no choice. When you walked in - it all went wrong, If I hadn't finished your brutal boxing match there'd would have been a much higher price to pay."

"Boxing? Is that all it was to you? A boxing match!"

"Keep your voice down. I know it must seem callous but a lot of people could have been exposed if he'd lived. Including me. I made it look like suicide. The British authorities probably won't buy that but at least there'll be no traces. One of those great political mysteries that the press love so much."

"Who was he?"

"A rising junior minister, in defence. I was supposed to befriend him, to gather useful information."

He recalls fragments of his encounter. The white flesh of a man bearing down upon him. The smell of sweat. The man he effectively condemned to death. "But why did Ed take you there? Is he in on this too?"

"Alec, we don't have time."

"I want to know."

She drops her head. "He's a distant cousin who has acquaintances in high places so I used him to get close to people. I sold myself as a girl who likes a good time but doesn't like to get involved. He bought it, bless him. I think a part of him fell in love with me though he never said. I think he'd have done anything for me. He became a kind of chaperone. I didn't tell him what happened when he picked me up that night. I just said I needed to get back here urgently, a personal matter. He thinks I live in the Western Sector of Berlin. He's too polite to ask any questions so he drove me straight to the airport."

"What he told me - about you and other men…"

"I guess he was either trying to protect you or prevent you getting closer to me because he was jealous. Is that why you came down to London?"

"He told me he was driving you down to the Dorchester. He'd tried to warn me off. I got drunk. I just couldn't believe what he was telling me. I took the train to London and waited in the foyer. I followed you both to his car. When you drove off I thought I'd lost you but then you parked only a couple of streets up. I watched you walk to the flat, and some others arriving in taxis. When they left and you didn't..."

He's aware of her fingers wrapping around his. She's dropped to the floor in front of him. "Darling, I'm so sorry. Because of you, I made mistakes. I hadn't meant this to happen. I was trained not to let it, and for a while I thought I was invincible. But all that's changed now. And because of that I've got you in to trouble."

He reaches forward, finding her lips, her delicate perfume, even the scent of fear. It's intoxicating.

She pulls back. "They'll be up here any minute. They already know you didn't murder Buchanan-Smith. I told them that when they picked me up. Convince them you're a committed Marxist, you're halfway there already. Tell them you admire this country even if what you see makes you think otherwise at first. They won't send you back to England, they won't want to risk it, so do as they ask you and don't ask questions. If you do that, there's a chance we can be together again."

"I won't let them touch you."

"Just do as I say. Please, it's our only hope."

"I shouldn't have come to London, I…"

"No, don't think that. I'm glad you did."

He feels her hands in his again, aware that she's shivering now. She smiles. "I'm tired."

"Remember everything I said and say nothing about this to Ursula. If she knows anything it'll put her in danger."

He rises from the chair, releasing her hand, desperate to gain some sense of control. "Christ, there must be something we can do. Is there a back entrance? Surely we can…"

"Alec.."

Before she can say more the door to the apartment opens again. Ursula hovers at the entrance, her boiler suit covered in oil and paint, her face etched with fear. "Katja darling, these men insisted…"

Two men push past her into the room, each brandishing a pair of handcuffs. "Kommen sie mit, Fräulein. Sie auch, Herr Carter."

Ursula remains at the door. "Why are they here, Katja?"

"I'm so sorry, my darling." She steps forward with almost hypnotic dignity. "No need for bullying, gentlemen. We have no intention of running."

She accepts the handcuffs without a struggle and advises Alec to do the same. He notices a look of disappointment cross his assailant's face. Kitty has stolen their thunder.

He feels his arm grabbed, then a shove towards Kitty and the door. Ursula is blocking their exit. "My God, Katja, what have you done?"

"I made a silly mistake. Don't worry, my darling, we'll be together again soon."

Before she can say more she's dragged into the corridor. Alec follows, the grip on his arm so tight he imagines the flesh will bruise. He turns his head back for a last glimpse of Ursula. Her face is blank. Unreadable. She steps back and closes the door.

He's pushed roughly in to one of two Trabants parked outside. Turning around he sees Kitty manhandled into the car behind, where two more companions await her. He wants to catch her eye but his car pulls away, leaving a trail of exhaust fumes; poisoning his view. A moment later the car turns a corner and Kitty is gone. He thinks he might die. Perhaps it would be best.

"Where are we going?" He asks in German, rationalising this choice before speaking. Pretending he doesn't understand might have benefits; he could eavesdrop, pick up snippets, but there's pride at stake; he doesn't want to appear weak, disadvantaged; a victim.

The skinny passenger answers without enthusiasm. "Headquarters."

He revisits his conversation with Kitty; what he should say. Watching the catastrophic scale of destruction pass his window he's not without empathy for the East German mindset. It's a new country, vulnerable, the epicentre of American and Russian power play; a country that's been decimated then pillaged. Abandoned by the West, assimilated by the East. Who can they trust? Communism's still work in progress. Perhaps Kitty's right, with the rout of Fascism and the outstretched hand of Russia maybe they really will become the shining beacon of a fairer world; given time, and reparation for everything that was destroyed.

The Trabant pulls up outside a long, municipal building. The skinny one escorts him by the elbow again, turning left through double doors to a functional corridor. It reminds him of hospitals. Columns of sunlight cross the floor from a line of rectangular windows. A clerk sits behind a desk at the far end, a row of empty chairs against the windowed wall. As they walk towards him Alec notices that the doors are numbered, but no names. His driver removes his handcuffs and tells him to sit. The skinny assistant explains to the clerk who they've brought before leaving without a glance back towards their captive. Alec rubs his wrists, the bruising already evident. The clerk stamps a document on his desk then rises from his chair.

"This way, please." He knocks on door twelve; one short, decisive note.

"Komm' rein."

The clerk lays a hand on Alec's shoulder, pushing him through the doorway into a dimly lit room.

"Ah, welcome, Herr Carter. Please take a seat." The man indicates a chair before settling at his large desk, a venetian blind obscuring the view behind him. "Smoke?" He offers an opened silver case. Higher quality cigarettes than his bunch of minions. Alec accepts, putting it to his lips as his host rises again proffering a polished, wooden lighter. His host switches to German. "I believe your German in excellent."

"I get by."

"Allow me to introduce myself. My name is Herr Ehrmann. I work for the government, director of operations relating to our overseas guests."

"Guests?" He runs his hands around his wrists.

Ehrmann glimpses at the raised skin. "My apologies. I admit sometimes our escorts can be a little too keen but I'm afraid they need to be cautious. Occasionally we have incidents where guests are somewhat, shall we say, uncooperative. These are still fragile times, you understand."

"So I've been led to believe." His instinct is to be humble, here at least. His own predicament is fragile enough. He wonders what the English headlines will be saying. Whether anyone here has seen them yet.

"I won't '*beat around the bush*'". Ehrmann has broken back into English for the phrase. "I love this expression, to beat the bushes, coming from your British love of hunting, I believe." He exhales with a smile. "Now, Herr Carter, you are an enigma to us. We have no record of you and yet you turn up in our country at the suggestion of Fräulein Bernstein because she says you're sympathetic to our cause?"

Ehrmann's expression suggests disbelief. Alec's instinct is not to try too hard; not to look desperate. He draws the smoke into his lungs before exhaling. "That's correct."

"Perhaps you could tell me what you know about Fräulein Bernstein?"

"She's a friend, a German teacher. We met in Cambridge."

"You were having an affair with her?"

He's not sure how to answer. Nor if he even knows. "I liked her. We got on."

"Yet a senior politician was murdered in London because you discovered Fräulein Bernstein was sleeping with him. Apparently you were jealous and assaulted him. And then you flea to East Berlin."

Had Kitty slept with Buchanan-Smith more than once? Until now he'd assumed not. At any rate Ehrmann's playing games, plainly wanting to unnerve him. "It was an unfortunate accident." As an explanation he knows it sounds lame.

"An accident? Then I assume a decent citizen such as yourself, Herr Carter, would call the police and face the consequences. But instead you chose to run away…"

"…I didn't choose!" The accusation of cowardice stings. He can't help rising to it.

"Then what, Herr Carter? I repeat, before I lose patience for wasting my time, what do you know about Fräulein Bernstein?"

He sees no advantage in lying now. He needs to resume some control. And dignity. "Very well. I know she's an agent, working for the East German government. But I only found out when she came to the apartment this morning. She never mentioned it before. She never betrayed you or any of your secrets."

"No. But she betrayed you, Herr Carter."

"What? Not in the slightest."

"Come. You don't think I'd expend valuable time if I hadn't read her dossier on you. I know you were born in…" He pulls across a folder from his desk, consulting the neatly written pages within. Handwriting Alec can't help recognising. "…Imber, on Salbury Plain. I know the Americans pushed the inhabitants out without recompense. I know your mother died soon after, of a broken heart, and then your father too. I know you're quite an angry man. Which is why you assaulted Fräulein Bernstein's lover when you were drunk. So there's no need for any more secrecy."

The shock cuts like glass but he has to contain it. Ehrmann wants to drive a wedge between them. Kitty had begged him to trust her, and he desperately wants to, despite the niggling doubts. "Her dossier's very accurate. Except it's Salisbury Plain, not Salbury."

"My pronunciation. Again, apologies." Ehrmann shuts the folder and throws it back to his desk. "Herr Carter, please tell me why I should trust you rather than returning you to the British authorities. It would be easy to frame you for the murder and no doubt your police would love to prove how clever they were at chasing down their wicked villain."

"If you did that surely you'd be in danger of exposing your own operation? If they asked me questions."

"Perhaps, but the only name you have is Fräulein Bernstein's and I'm not sure you'd want to put her in danger. As for myself, I'm a respectable, government employee. No more, no less. The alternative is that I just lose you somewhere. Otherwise you're another mouth to feed, and the GDR already has a burden of unwarranted costs. You see we don't like scavengers or leeches. Every citizen plays their part and so I have to wonder what part you think you could play."

Alec inhales the smoke, playing for time, feigning composure. Ehrmann's put his cards are on the table and suddenly he finds himself bargaining for his life. Be a Marxist, Kitty said, nothing less will save you. He flicks the thread of ash into the tray on the desk, his eyes fixed on Ehrmann's. "I've no wish to steal from your citizens, Herr Ehrmann. Fräulein Bernstein told me a great deal about the hopes, but also the fragility, of your country. I have a great deal of sympathy. My parents, their friends, were forced from their homes, the community they cherished. It was their world. And it was destroyed without any compensation from the army or the government, either then or now. I decided I never wanted to live in a country where those with power exploit the poor or the vulnerable. I believe here, in East Germany, you share those values. If there's any way I can play a part to help you, I would unquestioningly like to do so."

For the first time since entering the room he thinks he detects a softening in Ehrmann's glance. Brothers in arms, perhaps. His interviewer relaxes back into his chair, pressing his stained fingertips together. "Fräulein Bernstein informed us of your convictions, it's true. Had she not done so, you would have been quite a problem for us. But of course we still need to be persuaded that your beliefs are sincere."

Despite his heavy-handed capture, he genuinely feels an element of sympathy for Ehrmann and his newly formed country. Pulverised in the war by the Americans and Russians, ravaged by all, who wouldn't be paranoid about their fragile re-birth? And they might easily believe he was spying for British Intelligence, using Kitty as cover. He'd heard such stories. Burgess and Maclean might have been infamous defectors but there were bound to be dozens of British operatives actively engaged in undermining the Marxist states. He stubs his cigarette out in the ashtray. "I fully understand your predicament, Herr Ehrmann. I'd like to assure you that I'll do whatever's necessary to persuade you of my convictions."

Ehrmann finally smiles. "Excellent. I have a task in mind. But for now you will return to your current address and await further instructions. May I assure you that our drivers will be more courteous this time."

He rises from his chair, navigating his way around the broad desk to shake Alec's hand.

The flesh is warm but dry. Alec feigns a smile. "Thank you. I assure you, you won't be disappointed." Moving toward the door he's still desperate to hear of Kitty's fate but knows his enquiry must appear casual, uncommitted. "I assume Fräulein Bernstein will return to her duties?'

"We need to compile a full report on her experiences in England. I'm afraid she will be detained a little longer."

He wants to ask more but aware he must refrain. "Of course."

"Please remain at your current residence. Someone will call for you." Ehrmann's hand reaches out for the handle, holding the door open. "Oh, I almost forgot, Herr Carter. I trust you have your passport with you?"

"Yes, it's in my…"

"…Excellent. You'll please leave it with the clerk. We'll need it for printing some identity papers."

Ehrmann smiles again before retreating within his office. In the corridor the clerk is rubber-stamping a pile of single page documents. Fear grips at Alec's heart, despite the bureaucratic drudgery he's witnessing. He toys with the idea of fleeing from the building but knows it would be futile. He'd probably never see Kitty Bernstein again. He reaches inside his pocket, offering his passport to the clerk who accepts it with excessive courtesy.

19

Watching Alec's car disappear around the corner is in some senses a relief. She's done all she can to protect him, her burden of responsibility eased a fraction. This she tells herself despite her lurching stomach; wiser to focus on salvaging her own reputation if she wants to facilitate the slightest chance of re-union.

She makes no attempt to converse with her escorts. She knows now it's pointless and trying to make small talk with your wrists in handcuffs feels frankly absurd. Watching the broken city pass by, she realises the driver's not taking the same route that first led to her encounter with Ehrmann. The car's speeding further east. Perhaps a bad omen. She's heard rumours of unofficial employees being executed for the slightest mistake. A dubious consequence of a hazardous job. Observing the back of her captor's scraggy neck, she wonders how much longer they must wait before the foundation blocks of the promised Utopia begin to emerge.

At a crossroads they encounter a line of Russian transport vehicles heading south along one of the broad, treeless boulevards. She's never quite got used to the sight, a part of her still uncomfortable with the sense of occupation; the horrendous testimonies of multiple rape and vengeful humiliation to which Berliners were subjected, before and after the surrender. Flesh to be picked by vultures. But the young soldiers sitting in the open-topped trucks just look bored and cold. Probably wishing for their homeland.

Her driver steers the car off the main road into a courtyard. A group of brick buildings with no discernible hierarchy encircles it. They could constitute a small factory or supply outlet; bland and uninviting. Her heart skips. She'd lulled herself into a state of objective reflection in the car but now her palms are clammy, the handcuffs irritating her skin. The driver's assistant, reeking of sour sweat, escorts her to one of the smaller buildings. Inside, a concrete staircase leads them down to a windowless corridor. It appears to stretch further than the building above. A line of bare light bulbs leads the way past heavy, metal doors, each housing a grille.

"Wait in here, Fräulein. Someone will fetch you."

He removes the handcuffs and pushes her in to the cell. She hears the door lock and his footsteps retreat. A grille, high on the wall, provides a meagre stream of daylight and fresh air. She's grateful for it, it counters the acrid creep of bleach. A metal chair stands in the corner and against the wall a long, hard shelf suggests a bed. Beside it a tin pot, stained and tarnished. She assumes it's for pissing in. The walls are painted in shiny, grey gloss; there's no graffiti, not even a scouring of the plaster. Sitting herself on the chair, she listens for clues to give her some sense of where she is or what to expect. Occasionally footsteps pass and then stop, sometimes two sets returning. But there're no words she can discern. She watches the thin band of daylight slide across the wall, slowly losing any sense of time. Perhaps three or four hours later she hears keys again, the door opens, and a middle-aged woman enters, unsmiling.

"Come, Fräulein."

She's escorted back up the stairs, passing through a labyrinth of corridors, where office staff cross between one office and the next, papers in hand, but never conversing. The woman leads her into a narrow room, one side a wall of loose brown files, the other a patchwork of peeling grey paint. At the far end a man scribbles at the margins of a typed page. He looks up as she enters.

"Fräulein, step forward, please. You will remember me."

"Good morning, Herr Kirsch." She recognised him immediately. Though he looks a bit fatter. The ceiling light adds a gleam to his bald head, an inoffensive family man if she didn't know him. She hadn't taken to him the first time they'd met in Ehrmann's office. An unpleasant bureaucrat. No chair is close to hand, nor even offered, so she stands, hands crossed in dutiful repose.

"I have your report here, Fräulein. I'm afraid it's disappointing. We had very high hopes but sadly you can never ascertain an agent's true character until they're put to the test in the field. An unfortunate risk we are forced to take but of course if something goes wrong, our first duty is to protect the state." He consults the page before him. "When did you first have sex with Herr Carter?"

"I don't see that's…"

"…Fräulein, please, I'm not interested in lurid details. I just have to file an accurate report."

"We haven't. But maybe that doesn't make a good report."

"Playing silly games won't help you."

"I fell in love with him, that's all, but perhaps you consider that a game, too."

"Fräulein Bernstein, I'm not sure you appreciate the gravity of your situation so I would advise you to answer questions accurately and without a pejorative inflection. Is that clear?"

She conjures herself to obedience, knowing anything short will prove fatal. "Of course, Herr Kirsch. I apologise. I've not slept."

His eyes stare, unblinking from behind the wire frames. "By falling in love with him did you compromise your mission and the security of the state?"

"I think," she hesitates a beat, but there's no point in denying it. It won't help her cause. "Yes, I'm afraid I did."

He scribbles a tick against a paragraph. "Good. Now I will ask again. When did you first have sexual relations with Herr Carter?"

"About a week ago. We were in a park by the university. We sat on a bench to avoid the rain. He kissed me then, for the first time."

"This is when you made the mistake with the lighter from the hotel?"

"Yes."

Another tick. "And?"

"That was it. We kissed again briefly at my apartment this morning before we were collected."

"You never had penetrative sex?'

"Sadly not."

He looks up again from his notes. "Please stick to the facts, Fräulein. Your personal feelings are repugnant and of no interest to me."

"An error of judgement, Herr Kirsch. Once more I apologise

unreservedly." He ticks another box. She steels herself, desperate not to shiver despite the insufficient warmth of her blouse. In contrast she notes a crease of sweat beading on her interrogator's brow. "May I be permitted to ask one question?"

His chair creaks as he sits back, his body language suggesting it's contrary to form. But she pursues it anyway. She needs to know. "About my collaborator, Herr Grant?"

"He's a fine agent. Young but promising. Again, I'd caution you not to jeopardise your own case by slandering others."

"Were his instructions to kill me?"

If he's surprised by the question he doesn't show it. But there's a heartbeat of delay before he responds. "That you even pose the question makes me believe your training was insufficient to iron out your emotional weaknesses. It's a pity. We will have to evaluate our processes. Herr Grant chose not to kill you for two reasons. Firstly he considered the disposal of your corpse an insurmountable problem and secondly a dead call girl recognised by staff at an expensive London hotel might set the British press on a grubby mission to link her to the suicide of Herr Buchanan-Smith."

She finds this answer hard to believe but presumably it's the excuse that Ed gave. She has him down as a coward. Lucky for her really, otherwise she'd be a rag in a field.

"I assume you didn't pass any information to your beloved, Herr Carter, concerning Herr Grant's occupation?"

"I'm not a fool, Herr Kirsch."

"If you're lying we can retrieve the information from him. As I'm sure you're aware."

She will not shed tears though she's sure he'd love it, instead pondering how she might kill him before resisting the urge. "I give you my word."

"Let us hope your word is more reliable than your service. It may help at your trial.

"Trial?"

He smiles for the first time. "This is a country of principle, Fräulein. We are not in the Imperialist West. We would not presume to condemn you without a fair trial."

"If it's fair, I hope I'll be able to prove my loyalty and my innocence."

"Fräulein, I'm afraid you've already disproved your innocence. The rest is for the court to decide."

"But if charges brought against me are found unwarranted, presumably I'll be free to go?"

He smiles. It's unnerving. "Of course. But for now I'm afraid you must stay here until you're called. We have to be meticulous in protecting our security. As I'm sure you understand."

Returning to her cell she waits for the door to clank shut behind her before falling on to the shelf-like bed. Someone added a pillow and two coarse blankets while she was upstairs. How very thoughtful. All she can think of is to get some sleep, having barely rested in the last thirty-six hours. She tries to empty her mind, a trick her mother taught her as a child, to empty her bag of worries leaving only the things she could solve at that moment, the rest filed away, unbidden until a solution appeared. But the thought of her parents distresses her more. She's been out of contact for so long; part of her training had demanded the separation from all loved ones: compliant anaesthesia, they'd called it, to procure stronger agents. Plainly it hadn't worked. She can almost recall her last letter to them word for word; don't worry about me, I'm living with Ursula again. I have a new job but we have no phone and post is unreliable so I might not be in touch for a while. I love you both etc etc. She turns her head to the wall. Perhaps her re-educators were right. She must now file her parents away.

The same woman brings her some lunch; a slice of corn bread, raw onion and a slab of greasy cheese. She's most excited by the glass of water, even though it's warm and cloudy. She leans back against the wall, determined to maintain a structure to the day despite the four battleship grey walls that envelope her. Another meal comes later, a thin stew, the patch of light drifting to the floor then extinguished. She counts three days passing an identical routine until on the fourth, the woman brings in clothes in addition to the breakfast of stale bread. The first change of clothing she's been offered. Grey trousers and a coarse shirt. Also a stained towel.

"Put these on please. You can wash in the toilet. I will be back in fifteen minutes to escort you there."

She asks no questions; she's tried and failed to establish any kind of rapport. Exactly fifteen minutes later the woman returns and escorts her to the toilet. A small porcelain sink, cracked and stained, stands on the tiled floor. There's a single, cold tap; above it a small mirror. More from curiosity than vanity she stares at it, shocked by what she sees. She looks away, forcing her head under the tap, rubbing at her scalp until it hurts, slapping her cheeks with the water until some hint of colour appears. It'll have to do. It sharpens her mind at least, which is her only immediate requirement.

Both the trousers and the shirt are a size too large but she has adapted them as best she can, conscious that though they might want her to look like a broken renegade she has no intention of doing so.

The woman escorts her back to her cell. "Leave the towel on your chair." She does as requested, aware that the woman is observing her more keenly than usual. "You look better for a wash. I'd let you borrow my lipstick but they won't allow it."

"Thank you."

"Come. Hands together please."

She walks forward, relinquishing to the cold metal encircling her wrists. It feels good to be out of the cell, even though their route only takes them back through the labyrinth of corridors to another part of the building. But along the way she glimpses a world outside. The sun's shining, guards lob a ball around a courtyard. Weeds force themselves through the asphalt, despite the cold.

They approach a double set of doors. Two guards either side push them open and she's forced through by her escort. The courtroom is larger than she'd expected, like a small gym, with a parquet floor. A long, trestle table stands at its centre with two more adjacent at either end. She counts seven men sitting before her at the head table, she recognises Herr Kirsch only; at the side tables a mixture of solemn-faced individuals, some in uniform, some not, more men than women. A jury perhaps? Onlookers have been herded to the back of the room, a bedraggled bunch from the street? Assembled to vilify her, no doubt. Four microphones sit on the central table, their wires trailing to a coiled heap on the floor. A fifth stands a respectful distance away. Head height. The man seated at the centre requests her to step before it, a distinguished figure, lean, early fifties she guesses, a goatee beard and hollow cheeks. Immediately a camera flashes in her face. Two more in quick succession. The photographer steps back. She thinks of her father's trail. She can't imagine hers will be any fairer. But the thought of him strengthens her resolve. In this moment, even at an insurmountable distance, he brings her comfort.

The leader lists the charges against her; his voice melodic, almost avuncular; dereliction of duty of Comrade Bernstein to the state, wilful misappropriation of state funds, inappropriate collusion with enemies of the state, failure to act responsibly in management of appropriated firearms.

She almost gives up listening but can't help admit they've conjured an impressive list.

"Will the accused admit to each of these charges?"

She takes a step forward. "No, comrade, I will not." Her words echo around the room.

"Will the accused admit to any of these charges?"

"No, comrade, I will not."

She observes him consulting with Herr Kirsch and another bureaucratic type to his right; aware her thin veneer of blowsy confidence could easily be blown to dust. It wouldn't take much. Their whispered conference feels interminable, her energy already draining, all part of the plan she imagines. She avoids the peripheral faces at the adjacent tables, it would distract her and she has no hunger for their pathetic contempt.

The council of three lift their heads in unison. Their leader speaks for them. "The comrade may speak to defend herself. Speak clearly into the microphone. And briefly. This court will not tolerate time wasters."

She steps closer. The microphone hums before emitting a wild screech, like a flock of starving gulls. She winces, waiting for its echo to ebb away across the room. "Comrades, I thank you for giving me the opportunity to prove my innocence…"

A wild shout from one of the seven. Surprisingly high-pitched. "You may prove nothing, Comrade! That is our duty not yours. Continue."

"Thank you, comrade. I am humbled." She takes a breath, lets her head fall before raising it again. "When I became an unofficial employee of the State I vowed that I would do all in my power to promote the welfare, and political and economic ambitions, of the German Democratic Republic. I continue to believe in the Marxist foundations that will enable our country to flourish as a modern, Socialist, egalitarian state."

The leader interrupts. "Fine words comrade, but we are all aware this was your vow. I repeat. Don't waste our time!" His voice has lost its mellow note. "Continue with relevant facts. If there are any."

A flutter of assent spreads across the room. As humiliating as playground abuse. She bites her lip, turning her attention to the broader audience for the first time. "Comrades, my crime, as you label it, is that while fulfilling my duties to the very best of my ability, I had the apparent misfortune to fall in love, with someone who, like us, believes in the Marxist cause. He currently awaits his own fate at the mercy of the State, because he trusted me with his heart and hoped with all sincerity that this country, this paradigm of virtuous, socialist principles, would offer him sanctuary."

Another interruption. "He's an Englishman, Comrade. An Imperialist!"

"He's first and foremost a Marxist. I was under the impression that our beliefs stretch beyond the boundaries of nationality."

Pettily, she knows, she's scored a point. The man resumes his seat. "Continue."

"If I have failed in my assignment, it's not for lack of belief or faith. It's because I'm human, and fallible, as we all are…"

"…You do not speak for others, comrade! I have already warned you of this arrogance! The same high-pitched aggressor, his face redder than fire.

"Forgive me, comrade. I was trying to explain the position…"

"…Your position is that you failed the state, at great cost to your fellow comrades and citizens! You spent lavishly on clothes and hotels…"

"… I was supposed to be playing the part of an American heiress…"

"Silence, comrade!" The leader resumes control. "You are not here to argue. You are here to atone. My comrade is right. You displayed far more avariciousness than necessary. Plainly indicating the germs of Capitalist greed still linger within you. And you failed in your main assignment, not because you fell in love but because you were careless. If you hadn't shown your lover the lighter he would never have found your hotel and you would not have been forced to kill a highly promising source. Lust and greed, comrade. These are the traits of a whore! This is an odious case of betrayal of the State and all that it stands for. Before I sentence you, will you at least atone for your crimes?"

She feels his gaze demonise her, not just his, the entire audience, consumed with their own self-righteousness. She thinks again of her father. What would he do? She lowers her head, marvelling at the beauty of the patina on the wooden flooring. "Forgive me, Comrades. I apologise unreservedly."

A murmur flushes the room. "Silence. Please lift your head, Comrade Bernstein."

She does as he asks. The camera flashes again. She drops her hands before her, thumbs caressing the soft flesh on the underside of her fingers. A second flash. This time closer.

"You have been found guilty of all charges and will be escorted from here to prison where you will serve a sentence for life, to be reviewed twenty years from this date. The court is dismissed. Please take the prisoner away."

The moments following barely register. She's vaguely aware of a river of voices as the two guards grab her arms, pushing her to the doorway. Numb to pain when they press hard at her flesh, her breasts somehow a legitimate place to spread their fingers. The corridors merge to one. Snatches of daylight. One of them opens a door leading to the weed-ridden courtyard. She winces, unused to the bright light. They push her on towards a lorry, grey and indistinguishable, parked beside a metal gate. A third guard stands at its rear, opening the door as they approach. She feels his hand on her bottom, shoving her into darkness, the door sealing behind her. Metallic footsteps retreat. She waits for her eyes to adjust but they are stubborn. Nothing reveals itself. There is no air. Only the scent of fear makes her realise she is not alone.

As the engine starts up and the lorry lurches forward, one voice raises itself from the darkness. A woman's voice. "Do not speak. We must conserve oxygen."

She doesn't reply, lowering her head to her knees. Despite her best efforts, she has no idea of their direction of travel, their metal tomb impervious to an outside world. The air seems to grow thinner by the mile, and despite the number of bodies, from shifts of movement she calculates about seven, her teeth chatter with the bone-chilling cold. No one thought to provide a coat. But why should they care? She wonders if her supposed crime was really much simpler than the court suggested; she was a Jew, a half-Jew in truth but a Jew nonetheless.

Perhaps an hour later the lorry draws to a halt and the engine cuts out. No one speaks. She awaits in darkness but it seems an eternity before the lock is released. The guards' sick little game. As the door draws open she's forced again to shield her eyes, the sunlight throwing her fellow travellers in to stark relief. There's eight of them. All women, young and middle-aged. All stare at the floor. None of them will make eye contact. Not at least, while they're in full view. Orders are shouted. Somewhere a dog barks. She steps down from the lorry, assessing her surroundings, her breath curling from her lips. They're in a broad, gravel courtyard, such as would belong to a country estate. Beyond it stands an imposing brick building, rectangular in shape but fortressed, like a castle. Its walls rise metres above them, defiant and impenetrable, except for a gated, arch entrance at its centre. Two local guards arrive to join the others. One holds a German Shepherd at the end of a leash. She finds herself corralled into a line and marched across the frosted gravel towards the building. It seems minutes before they reach the mediaeval-looking gate, such is the scale of the courtyard. When she finally crosses the threshold she pauses to look back. Beyond a perimeter wall she can see a dog-tooth ridge of pine trees, spreading across the horizon. It reminds her of a time, long ago, when she used to go cross-country skiing with her parents. A time when ignorance and innocence were her best friends. One of the guards shouts at her for lingering. She turns around, following the line into the dim chamber, recalling that her family's last skiing trip must have been in the winter of '35.

Cold Road to Imber

20

Twenty-four hours after his detainment, there's a rap on the apartment door. He opens it, without hope, to see his two chain-smoking escorts, blocking his exit, shaded against the light.

"You must come with us now, please."

He's barely seen Ursula since his return, her shifts at the printing works taking precedence over his own anguish. It's clear that life's harder here. He won't wake her before he goes. She needs the sleep and it's better she doesn't get involved. Grabbing his jacket from the chair he follows them to the car. No handcuffs this time. Progress of sorts, though until he finds out what's happened to Kitty he can't relax. He hadn't slept, waiting all night for a key in the door, the approach of her footsteps. It came at about three, his heart leaping, but then a desultory cough, the blandest clue, and he threw his head back to the pillow, realising Ursula has just returned from her night shift. By five he could lie down no longer; grabbed his cigarettes and rose to make coffee.

The driver takes the same route. A thin layer of grey stratus straddles the city, rendering a weary bleakness to the promise of the day. Or perhaps it's just him. Even the few modern buildings, brutalist blocks of Modernist concrete, show less conviction of their glory. The same clerk delivers him into

Ehrmann's office.

"Herr Carter. I trust you slept well."

He's unsure from Ehrmann's flat tone whether it's a genuine enquiry. There's been no peremptory handshake, no offer of a cigarette which along with coffee is the only thing keeping him upright. "Not really."

Ehrmann indicates the chair opposite and settles himself behind his desk, yellowed fingertips pressed together again. "A guilty conscience perhaps. Are you familiar with Dostoevsky's Crime and Punishment?"

He's in no mood for intellectual games. Sits forward, impatient to wipe the unctuous smile from Ehrmann's face. "Tell me what's happened to Fräulein Bernstein."

The fingertips separate. If his captor finds the interruption discourteous, Alec doesn't care. Kitty's safety is the only thing on his mind.

"She's been detained. There are procedures when an agent loses their way. We have to evaluate her threat to our security and while we do that, it's vital that she neither operates in the realm, nor is vulnerable to approach, nor foreign interference. We protect her for her own safety."

"Where is she?"

"In one of our holding residences. Not far from here."

"Can I see her?"

"As I explained, Herr Carter, we have a duty to protect her."

"So when? A week? A month? For Christ's sake, how long does it take to evaluate someone?!"

"I see you can blaspheme in German too."

Alec shrinks back for a moment, annoyed with himself for losing his cool. He knows it won't help his cause.

"I understand your concern, Herr Carter, but please be patient. She's quite safe, but I'm afraid I cannot yet say when you will see her again."

Ehrmann's mock sympathy cuts deep into his flesh. He feels his energy ebb, days of adrenalin overloading his veins suddenly washed away by a bureaucratic wall. Except it's more invidious than that. It smells, not of paper and ink, but of fear and sweat.

At last his captor offers a cigarette. He takes one from the silver case, inhales the smoke deeply, hoping for some momentary elixir. He needs to calculate his position. But Ehrmann offers no room for scheming.

"I have a proposition for you, Herr Carter, which I will come to. But first I must confess I've been impressed by your political awareness, which Comrade Bernstein, despite her mistakes, had informed us of. But also you've demonstrated loyalty towards her. Whether that is misplaced or not I will not comment, but the ability to feel and demonstrate loyalty is I think a valuable commodity, particularly when it comes to supporting the State. Wouldn't you agree?"

Alec glances down at the cigarette curled between his fingers. Hot to his skin. "Whether to a person or a State, loyalty is always earned. I've only been in East Berlin twenty-four hours."

"Then you have much to learn. Loyalty is not just a system of checks and balances, of beads on a counting rack. It is a step of faith. And of your faith we are yet to be convinced."

He brushes ash from his trousers, hoping to regain a sense of composure. "What exactly is it you require, Herr Ehrmann?"

"We have an assignment for you. Your impeccable English manner and useful knowledge of German are perfect qualities for operating as a private tutor. There are many families in West Berlin who think their children need tutoring in English. They believe that America will win the war of ideology and they fall over themselves to prepare their offspring. Like sending rats to the Pied Piper."

"The Pied Piper of Saxony."

"Very good, Herr Carter. Saxony which is now in West Germany. From which he drew not only their rats but their children too. But we digress. The point is these wealthy families have much influence. Many of them are successful industrialists, entrepreneurs, who we believe are stealing commodities and intellectual property from the East. You will take up residence as a tutor in a household we believe will give us useful information. Use your time to find out about the father's business and his connections by whichever means you think expedient. The child should prove a good source. You will be assigned a contact to whom you will report. You will inform no one else of your task. If you do, there will be very severe consequences. Do you understand?"

Alec taps a thread of ash into the tray on the desk, unwilling to display any sign of intimidation, though his pulse throbs in his temple. "What if I refuse?"

"We hand you back to the British authorities. As I said yesterday, they have an unfortunate murder to solve. We can provide them with a suspect. I think on balance you'll agree working here as an English tutor is a more rewarding prospect."

A part of him would willingly return to England and accept his fate. Morally it would be the right course of action, and perhaps he'd be spared the death penalty by confessing the truth. But then he'd have to implicate Kitty. At which point what would happen to her? Ehrmann would no doubt have her disposed of; bury the evidence. A cold line of sweat trickles down his back. He can't leave Germany without finding her. It's not an option.

He glances at the wall, affecting nonchalance. "Is it a girl or a boy?" Not that it makes much difference.

Ehrmann smiles. "A boy, ten years old. His name's Stefan Rosenberg. His family returned after the war. They were lucky to escape."

"But they returned."

"Money is a terrible vice, Herr Carter. Those who worship it are also blinded by it." He smiles again. "You'll meet his mother first. She'll want to see everything is in order so we'll return your passport with a work permit. You are a history scholar at Cambridge University who's taken a year off to study in West Berlin. Your contact will give you more details. Please be ready on Thursday morning at nine o'clock. He will call for you."

"I trust he'll be more agreeable than my usual escorts."

"I suggest you get some sleep on your return, Herr Carter. Plainly you need it."

Climbing the stairs to Kitty's apartment he wonders what he should tell Ursula. Presumably she'll be getting ready for her next shift. Worrying about her friend. Yet Kitty swore him to secrecy. He knocks gently on the door, hoping against hope that no one will answer and that he can go straight to sleep. Let his mind rest. But a second later Ursula stands before him, looking over his shoulder.

"Where is she? I thought she'd be back by now."

"She's just helping with enquiries."

She takes a step back to let him in, closing the door quickly behind him. "I thought I'd wake up to find her here. Now you return without her. I'm so worried."

He rests his arm on hers, anxious to calm her. "There's no need, I promise. I think they're frightened she's brought in a Western spy unwittingly. Nothing could be further from the truth."

She gives a weak smile. "Everyone's so paranoid. You hear stories, you don't know what's true and what's not. They say America will drop a nuclear bomb on us. Maybe they will, who knows? We live on a diet of fear. It gives me constant indigestion."

He smiles. "Let me make some coffee."

Alec steps past her towards the sink, washing his hands before taking two cups from the cupboard; mindful of this ridiculously domestic scene. Ursula has sat in one of the chairs to finish her slice of bread. A book of crossword puzzles lies open beside her, a pencil hovering in her hand but never committing to the page. He has no idea what to do, so he settles in the chair adjacent to hers, sipping the coffee.

"Do you like crosswords?" He can't find anything constructive to say.

"It fills the time." She smiles weakly. "What will you do now?"

He wants to sound positive. Give her some hope. Or at least the possibility of some rent. "I've been offered a job, teaching English."

Her expression is ambiguous, surprised but somehow fearful.

"Did Katja arrange it?"

"Not exactly. It's not in a school. I'll be working as an individual tutor. A young boy. I start on Thursday."

"And they'll pay you?"

"A bit. Enough so I can pay you some rent."

"But when Katja returns…"

"…Then we'll have a reason to celebrate. And I'll make other arrangements."

He has no idea what these arrangements will be but it seems to satisfy Ursula. She rises from the chair, swilling out her cup in the sink.

"I must go. It's a long shift so I won't be back till late this evening. Help yourself to what you can find."

"Thank you."

She stops at the door. "Do a crossword if you like. They're a useful distraction."

After her footsteps retreat his ears tune to a different noise, a dull thump issuing from the courtyard. Looking down from the window he sees a woman beating dust from a rug. It flies up and out to the sky, like a murmuration. When she retires he feels an acute absence; an emptiness. He picks up the crossword book then throws it back to the table. Why did Ursula ask so few questions? He lights a cigarette instead. He replays conversations which shift and blow like sand until everything reeks of deceit and artifice. Who can he trust now? Ed had warned him about Kitty, but that turned out to be a story she spun to deceive. He must have guessed at least that they'd run away together. Their mutual disappearance would be too co-incidental. Maybe he's already searching for him. He hopes he is. He could use a friend.

He showers in cold water. From Ehrmann's obfuscation he guesses Kitty won't return for a day or two so he needs to keep himself motivated and alert. A walk should help.

Stepping into the cool air, he feels a palpable relief, his paranoia retreating as he begins to construct a tentative scaffold of hope. Kitty had promised things would work out. He's desperate to believe her.

His first task is to find a newsagent, so he chooses a southerly route towards the city centre. At the end of Fehrbelliner Strasse he encounters two young mothers chatting idly across their prams. He apologises for interrupting. Where could he buy a newspaper? The bolder of the two points along a narrower street. It's a fleeting interaction. She avoids eye contact. He's not one of her pack.

He follows her directions, finding what looks like a junk store on the corner of the street, its walls pockmarked in a form now so familiar to him. The damage has lost its power to shock. A rack of newspapers stands on the pavement outside but there's only one title. Neues Deutschland. He joins the queue. The shelves are bare apart from a desultory collection of bric-a-brac: fountain pens, dusty books, kitsch paintings of children or pastoral scenes, all he assumes raided from destroyed apartments. Nobody converses, empty shopping bags looking for bread or potatoes. Pasty faces. Locked in their own thoughts. The sullen-faced shopkeeper bridles at his request for an English newspaper. Why would she stock such a thing? He leaves with a copy of Neues Deutschland, choosing to walk on another block, rather than return the way he came.

In his peripheral vision he's aware of a young man in a donkey jacket, setting off in the same direction, on the other side of the road. Alec takes little notice but as he rounds a corner, he realises the young man is keeping pace, not very discreetly. He crosses the road and doubles back, hoping to thwart his companion, but still the shadow pursues him. There seems no harm intended, it's almost like a game; he could even be amused by it, and yet, when he finally steps back into the apartment, his mouth is dry and he shivers involuntarily.

Without removing his coat he scours the pages of the paper, fingers trembling at each page. Headlines praise the policies of the SDP, blowsy stories of commitment to the state. Slogans are printed in bold. *Vorwärts Deutsche Jugend für Frieden, German youth advance for freedom, Wir erkämpfen den Frieden, We fight for freedom.* Nothing about the murder or suicide of a junior minister in London. It's a relief of sorts.

The following day he takes the identical walk. His shadow already lies in wait as he leaves the apartment. He buys another copy of Neues Deutschland and chooses a longer route to return, an hour of exploration through cratered streets north-west to the border with the Western sector, but his accomplice never bores of him. He doesn't mention it to Ursula when he sees her that evening. In fact she barely talks, listening to her beloved wireless, head buried in crosswords. He supposes he's become a hindrance, at worst perhaps a threat to her safety. When he finds the courage to ask she deflects him. Better, she says to deal with practicalities than speculate about abstracts. She bids him goodnight.

On the Wednesday he walks for three hours, a circular route that takes him on a radius around Alexanderplatz towards the southern sector. He peruses shop windows. What goods there are look forlorn and unappealing. On a sudden impulse he rides a tram four stops in an easterly direction, crossing the road to return the same way. Always his shadow is there. Oddly it's becoming reassuring. He'd like to approach him for a pennyworth of company; in his mind he conjures a convivial acquaintance; but it's a hapless deceit.

On Thursday morning at precisely nine o'clock there's a sharp rap on the door. He's been up since five, eager to start, praying the work will occupy his churning mind. A rake-thin man stands before him, his white-blond hair receding from a bony skull. Eyes that never see sleep. "Herr Carter?"

"Yes."

"Put these clothes on. They'll be more acceptable. And they don't stink." He hands across a small suitcase which Alec accepts without comment. Returning to Kitty's bedroom he opens the case to reveal a tweed jacket, a cream shirt, a pair of grey trousers and dark socks. Buried underneath the clothes he discovers a pair of dark brown Brogues. The sizes are perfect. He can't remember the last time he looked so smart.

The wiry man appraises him on his return. "My name is Horst Klausen. My car is downstairs. I will give you further instructions on the way."

Outside his new companion steps towards a shiny VW Beetle, closing the passenger door with surprising courtesy once Alec has climbed in. The interior is equally spotless, a welcome relief after the soiled Trabant his previous accomplices had forced him to endure. They head south to Alexanderplatz, turning right onto the broad boulevard of Unter den Linden towards the Brandenburg Gate. Two guards stand on duty at the foot of the stone columns but show no concern as Horst steers them through into the Western sector. They pass the Soviet Memorial standing tall and proud to Alec's left, the skeletal Reichstag to his right, and looming in the distance, the Victory Column, symbol of past glories, so revered by Hitler and his cronies. It's only a couple of days since he walked this route, in the opposite direction. Returning feels like a welcome change of air, a heady assault of oxygen.

Horst drives fast, his eyes glued to the road. "You will be interviewed by Frau Rosenberg. Please give a good account of yourself. She is particular. You may embellish your credentials a little, but there's no need to lie. It's enough that you study at Cambridge. Be nice to the boy. They say he's too sensitive. You will arrange for the tutorials to occur twice a week, once in the daytime, once in the evening when Herr Rosenberg will be at home. Is that clear?"

"You're assuming I'll get the job."

"You don't have a choice."

As they steer around the Victory Column he glances up at the gilded form of Victoria, Roman goddess of victory, perched on top, before they continue west.

"In the daytime sessions you will quiz the child about his father's business and daily routine, anything you can gather. If you find an opportunity you will also investigate Herr Rosenberg's office. Sometimes the mother goes out for coffee. In the evenings you will establish a courteous relationship with Herr Rosenberg and find out all you can from him."

"What exactly am I looking for?"

"Information about his business practices. We know he has contacts in the East who sold him our heavy machinery for his factories after the war. They were traitors, profiteers. Vermin. He and they are just the same. We think he also buys sensitive information from them which he sells to the West German government. His personal wealth is built on exploitation. You should not feel ashamed of your assignment, Herr Carter. You should relish it. These people are Jewish shit."

They head north-west, the grand boulevard replaced by more intimate roads with boutique stores, cafes and nineteenth century town houses. There's a distinctive bustle to life, couples walking dogs, delivery vans, men in bars hunched over card games. Berlin seems to be a reservoir of fluid principles, claims and counter claims, shadows and mirages. Perhaps not just Berlin.

Horst pulls the car up at the end of a narrow street, the buildings either side a paradigm of fin de siècle elegance, graceful wrought iron balconies fronting louvered first floor doors, walls rendered in a variety of subtle shades.

"Go to number twenty-three." He points. "That one over there with the double balconies. You'll need these but you return them to me as soon as you're finished. I will be waiting outside in an hour." He hands Alec his passport and a working permit. "You charge twenty Deutsche Marks for one hour. Payment in advance. You will give me the money on your return."

"All of it?"

For the first time Horst smiles. "Don't try to cheat me, Herr Carter. It won't be worth your while."

Once out of the car he quickly runs through his possibilities. He has his passport in his hand, he could just run. But that would mean leaving Kitty behind. Glancing back at the waiting car he presses on the brass doorbell. At least if he meets Herr Rosenberg he can formulate his own judgement.

A maid delivers him to a drawing room on the first floor. His first impression is of opulence. Grand, gilt framed paintings adorn the walls, two high-backed sofas sit either side of a marble fireplace. Light dances across the room from a set of three balcony doors. Wafer thin curtains stir in the draft. Sitting opposite each other on the sofas are mother and son. Frau Rosenberg hovers over a silver tray, pouring coffee, raising her head with charming elegance as he performs an elaborate bow.

Such formality he knows plays better in Germany.

"Herr Carter, thank you so much for coming. You found us without difficulty?"

"Yes, thank you, Frau Rosenberg, it wasn't a problem."

"Ah, your German is excellent, as I'd been led to believe." She waves across at a young, dark-haired boy who sits awkwardly on the edge of the opposite sofa. "This is Stefan. Say hello to Herr Carter, Stefan. We hope he's going to help you with your English."

The boy mumbles a greeting and, complying with Frau Rosenberg's wishes, Alec settles beside him. "Before we proceed, I do apologise, Herr Carter, but would you mind if I see your paperwork? One can't be too careful these days."

"Of course." He stretches across to present her with the passport and work permit.

"Excellent. Some coffee?"

"That'd be kind. Thank you."

The pouring feels like an elaborate, beguiling ceremony. "Please tell us about yourself, you're currently studying at Cambridge, I believe?"

"I'm a history scholar. I'm taking a year out to study German social and economic policy in the early nineteenth century. Berlin seemed a good place to start."

"Our wonderful city has of course suffered but we have to make amends. Better to face your sorrows than run away from them, my husband likes to say. I hope he's right. But I'm glad you're studying a more honourable time. Sometimes I fear the world will only ever think of Germany with distain."

He sips the coffee. "Germany is not the only country with a stain on its conscience, Frau Rosenberg."

She smiles. He imagines she thought he said it to make her feel better. "Perhaps you're right." She turns to her son. "But we're not here to discuss politics, are we Stefan? So why don't I leave you two to get to know each other a little and then perhaps we can discuss some details afterwards."

"Of course." He places his cup and saucer carefully on the table, standing as she leaves the room, before falling back to the thick cushion beside his pupil. Stefan barely registers him, his eyes fixed beyond the windows to the apartments opposite. The task feels both arduous and insidious but he has no choice. He begins in English. "Do you speak English, Stefan?"

"A little." His accent is strong, hardly comprehensible.

"How old are you?"

"Ten."

"Very good." He wonders what to ask next, remembering Horst's words. It's vital the child trusts him. "What do you like to eat?"

For the first time the boy looks at him. Plainly he hasn't understood. He repeats the question in German. Was magst du gerne zu essen?"

"Chocolat."

Alec continues in German. They'll be starting from scratch. "They next time I come I'll bring you some chocolate. Would you like that?"

The boy smiles broadly, an assortment of teeth that haven't yet found their rightful place. Ten minutes later, after a brief foray into English nouns and adjectives, Frau Rosenberg returns, clearly delighted at the progress her son has made as Alec points to objects in the room for him to name.

"Excellent, Herr Carter. I'm sure Stefan will make huge progress. When can you start?"

As instructed, he arranges two lessons a week, one after school and one in the evening. He agrees his payment terms, fighting back his own discomfort, although his new employer seems more than happy to remove crisp notes from her purse and thrust them into his hand.

Stepping back outside, the notes pressed into his jacket pocket, he sees the VW Beetle has not moved. He feels his stomach tighten. A part of him had enjoyed his time with the Rosenbergs, whether it was just a brief moment of relief or whether because he was surprised to find he liked the boy, he wasn't sure. He climbs in, confronted by the smell of onions. Horst tosses the remnants of a bratwurst from the window.

"You did as I asked?"

"All the arrangements are made."

"And she paid you?"

Alec removes the notes from his pocket. Horst counts them before returning five Deutsch Marks, instructing Alec to give them to Ursula for his upkeep. "Your passport and work permit as well please. For safe-keeping."

Reluctantly he hands over the items requested. Horst executes a U turn and speeds away from the cosy, residential quarter. They haven't gone far before Alex spots a newspaper stall at a crossroads.

"Could you stop? I'd like to buy a paper."

 "I'm not a chauffeur, Herr Carter."

"Better a chauffeur than a thief."

Horst stamps hard on the brake, throwing the VW into reverse. He pulls up sharply beside the stall. "Be quick. If you run, I will find you."

Stepping from the Beetle, he locates the English language papers tucked in a corner of the stall. The Times and The Washington Post. The Times was printed on Wednesday. He buys it with the coins he has left in his pocket and heads back to the car. "Thank you."

Horst has lit a cigarette. "When's the next lesson?"

"Tomorrow. Three o'clock."

"I'll pick you up at twenty-five to three. You will wear those clothes again."

Conversation falters as the car swings back east, on to the boulevard. There seems little point in small talk, what the Hell do he and Horst Klausen have in common? Perhaps more than he cares to acknowledge. The newspaper curls in his damp palms. He deliberately avoids glancing at the front page; he'll wait till he's alone, but fear cramps his gut and tightens his sinews. Anxious to be back at the apartment he hopes the border guards don't stop them. But they're waved through without question. Either it's some magic spun by the lustrous Beetle or Horst is known to them. A little flick of Horst Klausen's index finger suggests it's the latter.

He finds Ursula wiping the floor with a mop when he returns. She wears an apron, shifting the furniture from one spot to another as if it had no right to be there. He imagines she's equally efficient at work. He'd hoped he could have let himself in with the key she'd given him and gone straight to Kitty's bedroom but some ill-placed politeness prevents him. The newspaper will have to wait.

"Have you heard anything?" He knows it's a hopeless question but he asks anyway.

Ursula deigns to lift her head. "She'll be back. I know she will. Sometimes it takes a little longer."

Her change of tone is both surprising and shocking. He wonders if she knows something but isn't telling him. "So, you're sure of that? You're not worried anymore?"

She shifts the bucket of soapy water across the floor. "It was a shock, seeing her so briefly before she disappeared again. But Kitty knows how to look after herself so I must trust her. Everything will be fine."

She spins around to mop the kitchen area. Her manner convinces him she's lying but he feels too uncertain of his ground to challenge her. "I've got something for you." He steps forward, neatly avoiding the wet patches of the floor, and removes the five Deutsche Mark note from his jacket pocket. "My wages. I was told to give them to you for housekeeping."

She takes the note and folds it into the pocket of her apron, her face softening a little. "You look very smart. Very English gentleman."

"Thank you. I was told I had to make a good impression so they gave me some fresh clothes."

"And did you? Make a good impression?"

"I think my pupil enjoys chocolate more than he enjoys learning English."

"I believe he and I would get on."

He smiles. Stirring an ounce of Ursula's heart has become a strange pleasure when there's little else to bring comfort. "His family's very wealthy. They could buy a factory of chocolate."

"Then the child would be sick from over-indulgence. All children are born Capitalists. It's only through the teaching and wisdom of Marxism that they learn not to be greedy."

Her derision shocks him. Or perhaps he's too sentimental. "I thought all children were innocent."

"Innocent of morals. These they must learn."

He sees no point in arguing. Nor does he feel he has much right to. "Perhaps. You're not at work today?

"Not till later. I'll make some soup once I've been shopping."

It's obvious she resents him, thrust suddenly into the role of his housekeeper. But to interfere with her routine, take control of any aspect of the household, would only bring further disharmony. He makes his excuses and returns to the sanctuary of Kitty's bedroom, closing the door behind him. Conscious of stale sweat dried to his back, he throws off the tweed jacket and removes the shirt, grateful for the cooling air. The newspaper lies on the bed beside him. He unfurls it, scouring the frontpage headlines. *American H bomb plans berated by Attlee. Churchill to resign?* He doesn't bother to read on, turning the pages until halting at page four. *Buchanan-Smith suspected heart attack.* He reads on. *Investigations into the sudden death of junior minister, Mr Buchanan-Smith, suggest that he might have suffered a fatal heart attack. Results from a post-mortem are expected shortly while the police continue their investigation. Evidence of a break-in has led to speculation that Buchanan-Smith might have experienced heart failure in an altercation. Mrs Buchanan-Smith was out of London with her children...*

He discards the paper and steps to the window, his gaze fixed on the tenement block opposite as if it might reveal some semblance of truth behind the words. Surely the results of a post-mortem would be established by now? He can only assume it's some sort of cover up. The establishment closing ranks to prevent the reputation of one of their own being tainted. Whichever way, he feels nauseous. Despite Kitty's emollient words he feels responsible for the death. Maybe her training's taught her to isolate her emotions, but he's floundering, with nowhere to run.

The following day, driving across to the western sector, Horst glances down at the newspaper, folded in his hand. "You like your paper, huh?'

"I thought I'd use it for English lessons. No one seems to have any textbooks."

"What does your English paper tell you?"

"Not much. Just that Winston Churchill's too old to be Prime Minister and our previous Prime Minister thinks the Americans are getting trigger happy with their hydrogen bomb."

Horst smiles. "Never go to bed with an American. You won't wake up in the morning." He laughs. Alec forces a grin.

The car speeds down the boulevard, leaving the Brandenburg Gate far behind them. Horst flicks ash from a crack in the side window. "Today will be a good day to explore the apartment. Frau Rosenberg will be out playing bridge. You must deliver a little something. They don't employ me just to be your dutiful chauffeur. And they know I get bored very easily if things don't happen. I trust you understand me."

He pulls the car up at the end of HaubachStrasse and reaches in front of Alec to the glove compartment, pulling out a small, rather battered metal case. "It's loaded with film. Just press and wind it on like this." He demonstrates the technique with ease. "No family snaps, please. I'll see you in an hour."

Alec had heard of the fabled Minox camera but never seen one. He slips the aluminium rectangle into his pocket and steps out of the car.

Frau Rosenberg greets him effusively in the drawing room but shows no intention of staying. She is dressed impeccably, her hat already in place, a handbag over her arm. Stefan sits in exactly the same place on the sofa, hands in his lap, dressed in shirt and tie as if he might be going to dinner. It's hard not to feel sorry for him.

She hovers at the door. "If you need anything please don't hesitate to call the maid. Her name is Doethe, she'll bring you whatever you request. Have fun, Stefan, and make sure you do as Herr Carter tells you. Auf Wiedersehen." The room falls to silence. Alec consults his surroundings, wondering if anything shows promise for mad Horst, but his eye falls on nothing other than the tasteful trappings of the bourgeoisie. He turns to his meek pupil, addressing him in German. "Well, Stefan, I think a coffee might be nice to start our lesson."

Stefan points to the brass button next to the fireplace. "Press that bell. Then she'll come."

He does as the child suggests before joining him on the sofa. "I brought this English newspaper. I thought we could read bits and learn some new words and phrases. Do you remember the ones I taught you yesterday?"

Again Stefan raises his finger, thrusting it around the room. "Door. Chair. Table. Glass. Books."

"Very good. Do you like sport, Stefan? Maybe we could read something about sport?"

"I don't like football. Papa says it's a game for the uneducated."

"Well in that case let's read about cricket. It's an English game. I think your father would approve."

He opens the paper to the sports section just as Doethe appears at the door. "Is there something you would like, Herr Carter?"

"I'd love a coffee, if that's not any trouble."

"Of course."

As she leaves Stefan glances up to him. "You're too polite."

"I was brought up like that."

"But not with servants."

"We didn't have any servants."

"Then who took you to the park?"

He smiles. "No one. I ran around the hills until it was time for tea. At your age I thought those hills went on forever and my friends and I were the only children in the world."

He watches for some reaction in Stefan's face. What he sees is a stillness, a moment of deep contemplation before the child speaks. "I can't imagine that."

"It wasn't perfect. No life is. But now I believe you're deliberately distracting me and we have work to do." He conjures a smile from the boy which kindles even deeper satisfaction than his moment of lightness with Ursula. Of such small things his life is now made. Clinging to the wreckage.

Spreading the newspaper in front of them he runs through the back pages to find an article he thinks appropriate. Most are analytical pieces covering county cricket club matches but there is one that describes a day at a local village match, written with a tongue in cheek affection for the quirks of English summer rituals. It starts with the preparations for tea. Although the tone is wistful he feels the aching emptiness return, a yearning for something which now seems remote and unreachable. The maid enters with a pot of coffee on the silver tray, jolting him to the task in hand. He thanks her and switches his attention to Stefan.

"This article is about a summer day in England. I'll trace my finger over the words as I read the first sentences and then you tell me if you understood anything. How does that sound?"

"Horrible."

He smiles. *"Many will argue that there is no greater pastime in this fair land than a day of village cricket, set on an idyllic green under a summer sky. While the tea urns hiss and rattle, and ladies prepare scones, their fingers speckled with jam and cream, drowsy spectators spring from their reveries to cheer a four across the boundary…"*

He reads another paragraph, aware that Stefan has understood nothing. But it doesn't matter. Although he'd be happy to improve his English it's not why's he's here. Though he wishes otherwise. "Did you understand any of that, Stefan?"

"Sky." The boy reverts to German. "Last time you pointed to the sky and you said it again just now."

"Excellent detective work. I can see we'll make a good team."

The boy smiles a broad, toothy grin. Alec finds himself unable to respond, dismayed by his own fraudulence. "I'll tell you what, I want you to underline any words you recognise in this article. Do you have a pen?"

"Yes. In my blazer." Stefan produces a smart fountain pen from his inside jacket pocket.

"That's a lovely pen. Now while you do that I just need to talk to the maid about something. I'll be back in a minute. Make sure you concentrate as long as I'm gone." He smiles. "If you do, there might be chocolate." In the same moment he realises he's forgotten to bring any chocolate but hopefully Doethe can help him. "Don't disappoint me, will you?"

Stefan shakes his head, taking his pen with glee to the word "*sky.*"

Heading out to the hallway, he observes doors to his left and right, some half ajar, others closed. He walks slowly, noting what he can through the cracks. One appears to be a dining room, another a small library. He treads on the soft rugs to muffle the sound of his footsteps, the courage to enter any of the rooms not yet stirring within him. Three wooden steps lead down to a much narrower passage which abruptly turns to the left. It opens to a small kitchen, crammed with cooking utensils, and smelling of fried onions and garlic, far more appealing than anything he's experienced at Ursula's. There's yet another room past the kitchen. He can hear music, light melodies, sounding like Frank Sinatra in German. It warms his heart.

He calls out. "Hello? Excuse me?"

No reply. He takes another step to the doorway. Doethe has her back to him, singing along to the music as she irons a shirt. The room steams from lack of air. There's no window. An open door beyond reveals a tiny boxroom, a single bed narrower than his own frame. "Excuse me, Fräulein?"

She turns and jumps. He apologises immediately stepping back a couple of paces. "I'm sorry if I startled you."

Quickly she regains her composure. "Not at all, forgive me, Herr Carter."

"The other day, when I came, I promised Stefan some chocolate. Unfortunately he remembered and I forgot."

She smiles, returning the hot iron to the board and stepping past him to the kitchen. He catches a waft of fresh linen. It reminds him of his mother. Opening one of the cabinets, she pulls out a jar, burdened with lollipops and shiny sweet wrappers.

"Take whatever you want." She offers the jar to him. "I promise I won't tell Frau Rosenberg that you bribed him." She smiles again. He's unsure whether she means it seriously.

"That's very kind. Oh, and the bathroom?"

"Second door on the left in the hallway."

"Thank you. You're very kind." He drops the sweets in to his pocket and retreats across the kitchen, looking back as he rounds the corner, to be certain she's returned to her ironing.

By process of elimination there are only two rooms in the hallway unaccounted for. The first he opens is a disappointment. A store cupboard, full of suitcases, clothes and an assortment of boxes. Moving to the second he stops at the door, listening for any sense of movement in the drawing room but Stefan gives no hint of restlessness. He turns the handle and steps in. Someone's study, presumably Herr Rosenberg's, as he'd hoped. The hallmarks of success abound; a mahogany desk decked in silver-framed photographs, a row of trophies on a shelf, expensive oil paintings, a matching, mahogany bookcase that swivels on its base. He leaves the door slightly ajar and walks across to the desk. The window behind looks over a communal garden, an urban oasis. Taking the Minox from his pocket, he scans the paperwork spread across the surface. There are figures and handwritten notes; he touches nothing but photographs it all, aware of the speed of his heart and trembling fingers, his ear bent to the door. Not a whisper. He feels bolder now, checking the drawers, most of which are unlocked but reveal only stationery. The central drawer doesn't yield. He checks the study door again before running his fingers along the inner edge of the drawer support, stopping at the sudden cool of metal. He'd seen people hide keys here in films, not thinking for a moment that he'd find anything, but then Rosenberg probably wasn't expecting his office to be violated. Ignoring his own self-loathing he places the key in the keyhole. It turns. The drawer slides open. On the left he sees a small pistol, to the right, what looks like a diary. He lifts it out, fumbling through scribbled pages until he reaches November, the most recent entries he supposes, being of most use. Starting at the first page he takes a photo and turns to the next, working as fast as his nervous fingers will manage. Turning the third page the camera falls from his grasp. It clatters to the parquet floor. He picks it up, slaps the diary closed and pushes it back into the drawer. Footsteps approach quickly from the kitchen. There's no time to retreat. He waits for Doethe to appear, certain she has heard his pounding heart.

She halts in the doorway; her kind smile replaced by loathing.

"Forgive me, Fräulein, I was looking for inspiration…I thought somewhere there might be some books that I could use for Stefan." He steps away from the desk. "But maybe you know of somewhere better."

She remains at the door, blocking his path. "Some people think because the Rosenbergs are wealthy that it's permissible to steal things. You wouldn't be the first tutor to disappoint them."

"It's not like that, I promise. Please. I was just curious. I've never been in a house like this. I wouldn't steal anything."

"You should leave."

"I swear, Fräulein, please, I beg you. It's not what it seems. I have no money. This job is the only way I can get by. Please, I swear I'm not like the others."

She considers for a moment, her face still held in a portrait of contempt. "You better give Stefan his chocolate. If it happens again I'll call the police."

"It won't, I promise. You don't know what this means to me."

She steps aside, allowing him to pass and return to Stefan, who has given up with the newspaper, oblivious to the world, as he plays on the floor with a figurine dog, that had previously sat on the mantelpiece. He looks up as Alec enters.

"I didn't find any word after *sky*. Then I got bored because you took so long."

Passing the camera back to Horst, he is overcome with self-loathing, a visceral state that turns his stomach sour and his breath rancid. But Horst doesn't seem to care.

"So, Herr Carter, you have the weekend free. Don't go far. I assume by now you know our slugs will trail you."

"It's come to my attention. Yes."

"Maybe now Fräulein Bernstein is unavailable you could find another pretty young maiden to fuck."

He ignores the comment, watching for Horst's index finger to rise as they pass the East Berlin border guards. The nail, he notices, is black with dirt. He wonders how to get through the weekend. Worrying about Kitty, appeasing Ursula as best he can, wondering what Doethe might say. If she tells the Rosenbergs, he's finished. Horst will have no qualms. Perhaps his driver is right, he should find a pretty girl. She might be his last.

Cold Road to Imber

21

He's woken early by a scraping sound, again like the shift of a chair, but there's no one else in Kitty's bedroom. He's heard these scrabbling noises before, wondering if there's a large rat in the apartment next door. Maybe some lonely pensioner's died and been forgotten, nibbled to bone. It wouldn't surprise him. But there's no smell of decay, just the lingering scent of Kitty on his pillow. Initially it brought comfort. Now it makes him want to retch.

To his surprise Ursula is already in the kitchen. For once she's abandoned her blue work overalls, her hair lapping her shoulders instead of trussed up in a scarf. She turns from the sink, her rubber-gloved hand the one clue to her work ethic. Her shorts and T-shirt show off a muscular form, hardly refined but not unattractive. "I just made some coffee."

He lingers, unsure of his place, wishing she were at work. "Thank you."

She brings the coffee pot to the table. Marital bliss. He attempts to smile, finding appropriate words. "No shift this morning?"

"I've got a free weekend. Once I've finished cleaning I thought I'd go to the park. It's a beautiful day if you like the cold."

He sips the coffee as she settles in the chair beside him.

"Why don't you join me? I can show you Berlin in the sunshine."

The idea of ambling in a park seems so hopelessly domestic, the antithesis of all that absorbs him. He fumbles for an excuse but conjures nothing convincing. "I'm afraid I left my overcoat in Cambridge." It sounds ridiculous, he knows. And she must sense it too because she's laughing at him.

"Katja told me Englishmen are very polite. But they don't always say what they mean."

"I'm sorry. I'm a bit…I'm not sure I'd be the best company."

"I think it would do you good. What else are you going to do today except mope in here worrying about Katja?"

"I might read the paper." Which he knows is a lie, but her mention of Kitty jars. He'd rather they pretended she didn't exist, or at least not involve her in such a frivolous conversation.

Ursula's gaze remains obstinately fixed upon him. "It's a big park. There's lots of space to explore. When you're not cooped within these walls, it's easier to breathe. You can borrow my father's old coat."

She sends him on an errand to the shop to buy some bread, wrapped in the moth-eaten overcoat coat that is a size too large. But it does its job though he's still dubious about a picnic in such ball-breaking cold. As usual his shadow is waiting across the road, his frosted breath rising to the sapphire sky. Perhaps it's a hopeful sign. If Doethe, the maid, had confessed what she'd witnessed to Rosenberg, presumably there'd be no need to spy on him anymore. Instead he'd probably already be in the back of Horst Klausen's car waiting to be dispatched. Forgotten. Like the pensioner.

Sitting next to Ursula in the tram, a string bag containing lunch on her knees, he plays the dutiful part of an East Berlin couple, mirroring those around them, who by the look of their own laps, have the same intention. At each stop he thinks about running, finding a way to escape, aware it's just fantasy. The best idea would be to spend the weekend anaesthetised. Perhaps Ursula packed a flask of cheap schnapps. At least it would fight the cold.

The tram slices south-east, metal grinding against metal. When the conductor announces Treptower Park most passengers disembark. The air bites hard as he steps onto the pavement. Instantly the crowd dissipates, spreading to distant corners of a vast, frozen park. He's not seen any recreational space since arriving in East Berlin. But these frosted fields, flat and broad, give aching comfort. An echo of Cambridge.

Ursula strides out along one of the broad avenues banging her gloved hands together; not a stroller, thank Christ. "We'll eat by the river but first we must get the blood flowing."

He marches with her, following a route which dissects the fields in perfect symmetry. Trees have been planted, still young but already they enhance the view. He finds his fears subsiding, the touch of warmth from the sun on his back a welcome elixir. Fathers play football with sons in frozen bubbles of steam while mothers and daughters crack puddles or rescue errant toddlers. It's a familiar, joyous scene yet it doesn't feel like an English park; he can't quite figure the difference, perhaps it's just quieter than he'd expect.

Ursula seems unmoved by the family pleasures. Her gaze hasn't shifted from their path. "The Russians turned the park into a memorial after the war to honour their dead. Everyone comes here when they have days off. But not so many come to see the memorial."

She leads him down a narrower track, which, beyond a line of bushes, broadens abruptly to a rectangular arena, laid in vast concrete slabs. Its scale is both brutal and impressive. Two triangular towers, carved from granite, rise above, climbing inwards towards one another to form a portal. Beyond them, his eye is lead past a series of stone-rimmed squares, laid in the concrete, to the statue of a soldier standing in the distance, on top of a pedestal, at least a hundred feet above the ground. Ursula says nothing. She draws him closer to the statue until he can see that the soldier is carrying a small child in his arm. In his spare hand a vast sword sweeps down to the steps. A crushed swastika lies at his feet.

Despite its starkness he finds it moves him. He's aware of Ursula's breath, distilling in the air as she hovers close by, as if she might catch him if he falls. At least, this is how it feels.

Her voice, when she finally speaks, is almost a whisper of reverence. "Eighty thousand Russian soldiers died trying to rescue Berlin from the Nazis. We have a lot to be grateful for."

He says nothing.

Suddenly she smiles. "But such a beautiful day isn't the time to dwell on the past. Come on, let's head to the river." She takes his arm to steer him away, only letting go once they are clear of the memorial. The Spey borders the eastern edge of the park. It doesn't take long to reach but it's in mournful mood. Standing on the bank, Alec observes the sluggish drift of thin ice, breaking and reforming like a watery kaleidoscope. He can't help comparing it to the Cam, nostalgic for the punting that will start in spring. They settle on a bench facing the river; an idyllic Brueghel scene were it not scarred by the noxious clouds of industry spilling in the distance. A sense of despair rekindles itself. Turning to watch Ursula unpack the bag he's glad to see she's brought two hip flasks. Otherwise there's little to celebrate in its contents.

"This will warm you up." She hands him the flask. He drinks copiously from its mouth, aware that she's watching him. He doesn't much care. Getting drunk is his sole objective.

"You're in love with Katja, aren't you?"

He's surprised by her directness. Vodka burns his belly. "Is everyone here a detective?'

"I wouldn't blame you. She's a beguiling woman. But she'll never be what you want her to be. Pursuing Katja will condemn you to misery."

He swigs again, wincing as it burns. "Happy thought on a beautiful day. But I don't have a choice. I can't just forget her."

"You might have to."

"They'd have to shoot me first."

"That would be a waste of two good lives. Which I won't let happen. Now hand me that bottle before you finish it off. The other one is schnapps. Our pudding."

Her request makes him smile. His turn to watch her drink. "I must thank you, Ursula. For everything you've done for me."

She slips the flask from her mouth and wipes her lips. "Don't flatter yourself. I did it for Katja. We all do everything for Katja."

In the morning he wakes again to a strange sound, but not the scratching next door. He prises open his eyes, it's early dawn. Ursula is gathering her clothes at the end of his bed. His head aches, his mind befuddled, dull, slowly awakening. He closes them again, thinking it best not to watch her but she's seen him.

"Go back to sleep." Still naked she carries her clothes out of the room as he slumps his head back to the pillow. He barely remembers. Perhaps it's best. A sick man's darkness envelops him, luring him back to oblivion.

When he eventually emerges he finds her cleaning again; this time the window above the kitchen. She scours as if her life depended on it, every crevice purged of grime, water dripping from the pane in a stream of tears. He wonders how so little can take so much of her attention.

"I thought Sunday was a day of rest."

She turns around, a wet rag dripping between her fingers. "Only if you believe in God."

He runs his hand around the back of his neck, erasing non-existent pain. But it at least massages his self-loathing. "Shall I make some coffee?"

"Sure."

He steps to the sink, aware of her body close to his, the smell of disinfectant overriding any sexual urge that must have crept upon them the previous day. "Thank you for showing me the park."

She has returned her attention to the window; a drier cloth collecting the smears of soapy water. "It was fun." She says it without any emphasis. No reference. He hopes it's a good sign. Yesterday was a different world.

He makes the coffee in silence, taking the pot to the table and lighting a cigarette. There's little to do but watch her. Finally she seems satisfied, a clearer view of the tenement block opposite, for what it's worth. She slumps into the armchair adjacent to his; her fingers are raw, red. Ink stains interspersed with bruised flesh. He wonders whether her body is the same. He can't remember. She makes no attempt at conversation, seemingly more at ease with the silence than he.

The ash on his cigarette hangs precariously. He taps it into the ashtray, mindful of any spillage that might upset her cleaning operation. "I can't help thinking about the memorial. So many Russian soldiers. I hadn't really thought about it like that."

"Don't feel too sorry for them. They took their reward. Everybody did. But how could we complain when they overran the Nazis?"

"I was under the impression, I imagined you thought of the Russians as heroes."

She fixes him again with the intense gaze he now finds familiar. "There are no heroes. Only hope. I could still point out Nazis who live round here. The people who pretend they always hated Hitler. And others who bear the scars of being raped by Russian soldiers. It's not a simple story with a happy ending. My hope is that Marxism will teach us to respect one another, share common values of humanity. For that, at least, I feel grateful to Russia for overthrowing Fascism. But for now the world is ruled by men who believe they are perfect and their enemies evil. Because men are flawed humans, not heroes."

He wonders how she can feel any hope at all when his own experience has been so squalid. But he feels closer to her, whether because of their lovemaking or her honesty, he's not sure. But something has changed. He feels a sudden urge to confide in her. In truth, he has no one else to turn to. "The boy I'm teaching English, in the Western sector, it's a cover. They want me to find out about his father, he's a successful businessman who they think's guilty of extortion of GDR property after the war."

"A lot of Westies took things that weren't theirs. You can hardly blame the GDR for wanting them back. Look at your British colonies."

"This family's Jewish. I wondered if they'd been singled out for that reason."

She hesitates, her coffee slipping back to the table beside her. Stepping to the wireless, she waits for the music to emerge before sitting down again. "Anti-semitism didn't just evaporate after the war, it went underground. The Nazis are now dormant, waiting for a better day, but I've no doubt some have bagged themselves key roles in the East German government. Which is why you can't trust anyone. No one does. It's a volatile situation. So in answer to your question, I think the Jews will never be safe. But for now, we hope the storm will pass. That decency will win out over depravation. You really shouldn't be here, Alec, but while you are, please be vigilant. Do as you're asked but don't take risks."

"I appreciate your advice. But I can't leave without Kitty."

She smiles, surprising him. "Not very flattering to say that to the woman you just slept with."

"Forgive me. I didn't mean to..."

"...You don't need my forgiveness. We did what we both wanted. None of us are immune to the perils of loneliness."

Hearing her label their plight so specifically is almost more than he can bear. He wants to hold her again, to seek comfort in her warm flesh, but he has to resist; it would only add more complication, and suffering. Deliberately he returns the conversation to Kitty. "When do you think you'll hear from her?"

"I don't know. You must be brave. Sometimes people just - disappear."

"Jesus Christ."

"You should leave. The sooner the better."

"I can't. They've got my passport and anyway, it's complicated. I can't go back to England."

"Then you have no choice. If you want to survive long enough to see Katja again you must do exactly as they tell you." She stands up, the intimacy of their conversation now broken. "Why don't you buy some rolls while I finish cleaning? We need food. It's one habit we all have in common."

More bloody rolls. He barely notices his shadow on the way to the shop. Or the sunlight that drizzles irregular shadows across mortar blasted walls. After their lunch of bread and cheese he takes a longer walk, mulling over what Ursula has said. He still hasn't been arrested; maybe he can formulate a plan of escape should he need it, though as yet he has no idea how. In the evening he asks Ursula about her family. The vodka helps him relax, but he's careful not to drink too much. She tells him about the bomb that dropped on her house. How she was lucky. And in response to her own questions, he recounts his story of Imber. Like their lovemaking, it feels part of another world. Parting at bedtime she kisses him on the cheek, and despite the tingling in his cock he resists the urge to embrace her.

When Horst bangs on the door, early Monday evening, he feels prepared to face the worst. A weekend passed with Ursula has given him some resilience, if not hope. But Horst shows no sign of changing their routine, as obnoxious as ever, leery, confident, self-serving. He can't think of many positive adjectives to describe his driver. They pull up at the usual spot in Haubachstrasse. Horst reaches for the Minox camera in the glove box.

"Get some more pictures of his diary, the earlier months. Don't get cocky but they were very pleased with the last lot."

"I won't need the camera, you idiot, Herr Rosenberg will be there. I'll concentrate on him and try to win his trust."

"Have it your way. But call me an idiot again and I'll kill you. Now piss off. I'll see you in an hour."

The maid, Doethe, opens the door. Her face gives nothing away but he assumes she hasn't told anyone about the incident in the study. Before she leads him into the drawing room he catches her arm. "Thank you, Doethe."

She says nothing, disappearing back to her kitchen. He's surprised to find only Herr Rosenberg when he enters the sitting room. A slighter man than he'd expected; he stands at the fireplace snipping off the end of a cigar, turning around with an effusive smile on hearing his guest enter. "Ah, Herr Carter."

Rosenberg walks to greet him, hand extended. His face is sallow, the skin prematurely aged though his hair is still dark, neatly cut. Everything about him is neat, refined. "Would you care for a cigar?"

His hand is warm, surprisingly soft. "Thank you. But perhaps not before a lesson."

"Then a cigarette, surely?"

He accepts. It's obvious there'll be some sort of chat before Stefan appears. Though he has no idea what it'll entail. He settles on the stiff sofa, Rosenberg sitting opposite, just as his wife had done. "Forgive me, Herr Carter, I was curious to meet you. Stefan says such nice things about you. I can't believe how much he suddenly likes to learn English. Plainly he wants to impress you so I must express my gratitude."

"The pleasure's all mine, Herr Rosenberg. He's a bright fellow." He hadn't expected Rosenberg to be so magnanimous, wondering if it's a trap or whether the entire family are genuinely so delightful.

"He tells me that you're studying at Cambridge. Such a beautiful city, I spent some time there in my youth. But he's a bit confused about where you come from. He tells me you lived in hills and ran forever."

He can't help smiling, recalling his conversation with Stefan. "That's partly true. I was born in a village a long way from anywhere. But the Americans commandeered it for the war effort so we had to leave."

"I'm sorry to hear that. And now you find yourself living in West Berlin which I imagine is a very different world. Where are you staying?"

He knew he might be asked this at some point. "In the Brunnenviertel."

"Ah, quite near the border with our friends in the Eastern Sector. Have you been over there?"

"Yes. Once or twice."

"And what did you make of it?"

He wonders where he's being led. Or whether Rosenberg is just naturally curious. But still he has to be careful. Neutral. "It seems... more damaged."

"It took the brunt of the fighting, that's true. I only wish they would let us help them repair it."

He senses an opening, a scrap that might feed Klausen's greedy stomach. "That's something you could do, Herr Rosenberg?"

"I've offered but I meet a wall of silence. I have a lot of contractors working for my company. They're all hungry for work and I've offered the East Berlin government very good terms but it seems they don't want to do business with me."

Alec glances about the room; at the wealth of objects. "You must have a very successful business but I imagine it must have been hard – after the war I mean."

"I started young. I had a good business manufacturing pre-constructed housing units before the Nazis took over. Then of course, things got difficult. We had to abandon everything and my factories were used for war machinery. Afterwards the Americans took them over briefly. They gave them back to me when my family returned. Everything had been destroyed by Hitler's henchmen. I spent five years sourcing materials and machinery. At times it was an unpleasant business, black marketeers, blatant extortionists, but I was determined the Nazis wouldn't beat me. I had people to employ and, in some ways, I had a debt to pay. I've seen a lot, Herr Carter, so nothing surprises me or takes me unawares."

Rosenberg's eyes hold his for longer than he finds comfortable. But suddenly Stefan launches himself through the door, throwing himself on to the sofa beside Alec. "Alec, did you bring some chocolate? I can count to one hundred in English now. See, one, two, three, four …

Rosenberg smiles with pride. "…You see, Herr Carter, my son is very fond of you and he's learning fast. I'll leave you both to it. Perhaps we can talk again, when you next come. I think an evening visit, this time, would be preferable. Is Friday acceptable?"

"Of course, Herr Rosenberg. Thank you." He stands up, mindful of formalities, as Rosenberg leaves the room. "So, Stefan. No chocolate until you name eight different colours in

English." He remembers he still he has a few of the sweets left in his trouser pocket.

Horst is plainly irritated when he returns. "You're late. One hour and nine minutes."

"Herr Rosenberg wanted to introduce himself. We got talking. It was useful. I thought that's want you wanted."

Horst swings the car around, seemingly too impatient to go around the block. "An hour. No more. If he abuses your tutor time bad luck for the boy. If you're late again bad luck for you."

Aware that Horst Klausen could be capable of anything, he tries to calm him down, stringing out Rosenberg's story, embellishing where he can, convincing him there's more to discover. The dirt that Horst and his cronies crave.

Crossing back into the Eastern sector he's relieved to escape from the car. He watches the Beetle speed off down Fehrbahnstrasse, presumably on another specious mission. His mouth tastes bitter, the repellent association with a monster like Klausen. And to what purpose? To feed some waning hope of re-uniting with Kitty. He wonders what it would take to murder his accomplice. A few well-aimed blows to the head as Klausen pulled up the car. It could be done. He doubts Horst Klausen's much of a fighter unless he's armed with a pistol. But he's already got Buchanan-Smith's blood on his hands. The stain seems to be spreading. Beyond his control.

He finds Ursula slumped in one of the chairs. It's obvious she's been crying. A handkerchief clutched in one hand, some morsel of paper in the other. Instinctively he knows.

The sweat gathers at his collar as she hands him the tiny scrap of paper. It could be cheap toilet roll. Three short sentences are scribbled in pencil. Kitty's hand. *Life sentence. Alec must leave. Not safe!* He falls into the chair beside her, reading it again, scouring for hope between the words but finding none. He crushes the note and throws it to the floor.

Ursula lifts her head, her eyes puffy and swollen. "I found it in my letterbox this morning. Somebody must have smuggled it out for her. How can they treat her like this? She's not a criminal."

He sits forward on his chair, beginning to think now. Mapping a path to avoid despair. He takes Ursula's hand in his, unsure whether he can trust her; knowing he has no choice.

"Do you know why Kitty's in prison?"

She doesn't answer immediately, instead rising again from her chair to switch on the wireless, waiting for the glow of the valves to highlight the radio stations. The band plays on, bellicose and unrelenting. She increases the volume before returning to her chair, her eyes clearer now. "When you sleep in Katja's room, do you hear odd noises next door?"

"I thought they might be rats at first. But it's too specific."

"The room next door is for the caretaker. But the Stasi use it. You've met them of course, the secret police."

"I wouldn't call them my friends."

"They spy on us all the time, ever since we moved here. They listen through the walls with a stethoscope. They even use a camera. There's a small hole high in the wall. They must stand on a desk. Kitty thinks I don't know all this. But you don't get upgraded to a bigger apartment just because you're a civil servant. I always had my suspicions that Katja was more than that but it's safer not to say anything. To pretend you don't know."

"She didn't choose this life, Ursula. You must understand that.

They forced it on her."

"Perhaps. But her mistake was that she began to believe in her work and to revel in her status. For that they will punish her. She flew too close to the sun."

"I know she made mistakes, she wouldn't deny it. But to punish her with a life sentence. That can't be right. Surely she must be able to appeal?"

To his surprise she smiles, though it's joyless. "You're a gentle man, Alec, but you're naïve. We live in a dangerous place. The GDR has had a difficult beginning and it's still wild, like the West in all those Yankee, cowboy films. Like I say, I live in hope that sanity will return. But I can't say when."

"And Kitty…?"

"…She'll probably remain locked up until that time occurs. And your life will always be in danger."

He picks the crumpled note from the floor and unfolds it, staring again at the scribbled words. "You really think this is true?"

"Katja knows more than us. If she's risking her own life to tell you, she can't be playing games."

He hangs his head, blood draining from his limbs. A rag doll. Ursula fetches a glass of water and hands it to him. "Sip slowly. It's just shock."

"I won't abandon her."

"You have to. Go back to the West. Where you belong."

He sips the water. It calms him. And now he must tell her. His

361

only ally. He lifts his head. "It's not that simple. Something went wrong with one of Kitty's assignments in London. Someone high up in government she was supposed to crack for information. I got suspicious and jealous and followed her. When I saw him…touching her…I was drunk, I lost my mind. I tried to kill him. But I failed. Kitty had to finish my fuck up to protect the trail, she thought it would be safer for me, for us both, to come here. No one in England will trace her but if I return and they pin enough evidence on me I'll probably hang…And I suppose, thinking about it now, that's the right decision. It was my fault, not hers. I should be the one atoning instead of fleeing like a coward."

She takes his hands in hers. They are calloused and cold but nevertheless he finds the gesture comforting. "Katja is not innocent. She made her choice. You got caught up in something you couldn't understand. You're a good man, Alec. Accidents happen. Especially when you choose to live dangerously."

Suddenly he feels an anger, resentment. "I didn't choose it."

She takes her hands away. "Perhaps. Falling in love is never a choice. But ignoring the warning signs makes fools of us all."

He has to laugh, short and hollow. "So now I'm a gentleman and a fool."

She smiles. "A handsome fool. Do you still have your passport?"

"They took it from me."

She drops her head; like someone taking confession. Then she draws closer, her voice barely above a whisper. "I know someone at the printing factory. He does very good copies, all sorts of things. Perhaps he could make you a new one."

"I can't. I won't put you in danger."

"You wouldn't. No one would be surprised if I spoke to him. And the machinery is too noisy for anyone else to hear. I wouldn't be the first. After that it would be up to you."

"It's still too dangerous. Ursula. What if they traced you? You don't owe me anything, you've been too kind already."

She smiles, lighter this time, and he feels quite overwhelmed, working hard to restrain himself from embracing her. "Your heart will always belong to Katja, not me. I might as well send you packing. At least with a passport, you'd stand a chance. And maybe, if this country finds its way to freedom, Katja will be released. And you will be there to embrace her."

The following day, Ursula returns after her shift, drawing her finger to her lips as he greets her. She bids him to come closer, whispering into his ear as she grips his arm.

"It's arranged. You'll meet him tonight. First you must go for a walk to see if you're still being trailed. Then we'll make a plan."

He does as she requests, leaving the apartment block in the early afternoon, his head spinning with a mix of elation and fear. At first he sees no evidence of his regular companion and dares to hope that they might have lost interest. But once he turns the corner, his hope dissolves. A taller individual in a black jacket falls into step behind him on the other side of the street. His brief elation vanishes. He throws a half-smoked cigarette to the ground and returns to the apartment.

At seven o'clock, after meticulous instructions from Ursula over a light supper, he dons her father's overcoat and creeps out into the corridor again, turning right to avoid the Stasi spy den. She'd told him to leave the bulb on in Kitty's room. Near the stairs he locates the door she drew on a piece of paper. It has no number, just a bolt which is fastened but apparently not locked. There's no one about. He slides it back and steps out on to a metal fire escape which zigzags down to the courtyard. Light spills from curtainless windows but not enough to capture him. A blanket of cloud dispatches any moonlight. He hurries across the broken, weed-strewn concrete, targeting a dim ground floor window in the opposite block. A dog barks. He leans back against the wall. Someone draws back a curtain, searching, then scolding the dog before retreating. He breathes again, running his fingers up and down the rusted casement frame, searching for a faulty latch which yields to a heavy blow. He checks his hand; bruises but not cut. Climbing in, he gags at the air, fetid and rank, as if something died a week ago. He stumbles across the room until he finds a door which leads out to the corridor. There's no sound of activity, no hint of footsteps. Unclasping the latch he steps out, walking briskly to the exit, finding himself on a parallel street, virtually identical to Fehrbahnstrasse, except he sees no shadow lurking. He breathes deeply, the cool air filling his lungs, expelling all that was rancid.

He's memorised Ursula's scribbled map, in case someone stops him. The route takes him further east; about a fifteen-minute walk, she said. He hopes to do it in twelve. He walks purposefully but not too fast, head down against the cold breeze, anxious to avoid eye contact should he encounter anyone. But thankfully the streets are deserted. To his surprise he passes through an area of elegant nineteenth century apartments that are for the most part undamaged, but the apparition is short-lived. Further on, at the eastern end of the Botzowviertel, the tenement blocks are more derelict than anything he's seen. As if the war had just ended yesterday. He finds the narrow alleyway that Ursula had earmarked. The buildings either side are too dangerous to be occupied, a chaotic mound of brick and ironwork lies at their feet, almost concealing the entrance to the alley. He picks his way across the mangled heap, checking behind him before disappearing along the passage. It's so dark he has to feel his way, wishing he'd brought a torch, and grateful when a door eventually reveals itself on his right. He knocks twice, waits, then twice more. Footsteps. Someone climbing wooden stairs. The sound of his own breath, ragged, ridiculously shallow.

"Wer ist es?"

"Dein Bruder."

As the door opens he finds an older man than he'd expected. Perhaps sixty. Soon to retire, no doubt. He wonders why this man should put himself in such danger.

"Machen die Tur zu."

The man turns around to head back down the stairs, lighting their way with a torch. Alec shuts the door and follows him into the basement. They pass a series of coal bunkers, empty, presumably raided for fuel after the war. Rounding a corner, they enter a larger room lit by two paraffin lamps. An industrial-size porcelain sink stands in the corner, a laundry chute descends from the floor above. Before the war it must have been the residence of a wealthy family. A wooden chest, lined with narrow drawers, stands beside an iron desk. On the desk-surface there's an array of pens and ink, all neatly ordered and categorised. A large magnifying glass is screwed to the wall above.

The man coughs. Perhaps he's ill. Not as old as he'd first thought. "What is it you want?"

There's no interest in his voice, no room for pre-amble. It's just a question.

"I need a passport. A British one. As soon as possible. Can you do it?"

"It's an expensive request. There's the risk, of course, and the cost of the work."

"How much?"

"Seventy-five Deutsche Marks. But West German. In advance."

His heart sinks. There's no chance of finding such money. Bluff is his best call. "How do I know you'll honour the deal? I need proof before I'll pay anything."

The man removes his wire framed glasses, polishing them on his vest. Purple rings line his eyes, creases of grimy flesh cascading to the edge of his hollowed cheek bones. He turns to his cabinet, opening one drawer after another until he finds what he's looking for. Alec glimpses passports stacked on top of each other; varying colours and sizes. He pulls out two dark blue ones. British.

Alec reaches out but the old man holds them tight. From what he can tell, they seem authentic enough. "Where did you get these?"

"People scout for me. Tourists lose them or sometimes I buy them from an obliging policeman. We all make a living. One I think is for a man. Yes, this one. I can sell it to you for less if we just change the photograph but I acquired it only recently so we must assume he is still alive, which might cause you complications, if you want to get back to England. Or we start from the beginning, change everything and then…" he spreads his hands in to the air like a bird taking flight, "…you are a free man, ready to fly." For the first time he smiles, his mouth a cavern of decay.

Alec recoils. The breath escaping as rotten as the old man's teeth. He unfastens the strap of his wristwatch. "This is all I have for now. It was a gift from my parents. It's not worth much but it means a great deal to me. If I leave it with you it's a promise that I'll keep my word and return with the money."

The man accepts the watch, turning it in his hand. Evidently unimpressed. He looks back to Alec. "You have nothing else?"

"No. There's nothing I value more. Please. I beg you."

The man considers his acquisition a moment before shuffling round to a smaller cabinet. From it he produces a box-shaped camera and a large flash bulb. "Stand against the wall please." Alec does as he requests. The man lifts his camera but drops it to his side again, stepping across to Alec. "May I?" He wets his fingers and slicks the errant strands of Alec's hair across his forehead before stepping back again. "Try to smile, please. You look so sad."

A searing white light blinds him temporarily before the dingy room reassembles itself. The man has returned the box camera to his desk, coughing again, as if the effort of lifting it had completely exhausted him. He pulls across a grubby little notebook and licks the stub of a pencil. "What will your name be?"

It isn't something he'd even thought about. He searches for an idea but nothing comes, yet it's such a simple request. Then one name conjures itself to the fore, James Atherton, his old teacher and carer.

"James – James Michael...Anderson."

The man scribbles it down. "Born?"

"Nineteenth of March." His mother's birthday. "1934"

"Eye colour?"

"Hazel. No, just put brown."

"Place of Birth?"

He has to think again. Part of him wants to put somewhere far away from Imber. For safety. But it feels disloyal. If he's going to be re-invented he'd prefer his birth place to be at least nearer the truth. "Devizes, Wiltshire." He spells it out.

The man writes slowly then drops his pencil stub. "Two days. Come back with the money at the same time on Wednesday. Tell no one but Ursula. Now you must go. When you leave the alley make sure no one sees you."

The route back is still quieter. He scurries across the city, seeking shadows where he can, stepping back from the road when he hears the whining two stroke of an approaching Trabant. Arriving back half an hour before his rendezvous time. To his dismay there's no reply when he rings the bell of the rancid apartment. He's early. Ursula can't be there yet. He slumps behind the wall, shivering with cold and exhaustion until he hears the click of the door fifteen minutes later. Without exchanging a word they scramble back, through the putrid air of the abandoned apartment, to the sanctuary of their own walls.

She whispers once the door is closed. "Was it helpful?"

He nods.

"Get some sleep. Make a bit of noise before you go to bed. As if you got drunk and stayed up too late."

But after switching out the light he cannot sleep. His eye fixes on the tiny hole in the bedroom wall, high above his bed. It looks more like a stain than a hole, presumably made before Kitty and Ursula had moved in. Clinging to the bedclothes for warmth, he wonders how such elevated and noble ideals, the promise and hope of which Kitty had spoken so much, with such conviction, could come to this. A shabby informer behind a bedroom wall. An invisible peeping Tom.

In the morning he returns to the bread shop. It seems a good idea to show his face to his shadow; to maintain their little routine. Ursula is still asleep when he returns; he remembers she has a night shift. Brewing a very strong coffee he sits down on the hard armchair and lights a cigarette, wondering whether he can trust the old man, whatever his name. Ursula never told him. In reality he has no choice, he's at his mercy. It's just the question of payment. He runs his fingers around his wrist, feeling the absence of his wristwatch. Like a soldier losing a limb. Except a soldier knows what he's fighting for. He drinks too much coffee, smokes too much, running over possibilities and getting nowhere, impatient for Ursula to wake up. Though he can't really see how she can help.

Eventually she strays in wearing a thin dressing gown. Her bare calves are nut brown, sinewy ankles. His mind reels back a couple of nights and he's shocked to find himself aroused. It's the coffee; too much adrenalin.

He lifts his eyes to her face. "How did you sleep?" It's an innocuous question but he wants to be grounded. There's barely anything left he can be sure of.

She slumps onto the other chair. "I didn't."

"There's a pot of coffee. I made it very strong." He walks to the kitchenette, wanting to distance himself. Break the flow of his thought. At least not see her limbs for a second.

She switches on the wireless. Loud enough. He returns with a mug of coffee, dropping it on the table beside her.

She covers her legs, as if reading his thoughts. "When will it be ready?"

"Tomorrow evening."

"I'll be here again so we can use the same route."

He lights a cigarette, offering her one, which she takes, shifting nearer to the flame for him to light it. "There's a problem. He wants seventy-five West German Deutsch Marks and I don't have it. I gave him my watch but he still wants the money."

She sits back in the chair and to his surprise she smiles. "For once you have some luck. Katja keeps money in her desk. I don't know how much exactly but hopefully enough. You'll have to force the lock, she always takes the key with her. And you better sing while you do it, we don't want to alert our friend next door with strange noises."

He wants to hug her. "You haven't heard me sing."

The lock yields easily. The wood is rotten. But he'd been unprepared to find quite so much money stashed in various, yellowing envelopes, all marked by their currency; a mixture of dollars, sterling and West German Deutsch Marks, easily enough to pay his passport man. Beside the envelope there's a stack of photographs. He doesn't want to pry but finds himself unable to resist. They're mostly of a young girl, presumably with her parents. Kitty is instantly recognisable, the beauty not quite yet fully formed but still apparent. On either side a man and a woman, probably in their early forties. They obviously adore each other. What strikes him most is the innocence, or perhaps not so much innocence as contentment. He passes his thumb across her face. One photo particularly grabs his attention; Kitty and her mother kissing large pink puffs of candy floss at a fairground. They look unbearably happy, maybe her father said something funny as he took the photo. He slips it into his jacket pocket and shuts the drawer.

Slipping out again on Wednesday evening he feels more nervous, not so much because he might be caught, that possibility always lingers in his mind and is still the most likely outcome. It's more the chance that he might not be; that the old man might deliver his freedom. It's an inconceivable thought, and one only conjured by Kitty's smuggled note. Without her sanction he would never have tried. He fantasies about their re-union, speculating where it might be. For now he imagines an old farmhouse, maybe somewhere in the South of France, in six months' time, when the vines will be heavy with grapes and the air swells with the scent of lavender. Because life imprisonment must surely be just a threat? An example to others. A public slap of humiliation before you're reconciled to the Party.

The door in the narrow passageway opens again to his knock. The old man leads him back down the steps into the laundry room. By the flickering light of the paraffin lamps he sees that he's wearing his watch. He wants to punch him. Perhaps he still will.

"You have the money?"

He withdraws the crisp notes from his pocket but resists placing them into the ink-lined paw of his potential saviour. "Let me see it first, then you get the money."

The old man turns to his cabinet, careful to keep Alec in his sight line. He selects a dark blue passport from the thin drawer, opening it at the identity page. "You should be very happy, I think. There are far worse copies in circulation. I believe if you do a job you should do it well, no? Now the money, please."

Scanning the page quickly he can see that it's expertly done. He hands over the notes, receiving the passport in return. Everything is as he'd wished. A border guard would have to scrutinise it under a magnifying glass to spot the tampering; a very slight coarseness to the touch where the details have been re-written. Nothing more. "Thank you. You've done an excellent job."

The old man folds the money and drops it into his shirt pocket. "Now you must go."

"First my watch. I only gave it as an act of trust."

"Consider it a down payment. I put myself in danger for you. If you hadn't returned I would have nothing to show for it."

"I've given you the money. That was the sum we agreed."

"Trust is expensive my friend. You will learn that."

"I'm not leaving without it."

The old man sighs, sunken with exhaustion. "You have no choice. Of course you may tell yourself, I can beat this man so he falls to the floor, it wouldn't be hard to steal back my watch. But then my wife would find me and I have already told her about you. She might tell someone else and then see how quickly they find you. You mustn't judge me too harshly, Herr Anderson. We all need to survive. I will sell your watch to pay for medicine to relieve her pain. She has lung cancer. Go now, please. The longer you stay, the greater the danger for both of us."

He turns abruptly, passport clenched in his hand, back into the freezing night air, wondering whether to believe the old man or not, despising his new-found cynicism.

To his relief, Ursula is already waiting. He says nothing until they reach the safety of her apartment, the wireless still playing its ceaseless repertoire of marching tunes. Despite the loss of his watch he feels elated, a small act of defiance to restore his pride, whatever obstacles may lay ahead. His chilled fingers reach into his coat pocket. "He's done a brilliant job. Take a look."

She turns on him, hissing under cover of the wireless. "Don't be foolish."

He returns it to his pocket, embarrassed by his error, born of naïve enthusiasm. Watching her step to the kitchenette to open a bottle of vodka he wonders how he might ever repay her kindness and bravery. If he and Kitty are labelled traitors, then Ursula, if she were ever found out, would be a sacrifice of their making. He wonders whether to suggest she defect to the West; before it's possibly too late.

"D'you think you'll stay here? If Kitty doesn't return?"

She stops what's she's doing, seemingly taken aback by the question. "Of course. Where else would I go? I might have to move back to a smaller apartment but that would be the right thing to do. There are families that need the space more than me."

He doesn't answer, unsure what to make of her optimism for the GDR's future. Clearly, she has more faith than him. And perhaps she'll be proved right.

He changes the subject. "Will I see you in the morning?"

"I've got a twelve-hour shift tomorrow, starting at seven. So maybe I should wish you good luck now. Just in case."

He hasn't yet formulated a plan. The idea of evading either his shadow or Horst in an escape seems absurd, beyond possibility. Yet, as Ursula steps towards him, he understands there can be no delay. He must leave imminently. The longer he stays the more dangerous her own predicament. "I'll buy some food before I leave for my English lesson. There'll be something to eat when you get back."

She steps away from the kitchenette and kisses him tenderly on the cheek. "Thank you, Alec. I really hope your lesson goes well." As she turns her back on him, towards her bedroom, he reaches in his pocket for his cigarette packet. It stops him walking after her.

The next morning he still has no cogent plan. Only one thought has occurred to him. He steps outside to go shopping, not surprised to see the shadow waiting as usual. A different one again. Three now. He deliberately chooses to walk past the entrance to the other tenement block to see if he could escape the same way; this time with a valid passport. It seems the best option. But turning the corner of the street he discovers his first shadow lurking at the door. As if they've guessed somehow. The shadow even smiles, an acknowledgment of recognition, as if he were meeting a distant neighbour in a street. He hurries past, sweat soaking his shirt, wondering who told them. Kitty had warned him that many citizens spied on their neighbours, either driven by paranoia, or money, or just nosiness. But his own shadowing feels more akin to imprisonment. At any rate his one idea is dead in the water. Back in the apartment, he takes a shower and dresses in the jacket and shirt lent to him for his lesson. As a last thought he removes the remaining West German Marks from Kitty's drawer. He'll repay her when they're together again. He'll buy her dinner in Monte Carlo.

Horst Klausen raps sharply on the door at six o'clock, sullen, untalkative, and driving like a maniac. Alec feels no inclination to find out why. Perhaps he's been dumped by a girlfriend. More likely, he's found out some prostitute's given him the clap. These speculations calm him. He almost wants to laugh. The hard edge of his new passport peaks from his inside pocket. He prays Klausen won't spot it.

The Beetle smells of acrid disinfectant. He winds down the window. It prompts his sour-faced companion to speak, his tone cold as gun metal. "They want better information. You gave me shit; stuff they already know about. Ask him details about his contacts in the East. People he works with or does deals with. They want names of traitors." He swings the car around Alexanderplatz, narrowly missing a tram.

"They can't expect me to get that kind of information straight away. He'll suspect something."

"I've had a shit day, Englishman, don't disappoint me. You're not the only one under pressure. You give me something, I save your butt. And you save mine. It's called teamwork. Like that American couple, the ones who stole from the rich to give to the poor. Bonnie and somebody."

"Bonnie and Clyde? They killed policemen and robbed banks for their own gain."

"Because the Capitalist pigs had made them poor through exploitation. Didn't you study at school? They were forced to kill to survive. Anyway, killing fat Americans is good sport."

He doesn't bother arguing the point. But he's grateful for the distraction. Passing through the Brandenburg Gate he watches for the grubby, raised finger as the Beetle speeds past the East German border guard. He wonders when or how he might return, stealing himself from turning around to watch the Gate recede, just in case Horst suspects something. A plan of sorts has woven through his brain. His heart quickens, daring to hope that Horst will let him out of the car without guessing his thoughts. The car skips north-west towards Charlottenburg, pulling up abruptly in Haubachstrasse. He wipes the sweat from his palms onto his trousers.

But Horst Klausen is barely looking at him. "You don't need the camera today. Just get the fucking information."

"If Rosenberg doesn't want to talk there's not much I can do."

"Everybody wants to confess their misdemeanours in the end. It's human nature. Make him confess. Dostoevsky said that. He's a writer."

"And he's dead, I daresay like a lot of people you've known."

He's about to shut the car door but Horst leans over, grabbing his arm.

"Don't be clever with me, Englishman. Out in the wild, who survives the night? The scholar or the sniper?"

Alec pulls away, crossing the street to the apartment, his legs so light and bloodless they barely carry him. He waits for Klausen to shout, or rush after him, but neither happen before he reaches the elegant, nineteenth century door, ringing the bell and avoiding a glance back to the car. Doethe's footsteps patter across the hall. She closes the door behind him and he prays he will never see Horst Klausen again. He follows her up the stairs to the sitting room; to his disappointment only Stefan is waiting for him, though he can hear voices emanating from the dining room.

The child seems genuinely pleased to see him. "Hello, Alec. I hope you brought chocolate. Father gave me a sip of wine at dinner. He says it'll make my English better."

He smiles. "Maybe it will. In which case I'll have to bribe you with wine as well as chocolate. Like a grown-up. Now, show me what you've done."

He settles on the sofa beside the boy, finding it hard to concentrate on the pages of homework. For half an hour he introduces new verbs, nouns and adjectives but his heart isn't in it and he can tell Stefan is dispirited by his lacklustre performance. Despite his intention, he repeatedly flicks his gaze to the carriage clock on the mantelpiece, aware of time passing and ebullient conversation next door which only highlights the unusually sullen atmosphere of their English lesson. But with twenty minutes to go, Frau Rosenberg skirts into the room, a little flushed with alcohol, and suggests that he come through to the dining room for a drink and some cheese. Perhaps her intuition told her the lesson wasn't his best. Whatever her reasoning, he knows it's his only chance.

She smiles at her son. "Go and play now, Stefan. I'm sure Herr Carter could do with a break and you'll see him next week."

Stefan shows no resistance, plainly glad the lesson is over. But his courtesy remains. "Thank you, Alec. But please bring chocolate. I like it better than wine."

He smiles. "I promise." Though he can't even think about next week.

The boy runs off and Frau Rosenberg smiles again. "Please come through, Albert and I were just thinking how nice it would be to hear more about your life at Cambridge."

He glances at the clock again. Fifteen minutes. Horst will be waiting.

The room is both opulent and cosy. Burgundy curtains of the softest velvet are drawn across the windows. A haze of smoke drifts in lazy curls in the warm light. Candles abound. He's never seen so many except at a church service. Herr Rosenberg rises from his chair at the far end of the mahogany dining table, another of his cigars in hand.

"Ah, Herr Carter, I'm so pleased you have time for us. Please. Sit down. We have cheese. Would you like a glass of port, like the English do, or I have schnapps?" He indicates the chair beside him and his wife settles opposite.

"A port. Thank you." He wonders how to begin, but a port might give him courage. Rosenberg pours three glasses and settles the decanter on the table, returning to the head of the table. "I know you have this tradition of passing the port but forgive me, I can't remember the detail. Perhaps you would remind me."

He tries to smile. "You pass it to the left. You pour your own glass and pass it on."

"Ah yes, clockwise. Very logical. I imagine in a noble institution like Cambridge University there are many such occasions."

"I suppose there are, but it's not often like that." He tries to relax, realising his hosts want to hear more. "There's a lot of what we call 'pub crawls' as well. Young men drinking too much and then jumping into the river for a dare after closing time."

Frau Rosenberg laughs. "It sounds quite dangerous."

"The alcohol numbs the pain." He's aware he's sipping the port too quickly, desperate to find the right moment to speak.

Herr Rosenberg pushes the decanter towards him. Alec refills his glass, unsure whether to hand it on to Rosenberg's wife. She looks too refined to play such men's games.

Rosenberg takes an ostentatious puff on his cigar. "So how did you come to choose Berlin as the city in which to study? I would say Paris and Rome are more beautiful, and perhaps not as troubled since the war."

"But you can't speak German." He knows he sounds too defensive, almost petulant. He wishes he had his wristwatch. The dining room mantelpiece lacks a clock.

"Yes, of course, forgive me." Rosenberg glances at his wife, a gesture that Alec witnesses, as if perhaps he is seeking permission. But her face never surrenders its elegant poise. "But I was wondering why a history student would be so keen to further their German. Unless you have another purpose. Or maybe you just enjoy languages. In curiosity I turned to one of my trusted friends, a Cambridge scholar himself. When I mentioned your name he seemed quite shocked, apparently your name is well known in Cambridge circles. The student that suddenly vanished into thin air. There's rumours that you're a defector, like your fellow alumnus, Donald Maclean. Indeed I gather you attended the same college as him…"

"…Herr Rosenberg, I can explain."

"Of course. I hoped you would." Herr Rosenberg's face is a study of dignified restrain.

In contrast he feels heat rush from his heart, prickling his forehead in a sticky sweat. "I'm not a defector, but I'm in trouble. And I need your help."

Rosenberg glances back to his wife. "You need my help yet you creep into my study and break into my desk."

"Please. It's not how it looks, you must believe me. I was sent here by the Stasi, they're hunting for what they call traitors using me as a cover. It wasn't my choice. I met a German girl in Cambridge, something happened, a terrible accident, and we came to Berlin. Now the Stasi have put her in prison and they're keeping me hostage, doing their dirty work. I was in your study looking for any information on your contacts or your routine. I took some pictures of your diary for which I sincerely apologise."

To Alec's surprise his host laughs. "They'll find nothing useful in there. Unless they want to know what I had for breakfast."

"My controller's waiting outside. He's expecting names of your business contacts in the East. If I don't leave in the next few minutes with that information I expect he'll terminate my contract. In other words he'll kill me."

He's spoken so quickly he finds himself breathing hard, desperately scanning Rosenberg's eyes for any understanding of his plight. But Rosenberg simply glances once more to his wife who reaches for his manicured hand, presumably showing sympathy for this violation of their family.

"Please, Herr Rosenberg, I'm begging you for help. Even if you don't think I deserve it."

"Was this German woman a spy?"

"Yes."

"Working for the Stasi?"

"They recruited her against her will. It's how they operate."

"Did you know she was a spy?"

"No. I fell in love with her. How can you really know anyone when you fall in love with them? You're startled by their light. Please, I know I've abused your family for which I'm truly sorry. But now I'm asking for mercy."

"I could call the police. They can keep you under protection until your return to England."

"That's not possible. After the accident in London, they won't be lenient. I made a terrible mistake for which they'll probably hang me."

"It seems to me you make quite a lot of mistakes."

"I was a drunken fool, blinded by love and jealousy. Fate will decide my future but whatever they accuse me of, it was love that made an ass of me. I don't think I'm a bad man, Herr Rosenberg, but I have been a fool."

Rosenberg's considers his port, swilling the viscous fluid in his glass. As if his mind is more consumed by the choice of cheese to select with his drink. Eventually his gaze returns across the table. "I don't wish to know anymore. It's up to your conscience what you choose to do. I've witnessed a lot of unpleasant things in the years since the war. And I admit, in some business matters my own conduct has not been perfect. So I'm not really in a position to judge you. In the brief time you've been here you have made a good friend for Stefan. And for that I am grateful, even if he might now lose you. Maybe it has given him a taste for friendship. If you think I can help, what do you have in mind?"

He's barely able to assimilate what he's heard. "Is there a different exit at the back of the apartment? A way that I can slip out unnoticed."

Rosenberg considers for a moment. "Through the maid's bedroom, but the courtyard's surrounded by high walls. You'll never make it to the road. The only way out is through the front door." Extraordinarily he smiles. "But that doesn't mean everything is lost." He calls for Doethe.

At one minute to eight Alec stands in the hallway, already sweating profusely under a heavy, dark overcoat. Doethe takes a black hat lined with fur from the back of the cloakroom cupboard and places it on his head. Next she selects an ivory topped walking stick which, when she hands it across to him, feels reassuringly cool against his hot palm. "I think you'll find some spectacles in the top pocket."

He searches inside the coat, his fingers finding a slim leather case inside which sit a pair of gold-rimmed spectacles. Herr Rosenberg stands at the entrance to the dining room witnessing the transformation with his wife. "I'd make you a gift of the coat but it was my father's before mine. Sentimental value, you see. Those are his spectacles. Perhaps you'll send it back when you reach England."

"Of course. As soon as I can."

Rosenberg smiles. "Try to walk slowly, like an old man. Use the stick to lean on."

Alec dons the spectacles, squinting to make sense of the world. It's just manageable. Doethe brushes down the lapels of the coat. "Remember, left down Gierkezelle then double back to Kaiser Friedrich Strasse. Then go right, south. Once you cross Kantstrasse you'll see the S Bahn. Take the train to Spandau. If you get lost, remember the streets are on a grid system. Just make sure you always head south."

"Thank you." He glances toward the Rosenbergs. His wife has grasped her husband's hand. "I won't forget your kindness."

Rosenberg grins. "Send us a postcard of Buckingham Palace. Good luck."

He descends the staircase with Doethe to the front door. As she draws it open, cooler air rushes in from the street, drying the sweat on his brow. She kisses him on the cheek and closes the door swiftly behind him. He avoids looking back to Klausen's car, setting off in the opposite direction, listening to his own faltering footsteps as he inches along the deserted street. How does an old man walk? Slowly unfortunately. He guesses the number of footsteps before he can turn left. Seventy perhaps, counting them under his breath, feeling his way through the myopic blur. In the dim light his glasses render him almost blind. The distant hum of traffic suggests he's not too far now from the main road. Fifty paces maybe? His confidence is growing; no sound of a car behind him. He's desperate to walk faster but knows it would be fatal. Despite the slothfulness he's hyper ventilating, dizzy with the amount of oxygen flooding his lungs. Thirty steps left. The intersection with Gierkazelle mirages in his restricted vision. Thirty steps. Twenty. Ten.

A shot fires, ricocheting off the stonework. The headlights of the Beetle bear down on him like searchlights. He throws the cane wildly in the car's direction, sprinting out of its path. A second shot grazes his leg. It stings like hell. He turns the corner in to Gierkezelle, tracking low behind the line of parked cars, aware of the Beetle spinning round the bend in pursuit. Doethe said double back to the main road at the next corner. If he can get that far, he's got a chance. A third shot shatters a ground floor window. Someone screams. He turns another corner, a narrower street, but the Beetle follows, metal scraping metal as Klausen accelerates. Alec flicks right, Kaiser Friedrich Strasse now just ahead. It'll buy him time; Klausen will have to wait for traffic. A fourth shot. It whistles past. He dumps the coat and hat, lungs screaming, lunging across the main road, oblivious to the screeching of brakes. Head south. Don't look back. He sprints on, aching for breath, stopping only when forced to by the retch of his gut. Holding for support to a wall he vomits onto the pavement. Blood trickles from his calf. The pain's like fire but the bone is undamaged. Looking up the street there's no sign of the Beetle. Perhaps he's lost him. He ties his handkerchief around the graze, hoping to stem the trail.

But something flickers in his vision, back on the far side, moving faster than the other pedestrians. Klausen. He's abandoned his car. Alec forces himself to run again, sprinting across Kant Strasse, pirouetting between traffic, not daring to turn round until he reaches the station entrance. Klausen is still in pursuit. Alec leaps the stairs to the platform, pushing past another traveller. The platform stands high above the city like a ship on a frozen sea. A biting wind blows from the east. There's no sign of a train.

Keeping close to the back wall, he walks briskly along its length, past a small pool of waiting passengers, praying a train will come. At the furthest end of the platform there's a door to what looks like a guards' room. It's marked Private; the small, unlit window, caked in dirt, suggesting it's unused. He turns the handle. It yields to his touch. Stepping inside, and willing his breath to slow, he listens and waits. Only a minute passes, before he hears what he dreads; footsteps, distant at first, but persistent and drawing nearer. But then there's another sound; a low, metallic rumble, building steadily to a sharp screech, drowning the footsteps. Carriages rush past, flickers of light, until the train draws to a halt. A handful of passengers disembark, collars turned against the cold. He waits as long as he dares, fingers clasped to the handle of the door. A gush of air signals the train doors are closing. He pulls on the handle and launches out towards the carriage, the doors sealing behind him, as he crashes to the carriage floor. Alarmed passengers stare then shift their gaze. Lifting himself up, he turns towards the window, watching the platform recede; deserted except for one man, Klausen, a revolver swinging from his hand, cursing into the frosted air.

He doesn't sit down, despite his aching leg, choosing to hover at the door, in case he's forced to make a sudden exit. If ticket inspectors board he'll have to disembark before they catch him. He stares at the road below, snaking a parallel route, west, looking for a glimpse of the Beetle but seeing none. Perhaps he can breathe now. Though Klausen's probably guessed he's heading for Spandau. If he can get that far, without Klausen finding him, he might be able to board a train west, back across the border of West Berlin into East Germany. Then on through the final border into West Germany.

At each stop he expects his persecutor to be waiting. But nothing. When the train finally pulls into Spandau station he scans the platform before alighting with his fellow passengers, huddled in their midst, until he reaches the ticket office. Still no sign. The next train doesn't leave for fifteen minutes so he's forced to hover in the shadows of the concourse, waiting for the platform announcement, watching the minutes pass with careless lethargy on the station clock; hardly daring to believe he might soon be a free man. To his left, a few metres away, he spots a newspaper stand. It might be useful. He reaches for the spare coins in his pocket, head buried low, and buys an English Times.

384

No news of a London murder on the front page. He folds it in two, searching the station again, heart racing. The tannoy echoes to life, announcing his platform. He moves swiftly, stepping aboard without looking back, choosing a seat by the compartment door and avoiding eye contact with fellow passengers. Out of the window, on the opposite platform, he suddenly spots what he feared; Klausen, hand in pocket, searching frantically, sprinting from one end of the platform to the other. Suddenly, as if he's sensed he's being watched, he stops and pivots his gaze towards Alec's train. For a moment, before the whistle blows and the train creeps from the platform, Alec believes their eyes meet. Though he can't be certain.

He lifts his newspaper, the words barely registering above the clamour of his pulse. The train begins to pick up speed but barely seems to have started its journey before the brakes hiss in clouds of steam and they draw to a halt at a makeshift platform. He looks out. It's a familiar scene. An East German guard walks the length of the platform, the German Shepherd dog held on its leash, teeth bared, pulling him forwards.

"Bereiten sie Ihre Reisepasse bitte!"

He hears a guard enter the next-door compartment. He lifts the newspaper higher. A young man, no older than himself, steps into his own. Handsome and proud, he looks like a remnant from the Hitler Youth.

"Ihr Reisepass, bitte."

He reaches for the passport in his jacket pocket. James Michael Anderson. He fears the ink may have spread on the re-worked surface. The young guard studies his photo and glances at the newspaper.

"Englander?"

He nods.

"Wohin fahren sie?"

He pretends not to understand, just a polite query crossing his face.

"Where do you travel?"

"Hamburg."

The young man glances at the details of the passport again before handing it back and leaving the compartment.

He folds his newspaper again, his pulse relaxing, dropping his head to his chest. If Klausen were on the train he'd have found him by now. The graze on his leg distracts him; it's stinging and there's a stain of blood on his trousers. He doesn't dare move for fear it'll start bleeding again.

Outside the city resolves quickly to darkness. He catches his own, hollow reflection in the window. A shell. Exhausted. Too shattered to hope or even care. He craves sleep and surrenders without resistance to the gentle rocking motion of the carriage.

He wakes to yet more shouted commands, opening his eyes, quickly alert. The train's pulled up at the East and West German border. He must have been asleep for well over an hour. Instinctively he scans for Klausen then breathes again. Guards board the train. He picks up the paper; the same routine. The East German guard's much older than the last one, like he might be about to draw his pension. When Alec hands him the passport he can smell alcohol and sweat. Chubby, nail-bitten fingers flick the pages. The guard scrutinises Alec's face then looks back at the photo. Perhaps he will say something. But his attention is diverted by a yapping dog, of which Alec had been totally unaware, hiding in the folds of a fellow passenger's coat. The guard is evidently drawn by the tiny dog, returning Alec's passport and falling into a brief conversation with its owner. Perhaps he's keener to engage with the West German travellers; the ones who by fate of history, now live in a place he can never reach, thought they might only live a mile apart.

When the West German guards board they barely glance at him. He breathes more slowly now. The train travels on through the evening, west then north towards Hamburg. So far luck has been with him. He lights a cigarette, the absence of imminent danger replaced by nagging doubt and apprehension. Should he have abandoned Kitty so easily? Was that more Ursula's wish than his; to which he succumbed? Leaving Berlin hasn't bought freedom. Just a different fate. His body aches. Exhaustion has taken its toll. He can barely think straight and the choices that face him too grim to contemplate. There's only one person he imagines could help him now. If nothing else it might quell the burden of loneliness.

Alighting on to the concourse at Hamburg Hauptbahnhof, he stamps out the cigarette butt, shivering in the icy air. Even if he wanted to catch the ferry to Harwich, he assumes it's too late now. The ornate, station clock hands click to quarter past eleven. He should have kept Rosenberg's coat; it wouldn't have impeded him that much. And now he's dumped the only thing to protect him from the bitter cold; the item which initially saved him and which he swore he'd return to its keeper. Rosenberg. His earthly saviour.

Walking towards the exit he still fears Klausen might spring from behind or the West German police apprehend him. But none of the good burghers of Hamburg seem remotely interested in his existence. He finds a row of telephone booths in the terminus and dials the operator.

"Yes, I want to make a call to England. Trinity College, Cambridge University."

He repeats it, eyes darting impatiently round the station, until the operator understands. He hasn't worked out yet what he's going to say. He just needs advice. He just needs a friend.

"Yes, I understand it's late but tell them it's urgent."

Again he waits. Interminably.

"Trinity College. How may I help?"

The familiar tone of the porter's voice generates a wave of longing, almost denying his ability to speak. He adopts a German accent. The porter won't question its authenticity. Even if he decides it's a student prank he'll probably err on the side of caution.

"I'm sorry I call so late. Can I speak with Edward Grant? I have some important personal news about accident in Germany, concerning his family."

"Of course, I'll try for you, sir. I'll put you through to the phone in his block. If there's no reply I'll connect you back to me."

"Thank you."

He hears a click, then a phone ringing. He pictures it hanging on the wall by the notice board, grubby and chipped. It rings several times before someone picks up.

"Yes?"'

He doesn't recognise the grumpy voice. "Can I speak with Edward Grant? I'm ringing from Germany. I have some important news for him. Tell him it's…tell him it concerns Imber."

"Concerns what?"

"Imber, tell him it's about Imber."

"I'll see if he's there."

He hears the phone drop, footsteps echoing up the stairs to his own room where he imagines Ed, lying on his bed, sipping whisky from his flask, in suitable mourning for his lost friend. A minute later he hears footsteps return. The anticipation is almost too much to bear. The sound of the receiver picked up.

But it's the same voice. "He says he's never heard of Imber."

"What? Please. It's very important. Just tell him…"

"…He said he doesn't want to be disturbed. He doesn't know anything about Imber."

Alec feels a shiver spread. A sudden ache. The beginnings of a fever. "I see. Could you ask…"

"…It's very late. You must have the wrong person." The phone dies.

He hangs up before the operator has finished her request for payment. She has his details. But James Anderson will never be traceable. He doesn't exist. The thought of booking into a hostel suddenly seems pointless. He wouldn't sleep.

Remembering the route from the ferry to the station, a journey he made only a week ago, he doubles back, looking perhaps to see if the same ferry is moored in the harbour; his return ticket to England, should he choose it. Frost already glistens on the pavement. He shivers. Turns his jacket collar up to the cold. His breath pressed to dense clouds. Arriving at the port, he sees several container ships docked at the far side of the Elbe, dwarfed by the skeletal cranes rising above them. But there's no sign of the passenger ferry. He steps down towards the water's edge. In the distance a church clock chimes midnight. In front of him the Elbe laps at the quay, its waters jet black, opaque. No moonlight to lighten its passage. A void. Why had he imagined Ed might help? He'd warned him not to get involved with Kitty. He'd be a fool, but all lovers were fools. And he couldn't regret it. Asking Ed to save him was pathetic; the mark of a coward.

He throws his cigarette into the river, watching it bob across the cold surface, wondering where the river might take it. Or him.

22

Breakfast arrives on a plastic tray at six thirty. No different to any other day. Her warden, Frau Leiter, leaves two slices of black bread and a dollop of meat paste on the desk, along with lukewarm coffee, which she pours into Kitty's mug from a metal flask. Frau Leiter is the friendlier of the two wardens. Kitty looks forward to her arrival; she's the nearest thing she has to a friend. But then they've known each other for nine years.

Frau Leiter pauses after pouring the coffee. She's never in a hurry. "Did you sleep well, Fräulein Bernstein?"

Kitty remains seated on the side of her bed. "I dreamt a lot."

"Nice dreams, perhaps?"

"I was on the beach in Santa Barbara."

"Somewhere you know?"

"It's in California."

Frau Leiter smiles, her front teeth, crooked and nicotine stained. "Dreams can very be cruel."

"I went there with my parents as a kid. My dad used to wrap me

391

in the sand, like a bed. I lay for hours just listening to the waves lapping."

Frau Leiter wipes drips from the metal flask. Unnecessarily. "You won't be exercising in the yard this morning."

"Now who's being cruel."

Her sarcasm forces another grin to the warden's face. "I have orders that you must have a picture taken. The photographer will come for you at eight o'clock."

Kitty rises to sit at the desk. The coffee has no aroma. It's too thin. But it's better than nothing. She drinks. "Why on earth do they need a photo of me?"

"Make sure you look nice. I've seen him. He's quite handsome."

Kitty smiles. "God forgive you, Frau Leiter. A married woman."

"You haven't seen my husband."

They laugh together. Kitty senses it's a tonic for them both. "Maybe he wants me to be the cover of a fashion magazine."

"Maybe you're dreaming again, huh." Frau Leiter shuts the heavy door behind her. Kitty listens for the key turning in the next cell. There's a brief conversation, too muffled for her to comprehend. Her neighbour is a young protester, angry and occasionally volatile. Ute Reinhardt. She's tried to make conversation but all attempts have been rebuffed. She doesn't blame the girl. According to Frau Leiter she'd been incarcerated for insulting a policeman, at the Alexanderplatz protest, four days previously. West German news reported over half a million East Germans attending, determined to push for greater freedoms. And now Ute Reinhardt sits alone for her misdemeanours.

The bread is stale. The meat paste stinks. She stares through the bars of her window to the wire-fenced courtyard beyond, her singular view of the world since she was moved to this room fifteen years ago. Above the high line of the perimeter fence she can just make out the tips of fir trees in the forest beyond. Her cell's comfortable enough. She has a bed, a desk and chair bolted to the floor, a bookcase filled with the political tracts of Marxist notables; in between them, well-thumbed novels by her favourite East European and Russian authors, Bulgakov, Hrabal, Dostoyevsky. Above her desk hangs a simple mirror. She considers her reflection more critically than usual, barely able to remember when someone last took her photograph. At fifty-seven she could look both better and worse. Better if she could see a bit more sun and style her smoky, grey hair. It's a standard short prison cut. Worse if she hadn't the good fortune to possess an elegant bone structure. Her skin has stayed aloft and taut, for which she's grateful. From her washbag she removes eyeliner and lipstick, both given to her by Frau Leiter. She last applied them a year ago, on New Year's Eve, when her fellow comrades gathered in the canteen to watch the fireworks on television in West Berlin. In recent years the rules have been relaxed and viewing of Western television is occasionally permitted; though only under the watch of the less ardent Communist, prison officers.

The photographer arrives promptly at eight. She's not disappointed by his looks. Frau Leiter has good taste. His hair is dark and wavy, his skin paler than milk, his brow set in a permanent furrow, as if the world had not delivered what he'd expected. In some ways he reminds her of Alec. He shows scant interest in her, avoiding any conversation as they walk through the labyrinth of corridors to an unmarked room, tucked away in a corner of the administration block.

"Stand over there, against that backdrop, please."

She does as he requests, stepping over light cables towards a large scroll of grey paper which hangs between two stands.

"Look into the camera."

She stares at the lens, urging her lips to a smile, though it's probably pointless. It's plain he's observing a prisoner, his visual curiosity unaroused, a middle-aged woman whose history is irrelevant to him. He's only following orders. She chastises herself for bothering to apply make-up. The shutter clicks. Three times.

"You're done. A guard will escort you back to your room."

"Aren't you going to tell me what it's for?"

He looks up from the camera, perhaps surprised by her audacity. "My instructions were to take the photograph, Fräulein. That's all."

She hovers by the doorway, hoping the guard won't arrive too quickly. "I've heard that everything's changing out there. Since Austria opened the border to Hungary in the summer. Now the head of the Party's stepped down. That demonstration in Alexanderplatz the other day. What do you make of it?"

"Nothing. Nor should you, Fräulein. Honecker's replacement comes from the same stable. Krenz was his deputy. He thinks the same way."

She hears the familiar jangle of keys. The imminent arrival of a guard. The photographer has turned his back on her, taking his Leica camera to a bench where it sits, unremarkably, amongst a bank of similar cameras.

His disdain irritates her. "I thought photography was all about observation. Anyone can press a button."

Switching off the lights either side of the tripod, he doesn't bother to look back at her. "If you make it out of here you'd be smart not to judge. I have a job and I have children to feed. I may press buttons. But I don't live in a cell."

The following morning she exercises in the yard again, a cold, ice blue, November day. The forests beyond the castle border are already flecked by early snow. There are the regular prisoners with whom she exchanges pleasantries, nothing too personal or political, just the quality of the food, gossip about the wardens. She barely knows these women, despite having shared dinners in the canteen with some of them for many years. Ute Reinhardt is walking in front of her. The girl marches alone, her stance angular and defiant, as if conversation with fellow prisoners would simply make her one of them. After lunch, in the workshop, Kitty solders joins to create metal barriers. She's a skilled worker, having practised it so long. Although she can't help questioning how many metal barriers a country can need. Perhaps they're exported to Hungary, or Czechoslovakia, or Poland, even Russia. Places she's never likely to see. Before the call to supper she reads Chekhov's The Seagull. She's read it several times since Frau Leiter smuggled it in for her. Works of fiction are forbidden. Frau Leiter has procured them all.

Her cell door opens again at five thirty. She follows the troop of women to the canteen, waiting in a line at the counter to receive a plate of thin goulash and boiled potatoes. The canteen is more a cavernous hall; thick stone walls and high, mullioned windows, denying any sense of life beyond, except for the stubborn draughts which ignore a change of season. Presumably built by a wealthy baron, he must have brought his house guests here, keen to exhibit his status after hunting boar in the forest.

She spots Ute Reinhardt sitting alone, watching the grainy images on the black and white television. Though she knows her

395

company will likely be rebuffed, Kitty makes her way to the bench, still stinging from the photographer's rebuke. He was right in a way, whatever the news that reaches them, whether from East or West German television, it's impossible to verify its truth. She lives in a goldfish bowl. Better just to keep swimming. But the young girl, who eyes her with unmasked hostility, has at least witnessed the modern world first-hand. Her allure is too enticing.

She drops her tray to the table, careful not to block the girl's view of the television behind her.

"You don't mind?"

"Your choice."

The girl doesn't shift her eyes from the television set. She eats clumsily, plainly keen to finish before any further conversation.

Kitty slices the potato in two, choosing to bide her time. A break in the television commentary signals an opportunity. She smiles. "The food used to be much worse. At least some things have changed."

"I don't plan staying long enough to care."

"Good idea. Do you have a lawyer working your case?" She's being disingenuous but the girl's bullishness intrigues her.

"I'll escape, even if it means slitting throats."

"Well, you wouldn't be the first to try that. But I've never seen it ending happily for either party."

The girl chews hard on the meat, her eyes still fixed on the screen.

"Did any of your friends get arrested after Alexanderplatz? I hear it was quite a defiant…"

"…Shut up a sec." The girl's interest in the screen is suddenly more acute, her fork empty, hovering in the air.

Kitty spins around, aware that the television has caught everyone's attention. Even the canteen staff and the guards. They're watching a press conference. Three grey-suited men and one woman sit behind a plinth, a featureless curtain draped behind them. She recognises the spokesperson, Gunter Schabowski, the party leader in East Berlin. He's announcing a relaxation of travel restrictions outside East Germany but when he finishes there's a barrage of questions from journalists. A sense of confusion or disbelief. Are the latest regulations repealing those made just a few days earlier? She watches, spellbound. Schabowski appears to ramble, unsure of his ground, until he confirms that the new law's been drafted to allow East German citizens to cross permanently between all borders, including East and West Berlin. The conference erupts, several questions fired at once again; he looks surprised by it, no longer in control, a note in his hand somehow the cause of his uncertainty. A journalist at the front demands to know how soon the new regulations will take effect. Schabowski looks bewildered. As far as he knows it takes place immediately, without delay. A British journalist asks what it will mean for the Berlin Wall. Kitty watches, barely able to comprehend what she's seeing as Schabowksi tries to steer around the question, insisting the Wall is part of a larger disarmament issue. But it's clear that the damage is done and he ends the conference abruptly; knowing he's just struck a pickaxe at twenty-seven years of concrete separating East from West.

There's scant sign of euphoria amongst her fellow prison mates, only muffled exchanges, confusion, disbelief. Turning back to Ute she looks for something more hopeful. The girl is quietly finishing her goulash, now cold and congealed.

When Kitty finally speaks she's surprised by the timidity in her own voice. "What does that mean? Are we now free?"

Ute lifts her face from her plate, wiping the bowl with stale bread. "Don't look so scared. It's what you want, isn't it?"

In the immediate days following, nothing changes in her routine. She exercises in the yard, welds barricades in the afternoon, and at dinner feasts on images of young East and West Berliners clambering up the Wall with pickaxes and hammers. Their euphoria is intoxicating. The border guards watch helplessly. Sections begin to crumble. The Wall's two facades reveal its split convictions; on the West a sprawl of graffiti, on the East, grey concrete pocked by bullet holes. Her sense of relief is overwhelming, of what might be, a joy she hasn't felt since before her father's trial. Yet her own circumstances haven't changed. The guards still order them about. The canteen workers still shiver as they serve brown slops onto metal plates like shit steaming on a pavement.

A week passes. More sections of the Wall crumble, aided by mechanical diggers. The city's heart appears to be healing even if her own fate remains stubbornly untouched. But after morning exercise, she has an unexpected visit from Frau Leiter. Occasionally the warden steps in for a gossip, which she would welcome, as she's finding it impossible to concentrate on Chekhov. Instead Frau Leiter remains at the door.

"You better brush your hair, Fräulein Bernstein. I have orders to escort you to Kommandant Etzenbach's office."

Kitty's met him once or twice over the years. An unlikely Senior Prison Officer, she's always thought. Cordial but unstimulating. She brushes her hair as requested and follows Frau Leiter along the winding corridors, up narrow twisting staircases, to the remotest corner of the castle. Her warden knocks on the door and announces Kitty's arrival before retiring. Walking into the office, Kitty observes a modest, if unusually messy attic room. She imagines he entered the job reluctantly, choosing somewhere as physically removed as possible from the fate of his prisoners. But it is also one of the coldest rooms. He pays for his chosen isolation. Perhaps it keeps him alert.

He invites her to sit, removing a series of files from his desk and dropping them to the floor behind his desk. He reminds her of a disarrayed academic, except he has nothing to study other than the turgid, monthly updates on his prisoners. Even his uniform is ill-fitting, the collar too wide for his neck, his bird-like face and creeping hairline reminding her somehow of an ostrich. Perhaps, in a way, he's more interesting than she'd given him credit for.

"Ah. Good morning. I imagine, Fräulein Bernstein, that you've been following the recent developments on television." His tone is relaxed. He even offers her a cigarette which she accepts, ignoring the slight tremor of his hand as he proffers a plastic lighter.

She inhales the rich smoke. Stronger than she's used to. "I've watched every night, Herr Kommandant. But I contain my enthusiasm. My world is here, and will no doubt remain so." She smiles thinly. Despite his polite manner she doesn't want to seek his empathy. He reaches to the cabinet behind him and removes a large buff envelope from the drawer, placing it before her on the table.

"I must tell you, you're quite wrong, Fräulein. That world will not be yours to dwell in much longer."

She looks to the envelope. The long-postponed warrant for her execution? She'd often pondered it. In the early years it would have both terrified and outraged her. But now? Now she's lived the life she was destined to. "I'm to be executed? Finally?"

A thin smile crosses his lips. He opens the envelope and pulls out a German Democratic Republic passport. Its blue cover is shiny and uncreased. Plainly it's new. Inside her photograph stares back at her. An older woman she barely recognises. "I hope you approve of the picture. I think he's captured you very well."

She feels her legs weaken at the implication of his gesture, a flicker in her spine. Her mouth is dry. His smile broadens. "You are free to go, Fräulein Bernstein."

It's not how she'd ever imagined such news. Tears of unrivalled relief. Jubilation. Euphoria. She feels a crushing apprehension, her mind suddenly stolen by practicalities. She says nothing. Can say nothing.

"You don't seem very pleased, Fräulein."

"Forgive me, Herr Kommandant. I don't know quite - I have no home, or money."

He averts her gaze, as if almost embarrassed by her plight. "You'll leave on the prison bus this afternoon which will take you to Alexanderplatz." He removes a key from the envelope along with a pocket-sized notebook. "Accommodation has been arranged. The address is on the label. And the State has paid your salary for work you undertook prior to your arrest adjusted for inflation. It's all written in this notebook. We ask only that you remain discreet. Information that you acquired during your service should remain undisclosed to anyone. No exceptions. There would be dire consequences. I trust you understand."

She can barely nod her acceptance. It's happening too fast.

"The money has been assigned to a bank account opened on your behalf. You will find your account booklet and details in the envelope."

She takes the envelope without question, like a child receiving pocket money. Her cigarette sits untouched in the ashtray. Etzenbach waits patiently but she still has no words for him. She cannot remember being short of words. Or so powerless.

"Are you quite well, Fräulein?"

"Yes. Thank you. What happens once I arrive at my accommodation?"

"That is up to you, Fräulein, though I would advise caution. The Wall might have fallen but the old order has not. For now at least. The State has shown you clemency so it would be simple good manners to appear grateful and not make a fuss."

She feels the energy seep back into her limbs; his meekness abhorrent to her, despite the fact he is one of the kindest men she has met since incarceration. "They're bartering for my silence."

"As I said, it would be wise to lie low, at least until circumstances have settled. These are unprecedented times. Our future might be less controlled but it will also be more unpredictable." He stands up, holding out his hand. "Now if you'll excuse me, Fräulein, there's much to do and you have to pack your things. Frau Leiter will escort you back."

She rises from the chair, shaking his hand lightly. Not a worker's hand. She'd like to remain for a while, to talk with him; to discover what lies behind his emollient platitudes.

Instead she picks up the envelope and turns for the door, but her curiosity forbids her to leave. "And what will your fate be, Herr Kommandant, once you no longer have the castle walls to protect you?"

He doesn't seem surprised by her question. "Like you I will go quietly. Though I can't pretend it will be easy. Before the war I lived a comfortable life on my family's estate. Perhaps too comfortable. The State took everything from us after the war. But managing a prison has many similarities to running a country estate. Once this job is done, which it will be, I'm not sure what will happen. Perhaps a return to the old ways, or perhaps I will have to atone. Good luck, Fräulein Bernstein. I wish you well."

"Thank you. Likewise." She reaches for the door.

In her cell she packs her belongings into a cardboard box in the company of Frau Leiter. They barely fill it; her washbag, a spare tracksuit and pair of trainers, and journals she had started to write but given up on. The books she will leave for Frau Leiter to distribute as she wishes though she cannot imagine who else might chose to read them. Perhaps Etzenbach. Her warden keeps up an easy chatter, then to Kitty's surprise, as they're about to leave, she embraces her tightly. It's the first physical affection she's experienced for over thirty years. But the moment is over before she can respond, her long-term companion leading her out to the forensic winter light of the forecourt where a bus awaits to take her and her fellow prisoners back to Berlin. In the company of others, Frau Leiter reverts to the detached formality of a warden, escorting her on to the bus without another word spoken.

Ute Reinhardt sits towards the rear, away from most of the prisoners, who huddle and converse, exhilarated by their sudden freedom. Kitty passes between them to settle next to Ute, smiling briefly but saying nothing. Small talk feels inappropriate. Beyond the bus window Frau Leiter shivers in the cold; an expressionless prison guard on duty. When the engine shudders into life a cloud of noxious fumes drifts past her face though she remains fixed to her spot. Kitty lifts her hand to wave. The display of warmth is not reciprocated. It hurts her though she knows it shouldn't.

She resists any temptation to talk to Ute on the journey; content instead to watch the forested landscape slip by in the sunlight, reassuringly unchanged. Even the small villages are as she remembers them. It's not until they approach the border with West Berlin that she's transported to a revised world, the border itself now a sophisticated fortress of look out towers and concrete barricades, guards emerging from angular brick buildings rather than the hastily constructed sheds she remembers. The bus halts, brakes hiss. An East German border guard steps on board but to her amazement he waves them on to West Berlin after the briefest of exchanges with their driver. A spontaneous burst of applause erupts among the women. The guard grins up coyly as they pass.

She laughs. "That's the first time I've ever seen a border guard smile."

Even Ute softens. "Poor boy wants the West to love him."

"Human after all."

Ute smiles. "I still wouldn't sleep with one. They'd never remove their shiny boots."

Kitty laughs again. More freely than she can remember. She leans across Ute, transfixed by a regenerated West Berlin emerging beyond the window; one she has only witnessed on television, like a science fiction film. She gawps at sleek cars, so many of them filling the boulevards; steel and glass offices topped by neon slogans, war damage metamorphosed to brash commercialism. Students fill the streets, some dressed as punks, the majority clad in jeans and puffer jackets, blurring any distinction between rich and poor. It's an egalitarianism of sorts, she thinks. Ute points out the latest trends; legwarmers, trainers, jumpers tucked into jeans, warming to Kitty's enthrallment. She reaches for Ute's hand, relishing this moment of intimacy with a stranger, yet aware it's no more than an illusion of extraordinary circumstance.

Twenty minutes later the bus crosses into the Eastern Sector at Checkpoint Charlie. Once more the border guards wave them through, the barriers now permanently raised, as if in salute to their new-found freedom. But it's immediately clear that the East is the less sparkling sibling, the contrast perhaps even greater than the days before the Wall. The absence of colour strikes her first. There are no advertising hoardings, no vibrant shop fronts; most buildings still pockmarked and forlorn, the cars more or less unchanged, since she was imprisoned. Even the pedestrians look pastier, many dressed in shell suits made from the cheapest nylon. It unsettles her optimism; the discomfort of seeing a former hero fall from grace.

Arriving at Alexanderplatz, she's encouraged to see greater evidence of renewal. The central grass square, around which the trams used to run, has been replaced by a concreted, pedestrian walkway; the surrounding buildings either repaired, or torn down and rebuilt, to create a drawing board of urban modernism. But it still lacks the conviction of the West. Stepping outside the bus, a nagging westerly wind blows across the concrete, unhindered in its course, turning the clear skies to lead. She turns to embrace Ute who has stepped down behind her, aware of the awkwardness of the young warrior, now they're beyond the cocoon of their bus.

"Take care of yourself." She doesn't ask where Ute lives, sensing that their relationship will remain forever locked within the prison. She is after all, nearly sixty years old, hardly the life blood of a young protester.

"You too. And don't let anyone make you afraid." The girl barely smiles before turning away.

She watches Ute head east across the square to catch another bus, then draws the notebook from her pocket in which her new address is neatly written. Heading north out of the city centre she cradles her meagre box of possessions in her arms. A refugee from the past.

The modernity of the square is soon displaced by a more familiar sight; the tenement blocks in poor repair, few cars except for the occasional Trabant resonating a high-pitched, two stroke rant as it passes; harsher on the ear than its sophisticated West German cousins. But at least there are more people out enjoying themselves than she remembers. A new tribe. Teenagers. Where once they were either dressed as children or adults, now the teenagers wear jeans, like their Western counterparts. In the past she might have found this mimicry shallow. Now she's not sure. She feels unqualified to judge; she can only observe.

The address is barely half a kilometer from her old apartment. It's nearer the Wall, although already large sections of the concrete divide have been destroyed or stolen. The tenement block is one of the most derelict she's seen, no doubt reserved by the State for the unclean, though she's grateful for a home. Her apartment is up ten flights of steps on the fifth floor. She sees no one in the dim stairwells. Pushing the key in the lock she opens the door to a narrow room with a window at the far end. In size and shape it's virtually identical to the apartment Ursula inhabited when Kitty first visited from America; a kitchenette at the far end, a hinged table hanging from the wall and a divan. The walls are stained by patches of damp. Cracks scribble across the ceiling. She places her bag on the wooden floor and walks to the window. A deep layer of grime cuts out the light. Outside, the sky has turned a yellowish grey, perhaps the hint of snow.

Feeling exhausted Kitty drops onto the frayed divan, her mind awash with thoughts of Ursula and what has become of her. Letters came for the first four years after imprisonment, always opened, and occasionally censored with black ink. They spoke of domestic life, Ursula's work at the factory, trips to the park, feeding the ducks, the weather. Nothing of consequence but they provided great comfort in the early years. Then they ceased, abruptly, and she had no idea why. Her friend had simply vanished. But now she's free her first intention is to find out.

The next day, after shopping for some basic provisions, she makes her way to Fehrbelliner Strasse. The snow never came, instead replaced by a pale, winter solstice sun. As she walks, she turns around frequently, her senses telling her that she's being followed though she never finds specific evidence. Perhaps it's just nerves. Arriving at her old apartment, she has no idea what to expect; it's highly likely that Ursula moved away long ago. She doesn't want to build up too much hope. A part of her feels she should just let the past evaporate but curiosity overrides what she knows is only cowardice. She owes Ursula a debt. Not only that, she loved her as a sister.

The entrance door has been replaced. Gone are the splinters of sniper damage. She studies the rows of doorbells, names written against each one. Ursula is not among them. But there are still numbers. She presses the bell; someone called Vogel.

"Yes?" A female voice, impatient and suspicious.

"I'm sorry to trouble you, I'm looking for Fräulein Meyer who lived here once. I wondered if you knew of her."

"No, nobody by that name."

"May I ask how long you've lived here?"

"Too many years. Please excuse me, I'm very busy."

She takes a step back, gazing upwards, wondering whether she should ring again, or try another apartment. Instead she turns around, her eye drawn to a man, who crosses the road and disappears down a side street. It's hard to escape the paranoia. She hesitates a moment before moving on. Maybe tomorrow she should head to Treptower Park. She knows it was a favourite spot of Ursula's. If the Gods are kind she might bump into her, if not there might be some welcome stranger, as desperate as her, for a little conversation.

After a frugal lunch she walks back into town to withdraw money from her account and buy herself a radio. It still leaves her with plenty to spare though she has no idea what else she might need. Her small kitchen is sufficiently equipped and though it would be lovely to have new clothes, nothing in the spartan shop windows appeals. Partly her confidence evades her; the smart sophistication of her earlier years seems out of place in this new world, and anyway, she's grown used to her tracksuit. In the evening she tunes into the BBC World Service, captivated by the news of a rapid thaw of relations with Eastern Europe. A Prague Spring turned to summer. In her own neighbourhood she witnesses students scrambling up the Wall, spraying graffiti on the bare East German face, defiance for which they'd have been shot a month ago. She can barely comprehend it. A less fragile optimism stirs within her, caught up in the elation, the intoxicating rush of unbridled freedom. Strangers share schnapps and laughter as they watch the Wall disintegrate; a feverish euphoria burning so strongly she wonders if she might be hallucinating. But then she sees others, standing in the shadows, either terrified or appalled by what they see. She understands what they're feeling; a fear of change, perhaps bitter disappointment at the East's failure to complete their political and economic dream. Perhaps some are just terrified of recrimination, of flying too close to the sun.

It's a cold, damp night so she returns to her apartment early, her mood faltering; no longer buoyed by the excited crowd. Turning back to her radio for company, seasonal carols and tales of Christian fellowship smack at her heart. How she misses Ursula.

Her thoughts turn to her parents, long buried in graves she has never seen. She will visit them when she's exhausted hope of finding her friend. Later, she drinks some vodka. It will help her sleep, she thinks, but instead her mind seeks out unwelcome memories, and despite her efforts to resist, they lead her to Alec, sitting on the bench beside her in Cambridge, a light rain drifting across the meadow. The cigarette lighter in her bag. Her single error. In prison she'd managed to freeze out all thoughts of him. But now, now if she chose, she could return to England. Ed never contacted her again after their acrimonious farewell at London Airport. Who knows what happened to either of them? She assumes Alec married and had the obligatory children, living the life he would have chosen for himself, were it not for her interference. It's the life he deserved after all, and it would be unwise for her to rake up the past. Not if she loves him, which she believes she still does.

23

In the week leading to Christmas the weather is unseasonably mild; dull skies hang low over Berlin like a grubby blanket. She takes the opportunity to explore longer walks, determined to cure herself of a festering self-pity which disrupts her logical brain. Occasionally she senses she's being followed again, though she never spots the man who hovered outside Ursula's old apartment. She regularly takes the tram to Treptower Park, still hoping that she might bump into Ursula, but as days turn to weeks she becomes more uncertain of her purpose. To renew a friendship after thirty years is fraught with difficulty. She'd only ever brought complication and stress to Ursula's life, perhaps even used her too much. Maybe her friend feels freer now, no longer trapped in her shadow. Not unlike Alec, perhaps.

On the radio, after a light supper, she witnesses political events unfold with startling rapidity. Already Eric Mielke, head of the Stasi, has resigned and his department been renamed the Office for National Security. She laughs out loud. As if that might fool anyone. But days later there's an announcement from the State that the department has been permanently dissolved, under orders from the Prime Minister, Hans Modrow.

On December 22nd she rises early, determined to bag a good vantage point at the Brandenburg Gate, for an event no one could have foreseen just weeks previously. Thousand have had a similar idea, braving the intermittent rain showers as they walk in excited clusters along Unter den Linden towards the eighteenth-century monument. Young fathers carry children on their shoulders, students wave home-made flags, the elderly look on from balcony windows. A large crane swings its claw to the Wall and begins to lift a section, raising the concrete block to the air so that passage between the Doric columns is finally restored. Cheers of jubilation swell through the crowd. Some are crying with happiness. Kitty links arms with strangers, drinking freely from the bottles of Sekt they press into her hands. Then a second cheer erupts as Helmut Kohl, the West German Chancellor, walks beside Prime Minister Modrow, from West to East underneath the Gate, a gesture of such symbolism she can barely comprehend its political significance, much less her own emotional response. West Germans can finally re-unite with their East German cousins; families that have been separated since 1961 by a concrete barricade three and a half meters high. Later, sitting alone again at her kitchen table, her euphoria having slipped away with the crowds, she stares out at the pewter sky and weeps freely.

Christmas Eve she tolerates without ceremony. It's easier. Although she'd always delighted in the festive glitter her mother so loved, quite ignoring her father's Jewishness, when the news of her death reached the prison, it killed any vestige of childhood. Another letter confirming her father's demise arrived less than a year later. But to celebrate her own release from prison she buys a pork chop and a cheap bottle of Sekt. On the kitchen table she lights a candle to remember both her parents and the victims of the Wall; those executed for attempting escape to the West, and others dispatched for treasonous crimes against the State, their tragic stories slowly surfacing since the collapse of the Stasi.

As the new year breaks she hears rumours, spread at first by mouth in shops and cafés, that former Stasi employees are destroying hundreds of documents and files; information the department amassed over years to sabotage the reputation of both eminent foreigners and suspected East Germans. The rumours gain traction when radio reports suggest Stasi employees have been seen entering their old headquarters in Lichtenberg, walking away with files under their arms. Kitty listens with a mixture of disgust and fear. She feels no loyalty to the institution which once employed her. But she cannot deny she was once a part of it.

Taking the tram east to Lichtenberg she's unsure what she'll do when she arrives. To protest with the growing crowd outside feels morally justified but hypocritical on her part. A part of her still wants to believe that the cause was worth fighting for, the actions she took defensible in the fight for a better world. Perhaps she was hopelessly naïve, believing the State to be some avuncular benefactor, determined to spread succour for its people. In reality she found it grew to be a bully, ruling by fist, dividing through paranoia, because like all bullies, its heart was weak and uncertain, fearful that subordinates might make friends elsewhere.

Outside the Stasi headquarters the crowd has gathered momentum, several rows deep, barely contained by the small number of policemen attempting to defend the modernist complex from assault. She observes from the outer fringes, stirred by the show of resistance but hesitant to partake. Perhaps someone will recognise her from long ago. A Stasi spy. In an instant she'd be the victim of a baying mob. And perhaps she'd deserve it. But suddenly the protesters surge forward, breaking the line of the hapless police, stampeding into the building; wolves seeking meat. She feels herself drawn in with them, their collective adrenalin igniting her own sense of injustice, her call to arms. Pushing past the barricades she runs with the crowd into the main building. It's a feeding frenzy; one breakaway mob bent only on destruction, their fury unbridled. Portraits are torn from walls; Erich Mielke, thirty-one years the Stasi boss, discarded to the floor, trampled upon, set alight.

She has no desire to join their frenzied attack, her only wish is to seek evidence of her friend. Ursula. It's clear there are others like her, desperate to retrieve information. Some seem to know exactly where to head. She follows them, guessing they must be ex-Stasi; the ones whose only concern is to corrupt any evidence against them. But if they lead her to Ursula she won't judge. The small group descends on a windowless back room, drab and insignificant, except for multiple rows of gun-metal filing cabinets, each coded in typed words on yellowing paper. A young man whips a crowbar from his jacket and forces the flimsy locks on each cabinet. The drawers fly open. Dust rises from long untouched surfaces. Folders pregnant with paperwork are thrown to vying hands. Chaos.

She closes her ears to the cacophony; shouts of triumph, metal scraping on metal. Her focus shifts to the files, decoding their system. Yellowed labels on each cabinet define four separate classifications. *Employees, Unofficial Informers, Crimes against the State, Accounts of Witnesses*. She must act quickly. Already the mob have arrived, ripping out fat reports while others discreetly fold thin pages into their pockets. She begins with *Employees,* seeking out her own file which is thicker than most. Without bothering to open it she thrusts it into a cloth bag that she'd held within her coat pocket. Next she turns to *Crimes Against the State*, assuming Ursula's another victim of manufactured treason. Her fingers reach folders listed under *M*, rapidly scanning each one, but there's no record of Ursula Meyer, despite her checking and re-checking. Her mouth dries. It could mean anything. Either Ursula chose to disappear or at worst, she might have been silenced. Dispatched without record. The airless room is so full of bodies she feels claustrophobic. Nauseous even. But she wills herself to remain, her glance shifting to the *Unofficial Informers* cabinets. It's what she'd feared most, deep down, but never believed. And it doesn't take long. *Ursula Meyer;* listed in perfect alphabetical order. She scans headlines on the page, heart fluttering, her spine cold. *Enlisted July 1954. Informer's main objective: reports on personal life of Fräulein Kitty Bernstein. Characteristics: Reliable worker. Information: low grade, limited detail. March 1955 Trial by jury: Guilty of collusion to provide false passport for British Spy, Herr Alec Carter. Relocated to USSR for remedial training in Siberian work camp. November 1973 Deceased: Sclerosis of the liver.*

She reads the report twice then lets it fall to the sea of unwanted and inseparable folders at her feet. It would be best to walk away, to leave the grubbiness of revenge to others, but her limbs refuse the request; as if they know she has unfinished business which she has yet to address. By now the *Employees* filing cabinets have been scoured and decimated, drawers pulled out so violently, most have crashed to the floor. One catches her eye, alphabetically listed under *G*. Crouching down beside it she begins to scrutinise its contents until she finds a dossier filed under *Herr Edward Grant.* She places it into the bag and leaves the building. No one stops her. All sense of authority has vanished.

Returning to her apartment by tram, her mind is numb. She barely finds the energy to walk the last streets to her door. Once inside she pours herself a large vodka. Her body shakes uncontrollably. She gulps down the spirit, harsh to her throat, winces and pours again. With each day that passes she's noticed that she's drinking more. A comfort of sorts. Ursula was always more of a drinker than she was. She swallows again, drinking for her friend; to her friend, if she still has the right to the claim. It's too hard, too tender, to contemplate. The two folders lie on the divan where she dropped them. She settles beside them, choosing first to pick up Ed's.

There are several lines of character assessment which, as she skims, appears mostly positive. *Disciplined, resourceful, collected, intelligent, potential to be ruthless.* The only negative suggests *a father complex, resentful for never reaching paternal expectations,* but it considers this trait *could be turned to advantage.* It's dated September 1952 and signed by one *J. Atherton.* She stares at the name, hand trembling. She should have guessed of course. The trip to Salisbury, fleeting images of a genial man smoking a pipe in his front room, his charming wife, Molly, baking an apple pie in her honour. How cosy and British they seemed. Ed conveniently forgetting his keys while she and Alec waited in the car. She should have seen it. But she was blinded by her faith in her own invincibility. Even that's not quite the truth. She takes another sip and reads on.

October 1954. Herr E. Grant's agent status withdrawn after failure to terminate Fräulein K. Bernstein. Her mind flits back to their farewell at London Airport. She's lucky he wasn't as ruthless as his report would suggest, or perhaps just not as competent. Staring at the faded, typed sheet, she recalls her last words to him. "Maybe we'll meet again one day. In happier times." It was a flippant comment, loaded with irony. She wonders if those happier times have finally arrived. It's not quite how she imagined them.

There's another page. After his fall from grace the Stasi continued to monitor him. He starts a fledgling pharmaceutical company and travels frequently. Regular trips to California, Thailand, and Tangiers. By the 1970s the information becomes very sketchy. Rudimentary even. As if someone has scoured the pages of foreign newspapers to glean anything they could write down. By the 1980s there's no mention of foreign trips nor any sense of a private life. There are snippets of articles pasted from what seem to be scientific journals or trade magazines. At any rate his fledgling company appears to have developed into a lucrative business. Clegmore Pharmaceuticals Ltd, based outside Cambridge, head office in London; a leading developer of erosion resistant industrial paints and now branching into the burgeoning market of natural beauty products.

She closes the dossier and slips it into the cutlery drawer. Reaching for a box of matches she places a metal wastepaper basket in the middle of the kitchen floor and sets light to her own dossier. The blackened pages crumple into the bin. When the job is done she falls back to the divan, closing her eyes, feeling the bite of exhaustion. Usually at seven she'd tune into the World Service, find something to snack on. But the vodka has suppressed her hunger and tonight she prefers not to listen to more reports of repressive intelligence agencies.

The news of Ursula's death weighs heavily on her chest. It will remain there for a while, the implications too delicate to unpick, a reluctance to dwell for fear of what it might unleash. Her thoughts turn instead to Ed Grant, replaying their separation at the airport so long ago, wondering why it bothers her quite so much. As the image plays about in her mind an idea stirs, a plan of sorts which begins to lift her spirits, feeling a younger Kitty Bernstein calling from her past. She begins to convince herself it's appropriate, even necessary; an old link restored, a positive symbol of the fall of the Wall. Like the meeting between Kohl and Modrow. It's a gesture of friendship, albeit a political one. More crucially it saves her mind from pending atrophy. That night, when she finally drifts to sleep, she dreams of Alec Carter.

She wakes early with a dry mouth and a dull head. But the plan she'd begun stitching together remains in place, its nagging persistence somehow a pointer to its veracity. Rising from the divan she knocks over the half-empty vodka bottle at her feet, catching it before it falls, pouring the remains down the sink. She will not let it seduce her. It's a route she's too familiar with, having seen its tarnishing effects in prison; the self-pity which she so hated and yet which was so slyly seductive. She thinks of poor Ursula; not blaming her for the betrayal; it was probably inevitable and beyond her friend's control, but the drinking didn't help.

She senses some of her wiliness return, a call to duty, if she can call it that. There's nothing she can do immediately about her threadbare clothes but a little make-up wouldn't hurt, just to lift her spirits when she's confronted by her reflection. She applies a burnt orange lipstick and brown eyeshadow. It's all she has, probably way out of date, but better than nothing.

Her first excursion is to the bank. There's more in her account than she'd remembered. Hopefully it's sufficient to enact her plan. Heading south through the city she crosses into the Western sector at Checkpoint Charlie. Nobody stops her. An Eastern border guard smiles. No bullets sever her spine. She takes the U Bahn, stepping out at Kurfurstendamm, transfixed by the abundant wealth displayed in the shops surrounding her. A constant flow of traffic fills the wide boulevard. Only the splintered remains of the Kaiser Wilhelm Memorial Church remind her of the past. She chooses one of the more modest fashion stores and buys a winter coat, a skirt and jacket, and a warm dress. She'd forgotten how much she liked clothes.

Asking the sales assistant if she knows of a public library, the girl directs her to a more sober street, away from the hubbub of shoppers. The building has an elegant, eighteenth-century facade, a lucky survivor of the war; serene yet defiant. Kitty imbibes the studious atmosphere, aware her heart is slowing to its rhythm. No one can follow her here, though so far this morning she's sensed no shadow. She asks to be directed to a list of European pharmaceutical companies, specialising in either paint products or beauty products, aware it's an unusual request, but the librarian's unfazed. In an unloved alcove, her eye glances along a line of thick encyclopedias, each labelled alphabetically. It doesn't take her long to find under 'C'. *Clegmore Pharmaceuticals. First registered 1962. CEO and founder Edward Grant. Maker of industrial paints. Head Office 110 Colemans Street London EC4 UK*

There's no reference to beauty products but she's undeterred. It's three years since the encyclopedias were published. A second search takes her to companies listed under 'V'. She's aware that Vogue magazine has had a German version for a while, either she read it somewhere or saw it on television, but she has no idea where it's based. The entry tells her it's Munich, opened in 1979. She scribbles the telephone number on a scrap of paper.

Not far from the library she finds a telephone kiosk. It's a quiet, residential street, perfect for the call she wants to make. Winter sun touches the glass panes; a false anthem of spring. She dials the number and requests to speak to their editor on beauty products. To her surprise she's put straight through. A young voice, enthusiastic, composed; and malleable, she hopes.

"Andrea Klaus"

"Good morning, Fräulein Klaus, my name is Fräulein Bernstein, I'm a freelance photo-journalist working in Berlin."

"Yes, how may I help you?"

"I wondered if you'd be interested in a story about natural beauty products. My cousin runs a very successful pharmaceutical company in England, based outside Cambridge and he's looking for some publicity about his products."

At first, as she'd expected, Andrea Klaus sounds non-plussed. Not her thing really. But polite enough.

Kitty persists. "I think it'd be a bit of a scoop to be honest. His products are not only gorgeous but very green. I've tried them, they look great. And he's working on a much larger scale than anyone's managed so far. But the thing is he's worried the British press will be too myopic and cynical, while here in Germany the green agenda is so much more advanced. I could take some pictures, he's an alumnus of Cambridge University so

417

I could get some shots at his beautiful old college. It'd make a great visual contrast with his state-of-the-art factory."

She feels her dormant training awaken; an absolute conviction of her latest truth. There's a hesitation at the end of the phone. She knows Andrea Klaus is ruminating; fearful she might miss out on a great story; one to impress her boss.

"I think your cousin's right about the British press, Fräulein Bernstein. In Germany we'd take a less cynical perspective. What's the name of his company?"

Bang. Target hit.

"Clegmore Pharamceuticals. I'm heading over next week. Maybe if you sent me a letter of introduction and your business card I could suggest it to him. He loves clothes anyway. Very English gent style. I'm sure I could persuade him to give his first interview to Vogue Germany. He's very slick. And very credible."

Andrea Klaus is putty in her hand. She replaces the receiver elated and with the barest tinge of guilt about her easy slide to deception. The years in prison have not dented her skillset.

Before returning to East Berlin there's a couple more errands. A skinny girl with a ring in her eyebrow does a decent job on her hair; layering and snipping until her short, grey bob has more body. The girl says she looks gamine. She's touched by the compliment. Walking back to the East she chooses a route through the Brandenburg Gate. She'd imagined it would feel satisfyingly symbolic, but instead as she passes between the columns her hands grow suddenly cold; the scars of her experience still too fresh. At Alexanderplatz she buys a cheap suitcase; no one important will see it, and some toiletries. From now on she must live frugally, waste nothing, eat sparingly and avoid alcohol. Her State backpay must be conserved for more important objectives.

Two days later a large envelope arrives from Munich. It contains a letter addressed to Ed from Andrea Klaus, and attached to it by paperclip, her business card. The letter, in English, is effusive; praise for Ed's work in green beauty products, a summary of Vogue's elite distribution in Germany. The two ideas seem incongruous but no matter. And to Kitty, a short note. *Can you take a nice shot of him in front of the beautiful buildings so we can get an idea of how he comes across?* Kitty senses the young Andrea Klaus has gone out on a limb, probably not running it past her boss, till she's more certain. All the better.

At a West Berlin travel agent she books a flight to Hamburg which will connect with a Lufthansa flight to London.

The following morning she boards the first plane. She's never been on a jet, nor seen one except on television. The force with which it accelerates down the runway astounds her. She feels giddy with intent.

She slips through passport control at Heathrow without a hitch, boarding a coach to the city centre. Like West Berlin, London has changed immeasurably since her last visit, back in '54. Beyond the toxic fumes of Victoria bus station, she senses a lightness about the city, both in its architecture and its bearing. Buildings rendered black by decades of soot, now exhibit a honey stone, Georgian elegance. Londoners seem more relaxed, more diverse, a melting pot of cultures. But another change shocks her. There's an extraordinary number of young homeless, either sleeping in the shelter of doorways, or begging on the streets. They're hard to avoid, though most locals try.

She spends the rest of the morning walking the city streets, observing this contrast of fortunes. At lunchtime she buys a sandwich in Soho and walks down to St James's Park to find a bench. At least it's mild despite the leaden sky. Later she takes the tube to King's Cross and checks in to a bed and breakfast. Her guidebook explains that the area behind the station is cheap. She can see why. Gas storage tanks dominate the horizon, in front of them a patchwork of railway lines and dilapidated, nineteenth-century housing. The room is basic and damp. Not so different to her apartment in East Berlin. She settles on a thin mattress, strangely amused by her own fall from grace. Memories of the Art Deco splendour at the Dorchester rush in; the champagne baths, the glamorous clothes. Barely conceivable that this was her life in the same city three decades ago.

In the morning she rises early, dressing as elegantly as her new clothes will allow. It's not Chanel but it will do. She applies make-up with more care than she's done since entering prison. Wiping condensation from the mirror, she recognises something of herself, a ghost of her past, but a welcome one. She declines breakfast and travels the underground to the City where she hopes to find a café in Colemans Street. It's a long narrow road, typical of the area and although it's only 7.15am, she assumes cafés will be open. London City workers, she recalls, are famously early birds. Discreetly she observes the numbers on the buildings until she reaches 110. It looks no different to the others, part of a terrace of three storey houses, presumably once a rich banker's home. There's a shiny plaque on the brickwork, small but well-polished. Clegmore Pharmaceuticals Ltd. She barely glances before walking on. On the other side of the road, a little further north, she spots an unremarkable café; the kind that survives on lunch time trade from office staff, never having to work too hard for custom. Inside there's a steady flow of coffee junkies, winter coats turned up against the fine rain. She takes a seat by the window. If she cranes her neck she can just see Clegmore's. Now all she has to do is wait. Taking out her notebook, to feign work, she orders a cappuccino. It arrives boiling hot with barely a hint of coffee. Whether Ed will turn up

or not, she really has no idea. It's a gamble. He could be at the
factory in Cambridge, or on a business trip, or in bed with a
lover. But if he's due at the office she's calculated that he won't
be the earliest to arrive, he's the CEO after all, but neither will
he want to imbue his staff with an impression of tardiness. She's
estimated he'll arrive somewhere around 8.30am. If he doesn't
appear by 9am she'll give up for the day.

Watching the spots of rain spin to webs on the glass, she tries to
slow her breath. But there is little to occupy her. She begins to
write nonsense in her notebook, to expel the growing
nervousness; parts of poems she remembers: Rilke, Whitman,
Blake, all bound together. She assumes they'd be horrified. The
coffee still burns her throat but it's an excuse to drink slowly. By
8am the rush of workers has subsided and she wonders how she
can least draw attention to herself. But the Italian owner shows
more preoccupation with cleaning the chrome coffee machine
than any lingering trade. At 8.15am she glances again to the
window. A large, black car has drawn up outside Clegmore's. It
hovers for a moment before a man steps out of the passenger
seat, lifting his hand as the car pulls away. It's unmistakeably
him; the stature, the hair, the elegant, gentlemanly style. She's
surprised how young he looks. He steps deftly into the office.

She waits another fifteen minutes before rising from the table.
Outside she checks her make-up and hair in a vanity mirror. It's
crucial she makes the biggest impression. Had she attempted to
contact him directly, by phone or by letter, she's certain he
would have rebuffed her. And anyway, this way's more fun. But
now, witnessing a glimpse of his persona as he left the car, the
apparent eternal youthfulness, she is mindful that in essence his
character has not changed. Her subterfuge is warranted. And she
must be vigilant.

She presses the brass bell plate. An intercom squawks.

"Can I help you?"

"Good morning, my name is Andrea Klaus." She adds a German tinge to her English. Just for authenticity. "I work for Vogue magazine in Germany. I don't have an appointment but I'm on holiday in London and my editor cheekily asked if I could secure an interview about your natural beauty product range while I'm here."

There's a moment's hesitation before a buzzer releases the door. She enters, poised, assured, mustering all the gracefulness she imagines Andrea Klaus to possess. The receptionist sits behind an ornate, cherry-wood desk, the foyer resemblant of a grand family hall with stucco ceilings and elaborately carved, Oriental wooden cabinets. A large palm completes the strangely exotic display. The receptionist smiles encouragingly, young and attractive of course. Fresh from graduating.

"Good morning. How may I help?"

Kitty breezes to the desk, immediately holding out Andrea Klaus's business card for inspection. "I'm so sorry to barge in like this but my editor never misses an opportunity. She wondered if it would be possible to get a short interview with Mr Grant. I'm sure he's very busy but it would just take ten minutes or so. It's just that his company's big news in Germany. We're very motivated by the green agenda, and obviously particularly for beauty products…"

The receptionist cuts in. "…I'm sure you understand, but Mr Grant's a very busy man. If you'd like to leave your card I can ask his PA to call you."

"That's very kind but unfortunately I fly back tomorrow. Maybe it would be possible just to have a quick word with his assistant?"

The girl holds her gaze, less amenable now, before picking up the phone. After a short exchange she invites Kitty to take a seat in the reception area. "His assistant will be down in a moment."

It's more a parlour than a reception area; a sash window looks out to the street, a stone mantelpiece surrounds an open fire. On a glass coffee table there's a fan of trade magazines and a row of glossy picture books on faraway places; Tangiers, Singapore, Thailand. Her mind flits back to the notes on his travels in the Stasi headquarters. A plumpish woman arrives in the doorway, in her fifties she guesses. Grown-up children. Heading for retirement. Maybe a school governor and a seat on several charity committees. "Miss Klaus, I'm Barbara, Mr Grant's assistant." She extends her hand. "How do you do? I'm so sorry to disappoint you but Mr Grant's in a meeting all morning and has to be at the factory in Cambridge this afternoon. So hopefully I can assist you in some way."

Kitty smiles. "Well as I explained to your delightful receptionist I'm on a rather cheeky errand to secure a scoop on your beauty products. I was so hoping Mr Grant would have a few minutes. Our German readers are very environmentally aware, and of course there's his history with Cambridge University and all that British tradition. I'm convinced we publish more articles on the Queen and her family than anywhere else in Europe." She smiles again, as brightly as she can.

Barbara gathers her hands together. The body language isn't positive. Either she doesn't believe the story or she's fiercely defensive of her boss. Kitty suspects the latter.

"You speak excellent English."

"My mother was English. She married a German."

"Oh. I see. Well I can see you've done some research. Perhaps as you're leaving tomorrow I could help you with more information, if you tell me exactly what you're looking for. Then maybe we could put a future date in Mr Grant's diary."

More positive than she'd expected but not the outcome she needs. Time to come clean. She leans in, almost a conspiratorial whisper. "The thing is, Barbara, I haven't been entirely honest. All that I've told you is true, but what I omitted to say is that I'm Ed's cousin, because I wanted to surprise him. We haven't seen each other in years because I was stuck behind the Berlin Wall. But now. Now I'm finally free again."

It's clear the woman is perplexed, unsure whether to show delight or maintain her cautious professionalism. Kitty feels mildly ashamed of her own schoolgirlish pleasure. But by gaining control of their encounter she feels her nerves abate; a surprise benefit of her Stasi training. "I'm sure he'd be really upset if he found out he'd missed me."

Barbara draws herself together again. "But I gave him your name. He didn't seem to recognise it."

"An old childhood joke. He's plainly forgotten. Just tell him it's his long-lost cousin from East Germany. He'll remember."

The assistant glances back through the door to the receptionist. "Please take a seat, Miss Klaus."

She sits down. The waxing smile never waning.

Barbara turns to the door, closing it behind her as she exits. Kitty steps to the window, seeking distraction, but there's scant activity on the street. A pigeon pecks at a flake of pastry before fluttering out of sight. She can hear the phone ringing beyond the door, the emollient tone of the young receptionist. A picture above the fireplace catches her eye. Modernist. A rural scene, reminiscent of Grant Wood. But it's clearly an English landscape, flat fields, hedges, a farmhouse in the distance. It could be Cambridgeshire.

"Hello, Kitty."

She'd become so absorbed in the painting she'd missed the door opening. It must be well-oiled. Ed stands before her, his smile revealing well-polished teeth. Her first fleeting impression had not been inaccurate. He's still slim, hair flecked with grey but hardly. Impeccably dressed. Savile Row suit. Cuffs neatly extended from the forearms. Expensive cufflinks, sapphires set in silver.

"Hello, Ed."

She waits by the fireplace as he closes the door, stepping forward to kiss her on both cheeks. A surprising gesture. His aftershave smells of pinecones. His gaze is intense. Direct. "You look well."

"You too." For a moment she's lost her assuredness. Startled.

"This is quite a surprise."

She smiles. "I didn't want to disappoint with my stage entrance."

He nods, appearing to appreciate her joke. "Take a seat. Did Barbara offer you some coffee?"

"No, but I just burnt my mouth off with coffee in that café opposite."

He smirks again. "Some water then."

"I'm fine." She doesn't want to be a receptacle for his hospitality. It's a weak position.

She settles again in the chair with its back to the window. Ed sits adjacent on the other side of the coffee table, oddly formal, both facing the fireplace. "I like your painting."

425

"Thank you. I commissioned it from a young student who was studying at Cambridge. He's making quite a name for himself now. It's soothing to be reminded of home when you're stuck in the City for days on end."

"Well, the business seems to be thriving. You're obviously making quite a splash in the market."

"I do my best."

He says no more. It's clear he's bored of the small talk. But she decides to wait, keen for him to lead the conversation now. She's an unexpected, and she suspects unwelcome guest, after all. Eventually he complies. "So. It's been a long time."

"Thirty-five years. When we last met. I was holding a gun to your head."

He feigns a smile. "It's not one of my fonder memories. But perhaps I should thank you for not pulling the trigger."

"On the contrary, it's me who should be thanking you. You were supposed to shoot me and dig a shallow grave. But even if I hadn't found that gun during your call with Atherton I don't think you'd have gone through with it."

He shifts uncomfortably, as she knew he would. Looking for a way out, his eyes glancing to the door. She persists anyway.

"From the East German Intelligence point of view, that was your weakness, Ed. Not ruthless enough. So in the spirit of Glasnost I felt I wanted to thank you, in person. You may recall my last words to you, at the airport, were that hopefully we'd meet in better times. Then I meant them flippantly. Now I just want to kill a few demons, have some closure as the Americans would say."

"Well I hope this helps in some way."

"I hope so too. I found you quite charming all those years ago, but in prison, all that time, I turned you into something of an ogre. I blamed you for my circumstance. But I realise now it was always my choice. I don't want to go to my grave with bad blood between us. We don't have to be friends, Ed, but I didn't want our farewell at the airport to be a permanent stain. A question mark."

She waits for his reaction. His gaze shifts to the floor, a midnight blue carpet which looks like it should contain stars. "I'm grateful. For your understanding and this visit. It can't have been easy. I heard about your prison sentence from Molly before all contact was lost but of course I wondered what happened to you. How you were. But there was nothing I could do, even though I thought about you a lot. I never stopped really."

He looks up, his gaze falling upon her again. "But that's the past, Kitty. None of it's important anymore. The Wall's fallen, whatever we believed then, it was a different time. I suppose we were naively optimistic."

"Or we had huge egos and an over-blown idea of our own righteousness."

To her surprise he laughs. "Perhaps. In that way we were maybe similar. But certainly I don't think we are what we were then. I'm a successful businessman and you're - a survivor. Which is why I can't believe you've made all this effort just to tell me you're grateful for what you so charmingly called my weakness."

The smile has vanished. Plainly a part of his unrepentant ego is bruised by her comment. She remembers the details in his report. "That weakness was in the eyes of the Stasi, not mine."

Her words do little to ameliorate his rancour. "But you were a part of it."

"Of it but not wedded to it."

"Maybe that was <u>your</u> weakness."

His words are dusted with bitterness but she has no intention to get involved in a slanging match. "I did want to thank you, but you're right, it wasn't the only thing. I want to know what happened with Buchanan-Smith. And what happened to his family."

"For God's sake, Kitty, like I said, the past is the past."

"Maybe but I've lived all those years in prison. In isolation. For me it's the last thing I remember. Please, I just want to know."

He sighs, shifting again in his chair. "No one was ever put to trial. Word was put out that it was a break-in that went wrong. The public bought it. Occasionally it gets revisited but as far as I know there's never been any new leads."

"And his family?"

"His wife remarried. More happily I hear. She emigrated to Canada. I think the children went with her."

"I'm glad she came through."

"Well I hope that appeases your guilt."

He's getting tetchy now. Plainly she's outstaying her welcome. Digging up dirt he has no desire to touch. "It's a burden I think we share."

His face reddens, the youthfulness suddenly in abeyance. "It's history. Now if you'll excuse me…"

"One more thing. If the trail came to nothing then I assume Alec never returned to England? Or got in touch with you?"

She looks for clues. His expression softens. Perhaps the memory of Alec touches his heart. "He called once. From Germany. One of the other students in our block took the call. But I was out at the time. The chap told him to call back. But he never did."

"I see. Poor old Alec. You've no idea what happened to him? Where he went?"

"No idea at all, I'm afraid. I'm guessing he went abroad somewhere. I suppose we'll never really know."

"I suppose not."

"It really is time to forget all that, Kitty. Concentrate on your work at Vogue. It sounds like a fantastic job."

"I'm sure it is. But I lied. Just to get through your door. Even so Andrea Klaus would be very happy to hear from you. Your receptionist has her card."

She thinks she witnesses a moment of shock pass across his face, aggrieved that he's been hoodwinked. But then he bursts into laughter. "I assumed just the name was false, to keep me guessing. Plainly I'm no longer as sharp as you."

"She works for Vogue in Munich. It'd be great publicity."

"It's a very kind offer. But Clegmore's will get plenty of air time in a documentary on television next week. You should watch if you can. BBC 2. Thursday. It's all about greener industries."

"Congratulations. But I don't own a television."

"That's a shame. It should be good. So what'll you do? When you return?"

"Get a proper job. Teach again, if anyone will have me."

"Of course they will. Children love you. I remember when…"

"…When what?"

"I was just thinking, those children you taught at the primary school, they're probably parents themselves now." He pauses, his gaze steadfast again. "I assume you don't have offspring."

"No, not much opportunity."

He smiles again. "Me neither. Let me, if I may, give you a piece of advice, Kitty. Forget everything. You don't have to look behind you anymore. Only the future matters."

"I can see that's worked for you. You've created a very fulfilling life for yourself. For me it's not so simple."

"Teaching will help. Digging up the past will only cause hurt and possibly danger. For us all. You have to promise me you won't start turning over any stones."

She smiles. "I promise."

"One last thing. How did you find me?"

She wondered when he'd ask and there's no point in lying. "You probably saw it on the news. The Stasi headquarters was raided by protesters and I was among them. I found your file and took it back to my apartment."

"I hope it made interesting reading."

"Not really. The grammar was all over the place."

He grins. Not very convincingly. "May I ask what you did with it?"

"I burnt it."

"The truth?"

"Cross my heart."

She notices the creases at his mouth soften slightly. As if he believes her.

"Presumably you were sensible enough to retrieve your own file?"

She smiles. "I burnt that too."

"Good."

She'll burn his when she returns, now that she's achieved her aim. A peace mission of sorts. She'd only kept it as insurance really, just in case he turned nasty. Conjuring her most charming pose, she holds her hands together, like a child in expectation. "My turn to ask a last question?"

He smiles. "If you must."

"Did you ever marry, or find a partner?

"Fate never led me in that direction. I have several Labradors instead. You?'

"Not much chance for that either. Unless I fancied the prison staff. Who were admittedly tough to resist."

He laughs aloud. More relaxed than he's been throughout the interview. But as quickly the mirth evaporates. "I suppose none of them matched up to Alec. You were very in love, Kitty. Maybe you still are."

"I don't deal in hypotheticals. Alec no longer exists apparently."

"Probably better that way."

"So now I must leave you to your work."

"Thank you for coming. I very much appreciate it. But before you go. One last question, I'm curious. The ideology we held so dear at the time. Do you, despite everything, still submit to its creed?"

She hadn't expected the question after all his platitudes about moving on. It throws her for a second. Perhaps it's a question that she hasn't dared ask herself. Either way, she's in danger of looking a fool. She smiles at him. "I'm human. Imperfect, just like everyone. Ideologies will come and go but humans will always be imperfect. And thank God for that."

He rises from the chair, saying nothing. Her time is done. Opening the door to the reception area he kisses her on both cheeks, the studied role of a perfect gentleman, steering her artfully towards the front door. Even the receptionist is grinning. Two childhood cousins, separated for decades, finally re-united.

He waits on the step to see her off. "Goodbye, Kitty. And the best of luck with the future."

"Goodbye, Ed." She offers a last grin before heading towards the tube station. Her heart is lighter somehow. It's what she had hoped for.

24

JANUARY 1990,   DEVIZES, ENGLAND

He wheels a trolley along a deserted aisle of the supermarket, unloading boxes of lager to replenish stock for the weekend. Tiny fragments of gold tinsel still cling to the ceiling where the sticking tape hasn't yet been removed. There's a smell of disinfectant; his supervisor is washing off the check-out conveyor belts, cleansing the shop of any remaining festive joy. The rest of January will be bleak. Returning to the office, she slips Bruce Springsteen's greatest hits into the CD player. It screams out across the supermarket, filling the void; dispelling the gloom.

She emerges with a clipboard and pencil and stops by Alec in the alcohol aisle. "Any chance you can fill in for me Tuesday night, James?"

As far as he remembers he's not doing anything Tuesday. And supervising pays better. "Night out on the town, is it?"

She nods at the speaker above them and grins. "Hot date with the Boss. I was born to be in the USA."

He can't help smiling. She's a dedicated fan. "Then I better say yes."

"You're a sweetheart. Thank you."

She moves on up the aisle. He wonders what she's really doing. Every date is with the Boss. By 9.30pm the shelf stacking is complete and he steps out into the evening air. It's pleasantly mild. A well-mannered, English winter. A familiar bunch of teenagers hangs around the bench outside the supermarket; one encircles it on his bike, the leader of the troop. The others share a can of beer. One smokes ostentatiously. Up Maryport Street lights glow from the pub. It's overflowing with Friday night revellers. Men hover outside in shirtsleeves, fags hanging from mouths, pint glasses clutched to chests, jibes and counter jibes preceding howls of derision. Their mirth, sporadic but acute, echoes against the facades of the charity and coffee shops.

Alec's quite tempted by a pint; there's bound to be someone he knows at the bar, but he's running in the morning, and there's already an open bottle of wine to finish at home. He turns away across Sheep Street, past the mail delivery office; a brooding modernist carbuncle which leers at the elegant, Georgian bookshop opposite. He turns right into Morris Lane. The narrow passageway leads to a long terrace of Victorian cottages on the left, each fronted by a strip of garden. The one he enters is more desolate than the rest; the path cracked, winter-limp shrubs outgrown their space. He turns the key in the door, opening to a small front room. Opposite the fireplace, a fake leather sofa occupies most of the space; in the corner a portable television sits on top of a ring-stained coffee table. The walls are bare except for a line of books occupying a single shelf. Newspapers spread across a threadbare carpet. He switches on the television before walking through to the galley kitchen. Reaching for the open wine he pours himself a large tumbler and slips a supermarket lasagne into the oven. The microwave gave up a while ago and the thermostat on the cooker has fractured to a thread of metal. He adjusts it with the set of pliers that sit on the kitchen surface. He keeps forgetting to ask the landlord to sort it all.

A police drama flickers on the television but it's already halfway through. Nothing on the other channels grabs his attention; a quiz show, gardening tips, and some discussion about cannabis among a group of worthies. He flicks back to the drama, thinking he might be able to catch up, his mind drifting to tasks for the weekend. He'll run early, maybe four miles up on the Plain, try to patch the Fiesta's radiator leak in the afternoon, head to the pub for a game of pool in the evening. Sunday morning he'll spend at the boxing club in Trowbridge. He's never told anyone about it, most of the staff at the supermarket would laugh, given his age. But it keeps him sane. The tumbler is already empty. He refills it but doesn't take another sip until he's completed a short fitness routine on the kitchen floor. Press-ups, crunches, bent-knee push ups. Five minutes later the lasagne's cooked.

He's not sure what wakes him so abruptly.

His empty plate lies at a precarious angle beside him, the wine bottle, now finished, sits at his feet. It's the voice, he thinks, his senses re-engaging. There was a familiar voice. His eyes settle on the television, still droning in the corner. Images of a modern factory and its production line cut in quick succession. Some sort of documentary. There's a voice over, a woman's voice, warm, not the one that woke him. She's describing the process of manufacture and then the screen cuts to an interview; a middle-aged man sitting in a sleek office. It's pristine, almost anodyne. His words and manner are compelling, a familiar and unmistakable charisma despite the passing years. Handsome and forthright, age has not dimmed his spell. If anything, Mr Edward Grant is more alluring; sitting in Alec's front room, as if they'd met yesterday.

He can't concentrate on the words. The shock is too great. He feels his mouth dry, a bead of sweat on his forehead, his body pulsing. Too many emotions. But the interview passes, usurped by the woman's voice-over, soft and melodic against dreamy spires of Cambridge. And then the credits roll, taking Ed Grant with them.

For a moment he cannot stir from the sofa, his gaze still locked to the screen. He reaches for the wine bottle, remembering it's empty; searching out the cigarettes in the kitchen drawer instead. His hand trembles as he lights the cigarette. The smoke seeps deep into his lungs in a vain attempt to quell the fear, so long dormant, now stirring in his belly. There's a bottle of cheap whisky in the cupboard, which he takes to the front room, pouring a generous fill into the empty tumbler. He continues to pour until the wrench of sleep obliterates all thought, a womb of absolution that cradles him till five in the morning, when he wakes sharply with an acrid mouth and a dull head.

By eight it is still barely light. He has driven up to the Plain and parked off the track amongst the hardened dog walkers, some perhaps in the same fragile state. The route he chooses runs higher still, to the summit of the Plain where a keen wind blows from the north-east; perfect to clear his head. As he runs, his line of sight stretches to the curve of the Marlborough Downs in the distance, pin sharp under a sapphire sky. After four miles his limbs begin to scream, his breath ragged and desperate. He vows to train harder; desperate to push Ed Grant to the recesses of his brain. But the Plain evokes memories. Perhaps it was a mistake to run so close to Imber. He's never been back since he visited with Kitty. Before his world shattered. Still, he pushes on, knowing that by the time he's completed the circuit he'll be exhausted, and the dopamine and endorphins will have done their work. For a while at least.

Before taking a shower, he decides to fix the car radiator; it's another distraction, helping his mind relax, absorbed by the mundanity of his task. But later, as daylight ebbs, he feels the disquiet return, tightening the sinews that running had temporarily released. Staying at home is not an option. Better to head out, shoot a few rounds of pool with the guys in the pub. No demands put upon him, no questions asked. He takes the cigarettes with him, smoking more in one evening than he's done in two months. It doesn't go un-noticed but he takes the flak. And it helps him concentrate. He plays brutally, winning most games through sheer, bloody will, then leaving without having said much; at the point he's sunk enough booze to numb his thoughts but not enough to disarm him. That must never happen.

On Sunday morning he drives to the boxing club on the outskirts of Melksham. It's a hovel compared to the fancy gym that's just opened on the Devizes industrial estate but it's cheap. The booze has dulled his performance and he suffers for it. His sparring partner lands several bruising punches, abusing him for his paltry defence. He's in a muck sweat, water dripping from his body, his flesh pummelled and tender. But it's what he wanted, to be pounded, shaken up, reduced to the truth of his state. It's motivational.

On his return, he slumps on to the sofa, absolved of the urgent need for more booze or fags. A league football match plays out on the television but it barely grabs his attention. He rests a few minutes, feeling his strength return, then leaves the sofa to find a writing pad and a tray, sitting down again with a pen which hovers over the empty page, like a bird of prey above a field. Waiting. Watching. The wording is crucial. The decision to pounce was made after his run.

Dear Ed,

This letter will no doubt come as a surprise, as great as mine I'd imagine, when I saw you on the television a couple of days ago. You haven't changed that much which must be either good genes or a healthy lifestyle, or maybe both.

I often wondered what happened to you after Cambridge but it seemed prudent not to make enquiries. I realised after my call from Hamburg that you'd decided we'd be better to part company. Now by chance you've turned up again and I'm wondering if that rule still applies. Perhaps we should meet? I think it might help me at least, though of course for you I cannot say.

I'm aware I'm taking a risk and if I don't hear from you I shall understand. We were once great friends. You helped me considerably in my first days at Trinity College, country bumpkin that I was. There is a hole in my life that you once filled. Forgive me for the sentiment. Neither of us are spring chickens anymore.

Best regards,

Alec

He reads the letter back once then seals it in an envelope. Tomorrow he'll find out the address of Ed's company at the library. The name rings a bell for some reason, just about the only thing from the documentary that stuck in his mind; Clegmore Pharmaceuticals.

Monday morning is always busy; replenishing stock, putting in orders, price checking. He's grateful for the distraction. At lunchtime he finds the address he's looking for and writes it on a scrap of paper provided by the librarian. The letter remains on the sofa beside him until half past eleven that night when he finally switches off the television. Walking down the lane to the post box, the chilled air promises a hard frost. Stars pepper the night sky, a million points of light bleeding through a black canvas. His breath steams and unfurls, the heat of two whiskies. He posts the letter; the street sleeping so soundly he hears it drop to the metal floor. Tomorrow morning a postman will whisk it away. The rest is fate.

Each day he waits, his disquiet increases. Perhaps it was an unwise decision, a momentary pull of the heart; a lack of vigilance. Despite the passing of years he is still a fugitive, an alias, never having paid his debt for the murder of Buchanan-Smith. At least that's how Ed might see it. In his own mind he's convinced himself it was manslaughter, a reflex self-defence, a well of belief so bolstered by endless retellings it's deep enough to bury any counter truth. So why still seek Ed's blessing?

Four days later an envelope lies on the doormat when he returns from work. The handwriting is so elaborate and effusive, a graphologist would probably have a field day. He rips it open to find a card with an address neatly printed at its top.

Dearest Alec,

What a delight after all this time! I often wondered if you'd ever turn up. Please, please come this weekend! How about Sunday for lunch? You didn't mention a family but bring them as well if you have one. I shall look forward to it. No need to reply unless you really can't make it, but I shan't accept an excuse unless a sudden meteorite or something lands on Devizes! Address as above. Don't wear your Sunday best. Dogs etc, so very informal!

Yours in anticipation,

Ed

He stares at it, reads it twice. Is it what he wanted? The reply seems so ludicrously carefree, as if their separation had been a simple act of geography; two old mates distanced by work and families. Yet there is something distinctly Ed about the language, the bonhomie, the flippancy, the exclamation marks, as if nothing worth living comes without a degree of exaggeration. It almost makes him smile. But it doesn't erase the sense of unease. If he were looking for either apology or absolution it would be foolish to imagine Ed delivering it. Ed's the kind of man who polishes tin and persuades you it's gold, so what would his sanction mean anyway?

He drops the letter onto the kitchen work surface and reaches for the open bottle of wine. Perhaps it doesn't matter what his old roommate thinks. In the days since he spotted Ed on television a more visceral concern has crept into his consciousness. One that he has deliberately buried but now occupies an alarming part of his waking hours. The thought of Kitty; what happened to her? Where she is now? A wound which, previously he'd assumed healed, is now festering. The last memory of her, shoved into the car outside her Berlin apartment, glimpsed through a grimy rear windscreen. And now the Wall has fallen, their separation no longer bound by concrete, but by his own trepidation.

He asks his supervisor for Sunday off. He's done her enough favours. But wandering down the aisles, he's unsure what gift he should take; wine, flowers, chocolates? Nothing feels appropriate and anyway he's too nervous to give it much consideration. In what he realises is an absurd twist of logic, he cleans the Fiesta and irons his best shirt, despite the plea to be casual. Ed's sure to have pristine standards. In his own case 'best' means un-frayed. Glancing in the mirror, he inspects what's presented to him, not unhappy with the reflection; a middle-aged man still trim enough and healthy enough, thanks to the running and boxing. He's never been vain but it's crucial that Ed sees a survivor, even though he's one who's lived in the wilderness.

Driving into Sussex across the Downs, a canvas of winter serenity bewitches him; a feeble sun, crested on the horizon, draws tapering shadows towards the valleys where hamlets shelter under a haze of wood smoke. A landscape which appears untroubled by time. The village of Arbutt, nestling off the main road, proves the most idyllic of all of them. A thatched pub sits on the edge of the village green, a frozen pond at its centre in which someone's chipped at the ice to let the ducks play. An impressive Norman church stands on the far side, surrounded by a patchwork of timbered houses. The entrance to Arbutt Manor lies to the north of the green, along a short, sandy lane. A three-meter beech hedge, rusty leaves still clinging to its frame, lines the boundary. As he drives towards the high, wrought iron gates, they part slowly and silently. He steers the car down the long, curving driveway, a quickening to the beat of his heart, beseeching him to turn the car around.

The house, when it reveals itself, is chocolate box Tudor; the sort of thing he's seen on a thousand biscuit tins. Elaborate fluted chimneys rise to the sky above the lattice of beams and lead-panelled windows. It doesn't welcome visitors with ease, no light or sense of life reflected from within. He parks alongside a vintage Bentley and a muddy Land Rover. Plainly Clegmore Pharmaceuticals runs at a substantial profit. Running his hand through his hair he glances in the rear-view mirror, summoning the courage to step out. His vision is drawn to a man hurrying towards him from the entrance lobby door.

"Alec, Alec, I can't believe it. You found us then."

Ed Grant, unmistakably him, is waiting as Alec steps from the car, with his hand out-stretched. He's worn well, almost more handsome with age, more relaxed than he looked under the studio television lights. "I did. It's quite hard to miss."

"Yes, I suppose it is. But, my God, Alec, you haven't changed a bit."

He laughs in response. Unused to having someone address him as Alec after so long. It's almost painful. "You look pretty good yourself."

To his surprise Ed drops a hand across his shoulder, spinning him around towards the house. "Come, I'll show you the grounds later but first let's enjoy a restorative sherry."

He looks up at the weathered brick walls looming before him.

"It's quite a place."

"It belonged to a distant relative. Don't ask me the connection. I just remember coming here as a child and always loving it. When it came on the market I couldn't resist. You didn't bring any family with you?"

Ed's hand has not left his shoulder. It's both a comfort and an imposition. But to move away would seem churlish. "Never got round to that. Just me, I'm afraid."

"Well, no matter. I'm very happy you're finally here."

Three Labradors run out to greet them; two chocolate, one black, tails wagging with excitement. "My family of sorts. The chocolates are Abbot and Costello, Hardy's the black one. Laurel died last year bless him. That's us really, apart from Mrs B, my trusty housekeeper and cook par extraordinaire, who's fixed us some lunch, and Alfonso, my handyman, chauffeur and all-round smooth operator. Between you and me he's really a bit of a rough diamond. Brazilian born, but I've trained him well."

He smiles, inviting Alec across the threshold. "Anyway, I hope you're hungry. I'd imagined you with charming wife and two offspring so Mrs B catered far too efficiently and will be mortified if there's anything left."

"Apologies to Mrs B."

"Absolutely no need to apologise."

As he'd suspected, the house falls readily to darkness away from the windows. It smugly displays its noble lineage, gilt framed paintings of noble men, mediaeval armour at the foot of the stairwell, oak panelled walls ingrained with secrets. A house defined by its own heritage rather than the whim of its custodians. They pass several open doors to shadowy rooms before arriving at a library. Faded hardbacks line the walls, a shaft of welcome light bleeds through French windows from a manicured garden. In the middle of the room an elegant, walnut table is laid for five. Cold treats of every description adorn its surface; pies and salads, chicken drumsticks, a joint of ham, a variety of oozing cheeses. "It's more informal here than the dining room which is always bloody freezing at this time of year. Be a sport and clear those spare plates away while I get us that sherry."

He wasn't going to drink but even this room's cold, despite the fire crackling in the grate. He gathers the plates and cutlery. "Where shall I put them?"

"Oh anywhere will do. Dump them on that reading table."

He does as he's told and turns to accept the well plenished sherry glass from Ed's hand.

"Come, let's sit by the fire. There's so much to catch up on. Dear Alec, it's so marvellous to see you. You must tell me all about yourself. Romantic status first. Do I assume you live alone or is there a girlfriend you haven't yet mentioned?"

Ales smiles. So typical of Ed. The gruelling questions, but always posed with such grace. "Right the first time. The ladies come and go. How about you?"

"Like I said, the dogs and staff are really my family. Sadly I'm always too busy for anything else."

"The price of success, I suppose?" He watches Ed sip the sherry. Perhaps he's nervous after all.

"The business means everything really. I set it up about twenty years ago and haven't stopped since. But you're right, it has its own price. People envy you but they don't see the sacrifice. Do you like the name? I called the company after our chauffeur, Cleggy. The only man I could really rely upon."

443

It seems a strangely frank comment in the circumstances. "I thought I recognised it from somewhere. What happened to him?"

"Oh. Long gone. Dear old Cleggy."

There's a pause in which they sip, as if Cleggy's ghost had temporarily sat with them. Alec breaks the silence. "Do you do a lot of television stuff?"

"More and more actually. I seem to be getting a reputation as a go-to spokesman. Not that I'm complaining. It keeps the company profile high and I must confess I'm vain enough to enjoy the attention. It really was such a delightful surprise to hear from you after all this time. Cheers to an old friend."

Alec raises his glass in response, an unexpected warmth deep in his belly beginning to melt away years of hurt.

"But as punishment for making Mrs B cook so much you really must tell me everything about you. No holes barred. And no more clever deflection about the company. I can bore on about it to far less important people than yourself."

Plainly Ed's personality hasn't changed. They could be sitting on their beds at Cambridge, arguing over whisky-driven philosophies. But now, in this room, he doesn't know where to start, or at least he doesn't yet want to start at the beginning, when he was left abandoned in Hamburg. That's too delicate. To get there will need some stringent navigation. He doesn't want to frighten Ed off. It would lessen his chance of contacting Kitty. He'll mention her later, after they've had lunch. If Ed doesn't get there first.

"Well, I suppose the first thing to tell you is that I live in a small cottage in the centre of Devizes. And my car needs regular surgery. And sometimes the neighbour's cat visits me although really I prefer dogs."

Ed laughs at loud. "Christ, Alec, you always did paint rather a bleak picture of life. Why don't you get a dog then? Man's best friend and all that. Definitely mine."

"I don't know really. Maybe I will one day."

"Well cheers to that. We can walk them together." Ed drains his glass. "Now we must eat or I'll have Mrs B back from her sister's complaining about my appalling hospitality. Pile your plate as high as you dare."

He follows Ed to the table, doing exactly as requested. Rarely does he eat so well. It would be foolish to miss the opportunity.

"White or red?"

"A glass of red would be lovely." He reckons one glass can't hurt. Provided he eats enough and drinks coffee afterwards.

They settle opposite one other at the walnut table, Ed's portion considerably smaller than Alec's. "Now you've made me look greedy."

"Not at all. Mrs B serves this fare up every day. I have to watch my waistline. So, you live in Devizes, sadly without a dog. What else?"

Alec sips the wine, poured a little carelessly, but even he can recognise quality. A delicious Burgundy. Ed has tucked his napkin into the collar of his shirt. "Not much else. I work at the local supermarket."

"Manager?"

"General dogsbody. Occasional deputy duty manager. More often shelf stacker or till boy." He waits for a reaction, unsurprised when Ed drops his wine glass back to the table, for once seemingly lost for a response. "Well, you asked for no holes barred."

"My God, Alec. What happened?"

"Not much really."

"Nothing, except everything."

It's come around much quicker than he'd expected. But they could hardly small talk much longer without wives or kids to distract them. He takes another sip of wine. "I went to France for a while. I wasn't sure what to do. I'd managed to acquire a false passport in Berlin but I didn't think it would get me back to England. And what if it had? I guessed they'd have been looking for me after I disappeared from Cambridge. I took a train to Paris, stayed there for a couple of days to think things through. Then I went to Normandy and found a job on a farm. Basic pay and accommodation."

"I'm so sorry, Alec. Please, please forgive me. That night, when your call came through from Hamburg, I panicked. I didn't want to get involved. Kitty said you'd been in a fight, that it had got out of control, but she needed to protect you. I didn't know what to do or think. So I took her to the airport like she asked. She was pleading with me to. When I read about Buchanan-Smith in the paper next day. And then you disappeared. There was so much at stake. Not just for you and Kitty but for the government and Buchanan-Smith's wife and family. It would have been disastrous for everyone. So rightly or wrongly I decided to cover up what I knew. Unfortunately it meant you were the sacrifice."

"Did you ever try to find me?"

"I thought it was better to leave the dust to settle. Permanently."

"Yet you answered my letter. When you could've ignored it."

"I never forgot about you, Alec. I felt so desperately guilty. But now, I suppose things are finally changing. The Wall's come down, the Eastern bloc is breaking up. I'm optimistic. We live in a different world. And whatever happened that night, and I never want to know the details, you must promise me that, but it's a long time ago. All I seek now is your forgiveness, because were very close, but if that's asking too much, I will understand."

Alec sips from his wine glass, pondering Ed's words. He wants to forgive but can it really be that simple, after all this time? "I have to admit, I'd never imagined that we'd sit like this again. Face to face."

Ed snorts a laugh. "I don't blame you. If I were you I'd 've been an inferno of resentment. I really don't mind if you tell me you despise me. At least we deserve to be honest with one another."

He can't help smiling at Ed's bluntness. "Let's just say you weren't the friend I'd hoped you'd be. But I knew you weren't really responsible. You'd warned me off Kitty and I didn't listen. As a result you got caught up in something of which I'm profoundly ashamed. And for which you bear no blame."

Ed dabs his chin with his napkin, lapping up the juices from the chicken drumstick. "I appreciate your candour, Alec. And those are very noble sentiments, but the truth isn't as simple as that. I can admit it now, God knows how many years later, but I was jealous. If I'd left you and Kitty to get on with it, instead of desperately trying to keep you apart, you probably wouldn't have been so suspicious. You would never have followed her to London."

"Perhaps. But I was headstrong. And hopelessly naïve. Kitty said she suspected you were jealous. And who would blame you? She was a very beautiful woman."

"She was."

Alec feels a wave of longing rush through him, urgent and unfulfilled but he resists the urge to enquire after her. It's too soon. It'll look like he's just using Ed. And perhaps if he's honest he is. Glancing about him, it's clear their lives have nothing in common. A CEO and a shelf stacker. Hardly a marriage made in heaven. He thinks of something to say, something that'll tone down the dial. "Was she really your cousin, by the way?"

"Why do you ask?"

"I don't know. Call it idle curiosity."

"A distant one. But don't ask me the connections, they're too complicated. Now do eat up and carve yourself some more ham. Mrs B will kill me otherwise. Then I'll show you the grounds."

Over the course of their meal he discovers the rudiments of Ed's life since university, purposefully avoiding any touch points. He's already done some groundwork and at heart he does forgive Ed, suspecting he too would probably have rejected the plea from Hamburg in a reversal of circumstance. Or at least trying to convince himself that he would. It makes it easier; to adopt a neutrality. Ed divulges that both his parents are dead, his father plainly not mourned. As for his sister, they have little contact. She's a lawyer, married another lawyer. They have two girls and live in London and at Christmas and birthdays he sends them lavish presents. It doesn't conjure a particularly fulfilled personal life. Though he's hardly one to judge.

He takes another sip of the wine, enjoying it a little too much. "I never had you down as a corporate hotshot. Foreign Office more like, an eccentric diplomat in some God-forsaken outpost, but not business."

He makes Ed laugh. "I must say I surprised myself. It was Wilson's new Labour government in '64 that did it. I felt inspired by the breath of fresh air, sweeping away the Tory old guard, all of them married to a cousin or fucking their wife's sister. Then came Wilson's 'white heat of technology' speech. I really believed we could become a modern country."

"Put me off the scent again. I thought you loved all that toff stuff; affairs on tropical islands and cocktails at sunset with Mr Bond."

"Really, Alec, you always took things at such face value."

"Again I must apologise. My humble upbringing, I expect. My father didn't like surprises. He used to say, 'everyone should be true to themselves and plain to everyone else'. I suppose I thought I'd live by the same principles. How wrong that turned out."

"Don't be hard on yourself, old chap. We all have to adapt to whatever fate throws at us. And abiding by your principles can sometimes do more harm than good. Most of us obfuscate. Some hide in the shadows. Some seek the sunlight. There's not much truth that's free of damage."

Alec finds himself slow to respond, wondering quite what Ed means but not feeling comfortable to enquire further. Watching his old room-mate take a sip of wine he realises that his own glass is emptying more quickly.

Ed suddenly smiles, his tone lighter. "Now enough soul-searching, I need to hear more about your love life. Most women seemed to find you irresistible, unluckily for me. There must be a string of affairs you've yet to tell me about. I refuse to believe you're a reborn virgin."

He grins. "Not quite. I've had one or two relationships, but nothing really lasting. How about you?"

"Ditto, I suppose. Not so lucky in love. Anyway, let's console ourselves with a stroll before it gets dark, no point in getting maudlin. Good wine always does that I find. Great pity."

The sunshine makes Alec blink after the gloom of the house but the air is sharp enough to clear his head and, though not a gardener himself, he can see how well-tended the grounds are; paths neatly clipped, snowdrops bringing life to shadowed lawns, herbaceous borders hinting the promise of Spring. Ed calls the Labradors to heel, stooping to smell winter jasmine. "Such a consoling scent when winter's dragging its heel. Do you garden?"

"Not really. As I'm sure my neighbours would attest. But it's more a front yard than a garden."

"I do think you could do with a woman in your life, Alec."

"I wouldn't disagree, but it's very difficult. You must understand, when they want to know about my past I have to lie, which isn't the best way to build a trusting relationship. And they always sense it."

"Maybe you've never been sufficiently smitten."

"That's probably true, too. And just so you know, my name is James now, or Jim. Jim Anderson. When I bought my false passport in Berlin, in order to escape, I had to come up with a name so I thought of my old school master, James Atherton. D'you remember him? The chap we went to visit after going to Imber?"

Ed steps away from the borders towards to the open lawn. "Of course. Your history teacher, wasn't he?"

"He was, yes. History teacher and mentor. I often think of him.

450

He must be quite old by now."

"Sorry to break the news, old chap, but I think I saw his death announced in The Times quite a few years ago."

"Oh God, poor Molly. Did they say what he died of?"

"Not that I recall, died suddenly or some such ambiguous wording. Terrible shame."

"Poor man. He was one of the best."

Ed moves on. "You say you escaped."

"I was detained by the Stasi and made to work for them. I was a prisoner in all but name so I knew I had to escape. An old man made me a false passport and I managed to run." He purposefully hasn't mentioned Kitty's involvement, wondering if Ed will now seize the opportunity. But he doesn't.

"I'm sorry to hear that but at least you're here. And maybe now's the time to leave that story behind. Anyway, there's something I want to show you."

Ed grabs his arm and Alec finds himself thrust across the lawn towards a large barn, fronted by double hinged doors.

"I gave Alfonso the day off so he won't be able to fly into one of his Brazilian rages about my carelessness." He unlocks the double doors folding them back against the barn. Thin rods of light break through gaps in the wood, as if searching for something. And in that moment Alec spots it, the maroon MG Magnette, as polished and perfect as he'd remembered it. A lost friend, so emotive to his burden of loss that his heart skitters like a foal.

"She's as beautiful as ever."

He follows Ed towards the car. "I dumped her when I graduated. Appalling breach of trust. But after my parents died I suddenly missed her, quite more than anything really. So I tracked her down. It took me four years. Unbelievably she was still as pretty as ever. If not more so, at least to me. I paid far too much because I couldn't bear to be parted any longer.

He motions to Alec with his hand. "Jump in."

But Alec hesitates. For one they've drunk too much to go for a spin and for another; well maybe it's just too painful.

"Please, Alec. For old times' sake."

He steps towards the car, his fingers clasping around the passenger door handle, as if it were yesterday. Ed settles in behind the wheel. The smell of worn, cracked leather an adorably heady perfume. A locked memory.

"I've drunk too much to drive on the road but we can pootle around the grounds."

Ed eases the Magnette out of the barn, turning along a gravel track which borders a thicket of birch, the white bark skeletal in the low sunlight. It's a stately drive, more a Royal pageant than a mad dash along the A1. Alec flicks his eyes to the rear seat. He half expects to see Kitty but instead there's just a dip in the stretch of the leather. It's almost unbearable. He can picture her leaning forward, her breath on his cheek. Her scent. Perhaps this is the right moment to choose. Not too intense. When he and Ed are both staring through the windscreen. Two boys in the front seats, playing at being grown-ups.

He attempts to sound casual. By the by. "Did you ever hear again from Kitty? After she returned to Berlin."

"I wondered when you might ask."

"Well did you?"

"Not for years. Then she turned up at my office in London. Only a couple of weeks ago."

"What? And you weren't going to mention it?"

"I wasn't sure if you'd want to know."

"For God's sake, Ed." He realises he's been too forceful. Given his cards away. Still it's done now and his friend has pulled the Magnette up to a halt, switching off the engine. The veneer of charm replaced by a look of petulance.

"I'm sorry if I got it wrong, Alec, but I thought you might not want to dwell on the past. You must realise, up until two weeks ago I had to assume you were both dead, or at least as good as."

"Thanks for the vote of confidence."

"Don't be an ass."

Ed has a point. He mustn't sound bitter again. "Did you ever really know much about her?"

"Like what exactly? I knew she was a distant cousin, with a taste for the high life. And very beautiful. What more was there to know?"

"She was a spy, Ed. For the East German government."

Ed barely seems to blink, his fingers lightly tapping the steering wheel. "That doesn't surprise me, even if you think it should. The truth is, after you disappeared from Cambridge, rumours spread. You were seen as collateral damage, a victim on the run who might or might not have had some involvement in Buchanan's demise. But really the focus of investigation remained on Kitty. She made a prettier picture in the paper.

453

After Burgess and Maclean turned up in Moscow it started more speculation. Frightful business really. One of my father's friends had insider knowledge from Berlin. There were some suggestions that she was fucking Buchanan-Smith for information. But nothing tangible ever came to light. I never told anybody that I'd introduced her to him. I honestly thought she was just a good time girl. I've never mentioned it since. Until now. And nor should you, Alec."

"Why would I? My head still hangs in a noose. I was the one that attacked him to a heartbeat from death. Kitty just finished the job."

"I don't want to hear anymore, Alec. But I'm sorry. Truly I am."

"I'm sorry I brought it up. It's just I always wondered if she'd survived."

"She told me she was released from prison when the Stasi was disbanded just before Christmas. She seems to be in remarkably good health, considering all she's been through."

Alec tries to picture her but shies away from asking about her physical appearance. Hard to reconcile. "Why do you think she came to find you? It must have been a risk."

"I think she wanted to put a few demons to bed. She asked after Buchanan-Smith's family. I reassured her they were fine which seemed to help. His wife re-married. More happily I gather. I think Kitty's going to take up teaching again. She was very good at it. They'll be lucky children."

Alec waits to see if Ed will reveal any more but, unusually for his old room-mate, he seems reluctant to elaborate. "Did she ever marry. Meet someone?"

"Hardly likely in a Stasi prison. She didn't mention anyone."

"Did she mention me?"

He feels Ed's gaze fall upon him. Almost an admonishment. "Just at the end of our conversation, asking if I'd seen you, which of course I hadn't then. Then she left. I don't suppose we'll hear from her again."

He senses the door shutting. He must act. "I'd like to see her."

"I don't think that's a good idea."

"I loved her, Ed. I still do."

The pulse at Ed's brow throbs a little faster. Alec wonders what he might say. Maybe he'll throw him out of the car. Ask him to leave. He wouldn't blame him.

"You were just one of many, Alec, dazzled by her brightness."

"I won't believe that. I wrote to her old address in Berlin regularly after I escaped. I had no idea where she was but I didn't give up hope. There's not a day I don't think about her."

"You always were a ridiculous romantic. But you must forget about her. Digging up the past is fraught with danger. What happens if some jobsworth MI5 agent makes a connection from a tip off somewhere? After all these years, fighting for your freedom, do you really want to throw both of you to the gallows?"

He sighs. "I don't want to keep running. I'm tired of the deceit. With the life I lead, it's not really a life at all. It seems a chance worth taking. Without Kitty there's nothing. I find myself willing each day to end. Please help me, Ed. It's the one thing you could still do for me."

Ed returns his gaze to the birch wood, as if he might find inspiration there. Or, as Alec hopes, some sort of solution.

"So even if it ends badly, you'd be prepared to take the risk?"

"I've nothing to lose, Ed. My life's empty and meaningless. Why would it be a risk?"

Ed turns back to face him. "It might be for her."

"It'll be her choice to make."

"I can't promise anything. I'll write to her. She'll probably want nothing to do with you. You were much better looking thirty years ago." Alec is not averse to the teasing. It has lightened the mood.

"Thank you for your reassuring endorsement."

The car guns into life again, a deep, satisfying throb. "There she goes. I really do adore her."

Alec smiles. "We both do."

"Let's have some tea before you go. By the way, I meant to ask, have you ever been back to Imber at all?

"Never. I know there's been lots of campaigns to reclaim it from the Ministry of Defence but it always seems to come to nothing. All the villagers are getting older and I doubt there's much will left to return. It's a long time since it was evacuated and I suppose it'll stay that way, a relic from a different world."

"I think you should go. Maybe it would help. It's not the place you remember of course; there are some grim concrete blocks dotted around to replicate houses and streets in Northern Ireland or God knows where. But the church is still standing. And the pub. I'm no therapist but they say re-visiting the past can heal wounds. It's on your doorstep. Maybe it's time to stop ignoring it."

His instinct has always been to forget Imber but maybe Ed's right. Perhaps it's time to return. His parents are buried in the church graveyard, after all; they'd probably appreciate a visit. And where's his anger at the village's fate ever got him anyway? He brushes his hand against the cool leather of the glovebox. "Maybe. When the right moment presents itself."

Ed pulls the Magnette up next to his Fiesta. The invitation to tea is extended but it seems half-hearted, and his instinct is to refuse, to make some spurious excuse. He feels absurdly drained, and given there can be no more discussion of Kitty, he has little appetite for prolonging small-talk. Ed appears unbothered when he refuses the invitation, doubtless feeling the same way. Standing awkwardly beside the cars, unsure how to say goodbye, Alec proffers his hand, wishing he had the courage to hug his room-mate. He feels the coolness of Ed's two hands cupped around his, as if sealing a bond, though the easy bonhomie has evaporated.

"Thank you and Mrs B for your hospitality. I haven't eaten that well in years."

"I'll tell her when she returns."

Alec steps back towards his car. "And you promise you won't forget to write that letter."

"I wish I could persuade you otherwise. But you've put me in an impossible position."

Alec grins. "My mother always accused me of being stubborn."

"She wasn't wrong. Goodbye, Alec.

"Goodbye, Ed."

He crams himself into the driver's seat, a disappointing experience after the leather opulence of the Magnette. Heading down the drive he captures an image of Ed waving in his rear-view mirror. It doesn't strike him as a picture of a particularly happy man, despite Ed's wealth and success. A family built of dogs and ersatz relations; servants by any other name.

25

MARCH 1990,   BERLIN

The outside of the school has hardly changed since Kitty last saw it. Children scramble about the courtyard, certainly more boisterous and better fed than their previous generation, but there's no sense of a project revitalised. Windows are split, the brickwork still pocked with wounds and the paintwork drab; if anything, it's in a worse state of repair. It's a chance visit, a hope that where she last failed, this time fate will grant her a reprieve. She doesn't want pity, just a show of kindness will do. Finding a job as a teacher has proved much harder than she'd expected. At any level. Despite several interviews, the sympathetic reception soon falters when she's forced to explain her past. No one wants a treasonous criminal influencing their pupils, even if her crime was one concocted by the Stasi.

Drawing closer to the porch entrance, she feels the spirit of Frau Lehman looking down upon her, the elegant but cool headmistress who rejected her when she first returned to East Germany from the States. Presumably in Heaven or Hell now, or at least in her late seventies, if she's still alive. A buzzer releases the latch on the door. She pushes it open, stepping inside to discover a young woman standing in the lobby. She looks pleasant enough, but impossibly young; a first job maybe. "Yes, madam, may I help you?"

459

Kitty hints at a smile. She wants to portray an openness but nothing over the top. No American bonhomie. There's still a restraint or distrust that's woven through the burghers. "Thank you, Fräulein, yes, good morning. I wondered if I might have a word with the headmistress. I worked here many years ago and would love to renew my acquaintance with some old colleagues. I was just passing by and I thought …"

The girl looks at her curiously. "…Your name, Madam?"

"Fräulein Bernstein. I taught English and games." Lying still comes so easily. Force of habit.

"Please wait here, Fräulein. The headmistress is extremely busy." The girl disappears behind the familiar, panelled door, the sight of which fills Kitty with a certain dread. Several minutes later the girl returns. "You may have five minutes but no more. Frau Lehman has been very generous."

Kitty hesitates. "Frau Lehman?"

"The headmistress, as you requested."

"Thank you."

The girl opens the door again, with excessive fuss, Kitty thinks, then closes it behind her. Frau Lehman shuffles forward from behind her desk, her hand clasped to a thin stick. Despite the impediment she still cuts a formidable figure, dressed in a charcoal suit that on closer inspection has seen better years, with a jade brooch clasped at her throat. Her hair, ice white, is scraped into a bun, the eyes still bright, inquisitive. She holds out her free hand; it feels fragile, blood barely passing through the veins. "Forgive me, Fräulein Bernstein, so many teachers have passed through our gates, at my age it's a challenge to remember them all. Please take a seat. When were you with us exactly?"

There seems little point in pursuing the lie, now that she's through the door. "I'm afraid I wasn't, Frau Lehman. I came to you, many years ago, looking for a job, but you were unable to help me. Since the Wall came down, I'm finding it very difficult to get work, so I hoped this time you might find it in your heart to help."

The headmistress lets loose her hand, a thin smile doubling the lines of her face. "Of course I remember you. But I daresay you hadn't expected me to be here."

"It was a surprise. But I'm glad to see you're keeping well."

"Well at least you're honest. To a point. Take a seat, Fräulein Bernstein. Can I offer you some coffee?"

"Thank you." She watches Frau Lehman return to a small sideboard, pouring two coffees from a ceramic pot with a tremorous hand; fearing it may spill. "May I help you, Frau Lehman?"

"Despite appearances I'm not an invalid, Fräulein Bernstein. We must not let age wither us." She returns with a dull green cup and saucer, handing it to Kitty before settling in the chair opposite, studying her subject as an artist might study her muse.

"You haven't changed that much. Most women are unlucky enough to have their beauty diminish with age but yours is quite the contrary. I remember you very well. Indeed, had you continued to lie when I asked about your previous employment here we would not be sharing a coffee. I tolerate many misdemeanours but I don't tolerate being taken for a fool. One of the disagreeable aspects of old age is that people assume your memory is impaired. But curiosity is a timeless trait. And if you're curious, you remember. Which brings me to wonder why you came here at all. You said, a little euphemistically, that I couldn't help you all those years ago. I recall being more brutal. I think I suggested that your motive for moving to the GDR was an affair of the heart, or rather a rejection, rather than political enlightenment."

Kitty glances momentarily down to her cupped hands, chastising herself for a sign of weakness. But the chance of work is too important to contemplate walking away. "Please, Frau Lehman, that was a long time ago. I accept maybe I was naïve. Not long after I came here, I was inducted into the Intelligence Service. At the time I had no choice, and although with education, I began to believe in my work, I suppose in truth I was kidding myself. Running away from what I'd lost. And then I made a mistake and I paid for it. I was arrested for crimes against the State. It was a fraudulent charge cooked up by the frenzy of paranoia that existed at the time. I spent my life in prison until a few weeks ago. But all that's past. I'm just desperate for some work. I'm a good teacher. Please. I'll do anything."

Frau Lehman sits back into the shadows, hands, as if in prayer, beneath her chin. "I assume this isn't the first school you've tried."

"It's always the same, both here and in West Berlin. I've tried everywhere. As soon as they find out about my record there's silence and I'm shown the door. It's a label that sticks. Crimes against the State, written large across my forehead. A serial killer would probably fare better."

"You were a spy, Fräulein Bernstein. There will always be consequences for your actions. And looking for sympathy I would suggest shows a fundamental flaw. Perhaps you were recruited against your will but from what I understand you became a very enthusiastic recruit with little sign of resistance.

"What do you mean, 'understand'?"

"That is what I heard."

"I'm sorry, I…"

Frau Lehman leans forward, her voice barely above a whisper. "…My dear Fräulein Bernstein, it was I that suggested recruiting you."

Kitty places the cup to the saucer, a cold hand clasping her heart. She cannot speak.

Frau Lehman continues, her voice softly moderated. "Your school friend, Fräulein Ursula Meyer, sent you to me for initial assessment. You mustn't think ill of her, no one could refuse the work of the Stasi without serious repercussions. Not many were either brave or foolhardy enough to refuse. I knew immediately you'd be a good agent and back then, I must say, I was more certain of my own political convictions. I believed I was doing the right thing. Even if I, too, had little choice."

As the shock passes Kitty finds herself holding back tears. But she will not let them flow, not for this woman. "I spent thirty years locked up, Frau Lehman. I thought I would die there. There were times when I even wanted to but I persuaded myself that life of any kind was worth the fight. I survived. God knows how, but I did, when so many women I knew didn't. And now I'm left to beg from the woman who sealed my fate; who tells me there was nothing she could do. How dare you judge me?! How dare you?!"

The answer is slow in coming. She feels her heart slap at her ribcage.

"If you're seeking an apology, Fräulein, it won't be forthcoming. The answer to your question is that, with practice, it's become easier to make difficult choices. As a headmistress of too many years I'm particularly adept at shrouding my personal thoughts. Sometimes I'm not sure I even recognise them. I'm afraid it's not hard for me to tell you that I can't offer you a position, for the same reason all the other schools gave you. It's difficult to sell one's staff a traitor. A role which it was your choice to take, not mine to forgive. Even if I employed you, eventually one of my staff would find out, and then where would I be? I don't wish my school to become a cauldron of distrust and resentment. Therefore, unfortunately, it's more prudent to betray you than betray them. I'm well versed in human nature, Fräulein Bernstein. In that sense I think we're quite alike."

"Forgive me if I don't recognise the similarity."

"I don't doubt that you're a good teacher and that you have a natural affinity with children. Fräulein Meyer told me so. In fact she gave you a glowing report. And, of course, I appreciate you must despise me. But try not to run away with your hatred. The reason I'm still headmistress here is because I felt, in very difficult and tumultuous times, that the school and the children needed a steady hand. I was worried that if I'd retired when I was supposed to, I'd be replaced by a puppet, a party follower who would spout doctrine for the children to follow; with little room for their own thoughts to develop. I accept, in the early days, I too was zealous, judgemental, a slave to the cause, but with time and evidence my zeal waned. Since then I've tried my best to foster openness, discussion, ideas hopefully motivated more by love than fear, accepting of differences. I never expected to see you again but I'm glad you came. I can't offer you a job, nor can I offer you a genuine apology. I did what we all did. But I hope you find some way to reconcile your misfortune."

Kitty searches her inquisitor's face for signs of humility or vulnerability. But the cool glare still traps her in its sight. She draws a breath, summoning a veneer of courage.

"Well, thank you for being so frank with me. And you're quite right, Frau Lehman, an ingenuine apology would hardly be worth accepting. Why would you need to apologise when plainly you've already forgiven yourself? I think we all have the ability to re-imagine our past, to make the ugly bits fit and wash ourselves clean. The reason you've never retired is not for some act of benevolence to your school children, it's because you're terrified of losing control. You've spent your life manipulating others, you know no other way of existing. I apologise for not falling under your spell but I can hardly accept your good wishes when you've sucked out my blood and gorged on your own sanctity."

To her surprise and irritation, Frau Lehman's lips stretch to a thin smile. "You're a spy and I'm a leech. Where's the difference, Fräulein?"

Kitty feels her face flush. She will survive. Not let her future be blighted by Frau Lehman and her Stasi friends. She rises to leave, stepping out of the office without closing the door.

Walking back down Fehrbelliner Strasse, past her old apartment, she begins to regret her outspokenness. Word will spread, destroying any remaining chance of work at a school. Still, of the many regrets she has, it ranks low on the scale. She shouldn't have returned there; survival's easy without a moral compass. Even if she'd been offered a job, it would have been hypocritical to accept it, from someone she despises. Staring up at the familiar tenement façade, her thoughts return to Ursula; memories uncomfortably stirred. Best friends since kindergarten, so bound together that they share an apartment as adults. Two friends who end up betraying one other. Slaves to a dubious master.

After three more days, searching shops and bars and anywhere else she can think of, she finds work as a janitor in the local hospital. No one asks questions and she's good at finding her way around a cleaning cupboard, having done it regularly in prison. The shifts are long, starting at 6 am, but it pays and she's happy to escape the confines of her one-room apartment. The hospital treats infections and has a minor surgery unit but the facilities are rudimentary; shockingly so, compared to the wards she's seen on Western television.

To her surprise, she finds the work quietly satisfying, wondering whether she might re-train as a nurse. In quieter moments she chats with the staff in the corridors, eager to discover how she might go about it. They're sympathetic but she detects a nervousness, an uncertainty about their own future, after unification with the West. There's rumours of rampant inflation and the notorious job insecurity that they've heard exists in the Capitalist West. She tries to reassure them. Harder when they say, "how would you know?" She doesn't want to tell them about her previous life in America.

Weeks pass with the same, diligent routine. She rises at five, taking the tram to the hospital, observing her fellow passengers, who after the euphoria of November, seemed to have settled back to duller lives. They all share a pasty, exhausted pallor, in need of rejuvenation, whether by hope or simple sunlight. One particularly cruel day, when drifting snow whips away the promise of Spring, she returns home to discover a letter in her mailbox. She doesn't recognise the handwriting but the stamp is British; a profile of the Queen. Such archaism still baffles her, the British obsession with their past. The glorious Empire. But she knows such lofty thoughts are a mask for a more visceral response. She feels her heartbeat quicken, racing now. As soon as she's reached the safety of her own walls she rips open the envelope.

Dear Kitty,

I hope I find you well and that you've managed to rekindle your career in education since we last met in London. Although it was a surprise to see you, I'm very grateful that you took the trouble to contact me. Perhaps it put a few ghosts to rest. It was certainly good to see that you are in fine form and ready to forget the difficulties of the past.

There is, however, one delicate matter that has cropped up since we met. Not long after I saw you, our friend contacted me out of the blue,

Her mouth dries, her gut aches. Fear and longing spiralling a dance. She reads on.

apparently he saw me on television and managed to track me down. I invited him for lunch and of course we talked of the past. I think he found it cathartic. I must say I'd forgotten how much I liked him and admired him really. He always wore his heart on his sleeve, so different to the repressed upper classes of which I confess I'm a fully signed up member. The point is he expressed an interest to see you. More than that really, he's been badgering me about it with letters since. He claims he still loves you, which I've told him is a foolish notion as he hasn't seen you for thirty-five years, but I'm afraid he's unrelenting. So I promised I'd write to you. I refused to give him your address in order to protect you. My considered advice would be to reply to this letter stating, gently but firmly, that you'd like nothing more to do with him. It would only cause trouble as I'm sure you're aware. You know too well unfortunately what a loose cannon he always was. I think now it's imperative you secure your future, not open old sores.

I think you'll agree this is the best course. If you choose not to reply I'll understand. It will be an equally valid way of deterring him.

Fondest love,

PS Please dispose of this letter in the same way you disposed of those other documents.

She drops the page onto the divan and stares at the wall; her head numb, observing someone she knew long ago, the ardour of youth. Emotions which belong to the past but which she finds rushing up to find air, beyond her control. Her hand is shaking. She knows she should ignore the letter, as Ed suggested. But then why write to her? She steps to the kitchen cupboard, her legs ridiculously weak, pouring a large schnapps which she drinks so quickly she gasps. But it warms her, steadies her. The letter lies where she dropped it. She does not read it again, instead taking two sheets of writing paper from the drawer and placing them on the fold-down kitchen table. The pen is a cheap, black biro. She wants to use a fountain pen but that would mean going to the shops. And in that time her mind might change.

My dear Ed,

I'm afraid the indecent speed of my reply will suggest to you what lies in my heart. While I understand that you think it would be both irrational and unwise to meet him, I find I'm sitting in my small apartment unable to contemplate much else. I hope you don't think badly of me. While in prison I convinced myself that there would be no chance of seeing him again, so I tried to forget about him. It was the only way to survive. I suppressed it all, my deepest feelings frozen hard as winter. Now, though, I feel as bewildered as a schoolgirl, what I barely dared hope, rising in my heart at the news your letter brings. I think I loved him from the day you introduced me. It wasn't meant to happen, it was deeply unprofessional and it caused unforgiveable damage. I'm sure you realised what was happening, it must have put you in an impossible position and I profoundly apologise for the dangerous and damaging consequences. But now I feel both of us have paid the price and perhaps should be allowed a moment in the sun after years of darkness. Who knows? We might not even like each other anymore but I would desperately like to see him. I would be so grateful if you would convey that message and arrange whatever means is necessary and safe for us to meet. This is one last favour I ask of you, dear Edward. I won't trouble you again.

With fondest love and deepest thanks,

PS I will do as you requested of your letter.

She posts her reply the same evening, returning to her apartment through the deepening snow. Pouring herself another schnapps she settles on the divan and wraps a shawl around her neck and arms. Ed's letter still lies beside her. She picks it up, fearing in her haste that she might have misread it but the words are still printed indelibly on the page. *He claims he still loves you.* She knows she should burn it, as Ed suggested. She folds it in two and places it in the cupboard above the sink, inside the Stasi dossier on Ed. A part of her feels ungrateful, unfaithful even, for defying his request. But he'd always said never trust anyone, and even now, when it appears the scars of past misdemeanours are finally healing, her instinct is to protect herself. Perhaps Ed guesses this of her, assuming she will not burn it, despite her promises. Perhaps, despite his business success and breezy confidence, he's still a boy, running scared, terrified someone in authority might rap on his door.

A week later a second letter arrives. The same handwriting. She rushes up the lobby stairs, barely able to resist opening the envelope before closing the apartment door. Her mind has been scrambled all week, working through shifts at the hospital with uncharacteristic detachment; finding little time or desire to gossip with the nurses, eating and sleeping even less. She hates herself for it, this uncontrollable and presumably irrational desire. But she has no choice. It's devouring her.

Ed's letter is shorter that the last one.

Dear Kitty,

Thank you for your prompt reply. I wish I could persuade you to re-consider but it seems it's not within my power. The bond between you is obviously stronger than any rational argument I can impose to keep you apart and therefore I must be humble and bow to whatever fate lies in store.

I have been in touch with him and suggested that you meet somewhere remote, initially, just as a precaution. He mentioned Imber (he's never returned since we were last there) which I thought seemed a good idea. Perhaps even romantic? The army opens it for a few days over Easter. If you go on the Easter Monday at 4.30 pm most of the visitors will have left. They close at 5. After that, well I suppose that's your affair and no longer my business.

I will not write again. Goodbye Kitty, please know that I've always held you both in the highest esteem. In another world, or another time, I feel we could have been very dear friends. I say this despite my father telling me never to harbour regrets. Like Edith Piaf, he said.

Fondest love,

Please do as I requested last time. I have done the same.

Despite her mounting excitement she's somehow unnerved by the coolness of Ed's tone. But what had she expected? She knows he's right; she's chosen an uncertain path with unknown consequences. It might be anti-climactic, the spark may well have evaporated, and the danger is not insignificant, as he suggested. Some retired police officer, with an axe to bear, may still be poring over the Buchanan-Smith files, hoping yet to solve a notorious murder. And why shouldn't he? She reads the brief note again, her mind leaping to the practicalities. It steadies her heart.

She moves her index finger across the shifts written on her wall calendar towards Easter. The public holiday dates are printed in a dark, Gothic typeface. A week and a half away. She remembers she'd already volunteered for a long shift on the Easter Monday. It made sense at the time. She was hardly going to be on a tram with all the East Berliner families, bearing cakes for relatives. Someone might be kind enough to swap shifts. She places the letter in the dossier with his first and grabs her coat. There's time to reach the bank before it closes, and anyway she's desperate to get some air; to prevent herself succumbing to doubt.

Fighting a cold headwind, though the snow has at last melted, she makes her way into town. A young cashier scribbles her balance on a scrap of paper. A quick calculation suggests she has enough for a flight from West Berlin to London, the remainder should cover accommodation and car hire. She'll fly on Easter Sunday and drive down to Imber on the Monday. Beyond that date she makes no plans.

In between her shifts she spends the next week frequenting cafés in what was previously the American sector of old West Berlin. She bides her time, listening to the conversations around her, searching out American women, ideally with babies or young children to distract them. After three days she thinks she's spotted a suitable candidate; a mother with a fractious toddler and a disapproving mother of her own. The trick is an old one that the Bureau taught her, easily prone to failure if the wrong candidate is selected. But this looks promising. A leather bag sits on the table, probably the young mother's judging by the story book that peeps out the top. The toddler's fractiousness escalates to a tantrum. His exasperated mother sweeps him away to the ladies' room leaving the older woman to reach for a cigarette, lighting it with nicotine-stained fingers. Kitty wastes no time. She grabs her own handbag and follows the young mother in haste, brushing deliberately against the grandmother's table and knocking the large leather bag to the floor. Profuse apologies. She gathers the contents, thrusting them back to the bag, except for a small leather wallet which she drops into her own bag. The older woman sees none of this, her view blocked by the table, her face a study of bemusement but not suspicion. Kitty is all charm; foolish smiles.

Inside the Ladies she sees the mother washing her toddler's hands in the sink; calming him; probably needing comfort herself. Kitty provides emollient words before disappearing into one of the cubicles, listening to the mother's movements as she opens the wallet. It only takes a moment to find what she's

looking for, a paper driving licence folded neatly in one of the
pockets. She ignores the name. Just check that it's valid. Which it
is. The licence states *North Carolina*; the slogan below *First in
Freedom*. She tucks it into her pocket. Hearing the mother leave,
she waits a beat then steps out behind her. As the young woman
settles again at her table, Kitty's gaze returns to the floor below
it, bending down as if to retrieve something.

"Oh God, I'm so sorry, I didn't see, your wallet's still down here.
I foolishly knocked your bag on the floor as I was heading to the
bathroom. Anyway no harm done. Thank God I noticed it." She
rises from the floor, returning the wallet to its rightful owner,
tickling the child under his chin. "Yes, aren't you such a
handsome boy." Walking out of the café she can't help thinking
that Ed would be proud of her.

Having managed to swap shifts Kitty spends her last day at the
hospital cleaning more vigorously than ever. It doesn't go
unnoticed. The staff tease her. But it distracts her from thoughts,
doubts even, about her impending trip, and since she's not sure
when she might return, if ever, she wants to leave the wards
immaculate. Before she leaves she's especially attentive to the
patients she has befriended. She will miss them. Though she's
probably getting ahead of herself. More likely, she thinks, she'll
see them next week. Her mind vacillates. She can hardly breathe.

By Easter Sunday morning she has regained her composure.
Though she's aware this is an emotional journey, a quest to find
peace, a resolution of sorts whatever it may be, there is still
reason to be vigilant, as Ed suggested. She must not let down
her guard, not until she's certain. The flight from Berlin to
London is uneventful. She resists small talk with her fellow
passengers, watching over the Channel as container ships cross
paths on a milky sea. At Heathrow she chooses the busiest
looking car hire company. A young man serves her; furry upper
lip. She provides him with her driving licence on request, her

accent pointedly East Coast, blinding him with flirtation and bureaucracy to explain why the name doesn't correlate with that of her freshly issued German passport. He could ask his boss for guidance but Kitty points out how busy she looks; how she'd probably love it if he just showed some balls and took charge himself. He grins. She asks for an automatic.

It's over thirty years since she's driven, and never outside the States. It takes some adjustment but by the time she's on the motorway heading west, she's got the hang of it. Her father taught her well. She smiles at the thought of him then dismisses it. One day she hopes to return, to take flowers to the cemetery, thank her parents for all they did, and for all they must have suffered, but that will have to wait. And given the circumstances, she thinks they will be patient, and forgive her for her folly.

The late sun dazzles her view as she heads west along the motorway. Woods either side of the road burn amber to gold. By the time she reaches the broad Wiltshire plains dusk is settling. There's so little traffic she can't help imagining she's the last person left outside, navigating deserted highways while everyone else has fled to their lover's arms. To still her heart she listens to the radio, a medley of indistinguishable pop songs which clash with her mood, but she's grateful for it. Finally, after another half hour, the distant halo of streetlights signals the outskirts of Salisbury. She feels her spirits rise though she's tired now. More exhausted than she thought possible. The small hotel's easy to find. She'd rehearsed the roads on a map. The owner, a chatty woman not much older than herself, shows her to the room which is small and devoid of air. As soon as the woman's closed the door behind her she collapses onto the bed, which creaks, and the mattress is softer than sponge. But she doesn't care. Without bothering to eat, she throws off her clothes and drifts straight to sleep.

She wakes early, not long after six; starving, desperate for breakfast, which won't be served till seven. She lingers in the shower, washing her hair with the potions available, dressing casually before the mirror. She wears jeans and a beige jumper. Cheap East German clothes but they'll have to do. She takes longer over her make-up, enough to show she's made an effort. Lastly she applies a dab of perfume behind her ears and on her neck. On a whim she'd bought it at the airport, a cheap Eastern brand, the only one she could afford, but it has a pleasant scent. The days of expensive Memoire Cherie are long since over.

Descending to the dining room she's served by the same woman. There seem to be no other staff. Her hostess's chatter precludes any silence, perhaps that's its purpose, as on inspection there also seem to be no other guests. But Kitty is glad to devour the cooked English breakfast dropped in front of her, deflecting any questions the woman may have by asking more of her own.

After several cups of weak coffee she retires to her room, unfolding the Ordnance Survey map of Salisbury Plain on her bed. Her fingers drift along a line heading north-west, leading her eventually to Imber, within the contours of a shallow valley, roughly at the centre of the Plain. A row of little boxes marks its existence and higher up the hill the symbol of a church, presumably still standing, where she remembers seeing the graves of Alec's parents. To the left large red letters state DANGER AREA. She wonders if the village will have changed at all, whether it's now at peace with itself and the local community, or whether people still feel betrayed. More specifically, what Alec feels. But she will know soon. Provided he turns up.

The doubts rise again. She feels fragile, foolish even. She must distract herself. There are some hours to go before the agreed rendez-vous, though in hindsight it wasn't even agreed. Ed had suggested it and in her haste she had acquiesced, still somehow his puppet. Why had Alec chosen Imber? She understood the danger but surely they could have met somewhere more convenient. Perhaps it was Ed's persuasion, his warped idea of a romantic tryst; more likely his obsessive desire to manipulate. Well she won't need him again. Like he said in his letter, this is goodbye. Their friendship can take no further course. If Alec turns up they can make their own story, whatever that may be.

She checks her watch. Barely quarter to eleven. Folding the map back into her handbag she pays the bill at the reception desk and asks the woman what she'd suggest seeing in Salisbury with a few hours to kill. Her hostess seems taken aback, as if it should be obvious, but soon recovers her wits, drifting into raptures about the Cathedral and its tallest spire, and insisting that there's bound to be a Bank Holiday service. Kitty smiles and thanks her. Easter, the resurrection of Christ, had totally skipped her mind.

Stepping out into the narrow lanes of the town's centre, she finds little to distract her. Most of the shops are closed. Cafés have tables invitingly laid behind large, plate glass windows, but they'll have to wait longer for their trade. She heads, as suggested, towards the cathedral, easily navigable by its climbing spire which rises triumphantly above the city roof lines. As she draws nearer, into a pretty, Georgian square, she's aware of choral music, vaguely familiar to her, drifting beyond the confines of the cathedral. She follows a path around a large, manicured lawn, circumnavigating the buttressed walls, until a second path eventually leads her to a heavy wooden door at the far side.

The door is ajar. She pushes it gently, revealing a view down the extraordinarily long nave. A captivated audience occupies the cathedral pews, their faces lifted so attentively towards the choir at the farthest end, that they seem either blessed, or touched by something that has distilled all their fears. A chamber orchestra accompanies the impressive choir. There's an empty pew to the right at the rear of the nave so she drifts towards it, her gaze rising to the vaulted ceiling as she settles to listen. She recognises the music. It's Bach. St Matthew's Passion; notes rising and falling with such grace she feels tears, inextricably, uncontrollably, rolling down her cheeks.

When the concert draws to a close, she observes the subdued audience, filing out along the aisles. A part of her wants to remain, untroubled, surrendering to whatever trance the music has cast upon her. A young man approaches, presumably some kind of warden, asking if she's alright. She's desperate to confess that she isn't, that she's doubting herself, that perhaps she's making a mistake, deceived by an aching loneliness for which only now is she able to forgive herself. But she doesn't say any of these things. She asks him if he knows the best way to Imber. For a moment he falters, an unusual request perhaps, but he's able to give her precise directions, even suggesting she leave soon, as it closes before dusk. Kitty smiles, thanking him, then lifts her small overnight bag from the pew and exits the cathedral to a forget-me-not sky, full of Spring promise.

Throwing her bag onto the back seat of the car, she opens the map again, checking the route he suggested. It looks easy enough. Before she leaves Salisbury she buys mints at a petrol station and a small bunch of white roses, barely in bloom, but they'll do. She's not even sure why she bought them.

Her mind settles as she drives; the town surrendering to a bucolic landscape, grassy fields shimmering emerald-green in the warmth of the sun, lambs dancing in skittish circles around their mothers. As she heads north the wood bordering the road is replaced by a broader, uninterrupted landscape, stretching to the horizon. She's reached the Plain, figuring that Stonehenge must be to the east, but it's hiding somewhere beyond another rise. Which is probably for the best. Who knows what memories it might evoke? She sucks on one mint after another, an emollient distraction. She tells herself Alec most likely won't turn up, having seen sense. Declaring his love for her in a letter to Ed is very flattering, but he's bound to falter at the reality; aware it's a mirage, a memory that rises to comfort in a time of vulnerability, before turning to dust.

At Gore Cross, as the main road descends to the village of West Lavington, she turns off onto a chalk track. Beyond a row of houses and outlying barns an array of signs indicates she's crossing onto Ministry of Defence land. One of them declares that Imber's open until five. She checks the car clock. It's just gone four. She drives up the long, shallow hill, reaching its peak after about a half mile, but there's still no sign of the village. Three cars drive past in the opposite direction, all moving at a stately pace, chalk dust rising from the tyres and drifting east in the gentle breeze. Instinctively she checks to see if she recognises Alec in any of them but none of the faces seem familiar. The thought hadn't occurred to her that she might not recognise him. Stress takes its toll. She pushes on down the other side of the hill. A broad valley falls away to her right, on her left oak trees hint at first bud. After another mile the road takes a steep descent. She swings the car around a sharp right-hand bend to enter a valley, at the far end of which, she notices the first remnants of human occupation. At once it is familiar to her, as if she had been here yesterday. But the village is not the one she remembers; a sketch of a village, a patchwork of brick ruins which whisper of a once thriving community.

Up ahead she spots a small area for parking. Two cars leave, heading back to the main road. She scrutinises the occupants as they pass; maybe relatives of the Imber dispossessed, but still no one that resembles Alec. One car still sits abandoned in the layby; a mud-stained Renault. His perhaps? Her mouth is dry. She pulls up behind it and cuts the engine. Her eye falls to the flowers she bought in haste. They look pathetic now. A token, like a child might give their granny. What was she thinking? She leaves them on the passenger seat and steps out into the cooling air. Scanning the hill either side, there's no sign of any visitors. But three soldiers examine a map on the bonnet of a Land Rover, parked in the centre of a concrete square. Impervious to her existence. Concrete block buildings with holes for windows surround them, kindergarten renditions of two storey houses. She half expects to see a child's drawing of a spidery sun high in the sky.

She glances back to the cars. No sign of him. No arms outstretched, as she had dared herself imagine, like the finale of an afternoon movie. She contemplates heading back; to accept her own foolishness, thinking perhaps that Ed has played one last game on her. Looking up the hill she can see that the church, at least, is still standing; stubborn and defiant, inviting visitors to pay their respects. To reward it for its unflinching faith. She switches direction, heading away from the cars up the steep path that leads towards it. Halfway up the hill, she spots a couple on their way back down. In their fifties, she guesses. Someone's daughter? Someone's son? She nods a greeting, trying to contain her disappointment, watching as they descend and clamber into the dirty Renault. Shadows creep along the valley road as the sun dips towards the Plain. She watches the car drive off, wondering why she's still standing there. But she's not yet ready to give up hope.

Turning around she climbs back towards the church. He is instantly recognisable, despite the sun's low rays piercing her eyes, his sturdy frame silhouetted, rigid as a statue. She walks slowly, barely daring to trust her own instinct, wishing he might shout to her, or move at least. Some pitiful sign of recognition. Then suddenly he draws a hand through his hair, a touch of vanity perhaps, wanting to look his best? Despite the rebuttal of age. His arms part. She can't help herself, running the last metres to bury herself in his embrace, a hint of damp and earth and cigarette, mixed with his own scent, which she remembers now so vividly, clinging to him as he clings to her, unable to lift her face in case she needs to find coherent words, or kiss him, or just part again, like the best of friends. When she feels his arms finally fall, after how long, she has no idea, she knows she must lift her face. He is smiling. "Hello, Kitty," is all he says.

"Hello, Alec."

"I was beginning to think you wouldn't come." His hand reaches to his pocket, but then hangs loosely, more self-conscious now.

"I was about to go back. I just passed a couple who took the last car…"

He smiles again. "…I came by taxi. My car broke down this morning. It's a bit of a wreck."

"But if I hadn't come?" Immediately she regrets the foolishness of her question.

"Perhaps I was being arrogant…"

"Christ, I'm being an idiot. I didn't mean - of course I was going to come." She falters, unable to imagine what should follow. Observing his face, she recognises everything that she once adored. Older certainly, a little unkempt, but undiminished, features of stone.

He fills the void. "You look well."

It's a little underwhelming. But then he is an Englishman, the charm of which, in this moment at least, she finds frustrating. She yearns to kiss him, smother herself in him, but he shows no sign of complicity. Except his foolish grin. "You don't look bad either. You haven't really changed." What else should she say? How to tread beyond the foothills of small talk? "Did you visit your parents?"

He glances back to the graveyard. "I said a quick hello, you can barely see their graves it's so overgrown now. It's the first time I've been back since we came with Ed. I hardly recognise it now. They'd be devastated. It was Ed who suggested coming here. He thought it might help."

"Has it?"

"I suppose it's too early to tell."

She finds herself looking away, towards the church. His first acknowledgement of their circumstance has unnerved her, despite her wish to cut to the chase. But then she finds her resource, fragments of the past, physical and emotional, rolling up through her like spits of flame. She returns his gaze. "I've missed you. So much."

"Me too."

She reaches up to kiss him, smelling the tobacco though it doesn't bother her. But still there is reserve, from both, she realises. This is not the fantasy of her afternoon movie but the awkward dance of two people stretching across a flood of separation, of unshared experience, of trust eclipsed by circumstance. She lowers her head and feels the warmth of his forehead touch her scalp. He takes her hands. Large, cold and comforting. His breathing is slower than hers. Her body aches. How is it possible to be so tired and yet so alive?

"What now?" She's still staring at his feet, a pair of worn brown brogues, ridiculously inappropriate for their situation. "What happens now?"

"I've no idea. How about I invite you for tea to my tiny house?"

He makes her laugh as she lifts her head again. "Are you sure there's room for both of us in your tiny house?"

"You can have the armchair. I'll make do with the footstool."

He smiles again. It seems the most innocent invitation. But here, in the open, she's mindful of Ed's warning, and knows that Alec will be too. For a moment they can pretend. But experience dictates they be vigilant. And, as a once professional spy, she must be the one to ruin the party. "Thank you for offering me your armchair. But it's not that simple, is it? We have to be very careful, Alec."

"Christ, I know that. But I had to see you Kitty, no matter what happens. It's all I've ever thought about. I just didn't know if you'd still feel…"

"…I'm here aren't I?"

His gaze leaves her, glancing to the horizon before finding her again. "We should go somewhere abroad. France to start with. I spent a while hiding there before I came back. No one would ever find us." He kisses her forehead. "Let's talk about it at my place. We should leave, they'll be closing the Plain soon." He grins at her again. "Can I hitch a lift?"

"So long as you don't smoke. It's hired."

He smiles again.

She finds herself being led by the arm, back down the hill towards the car, acquiescing to his will. It occurs to her that it's an odd switch, the control for once, more in his hands than hers. But it doesn't trouble her. Her doubt has gone. The bond between them seemingly unscarred by their fate, perhaps even strengthened by it. For now at least. And she only wants to deal with the now. There's no point in anguishing over Buchanan-Smith's death. It's the past. A different land. And if some fragment of hope can be salvaged from its tragic circumstance, then there's at least a mathematical counter-balance, a ledger to accommodate all the suffering humans impose on one another.

"I'm sorry about your car."

He laughs. "It's pretty old, so it didn't surprise me. I thought I'd fixed the problem but this morning it wasn't going anywhere. It won't get us across the Channel so we'll have to catch a train to Poole this evening and get the overnight ferry."

His sudden referral to immediate plans throws her. She'd imagined a gestation period, the subject to dwell on after tea. After they'd slept together. Maybe even over breakfast. She attempts to diffuse the subject, to avoid running too fast. In case they trip.

They stop at the bottom of the hill for a moment. She's aware of his gaze falling upon her. Challenging her. "You sound so sure."

"Our time, now."

Turning up the valley road back towards the car, she can't help admire his confidence. Even stronger than his younger self. Maybe it sprang from his experiences in Germany. At any rate, it's probably only skin deep. An act, designed to protect himself, and who can blame him? But now is not the time to probe. She wonders how they might survive in France, whether he's even though about it. Perhaps, though she finds it hard to admit, he's more resourceful than her. The questions keep looming despite her desire to quell them.

She flicks the key fob to open the car. In the concrete square beyond, the soldiers watch them this time. Desperate to dispatch them, no doubt, so the Plain can return to its rightful owners. Alec picks the roses off the passenger seat before sitting down. She glances at them resting in his hand, looking faintly ridiculous. But it makes her smile.

"It was just a gesture. Pretty silly really but I'm sure they'll look great in your tiny house."

"Thank you. I'm sure they will. I've got something for you as well." From his pocket he produces a creased, black and white photograph, the edges browned through age. "I stole it from your bedroom, to remind me of you. It's never been far from my pocket."

She immediately recognises the photograph of herself, eating candy floss at the fair with her mother, having wondered in the past where she might have mislaid it. "Keep it. It's yours now."

"I'd hoped you'd say that."

She grins at him. "So which way do we go?"

"Turn round and follow the route you came in."

She does as he requests, glancing in her mirror at the remaining bones of Imber. In such an intimate space, she feels suddenly lost for words again, as if nothing will quite describe her state. The pop music on the radio seems an intrusion so she switches it off. "I was singing along a bit on the way down. Distraction therapy."

"Did it work?"

"Not really."

"If I'd burst into song the taxi driver would've ejected me."

She smiles. "Very James Bond. I don't think I've heard you sing."

"It wasn't exactly the right time, was it? But that was then. Since I saw Ed, and found a way to you, I feel I've been singing all the time. Only quietly, like a timid bird, but now you're here I…"

Her hands grip tight to the wheel, the horizon melting under her misty gaze. She cannot bear to look at him.

"…I'm so sorry, Alec. Everything I did. It was a mess. I ruined everything."

"I love you, Kitty."

She laughs through her tears, wiping them from her cheeks as they reach the crest of the hill, turning briefly to witness his smile. "I really fucked up."

"We both did."

"I wasn't s'posed to fall in love, the training and everything. I thought I was immune to all that. Jesus."

"I'm glad you weren't. A perfectly imperfect human. And now." He laughs again.

The last rays of daylight stream through Alec's window, softening his features so he looks thirty years younger. She flicks away a loose tear. "What's wrong with Greece?"

"Too hot. Christ, I love you, Kitty. You're still the most beautiful woman I ever met."

"Oh Jesus, I love you too." Tears stream beyond her control. She halts the car, leaning over to find him. This time without reserve. Remembering his lips; cool, a hint of sweet tobacco, as enthralling as the first time he kissed her on the bench, a soggy, Spring day, in the Cambridge meadows. Perhaps they have atoned now. Perhaps she can forgive herself, lose herself in the soul of his embrace. Perhaps she can stay there. Forever.

He draws back for a moment. "We really should go."

He's right of course. So predictably reassuring in his statement of fact. Withdrawing to her seat, she notices his attention suddenly drawn beyond the windscreen.

A boyish grin breaks across his face. "Bollocks, looks like we've already overstayed our welcome."

She follows his gaze. An army Land Rover has pulled out of a side turning and halted a few yards in front of them, headlights on, blocking an easy exit.

Kitty grins. "What do we do this time?"

"We apologise. And refrain from high-speed reversing."

"Well, that's kind of boring, but if you insist." She smiles at him. "And just for the record, I don't feel sorry at all." As the two soldiers approach, she winds down the window. One looks like an officer, the other a regular squaddie. The officer approaches her window and leans down to her level. "Evening, ma'm."

Her most charming self. "I'm so sorry, officer, we were just…"

A sharp crack, glass shattering. Kitty swivels to find Alec's body slumped on his seat, a single wound piercing his forehead. Spinning back, she stares down the barrel of a pistol, a moment long enough to notice it has a silencer. How could she have been so foolish? She hadn't atoned at all. She closes her eyes. Pointless fighting. Not now Alec is gone.

Cold Road to Imber

26

SOUTH DOWNS, ENGLAND

On a walk around the herbaceous borders of his estate, he's disappointed by the choice of flowers. It's the wrong time of year; the daffodils are all but past, the tulips will wilt too quickly and the perennials display promising green shoots, but nothing that would form a suitable bouquet. He doesn't want to visit a florist, for one it wouldn't feel personal enough, for another it leaves a trail. At the farthest end of the border, in the dappled shade of a plane tree, he spots some early flowering irises and a last flush of pale cream daffodils. He cuts both, dropping them in to the wicker basket, and adds a few sprigs from the neighbouring, white spiraea.

On the large, oak table in the centre of the kitchen, he starts to prune the harvest into shape, until his critical eye is satisfied. "Would you make some coffee, Alf, I'll have it in the drawing room."

Sitting across the table, Alfonso raises his head from the tabloid newspaper spread in front of him, and walks to the coffee machine beneath the kitchen window. He gazes out to the view of neat flowerbeds, his back to Ed. "Do you want me to take them?"

Ed lifts his face from his work and studies his chauffeur. The daylight highlights a few silver hairs in his dark mane. He'd not noticed them before. Though he supposes even Alfonso is ageing, as everyone does, an Adonis no more, though most of the women in the village still flush when they meet him. "No, there's more important things for you to sort out, I'll drop them myself. What time's your flight?"

"Six ten, arriving eight thirty."

The coffee machine begins to gurgle. Ed turns his attention back to the flowers. "I'll take the Magnette. You take whatever you fancy."

"I'd love the Magnette."

"Too bad. Today it's not negotiable." He watches Alfonso put the coffee on a mahogany tray, a jug of milk beside it and two lemon biscuits. He smells of strong cologne. "Thank you, Alf. And can you leave my paper beside the chair."

Alfonso has already left the room. "Consider it done, Mister Edward."

It brings a brief smile to Ed's face which dissolves again on returning to the task in hand. The flowers, now neatly arranged, lie on the table. There is no more trimming to be done, no more gentle distraction from the purpose of his work, no aesthetic consideration to dull the ache inside his heart. Reaching into his pocket he retrieves a long lace string, withered and tarnished with age, and ties it around the stems of the bouquet. Though it's too long he uses it all, reluctant to take the scissors to such a precious object. It seemed fitting to use the lace from Alec's boxing gloves. Though he had taken the lace without much thought, almost instinctively, as they lay by the Cam all those years ago, he had kept it safe. With the passing of years, it had become a treasure of sorts, a keepsake, which now he feels should be returned to its rightful owner.

The job completed, he settles in the drawing room, the tray beside him on an occasional table, and The Telegraph folded next to it. He's been dreading this moment, having purposefully avoided the news on television or radio. The front page holds a large picture of the Queen and her family attending an Easter service at Sandringham. He opens the paper, scanning each page briefly, before he finds what he's looking for. It's quite a modest report, plainly there's not much information to reveal yet. Nevertheless, he's aware that his hand shakes slightly and his heart is racing. *Couple found dead on Salisbury Plain.* Forcing himself to read further he discovers what he'd expected. It speculates about a suicide pact, both victims shot in the forehead by a single bullet, the handgun found in the man's hand. The man is believed to have lived alone in Devizes, the woman as yet unidentified.

Ed folds the paper again before throwing it onto the nearest chair. The coffee will remain undrunk. He opens the drinks cabinet and pours himself a small brandy, sipping it slowly in a bid to calm his heart. When Alfonso appears in the doorway he's grateful for the interruption. "Everything okay, Mister Ed? Early to be drinking."

Ed places the empty glass onto the side table. "It's still a shock, that's all. No matter what…" Witnessing the look of incomprehension registered on Alfonso's face, he falters. "I don't expect you to understand, Alf, why should you? But they were my friends. Perhaps the only real friends."

Alfonso's expression remains impassive. "You have me. And Mrs B."

Ed feigns a smile. "Yes. I do. How lucky I am." Stealing himself to regain composure, he gathers his reading glasses and walks past the chauffeur into the hallway. "Let's run through a final check before you go. You've packed your overnight bag, I presume."

"Of course."

"Of course you have." He withdraws a large, leather-bound notebook from the side cabinet in the kitchen, opening it on the table. "You've got the address?"

Alfonso pats his jacket pocket.

"If there's no service porter, which I expect there won't be, hover around until someone goes in or out. Just find an excuse, you left something with a friend or whatever. They'll understand enough English. I imagine the lock on her apartment should be pretty rudimentary, nothing you can't handle. If you need to use force, go and buy overalls to look like a locksmith and try again. Once you're in, search everything. It'll be a tiny place so it shouldn't take long. Any documents you find, bring them back. Anything at all. No matter how trivial it looks. Then go straight back to the hotel and treat yourself to a good meal. And don't stop anywhere else before you come home. Any questions?"

"None."

"And you're sure it won't look like his car was tampered with. Nothing anyone would suspect?"

"I'm a chauffeur. I know cars."

Ed closes the notebook, returning it to the drawer. "For a few days you might have to indulge my emotions a bit, Alf. When the stakes are so high, you can flatter yourself at your planning, even though it kills your heart"

Later that afternoon, when he's waved Alfonso away to the airport, he jumps into the Magnette, dropping the bouquet of flowers onto the passenger seat. The journey will take him about two hours and where usually he would listen to the news of world events and business developments, instead he plays a CD, hoping to calm his thoughts; to not worry, as Alf so bluntly put it.

Handel's Sarabande fills the interior of his beloved car, accompanying him to Salisbury Plain, where the dying light bleeds to the horizon. At Gore Cross he turns left, headlights now lighting his path and moments later, he spots exactly what he'd expected. A few, modest, bunches of flowers lie at the road to Imber, the village now returned to its enforced isolation. He stops the car and glances briefly at the assembly of flowers; messages written in haste which it's now too dark to read, for which he's grateful. He leaves his own bouquet amongst them, now indistinguishable, an anonymous outpouring of grief and sympathy, as keenly and bitterly felt as all the rest; characters, he imagines, who have lost a friend and who understand the unbearable pain he feels, if not his hopeless circumstance. He turns tail and drives away, far from an abandoned village, which he promises himself he will never re-visit. The past must lie to rest. In peace now, he hopes.

Cold Road to Imber

Acknowledgements

Like many people I'm drawn to the mystery of abandoned villages and all they evoke. Whether it's simply nostalgia, or something more complex, like secrets held within ruins or the ghosts of lives once lived, they tap into our collective imagination and as a result, despite their demise, they achieve a kind of immortality. Imber is one such village, not far from where I live, which is well-known in the Wiltshire community for the hardship it suffered during the Second World War. I am particularly indebted to Rex Sawyer for his excellent book, Little Imber on the Down, which gives a fascinating and insightful description of the village's history accompanied by many fine photographs. Without it, I would have been lost.

I also read many interesting articles about British spies after the war, the majority connected to the Cambridge spy ring. These also highlighted the lesser-known role of women at the time, (my inspiration for Kitty), both as Communists and as lovers. One article I found very enlightening was written by Natasha Walter for The Guardian in 2003, titled Spies and Lovers.

There are many books and articles written about the German Democratic Republic and the role of the Stasi within it. While it's fair to say that few are flattering about the Stasi, there are those who believe, that given time, the socialist system in East Germany would have survived and prospered. In particular, an article by Stephen Gowans, called Democracy, East Germany and the Berlin Wall, gave a useful, alternative view which contrasts significantly with the conventional wisdom of the West.

I would like to thank the many people who have been supportive over the excessive time it has taken to write this book. I'd like to mention Sarah, my wife, and my dear friend, Angela, for all their feedback and corrections, and also my village friend, Lambert, for never failing to ask how the book's going.

Last but not least, I owe a debt to my two dogs, Cubby and Max, for insisting that we go for a walk every morning and helping me resolve plot points, or other conundrums, which otherwise were resisting resolution at my desk.

Jonathan, February 2023

ABOUT THE AUTHOR

The name, Jonathan Part, is a writing pseudonym for Mark Pearson. When he published his first novel, Jarvis Goes Global, he found that he wasn't the only person writing under this name and, to avoid confusion, decided to change it. Jarvis Goes Global is available on Amazon.

Mark began his career at the BBC where he developed his interest in writing fiction. He lives in rural Wiltshire with his wife and two dogs, his two children having fled the nest and returned to the city.

He is currently researching his next novel, which is set in and around Tiger Bay, in Cardiff, in the 1960s.

Printed in Great Britain
by Amazon